3

Taming the Wilderness Historical Fiction Series

THE RED LANDS
THE JOURNEY

JOANN KLUSMEYER

innovo
PUBLISHING

Published by Innovo Publishing, LLC
www.innovopublishing.com
1-888-546-2111

Providing Full-Service Publishing Services for Christian Authors, Artists &
Ministries: Books, eBooks, Audiobooks, Music, Screenplays, Film & Curricula

**Taming the Wilderness
Historical Fiction Series**

VOLUME 3

**THE RED LANDS
&
THE JOURNEY**

ISBN: 978-1-61314-720-7

Cover Design & Interior Layout: Innovo Publishing, LLC

Printed in the United States of America
U.S. Printing History
First Edition: 2022

Has God called you to create a Christian book, ebook, audiobook, music album,
screenplay, film, or curricula? If so, visit the ChristianPublishingPortal.com to
learn how to accomplish your calling with excellence. Learn to do everything
yourself, or hire trusted Christian Experts from our Marketplace to help.

Contents

It was the land, actually, that had the power to draw the people from the four directions and even from across the ocean. It was the clarion call coming from the place of the red lands. It was a call from the dirt, red as blood beneath its cover of grassy green…yes, that was what drew them, and once there, it held them fast.

The little girl lost her parents at age five, and for the next ten years, she helped raise her cousins. Then the trouble really began. After a lot of work, two gunshots, and a trip of several hundred miles, she knew without a doubt that she had reached the place of her destination…the place where the cloud should show its silver lining. Where was it, anyway?

The Red Lands

One

M any people came to this red land all together on one day, and many others were already there. The new people staked out their claims, but too often, prior claims had already been made. Both of these groups would earn title to their land by their sweat and by the speed of their horses, but mostly by the strength of their endurance and the joining together of their forces.

Ben Green had made a promise that he would not let go of his portion of the red land that had been handed down to him by his people before him. He would keep it, be it by the speed of his horses or the accuracy of his marksmanship, and when Ben made a promise, the world itself could consider it kept... because that was the way his pa had trained him.

For Ben's father, the world had been very different... and cruel. But before that....

Lemuel LaGrone left his home in the lowlands when he was thirteen years old. He left the day after his mother was buried in the low land by the swamps and amid sharp-toothed alligators.

Total in attendance at the burying was young Lemuel, himself, and his father, whose continued abuse had hastened the death of his mother. Lemuel stood with bowed head as his father, now momentarily sober, mouthed laments and undying love to the deceased as the grave was filled in. They were laments that would drown, once more, any remaining touch with reality, and that day his son put action to a long-ago made decision The boy emptied a leather pouch and filled it with 12 gage shot, as well as his other pair of tattered overalls and a shirt, a cup, a shallow iron saucepan, and a bowl and a spoon.

He took, with him in his leather pouch, one other thing. A Book. The tissue-thin inner leaves of the Bible, whose cover had long since been shredded with wear, were wrapped in the remains of his mother's lace scarf. This was added to the pouch, and it was taken into the woods and placed by a large cypress tree, to which was moored the family pirogue.

Returning to the hut, he spent the day sharpening his long-bladed pocketknife. The sharpening was a needed action and one that would draw no comment as to why it was being done. Blades were sharpened when they became dull, and who would be a better judge of a knife's dullness than the owner of the knife?

Then, in a special place at some distance away from the hut, he dug the blade of his knife in the ground and pried up a small metal box. Raising the rusted lid, he took out the scrap of cloth that protected the string of perfect pearls, and he held them curled in his palm, the soft depth of their aged ivory color glistening in his hand.

Slipping them in the pocket of his overalls, he pitched the metal box away and scuffed dirt into the hole.

When darkness fell, and there was no sound from the dilapidated couch except bouts of fitful snoring, Lemuel lifted the shotgun from its place on the wall and stepped through the door of the shack.

The redbone hound raised an eyebrow, hesitating a moment to see if his hunting companion was actually leaving the clearing. When the boy stepped through the trees, the hound unfolded his muscular legs and trotted after him.

At the cypress tree, Lemuel shouldered the leather pouch and waited beside the pirogue until the dog had swum to it and had shaken the water from his skin. Then he stepped in beside the animal. It was a new pirogue. The log had recently been hacked to its core with his hatchet and then carefully burned out, until a roomy interior had been created. The partly hollowed log, naturally buoyant, now skimmed high above the water because of its lightness.

Boy and dog moved silently through the greenish water, hardly creating a whisper of a wake. They moved carefully, skillfully avoiding the cypress knees humping up from the water and the larger of the pairs of eyes that shone in the light of the full moon.

Ropes of gray moss hung from the limbs of the trees, and many of these ropes harbored fast-biting, deadly vipers, but the boy was not concerned for his safety as he knew that the coolness of the evening had lulled the reptiles into lethargy.

Pulling through the water without effort, Lemuel reviewed the plans he had made against this day. His reason for staying this long in the family shelter had been his mother. Twice he had suggested they leave in the dark of the night, but she would not go. After all, he was only a boy so who would care for them? She did, however, hand Lemuel the pearls.

"Hide them well," she had whispered. "When you leave, take them with you. I have no money to give you, but the pearls are valuable. Keep them until you can use them to buy yourself a chance in life, the chance that you never had."

Disappointed, he had nevertheless put them in his pocket, later transferring them to the metal box buried under the cypress tree.

So, what could he do but wait?

Then she had said, "Son, when your life is better, think kindly of me. I did the best I could."

He had sighed and nodded. Yes, she had done the best she could, and he had done the best he could. If she had been able to live a few years longer, perhaps he could have persuaded her that he could take care of her, and they could have gone away together. Maybe not.

The fact was he was only thirteen.

The moon made patches of light on the water, occasionally sparkling on the ripples made by a fish as it surfaced to feed on fallen insects. The dog lay patiently, waiting for the boy to decide the location of the hunt. It was not for him to be concerned that they were going an exceptionally long way. It was for him to lie quietly and conserve his strength for the chase, the fight or the cunning required of him in the hunt.

The moon completed its overhead arc and abandoned the sky to the guardianship of the stars, and still the pirogue moved northward. At first light, the boy pulled the boat to the muddy shore. Stripping a many-legged creature from a leaf, he dropped it into the water. Waiting above the surface with the hand dip-net until the exact proper second, he scooped it into the water and brought up a flopping, finned creature with many teeth.

He tossed the finny catch onto the bank and repeated the action. Then, with the strike of a flint in his pocket, the boy created a sliver of flame that he fed into a blaze with small twigs and dry leaves. Skinning the two fish, he roasted them over the blaze until they were browned.

As he ate, the boy offered meat to the dog but it was refused. When he had eaten all he could, he stepped into the boat, laid himself down and went to sleep. The dog made a small run into the nearby tangle of trees and vines returning with a swamp rabbit, more to his own taste than the fish.

After eating most of the rabbit, he dashed into the cover once more, and captured another one that he brought back to the smoldering remains of the campfire.

When the boy awoke, the sun was high. Patting the dog on the head, he told him, "A good boy you are, Old Red. That'll make a fine breakfast."

The dog whipped his tail into a pleased arc, and waited. When the boy had roasted and eaten the meat, the dog ate the choicest of the rabbit's bones and entrails, and jumped into the boat.

Poling his stick against the muddy bottom of the canal, Lemuel LaGrone moved the boat farther north, skimming himself and the dog along the water and into their future.

When the streams of water became shallow and too congested with vines for the pirogue to move along rapidly, Lemuel stepped out onto the bank. Then casting one longing and regretful look at the new boat, he walked away. He had a fleeting hope that it would be found by someone who needed it badly. It had been one of the best boats he and his father had ever made.

Walking through the vine-webbed swamp was much slower than poling through the water, but boy and dog plunged ahead, eating when they were hungry and sleeping when they could go no farther.

In the next twelve days, he had left the swamps behind and had trudged onto the higher ground. The cypress and live oak trees turned into pines, sycamore and pecan. Bramble vines, covered with briers and ripe berries, tore at his legs. Wild grapes hung in clusters, and edible greens grew, free for the picking, all along the way.

Once headed north, he hardly knew when to stop, and finally reached the land of the taller mountains and the tumbling streams of water, and he breathed the cooler air.

Occasionally, he saw traces of the other inhabitants of the new land, but he steered around them, attracting as little attention as possible. When he smelled the smoke of a campfire, he turned aside.

He savored the aloneness he felt after the strife and abuse he had known all his life. Now he was truly alone with only the dog beside him. He had long known this time would come, and now he felt only relief that it was actually here and that he need no longer worry about his mother. She was beyond his help and was surely in the better place she had taught him about.

Two

Often, on a quiet afternoon, he settled beside a stream and rested, holding the remnants of the Bible on his knees. He could read some of the words. When he was younger, his mother had taught him sounds, carefully and patiently, but as he grew older and his mother's life grew more precarious, the lessons had grown fewer and farther between.

As he marked the place with his finger, he sounded out the letters of the words and was surprised that he remembered so many of them. He seemed able to puzzle them, those he did not know, just by the structure of the sentence. This knowledge, the knowing that he had not completely lost the gift of written words his mother had struggled to give him, brightened his spirit.

He read about a man called Abraham who seemed to have been called by God to leave the land of his home and move to a place where he had never been. This call seemed to be a request to have faith in a Power that would protect him and tell him where to go.

As he read the words, slowly working out the sound of them, he came across another word that he thought may have been a brother word to the word "faith." Noting the way it was used in the sentence, "trust" and "faith" seemed to be interchangeable. In the recesses of his mind he remembered a few times when his mother had told him to "trust" her when she told him his life would be better someday. It did not occur to him to think that possibly his mother thought his life was so dismal and miserable that it couldn't get any worse. Rather, he had taken heart from her encouragement.

Expanding on that thought, if it had been true of his life with his mother, then certainly it must still be true of his present life. He had trusted his mother, and now she was gone. Whom did he now have that he could trust? The answer to that question must surely be in the book, and he would find it if he kept reading.

Looking away from the book and allowing his eyes to settle on the heaps of mountains, blue in the distance, Lemuel reasoned that what had been done for the man, Abraham, in the book could also be done for him. He took heart from the words and purposefully climbed into the blue hills and prepared to stay.

The air was lighter and cooler in the hills, and he knew he would need a shelter. He had seen many caves, and they seemed the best place to live. He would need warmer clothing, and that meant bringing down a larger animal. His precious shot must be conserved, but he had seen the weapons of the natives of the mountains, and if they could bring down a deer with an arrow, so could he.

A cave home was an easy thing, and he chose one with a south-facing opening. Enlarging it by scraping away the dirt from the back, and sweeping away the accumulation of rocks and trash with a pine branch, he deemed it livable, and Red scratched himself a place and lay with his face toward the opening.

They now had a home, he and the faithful dog.

The making of the weapon, however, was more difficult. It occupied his time for several days. There seemed to be a trick to sending the arrow to an exact spot with great force, but if the others could do it, so could he.

When the weapon seemed workable, he brought down a fawn and later an inattentive buck. Sewing with a knife punch the strips of the tough hide, he fashioned a coat and a cap and decided trousers would be next. He had seen those worn by the natives, and they did not seem unduly complicated. Then he would try the shoes.

Lemuel read in the Book about the son of Abraham, and then about the grandson. The grandson had an occasion to change his name at a turning point in his life, and that seemed to be a good thing for him to do. Therefore the thirteen years of the life of Lemuel LaGrone was terminated, and a new life would begin.

After a few days of thought, Lemuel LaGrone became Lem Green, a new person, and he lived in the mountain cave for three years.

Perhaps Lem Green would have stayed longer in the mountain cave, but other circumstances overtook him.

The natives of the mountains knew that a foreign boy lived among them, and they were not concerned. There was land aplenty, and who would be concerned about a mere boy?

Then he grew taller and became a man of sixteen years. Now he became a possible threat. He was too strange and different to be taken into the tribe, and it was too intriguing to suppose that one of their women would long resist a closer inspection of the newcomer, and perhaps she would be lost to them.

It was then that a decision was made. First, they would plunder his cave, and perhaps that would make him leave. If not, a well-placed arrow would take care of the problem. Permently.

Lem came in from hunting and saw the brush he had piled at the mouth of the cave had been torn aside, and he saw the store of food he had gathered and dried had been stolen. His precious pouch had been hidden in a crevasse of the cave, and it was still there, but the cast iron saucepan he used constantly was gone.

Red sniffed the ground, whining and begging to be on the trail after the interloper, but Lem held him back. This was a serious problem, and it would take some thought. It was not that he minded moving on, he had fully intended to do so someday, but he refused to be driven away before he had thought it out.

Keeping Red on a leash to curb his enthusiasm, he followed the thieves, staying downwind and silent, and from a safe distance, he watched their camp. They had tied their horses within a grove of trees and gathered around the cook fire to roast their meat and smoke their pipes.

The time was in the dark of the moon, and when the camp had settled into sleep, Lem tied Red to a tree, cautioning him into silence, and crept toward the camp. Retrieving the valuable saucepan was too dangerous, but there was something else of value he could take.

Patting and smoothing his hand on the rounded belly of a young black mare, he loosed her and walked her quietly on the grass beside the trail. Reaching the dog, he unleashed him, and the trio headed west.

Walking the dog and the horse in the water of a mountain stream to drown their scent and the marks of passage, he worked his way through the vine-hung trees. The darkness slowed his progress, but he tirelessly plunged onward and by daylight. He was miles away.

Traveling in the water of another stream, he walked on, leading the horse and keeping the dog nearby. In midafternoon, the hungry dog ran down a large rabbit, and after it was roasted and eaten Lem called a rest, letting the horse graze while he and the dog napped beside a stream.

Still following the sun, he continued west. With the morning sun at his back and the evening sun in his face, he leisurely moved along, eating, resting and walking. The animals that he killed for food, he also skinned, rolling the hides together and loading them on the rump of the mare.

Then the hills were no longer so high, and the terrain was not so rugged. A swift river, running red with silt, flowed east as he continued to the west, and he followed it into the land of the red dirt.

At a crossroad, he came onto a building with many men and horses around it, and pausing at a distance, he made out the words on the building. They said, TRADING POST. Presuming it to be a store, he proceeded.

Walking inside, he looked around at the shirts and trousers, blankets and tents, and the kettles and pans. There was a metal saucepan the size of the one he lost. It was a lot lighter to lift than the iron one. He really needed a saucepan, but as he had never had money and hardly even a conception of money, he put the saucepan back on its hook.

As those in the store finished their business and left, he was alone with the owner.

"Hello, young man. Brought hides to trade?"

"Huh?"

"The hides you got on your mare. Are you aimin' to trade 'em in? If you are, I need to look at 'em, first."

Hmmm... so the hides had a value. Well, he'd see how it went.

The burley man wallered the cud of tobacco to the other side of his mouth as he examined the hides and commented. "Could be cured out better. Good pelts, though. I could give you two dollars in trade for the lot."

"Huh?"

He raised his voice. "TWO DOLLARS. IN TRADE."

Lem lifted the pan off the hook and raised his eyebrows.

"You want that? It'll be a dollar. What else?"

Lem looked around. It had been years since he had used his language to any extent, and the spoken words of it seemed foreign, yet vaguely familiar, coming from the red-faced, white-whiskered man whose huge nose showed blue veins.

All items in the store had marks, which must be the price, but his education had not covered numbers above his own ten fingers. It was very confusing.

He came onto a shirt of bright red and black, and it was soft and almost furry to touch. If that shirt was worn under his deerskin jacket, it would be very comfortable. He pointed to the shirt, and the whiskered man nodded.

"Sold. Take the shirt and pan, and bring your hides around to the back."

Skins off-loaded, Lem ask the man. "Who lives here?"

"Here? Why, I live here. Me and my woman."

Lem shook his head and circled his arm widely. "Who lives everywhere here?"

"Oh, that. You ain't knowin' where you are, huh? You're in the land'a the Wichita's."

"Wichita's?"

"Yeah, red men. Indians. Wichita tribe. Some Caddo and Apache. Chickasaw up to the north. Some others come through. Mostly Wichita's, though."

Lem pointed to himself and to the man. "The people like us. Where are they?"

This brought on a guffaw laugh that brought on a coughing spell, and then the old man explained. "Folks like us, they come and go. Mostly they go. I see 'em goin' west to get away from other people, and goin' north to farm the red lands."

"Red lands?"

"The dirt...you know, the red clay dirt. Like in the river."

"Oh." The words became no clearer by being repeated.

"You from around here?"

Lem pointed behind him. "Off east."

"Where'ya headed?"

Lem shrugged. "Could be here."

"With the Wichita's?"

"I ain't lookin' for trouble."

"Never heard'a the Wichita's causin' trouble. 'Course, I ain't met 'em all, yet. Tell you what, young man… say, what'a they call you?"

"Huh?"

"Your name?"

"Oh. Lem Green." He had to think a minute to remember.

"So, Lem, they's plenty room here. You settle around here, bring in whatever furs you have, and I'll trade 'em out for ya. You seem to be a bit light on gear. I got good blankets and tabaccy and such. You'll be findin' somethin' to trade for."

Lem nodded. Since he wasn't headed anywhere, particularly, perhaps he was there already. Springing onto the horse he had begun to call Star, for the white blaze on her forehead, he set off, the dog at his heels.

Heading toward the north, he walked until he smelled the smoke of cooking fires and heard sounds of a village. He allowed he'd stop for the night and staked the horse in the good grass. Red disappeared and came back with supper in the form of a rabbit. While it roasted, the dog brought in a sage hen.

Lem heated water in his saucepan and used it to wash his face. It would be good to have the pan to stew a squirrel or to wilt a pan of wild greens. He had really missed having a pan, but possession of the black horse had softened the loss.

He stayed in that camp for three days, during which time the mare produced a wobbly-legged foal, dark, but with more of a reddish shade than his mother. Good colt. Lem figured the pair of them may have evened out the loss of the cooking pan. Almost.

A week and several animal skins later, he moved closer to the sounds of the village. He could see their large, roomy huts made of bent-over poles with clumps of grass overlapping on the roof to shed the rain.

Young men on horses rode toward him, circling him curiously, then riding away. Older men came and asked who he was. They seemed to have no better use of words than he had.

Lem gave his name, and they spoke together in a limited way, examined his horse, and then moved on. Lem assumed he passed inspection, so he began to try to build a grass mound hut. His attempts were unstable, and his grass blew away in a small windstorm.

Some of the women came toward him, watching his attempts and laughing as his grass clumps fell apart. On the third day, they came to him and took the grass from his hand, pointing that he should step away. He did.

While he watched, new stakes were cut and bent into the ribbed beehive shape, and they were circled with tough vines that made them rigid. Grass was tied into brushes and wedged firmly into a thatch within the vines, building it higher and higher until the sapling frame was covered.

When finished, it was a smaller hut than most of their houses, but roomier than the cave and best of all, was tall enough for him to stand comfortably in the center.

The women had pointed him into the house and walked away. He thanked him the best he could, knowing none of their language. They seemed to be satisfied with his words.

Lem was very happy with the house and determined that he would shoot a deer, or something, and take it to the women to pay them for their effort. Meanwhile, he'd build a fire and cook something to eat.

Red had caught a brace of prairie hens, and Lem was plucking the feathers when a young woman approached, shyly, leading a spotted horse. Not knowing what to say, he watched her as she tied the horse to a tree and knelt on the ground, taking the prairie hens away from him. Well, if it was hens they wanted, it was fine with him. He'd eat something else.

She did not leave, however. She plucked the feathers, gathering them together and covering them with her scarf. From her belt, she took a knife and expertly sliced the meat into portions, threading the result onto the green spits cut from a nearby tree.

When the meat was browned and spitting fragrant juice into the flames, she put some of it in his bowl and brought it to him, settling down to eat the rest of it herself.

Lem ate, as instructed, wondering what he should do next. But when night fell, the girl took a blanket from her spotted horse and wrapping up in it, she went to sleep against the wall of his hut. Lem stayed outside until after midnight and then came in and lay down, finally going to sleep.

He awoke to soft sounds of movement, and he scooped up his gun and sat up in one fluid action. The sound, however, was the girl blowing softly on the flames under the pan. Lem watched as she put leaves in the pan and continued to build up the fire.

Pouring dark liquid in his bowl, she brought it to him. Pouring more of the liquid into his cup, she settled down to sip. The dark brew smelled and tasted of the woodland plants and was very refreshing. In a flattish wooden bowl that he had never seen, the girl poured yellowish powder and water, mixing it with her hand. On a flat rock by the flame, she spread the mixture, turning the rock to face the flame so the pasty mixture would brown.

She picked the hot bread off the rock with her fingers and brought it to him. Blowing away the steam, he tasted it. It was crunchy and flavored with corn, and he ate while he watched her bake another one.

Lem left with the horse and dog and brought back a small deer. The girl watched him, obviously pleased, and insisted on taking possession of the carcass.

Puzzled, Lem relinquished the animal and stepped into the grass house, where he found his supply of skins arranged along one wall. The feathers of the grouse were bunched in a leather sack for a pillow. His pouch and his cooking utensils had been cleaned and stacked beside the smoldering coals of the fire.

With her knife, the girl expertly removed the deerskin and was carving the meat into portions, cracking the bones and removing the marrowfat. She served him strips of roasted venison and a soup made of cracked corn and marrow fat, seasoned with herbs.

Long into the night she worked, hanging strips of meat from the overhead ribs and over the fire, keeping it blazing high. He finally came in, and she directed him toward the skins and motioned for him to sleep. She obviously required no help in whatever she was doing, and he finally went to sleep.

After a week, the cured venison had lost its moisture and hung, board-like, from the wooden strips, making up the roof of the grass house.

A variety of other foods, familiar and unfamiliar, also hung on the inside of the hut, and when mealtime came, they were prepared and offered to him.

Well, if she was going to stay, she needed more cookware. Stepping up his hunting, he built a supply of skins that she cured immediately and with great skill. Loading them onto his horse, he went to the trading post and traded for two metal plates, another cup and bowl, and a metal stew kettle. He got two forks, two spoons, and a large long-handled dipper.

The trader wrote figures on paper and handed it to him.

At his questioned look, he told Lem, "Them's credit slips. Spend it on something next time you bring in hides."

Lem put the paper in his pocket. It must be some kind of money. Sometime soon, he must get the man to tell him about money.

Gathering his new items together, he returned to the hut and handed them to the girl. Her dark eyes sparkled with pleasure, and she set them at the side of the hut with the rest of his things.

If this was going to be a continuing thing, Lem really needed to know her name. He asked her, and maybe she understood, but he could not say the words she told him. He'd just have to give her a name he liked.

After a lot of thought, he settled on the bush of red roses that had grown beside his shelter back in the lowlands. Rose. That would be a good name. So, pointing to himself, he told her "Lem." Pointing to her, he said, "Rose." After several repetitions, she attempted the words.

Also, if this was going to be a continuous thing, he'd have to see about a preacher. Didn't it take a preacher to make a partnership into a... well, she seemed to want to stay and help him, so...?

He spoke to the man at the store. "That'd be me, friend. I got the papers here to register marriage. I fill 'em up, and I send 'em in. Cost you a prime deer hide for the service." He hesitated, and added, "Don't get too much call for the service, though. You'd be the first in a long time."

Rose may have fully understood what he had asked, and then possibly she may not. He knew a lot of what he said passed over her understanding of his language. She did, however, agree to go with him and help him do whatever it was he wanted done. She even agreed to make a mark where she was told to.

The storekeeper tilted his head in puzzlement over her name. "Didn't know the Wichita's to name their youngens a name like 'Rose.'"

"They didn't," Lem admitted. "I gave it to her."

The older man nodded, understandingly. "Likely easier for us to say than what she had. They's more and more of her people takin' names that suit us better. They's times some'a them take two names, one of theirs and one of ours. Me? It makes no difference to me what folks is called. If their hides are cured good, they'll bring me a good price, and that's all I care about." A pause, then, "And you can't best the Wichita's for good curin.' Seem to have a special hand with hides."

Rose looked around the trading post and picked up a red-checked tablecloth. She showed it to Lem, questioning with her eyes? Yes, he told her, she could have it. He didn't remind her she had no table to put it on.

When he next saw the cloth, it was wrapped around her body in a very attractive way. Just another thing to be pleased about... with the life partner he had chosen. Or who had chosen him.

She was such a wonderfully pleasant addition to his life, he wanted to give her something special. A gift that had meant something to him, so from his leather pouch, he took the string of pearls and offered them. She took them, silently, and tucked them away, but never wore them.

Then came the day she rode her spotted horse to the trading post with him, and she gazed at the glass jewelry beads. Reds and blues, blacks and yellows, the colors were a jumble of rainbow hues.

Eyes shining, she looked at him, and he added a handful of the beads to his trade items. Back in the grass hut, she took the string of pearls from wherever she had hid them and handed them back to him. Holding the glass beads to her chest, she smiled happily.

So she liked colors. He now knew more about her. The table cloth... The beads... A word or two here and there, and they made themselves known to each other.

Thinking back, it was hard to remember when she had not been in his hut, seemingly pleased to see him come back from the hunt, and ready with food when he was hungry.

The job of curing of skins, the one he had considered to be a hard tedious job, was accomplished effortlessly with her strong hands. The storekeeper was right about her people having a way with skins.

In the spring, she planted corn and tended it carefully. Eventually, the grain was harvested, and bags of it hung from the bent wooden strips of the hut.

Winter in the Wichita country was usually mild, and a deerskin flap over the low door insured the grass hut was comfortable in all but the most prolonged winter rains.

It was in this way that Lem Green lived in the land of the Wichita's for three years, and he had not yet reached twenty-one-years old when his son joined them.

The wrinkled red bundle was born in the winter, and his mother put him in the cradleboard she had prepared. She hung him from the wooden strips on the inside the grass hut where he solemnly peered out of his furs, surveying his proud parents. He seldom cried or even fussed and seemed totally contented with the way his needs were met.

Lem named his son Benjamin after his mother's father, whom she had spoken kindly of. Since the birth of his son, Lem often had thoughts of his mother and her people and wished that she had told him more… or that he had asked more questions and listened better. He often wished he had pressed his mother for more education in the only book he had. But what was past, was long past, and he looked forward toward the future with optimism.

A year later, Benjamin crawled on the floor of the hut, often falling asleep against old Red, feeble and arthritic by this time.

The boy learned to walk holding to the skin of the old dog's neck, but when spring came, Red walked away into the trees and did not return. The pain in the old dog's joints had taken away his pleasure in the hunt, and therefore he had little reason to live.

A new pup, obviously part coyote, was brought to the hut and was named Barker. Lem taught the dog to hunt by day and taught his son to speak his language by night. Both learned well.

It was when young Ben was five that his father heard of the gold that was found in a river in the western land. A restlessness consumed him to go to this land, and he collected maps and stories about the wonder of it all. Gold had beauty and was shiny, and surely Rose would like it. Or, if not, she would like the shiny things it would buy.

Rose was not interested and begged for life to go on as it was, but Lem would not be satisfied. Piecing together all the stories he had heard, it seemed best to travel due north through the land of the Pottawatomi and the Sac and Fox, and then strike out to follow the sun.

He had very little thought of the distance he would have to travel, for traveling had not been a problem in the past. There would be others going that way, and there would be safety and companionship in the numbers.

He also harbored a small thought. As well as he had gotten on with the Wichita's living around him, he thought it would be well to expose his son to the other side of his inheritance as well. There would be other boys to play with and further his language lessons.

So in the early spring, with Rose on her spotted horse and his son on the young stallion, Lem rode his steady old black mare toward the north country.

Three

It was in the Sac and Fox lands that Lem camped to prepare himself for the long trek to the west.

He located a cave to provide temporary comfort to Rose, and she was left with the stuff as father and son took the gun and went to hunt the wild game that would be cured and taken with them. Rose was heavy with her second child, and it seemed best she stay with the camp and rest. When the child was born, they would move out.

On the second day that they were apart, a storm rolled down from the mountains and across the prairie, piling up the clouds of gray, charcoal, and black, swirling them in circles. The swirling created rope-like strands that blew this way and that, building themselves up too quickly for the hunting pair to return to the cave.

These funnels of air dipped and spun and fell to the ground, pulling up trees and grass by their roots, leaving a swath of bare red dirt across the land.

Father and son saw the storm pass by and hurried back to camp in the drenching rain to gaze in horror at the bareness of it all. It was empty. No Rose and not a shred of their possessions remained, only the lone spotted horse, dazed and confused in a grove of trees. A few gouges and scratches on her hide showed evidence of the storm's damage.

The rain beat dismally down on the bare red earth, puddling the water in red pools like the blood of the earth's wounds, and it ran its rivulets of crimson into the streams and lakes.

For days they frantically sought for Rose, and then spent weeks of crossing and re-crossing the storm's path, but she was gone without a trace. When the knowledge of her fate finally became real to Lem, the last thing he wanted to do was to go to the land of gold.

He took his young son to the cave, having no mental strength to go farther. Among the debris they finally cleaned from it was the leather pouch, recognizable shreds of a blanket, and a sprinkling of brightly colored beads. Nothing else.

Father and son spent days sifting through the dirt for the colored beads as though they had some direct tie to the one they loved, and if they could find them all, it would, somehow, bring her back. This find had renewed their interest and they searched the land again, but nothing more was found.

Inside the pouch was the string of pearls that had belonged to his mother, the wrapped pages of the Bible and the tortoise shell comb he had bought for Rose at the trading post. For these few things, he finally found reason to be grateful. The comb had been treasured by his beloved Rose, the pearls still held the promise of a better life, and the Bible was essential, in this raw country, for teaching his son to read his language.

The two of them began their new life in the cave. Knowing the value of skins, Lem spent the days hunting. Knowing the ways of the world into which he had brought his son, he spent the evening teaching the child to read the words in the Book. He taught himself, also, and, stumblingly, they learned together.

The word "trust" continued to intrigue him, and he worked his way through the pages feeling certain its meaning would someday be clear.

In the fine dust of the cave floor, he traced the shapes of the letters, then of words, and finally the boy could make sense of the writings and could read about Abraham, the man who was called to make a trip. Together, father and son learned that it was the great God that the man trusted and obeyed, and to him it was "counted as faith." There was that other word, again.

When Ben was eight, Lem married a woman from the Sac and Fox lands, joining with her in the ceremony of her people. The woman had lost her husband on a hunting trip, leaving her with a daughter of about five. The family of four moved westward looking for the best place to live.

Lem had learned that others of his parent's race had stopped in this land, setting up here and there among the trees, growing their food, herding their animals and sometimes moving on. He felt a strange tug to see these people and possibly live among then. He began to spend his evenings thinking and planning.

So many people came! He found that he did not have to seek out his people. They were soon all around him. They came in wagons and on horseback, and many left the same way.

Many, however, stayed in the good red land, expanding their crops to the many things that grew well in the mineral rich dirt using seed they had brought with them and continued to live in the land of the Sac and Fox. It was good land, and the people of the Sac and Fox willingly shared their good land. There was enough for everyone who chose to stay.

This was what Lem decided to do, and he raised his son, his wife's daughter and their own children, teaching them the words of his people as best he could. He knew it would be well for them to know the speech of their neighbors.

Ben Green lived in the Sac and Fox lands with his father and his father's second family and saw the settlers stop for a while and then move on. He also saw others who went on west to the place called the Unassigned Lands. He was curious about their movement.

Small settlements made up of several families happened here and there, and they were located within the Unassigned Lands called the Oklahoma territory. Ben had a hungering to be around those who spoke his father's language and those who could add to the meanings of many of his words. This longing pulled him toward the west where the most of the new people were to be found.

The reading lessons learned from his father enabled him to puzzle out the words on the pamphlets and fliers from the far off eastern place called the Government. There were many strange words, though, and he sought help from any person who would give it, hungering with a strange appetite to learn everything he could.

Every scrap of information he could find was treasured, and he read and re-read the words, trying to make sense of them. The thirst for information pulled him along in the way the scent of a rabbit pulls the nose of a hunting wolf. Information he received was eagerly consumed and digested in much the same way.

Four

To the west of the Sac and Fox lands, there were miles and miles of open space, free to anyone for hunting, and the red dirt land was available to anyone with the desire and skill to plant, tend and harvest food crops. At least, that was the way it seemed.

It also seemed, however, that there were unseen powers somewhere in the east, and those powers had the right to rule over this land and either permit or prevent access. Meetings were held (somewhere far away, it seemed) to decide on what would be done with the hunting lands of those who had lived on it for as long as people had lived. These things had interested Ben as he grew into his teens.

He invented reasons to be over in the Lands, around the crossing of trails and at settlement trading posts where pamphlets were circulated and posted on walls of public buildings. He thirsted to be part of every gathering where he could add to his knowledge of the language of his people and learn their strange ways.

He had grown up learning the way of the Wichita from his mother, but his father had precious little of his own life to pass on. Ben knew it would be his own duty to learn for himself.

Sometimes there were odd jobs he could do, and these were sought out and treasured for their access to spoken conversation. There were short-term labor jobs or freighting assignments, and each of these provided its own kind of learning.

These jobs made it possible for him to be with groups of people and to hear about the attitudes and plans that were constantly coming down from the place called the Government, so far away to the east. It also made it possible for him to become proficient in their language, his own language… the language of his father.

It was this effort to be nearer to what was said that had finally brought him into acquaintance with the Bertrand family.

On the shortest route between the Sac and Fox land where his father lived and the center of information from the outside world there was a meeting place. It was where the trail crossed the rivers that a settlement had been created and it seemed, of sorts, to be the hub for the transfer of information.

The distance from his father's house to the center of his interest was a hard two-day journey and required a nighttime stopover somewhere along the way, preferably near a homestead and people. The best homestead that was located midway belonged to the Bertrand family.

The Bertrand's, Maurice and Elizabeth, had come to the Lands with a "boomer" band. It was about this time that the unsettled lands began to attract attention, and certain vocal elements felt that "the more said, the better" should be the motto concerning the settling of these lands.

Geographically, the place of the Unassigned Lands was an area totally surrounded by land tracts previously assigned to the Wichita, Chickasaw, Sac and Fox, Pottawatomi, Cherokee, and other smaller tribes of native Americans.

This fertile nugget of land was crossed and recrossed by rivers and streams, set thickly with solid stands of hardwood trees, and blessed with temperate winters and bearable summers. With these obvious assets, it was a puzzle as to why this parcel had not been legally settled when there were multitudes people needing land?

These boomer associations assigned themselves the duty of "booming" the good points of the land, much as salesmen "drummers" had traveled their routes, attempting to "drum up" sales for their merchandise.

These boomers had much to gain, both politically and financially. Much gain could be made if the lands became more settled. When that happened there would be those who would buy goods and services from them, and they would "improve" the land, but first they must be persuaded to settle there.

Certain eloquent ones among the "boomers" spent time in the halls of the eastern government persuading with speeches and promises, and they sought help from the President of the country to open the lands, legally, for settlement.

Not wanting to wait until that time, others began to attempt to settle the land themselves, promising those they persuaded to listen to their promises, that when the land was finally opened, it would certainly be theirs.

They were assured that they would have something called "squatters rights," due the improvements they would have already made. No one questioned whether these boomers had the right to make such promises.

The first trickle of settlers was in place long before legal ownership was possible, and the Bertrand's were one of these families. Maurice Bertrand with his wife, his four children, and his wife's mother came into the land from Missouri.

In this land between the greater rivers, there was a smaller river called the Deep Fork.

Compared to smaller rivers, the Deep Fork was an exceptionally long one, usually running full because of the many tributaries that entered it, many of them spring fed. The river seemed good to Maurice, as there were few other settlers within miles of that certain choice spot, and the red soil, overlaid with humus from the leaves of the many trees, was fertile and tillable.

All that was required now was a burning off of the trees to make pastures, or they could be chopped into logs for cabins and for fuel.

He selected a site near a large tributary to the Deep Fork, and it was lined with tall sycamore trees as well as cottonwood and blackjack oak.

There was also a wealth of the shorter redbud trees that grew in clumps, producing purplish blooms in the early spring before leaves appeared on the dark charcoal colored branches. Later, the bloom would create clusters of seed pods that attracted birds and varmints. A most attractive land for certain.

Hardwood trees of pecan and walnut were generously represented, and small fruits such as bush plums and berry brambles of several kinds were in abundance. These were important to his decision, as local food would be a concern until crops were brought in.

When Maurice Bertrand arrived on the creek of the redbuds, his family consisted of girls fourteen and twelve, and boys eight and six. He later said that if the boys had been the older of his children, he might have made it on the claim, but what can one do when their first children were only girls?

Then, as fate would have it, another girl was born soon after they arrived, and the survival picture became even more dismal.

It took much of the first year of their residence just to clear the land, during which time they lived mainly on wild game, plants and native fruits and nuts. After a hard winter with some loss of hoof stock to wolves and coyotes, he began to be discouraged.

Though his crop the second year was better, the family now expected still another child, and the enormity of the accumulated responsibility was more than he could overcome. He began to speak of returning to Missouri and "civilization." He would simply follow the course of many others who found the frontier too challenging.

The oldest girl, Emma, was sixteen at the time Ben Green began to be fascinated with the activity happening within the territory of the Unassigned Lands. The Bertrand spread being near to mid-point, he asked permission to stop, overnight, in the hayloft of their barn.

Permission was readily granted as a neighbor would do, but, even more than that, his visits were anticipated with pleasure. So remote were the settlements that the Bertrand family was continuously hungry for the sight of another face, and the humblest traveler would be eagerly drawn into the bosom of the household for any bit of news he might have.

And Ben Green often had news.

He was barely past twenty-years-old, now, and had become a strong, dark-skinned and bright-eyed young man with an open smile and a tall, broad-shouldered build. He was a person who was instantly seen in a crowd, and from his first greeting, he inspired confidence.

During the second year of the Bertrand's stay, Ben had stopped over at least a dozen times, and he was usually persuaded to stay a day longer to catch them up with the news. Certainly, on his return trip, he must tell the news that was talked about in the settlement where the rivers crossed the marked trails.

The older daughter, Emma with her pale skin, rosy cheeks and smoky blue, and sometimes blue-green, eyes, was fast becoming a person to attract attention in any group, especially to a lonely young man. She began to pile her curls higher on her head and to wear her prettiest dress when she thought Ben would be coming by.

Ben, on the other hand, tried to bring some small bauble to slip to her and studied for miles how he could manage to get her alone for conversation.

His spotted horse, a descendant of the one his mother brought to his father's grass hut, was the only listener as Ben rehearsed what he would say when he saw Emma. But then, when he was face to face with her, all his clever words quickly evaporated, and he could only stare at her with tongue-tied adoration.

So it was when Emma's father, Maurice, had a crop freeze-out in the spring and he was forced to replant, that a continuously wet month left him with a weak stand of plants in his fields. Because of this, a spell of discouragement set in, and he began to talk more seriously of turning back to Missouri and "civilization."

Emma's heart quaked with fear that her father would take her away from her precious moments with Ben, and she begged him to be patient a little longer.

But, like a snowball that grows larger the farther it's pushed, once the talk began, it continued. Her father forgot the difficulties back in Missouri that had tempted him to seek his own land in the first place. He forgot why he had thought he needed to be away from his family and a multitude of other problems. He forgot about the arguments he gave his family about why he should listen to the "boomers."

In the pit of his discouragement, all he could remember was the availability of more comforts back in Missouri, and the fact that he had never been lonely with his extended family around.

The attitude of his wife's mother was a different story altogether. His mother-in-law staunchly maintained from the time the first word was uttered, that he could go but she was not returning with him. She insisted that they could load up their plunder and leave, but they would be leaving without her. She refrained from adding, the quicker the better.

She had reasons for staying, not the least of which was the land. From her first sight of the land a pull of kinship had formed between herself and the red dirt she walked on. She marveled that this red land beneath their feet grew such a wealth of plants, both medicinal and savory, and now, at this point, her vegetable and herb garden had just been built up to the point of being useful.

Her many trips into the woodland and along the redbud creek had yielded herbs, roots and bark, which could be turned into medicine, as well as seasonings and soothing tea.

The tender plants grew readily beneath the protective shade of the redbud clumps. They had been fertilized by the droppings of the birds that came for the seed clusters, and mulched by the many leaves shed each year by the bushy limbs.

She also reasoned thus. Had the family not been exceptionally well and fit during the two years of their stay? Their diet of nuts and small fruits had been good for them, and they would be foolish to leave this wonderful land where the Good Lord had finally led them.

Emma watched the verbal exchange between her father and her grandmother, hoping her grandmother would prevail, but certain she would not. She knew, from experience, that when her father's mind was made up, it was hard for him to change. Likely, impossible.

She waited anxiously for Ben's next trip past the house, and made up in her mind what she would tell him what was about to happen. Ben was surprised and pleased to find himself alone with Emma, but dismayed with her news.

With tear-filled eyes, she had told him. "My Pa, he's sure enough gonna go, and Ma ain't never yet stopped 'im doin' nothin' he ever tried."

"Your Pa's leavin,' for sure?" Ben hoped he had heard wrong.

But Emma nodded rapidly, a frown creasing her petal-smooth forehead. "He sure is, and it'll be soon if'n the crop don't start lookin' better'n it does."

Ben sought for words of comfort and found none. "Well, I…" The tone of his words hung dismally in the air.

Emma continued, "So I wanted to say to you, how do folks around here make it from one year to the next without starvin'? What do they do if the crop don't come in? Pa, he says bein' eight'a us, it's too big'a problem, with the boys not grown yet. You think Pa's doin' the crops right, or what? Other folks live here…." She paused, hoping for answer.

"Yeah, they do. They's years they don't live too good, though, but workin' on it, and bein' good at huntin,' that carries 'em through the bad times, mostly always. Another thing, havin' a bad crop sometimes teaches another way to keep it from happenin' again."

Emma reasoned, "Your pa lives here, and he has a family."

Ben nodded. "But I think my pa's always been here, and he don't know no better. He never had it no better, so he thinks he's doin' good."

"Is he?"

"Is he, what?"

"Is he a'doin' good like he thinks he is?"

"For him, yes. Me, I got different ideas. It seems like good for one person don't always mean good for the next person."

"What different ideas you got?"

Ben paused and pulled his thoughts together, so he could say the words exactly right. This was a favorite subject of his thoughts.

"There'll be a comin' a time that I'll have horses. I figure horses to be the answer to livin' good on this land. I'll need to have lots'a horses. I see folks comin' into the land, bringin' animals with 'em and not tryin' to breed better ones. Mine… when I get them… they'll be the best there is. They'll be sired out'a animals that's lived here and done good when times was bad." He waited, thinking he might be telling her more than she wished to know.

But when he saw her eyes were locked with his, he continued, "Then they'd be cross-sired with them horses from the east for size and pull strength. They'll be good horses, like none that live here now, and when crops don't come in, or if the storm freezes 'em or the wind knocks 'em down, there'll be the horses for me to sell. Them horses, they'll be good as trade money in the pocket. Could be even better."

Emma watched him as he shared his dream with her. Her unblinking eyes took in every expression as her attentive ears heard every word.

"You thinkin'a havin' horses like the one you got?"

"That'n, and others. Pa, he's got some black ones that he's had the breedin' stock of ever since he come to the territory. Brought the blood'a that black mare with 'im when he came up from the swamp land."

Emma's blue eyes became serious, and she drew her lips into a firm line, meaning a decision had been made.

"Ben?"

"Huh?"

"If my pa was to leave, which he's gonna do, there'd be a good piece'a land here to start raisin' them horses." Emma was determined to bargain with every tool at her disposal.

"Well, yeah, that'd be right. Only there'd be nobody…."

"Yeah, there'll be somebody. My Gran, she says she ain't a'goin' when Pa leaves. I keep thinkin,' if Gran stays, whyn't I stay, too? I didn't leave nothin' back in Missouri that I got'a go back to get. I don't even have a memory of what it's like there."

Now, Ben Green was a young man of above average intelligence, born of hardy stock and was very observant, as well. There were, however, times that the most obvious facts slid right over his head

Intent as he was on her question, as well as being unaccustomed to the devious ways of a girl striving to get what she wanted, he missed the underlying point of her whole conversation.

While his mind dealt with the concept of Emma's old Gran being so brave as to state, flat-out, that she was not leaving her land, he was not open to any other thought. It was a new thought that a woman would refuse to follow the man who brought her here.

Emma watched him, and then continued, "My Gran, she has her plants that she got out'a the woods, that are medicine. I'm wantin' to learn all she knows about healin,' and if I leave here with Pa, I'll not get to learn." Studying Ben's face, she waited. Had she said enough? Too much…?

Sometimes Ben was a bit slow in catching up, but he got there eventually.

"You're a'sayin' you're for sure not a'goin' when your Pa pulls out?"

Not trusting her voice, Emma shook her head slowly from side to side, swaying the fountain of dark curls that sprung down from the precious red ribbon, her most recent gift from Ben.

"Nope," she finally answered, decisively. "Me and Gran, we'll stay here. There's things we want, and they're all here," and she flung her arm inclusively around the modest log house, the partially fenced cattle enclosures, and the fields with their sparse showing of produce. She had the air of a princess surveying the realm she would eventually rule.

This statement took some consideration, and Ben settled himself down onto a flat rock that lay at his feet. In a whirl of skirts, Emma was nestled down into the grass nearby.

Ben nodded to himself as comprehension seeped into his brain. "You're thinkin' there'll be a way for the two'a you to make a go of it here, all by yourselves? Two women. You thinkin' to do what your Pa couldn't?"

The bouquet of dark curls again swayed. "Not alone. We'd need to have us some help, and there'll be a way to get it. There'll be someone somewhere that'll want to be part'a the start we got here. They'll want to help us 'cause we can help them get their own start. We got a lot'a land we been workin' on. There'll be someone who'll want a garden spot with the stumps already grubbed out, and they'll want wire strung around to keep in their hoof stock from wanderin' off. I know it ain't all they'll want, but it'd be givin' them a good start.... well...." Her voice trailed off, meaningfully, as if to invite him to complete the thought.

There was only silence, except for the birds in the redbud blossoms, searching for small insects for their nestlings.

Then the girl paused, looking down at her hands, clasped over the faded plaid of her skirt. "That'll give us... me and my Gran... our own start, too. It'd be like we was helpin' each other." She paused, then added, meaningfully, "That'd be helpin' us, and whoever else wants what we can give him."

Ben watched her face, the sober shape of her mouth and the depth of her sultry, smoky gray-green eyes. He had never considered Emma to be anything more than a scene to be admired with his eyes, like the fleeting beauty of a pink and purple streaked sunset, a rainbow threaded through a cloud after a spring rain, or possibly an eagle in flight, screaming through the sky to paralyze its prey with fear.

His small gifts to her stemmed partly from his own generous nature and love for beauty, and, more practically, a token payment to insure a continued welcome at the Bertrand house.

Listening to her words he sensed that this was this new thing, however, and possibly he could help. During his activities, he came in contact with certain people, and if he was vigilant, he could likely locate someone who would be interested in the plan put forth by Emma.

Emma was not certain his mind was working in the desired direction, so she decided to give it a bit of guidance.

"I'm sayin' all this but I'd not want to be a pest to you. It's just that you was talkin' about horses…? I'm thinking they'd need their space, if you was to have a lot of them."

Here was a subject he knew, and Ben picked up on the thought. "Horses, you're thinkin' of? Your pa put up a fair stretch'a fencin' only one wire high. A pesky cow'd push her way through that, but a contented horse, now, he'd stay put inside the fence, to be took care of. I could maybe help…"

The sultry eyes of the girl flashed from dull and downcast to bright and wide.

Turning her face up to his she demanded, "You could? You really could bring what horses you got now, thinkin' they'd stay back'a the wire? Oh, Ben, that'd be the best help we'd ever want! My Gran and me, we'd know you'd be comin' here, time and again, to see after 'em. Havin' you to be lookin' in on us, that'd make us feel safe. How many horses you got right now?"

"Well, I ain't got…."

"Don't tell me what you ain't got. Say the number. You got three? Maybe, six?"

Cornered, Ben mentally inventoried his current stock. "Well, out'a pa's black stock, them that come with him up from the lowlands, I got four and two of 'em's mares, ready to drop foals. Don't have no grown up stallion out'a the black. This here paint I ride, he's give me the three I sold, but there's the two mares and a filly that I got left."

As he talked, Emma's shapely fingers kept count. "That's four and three, and the one you're ridin'.' That's eight, and two more to come. Seems to me it'd be time to separate out your stock from your pa's and get 'em somewhere on their own." Emma was amazed at her boldness, but she was eager to solidify any gains she may have made.

Ben, his thoughts still on Emma's problem, failed to catch the switch in strategy. Emma aimed again, focusing carefully on her target.

"You could bring them animals on over here any time, getting' 'em used to the place... here?" She made it a question to be answered.

Ben suddenly focused, shaking his head with concern. "Oh, I'd not expect your pa to let me put my animals in behind his fences. He's been so good to let me stop by...."

"Ben, listen at what you're sayin.' My pa ain't gonna be here. I told you that. If he was to stay here, then Gran and me, we'd not be in this problem. When he takes my mama and goes, who do you think's gonna have the say over what happens on this place?"

Ben's forehead frowned with concern. "Emma....you say he's goin,' for sure? And he's gonna leave you here?"

Finally, she felt she had his attention. "Sure as thunder comes after the lightenin.' Right now he's a'tryin' to get ma to quit cryin' all the time, not wantin' to go, and he keeps thinkin' he can talk sense into Gran and me. He's wantin' to get ma back to Missouri 'afore her time comes, figurin' she'll have another girl." Emma hesitated, not wanting to confuse him with more details.

Ben looked out across the fresh green of the early spring. His hand plucked a nearby blade of grass that his tense fingers slowly shredded.

Emmy studied his hands and then his face. It seemed he needed more facts. "Ben, Gran and me, we know what we need and we're gonna get it. I'm talkin' to you, 'cause if it's your horses that'll be here and you checkin' in on us time and again, there'll be no need for me to be lookin' no farther. I ain't really got the time to be lookin' around, and when he goes, I won't have as much time as I have now. I need to get this here settled. I need more time...."

"Time?"

"Yeah, on account'a the book. I got me a notebook, and I'm writin' down what Gran tells me about the plants. I got pictures drawed of what the plant looks like and what its best used for. My book's not even half full, and Gran's pushin' at me to get it finished. I tell her she ain't goin' nowhere, strong and healthy like she is, but she says someone over sixty'd be a fool if she was to think she had a lot'a time left. Says to me, Gran does, that I need to get everything wrote down, and that takes a mite'a walkin' here and there, findin' where the plant is drawin' it and diggin' it up to bring back."

It was a long speech, but Ben had seemed to follow it well.

"And so I thought, here was a chance for me to stay and learn. Gran likes the redness of this dirt, once you dig down a ways. Says it's got things in it that puts the good in the medicine plants. She says the red of it is closer to the top'a the ground here than where she come from, and she ain't goin' back there."

Ben was intrigued. "You're tellin' me you're studyin' to be a plant doctor? That's what I hear you a'sayin'? That's a thing that's important for a settlement to have. Over in the Sac and Fox where my pa...." His voice trailed off as his mind caught up to the business at hand.

Turning toward her, he told her, resolutely, "Emma, I can do that. If it'd be a help to you, and to your Gran, a'course, I can bring my stock on over. I'd not want'a be the cause'a you not gettin' the learnin' you want."

Emma waited for the sound of Ben's words to penetrate his own thinking. She leaned back, planting her hands in the grass behind her. A tickle on her fingers signaled a furry caterpillar's progress across her hand and up her arm, humping itself onto her dress sleeve. Extending her arm out in front of her, she held a leaf before the insect and when it had climbed aboard, she tossed leaf and worm into a nearby bush.

"Emma, when you thinkin' this'll take place?"

"Soon. Ma's weakenin,' and pa's worry now is about me. He's not likin' me bein' left here alone, maybe, on account'a how old Gran is."

"Well, now I could start stoppin' in, say every week...?"

"Ben, what'd be the use'a you makin' the trip all the way to the Sac and Fox, usin' a day goin' and a day comin'? This here spread it's big enough for you and us, too. How hard would it be to put up yourself a place, permanent like, to stay? It ain't like your pa needs you... nor nothin'...? Does he?"

"Well, I...." Ben searched his mind for an answer and found none.

"He's got more sons to help him, don't he?"

So, sometime later, when Ben Green left the Bertrand spread, he had heavy thoughts on his mind. It was evident his life was going to take a sudden turn, and he needed to make some solid plans in order to turn with it.

Five

Back when the century of the 1800's was young, a family from the old country settled in the attractive land just over the big river that divided this new country called America. Obeying the urge to follow the sun, that family had crossed the mountain range in several hitches. Each stop had left a part of the family where they took root, but some of the family continued on.

The family reached even farther back in time, sprinkled from the plains below the Mediterranean to the steppes of the north country. It tracked along the northern edge of the inland sea and settled on a fertile coast.

Not content to stay, the young of the family looked across the narrow water to the cluster of fertile islands with a temperate climate regulated by the ocean current. Still not content, they built tall ships and rode them to the new land, pulled ahead by a strange internal force, not even understood by themselves. The way a migrating bird knows its life plan at the second it leaves its shell, these people knew there was a new land for them.

So, like the rolling of a tumble weed, shedding its seeds as it rolled before the wind, so the families of the old, settled country in the islands, had sent their children in the tall ships to the new continent.

The Danen ships with the tall sails, like the wings of strong eagles, shuttled across the water, bringing along those who lived on the shores of the old country, and those families often settled on the shore of the new country, that being what they knew.

The tall ships brought families from the craggy peaks of the highlands, and these newcomers often spurned the relative comfort of the fertile shoreline of the new country and trekked into the mountains, reminiscent of their old homeland.

The mountain range of the new country spread from the northern parts of the continent, far to the south, and a journey westward brought them to the mountains where many of them felt at home, and they stayed.

Others, just like the wind-blown tumbleweed, moved on to the big river. Crossing it, they came to the green mountains of the land just beyond.

Weary travelers stopped, planted their seeds and raised their crops. Their animals grew fat and life became easier. Then there were those among them who answered the urge to move on.

There were new mountains, never inhabited by anyone from the old country. The new land of this country stretched, seemingly endlessly, into the future. Then they heard of the special new land called the Oklahoma territory.

Some were intrigued by the gift of land in the Oklahoma territory. Almost at the geographical center of the new territory nestled a nugget of land, rich in fertile soil, peopled with a few friendly settlers, and it was open to new comers.

There were those, eventually coming to be known as "boomers," who, by mouth and action, "boomed" the blessings of this small new territory. They gathered those who were restless and assisted them with words, and often other means, to come and settle the land. Not waiting for the legalities handed down by the eastern Government, they brought the settlers on, caring not that they were selling empty promises.

The family of Bridie McMahan came across the river and settled on the green knolls of Missouri, and in the first decade of the century, small Bridget was born. Growing up with those who had also crossed the river, as well as her mother's people who had lived on the green land for generations, young Bridie acquired a broad education.

From her father's people, she was educated as well as any girl of the period was educated, in the letters and numbers of the old country. From her mother's people, she learned survivability, flexibility and an appreciation of her surroundings.

She also learned about the value and use of plants. Herbs, bark and roots had their uses and had been arranged by the Creator to be available for those whom he had created.

Intrigued by this evidence of a caring Creator, she had applied herself to the accumulation of knowledge that would be useful to her family and others around her.

Young Bridie had married the handsome and well-placed Robert Scott and became a valued member of his family. When he passed on before old age, he left her with grown children, Elizabeth, Mary Ann, and Robert junior.

Robert had long since answered the western call, Mary Ann settled comfortably on the green hills, and Elizabeth had married Maurice Bertrand, a young man whose strongest trait seemed to be restlessness.

It was with Elizabeth that Bridie chose to make her life. As Elizabeth's children began to appear, it was evident that Elizabeth was the one who could benefit most from her mother's presence, as her young man's interest moved from here to there, not staying long enough in one place to achieve success.

Restless as a willow in a windstorm, he had often flirted with the idea of moving west, so he was a ripe candidate when the boomer's voice was heard in Missouri.

With a small group of the restless, such as himself, he had moved his growing family into the territory called Oklahoma. Bridie Scott came with him.

He chose a well-watered spread of land that was trans versed by a small, but spring-fed, stream. It emptied into a larger, deep-channeled river. He started his cabin near a sparkling fountain of water that flowed from under a rock ledge, crystal clear and cool.

Bridie Scott walked the length and breadth of the new land, and pronounced it the best decision her son-in-law had ever made. Beneath the spreading limbs of the clumps of redbud trees growing by the small stream, she found the mushrooms that supplemented the diet of the family.

Brambles and other small fruit bore in season, and nuts, rich in oil, grew in the trees more abundantly than the squirrels could consume them.

The squirrels themselves seemed to come on in an endless supply. Larger game was abundant in the wooded timber, and game birds clustered on the twisting waterways.

Like a blazing jewel in the crown of this new land was the red dirt. It lay there, rich and fertile, just under the roots and leaf mold of the timber, and it washed out of the ground in the rainstorms, streaking across the land, red as lifeblood.

The thickness of the red dirt caught and held the precious seeds of important medicinal plants, sending them upward to offer their lives for the health of animals and people. Truly, a gift from the Great Creator who promised He would furnish leaves for healing.

Bridie dug the roots and collected the seeds, creating a garden near the flow of the crystal spring. With only a little water, when the ground was very dry, these plants grew to amazing sizes.

When the Oklahoma sun blazed down, their beneficial oils oozed out, giving a shine to the leaves of the plant. They held their seeds to be gathered and used, and their roots grew fat in the colorful red dirt of this wonderful red land.

When she could be spared, young Emma followed after Bridie, her grandmother, carrying her basket and trowel. This girl, the oldest of Elizabeth's children, listened with interest to whatever was told her, and, to an old woman, what could be more flattering than to be listened to?

What was even better, this girl asked meaningful questions. She remembered what she was told and often suggested new situations where this knowledge might be helpful.

These new situations were usually something Bridie, herself, had not considered. It was certain that Emma had it within her to be a medicine person… or a doctor, as her father's people would have called it.

So when it came about that Bridie's will-o-the-wisp son-in-law began to speak of tossing away the dream of this new land, she set her mind toward what could be done about it.

Her daughter, she knew, did not wish to leave. She dreaded to be moved yet once more, and certainly with nothing to be gained. This wish was strengthened by the knowledge of the new child to be born. Bridie also knew, however, that her daughter would go where her husband went, as was required of a married woman.

Next in her mind was the welfare of her granddaughter. Emma, now sixteen years of age, was practically a woman, and she possessed more strength of purpose than her mother had ever managed.

In a more populated land, Emma would likely be managing her own household by now and perhaps her own child. As it was, her granddaughter's best brush with the outside world was the young man who came by regularly on his way to somewhere past the screen of trees.

The young man, with his wide-set dark eyes, and his pleasant smile had totally captured Emma's heart. It was understandable, of course, as she had no access to anyone else.

It could be, however, that the young man could be part of the answer for the girl, and for herself, as well. From the evening conversations over the supper table and around the evening fire, Bridie knew him to be an ambitious young man with dreams. Perhaps his dreams were not the best ones, as related to herself and Emma, but dreams could be changed.

It would be much easier to redirect the dreams of a young man than to build dreams in a complacent mind where none had grown. The redirecting of the young man's dreams could be a goal worthy of Emma, herself, and it would be Bridie who would instruct her to this effect.

"Emma, honey, let's take a walk out to the herb garden."

"Sure, Gran. I just got'a rinse out these things and put 'em on the line. You want I should bring my book, or is it just to look at somethin'?"

"You'll not need the book. I'm just needin' to pass on some words."

Emma's mother, Elizabeth, barely showing from the new pregnancy, sat at the table sorting through the brown beans, removing small pebbles and damaged seeds. She had heard her mother's words to her daughter and let them pass over. It was a normal thing for her mother to take Emma to the garden. Elizabeth knew it was a good thing to know about the plants, but she, herself, had failed to find herself properly interested.

When Emma's duties were finished, Bridie walked ahead, leading her into the garden that was fenced around with a border of piled brush. Fence wire was too valuable to be spared to enclose a garden that did not produce beans and corn. Her son-in-law thought.

That had not been a problem to Bridie, and she gathered the leafy ends of limbs from the woodlot, those that were too small to be cut up for fuel. These, she piled in rows around the border of her garden.

The piled windrows of brush protected the vines and other plants beneath them from the mouths of the animals, and the plants grew up through the brush fence. As the brush decayed and settled low, more brush was gathered and piled onto it, rebuilding its height.

The brush fence trapped fallen leaves and they decayed under the fence, creating a deep band of highly rich and fertile soil, spread thickly over the red dirt below.

As the dark rich soil built up in the fence line, Bridie and Emma scooped it up to circle around special plants like a protective collar, adding richness and conserving moisture.

"Emma, honey, it ain't plants I wanted to talk to you about."

"Then what, Gran?"

"It'd be your pa's idea'a leavin' here."

"I know, Gran. It'll be bad to leave the garden, once we got it a'goin'."

"Could be we don't have to leave it."

Emma smiled, sadly. "I'd like that to be true, but you know Pa, bein' more'n average stubborn when he gets a thought in his mind."

"I wasn't wantin' to talk'a your pa not goin'. He's got his own mind to make up, but he's not makin' up mine."

"What're you sayin,' Gran?"

Bridie had settled down onto a flat rock near the garden. She was not particularly tired, but she never used her strength wastefully.

"Sit down, girl, and we'll have us a talk. Now, what I say is not for your ma's ears. It's just so you'll know and not be surprised when it happens. I put hopes and thought into this garden, for the good'a you and the rest'a your family, knowin' I didn't have too many more years. I was feelin' it'd be a thing I could leave, and you'd have the knowledge in your head to carry on."

Emma sat beside her grandmother and bowed her head, sensing the pain the old woman's words were causing her. Bridie continued.

"Now, I can see it'll not work out like I planned. I ain't goin' back with your pa." Bridie made the words hard and blunt to pierce the thoughts of the girl.

"Not a'goin'? For certain?"

"That's right."

"I know you ain't wantin' to, but Gran, what'll you do bein' here alone?"

"I'll do the best I can with what years I got left. There's a house to stay in, and who'd want to bring harm on a useless old woman?"

"But ma, she'll not let you stay here...."

"She'll have nothin' to say to it. I done my best by your ma, and now I know what I got'a do for myself. I like this land, and this here's where I'll die."

Emma stared into the beloved wrinkled face and into the bright eyes that held her own while the terrible words came from her mouth.

"But, Gran, I can't hardly think about what you're sayin'!"

"I know, Emma, honey. That'd be one'a the reasons why I wanted to tell you ahead'a the others. It'd be somethin' you'd want to know, and you'll see they's reasons to fill up your book with words. Likely, there'll be a time you can make use'a what you wrote down."

41

Emma's mouth puckered and her straight, high-bridged nose sniffled, delicately. She touched the edge of her sleeve to her moist eye and stared out into the new spring greenness of the plants. A full minute it took her, and then she looked up with a hardness in her eyes.

"Gran, I'm a'stayin' with you."

"Oh, no, honey," Bridie protested, modestly. "You mustn't throw yourself away for a useless old woman. I'll make out fine, and your family needs you to be along with them."

"No, Gran. I'm past sixteen years old, now, and I can make up my own mind. I like it here, and I'm not leavin.' Pa can't make me if I don't want to. You and me, we can make it…? Can't we?"

The girl's words pled for reassurance. Bridie was tempted to agree, but that would not be the truth. Where she, Bridie, might be safe, a beautiful young girl like Emma would certainly not be safe very long in this raw country.

Here was where her well-thought-out plan would need to be put in place.

"Well, Emma, just bein' you and me to take care'a ourselves, we could likely get along. 'Course, there's the thing about safety and when the word got around about you bein' here…."

Bridie paused, meaningfully, but continued. Might as well be brutally honest, "with you bein' here, we'd not be safe, for maybe this reason or maybe that reason. There's things that are true of human nature, even when we don't want 'em to be."

"About me…? You're sayin' you'd be better off without me?"

"Oh, no, child. It's just that with you a'stayin,' a different kind'a plan needs to be made."

"What'd that be, Gran?"

"To start with, we'd need to take on help."

"You mean hired help?"

"In a manner'a speakin.' Only they'd be paid with what we got here, and not with money, which we ain't got. It'd be a good chance there's a couple, or maybe even a trusted man, and him alone…" She paused, significantly.

Emma waited.

"It'd need to be a person needin' land to grow crops or animals, and what your pa's done here, that'd look like a good start to a person needin' it."

Emma nodded. "But, Gran, how'd we go about findin' that someone?"

"Oh, we'd wait and see. Likely someone'll be by. You noted surely that more folks come by here than did when we first come. Why, there's almost a road wore down in the grass, all the horse traffic that's gone past your pa's place."

"Ah, Gran, that's mostly been made by Ben, a'traipsin' back and forth from the Sac and Fox to the goin's on in the ranchin' spreads and the tradin' posts. Likely most'a the path was tromped down by him'n his horse."

It was Gran's turn to be silent. She inspected a small cut on her finger that had been made by a brier vine. She'd need to split open a thick leaf of the aloe plant and clean it out before it became infected.

"Gran?"

"Yes, honey?"

"How old would that person have to be?"

Gran hesitated. This was a very important part of the conversation. "Why, honey, I wouldn't think the person's age'd be that important. What'd be necessary would be a need in 'im for what we got. Like, maybe there'd be a young man with a dream to get started with somethin'...: Or other...?" She needed to give the girl's thoughts time to come together.

"I was just thinkin', Gran. There's Ben, and he's always got dreams."

"Has he? What's the biggest one that he's told to you?"

"Well, it's hard to think right off. I know he's always wantin' to know what's goin' on, everywhere. Seems there ain't a thing that don't interest 'im."

"Is that the truth, now!" Gran pretended the knowledge was new to her.

"Yeah, Gran. You know that spotted horse he likes to ride? He says that'n's been bred up from a pony that come from the Wichita land down south. Said his ma brought it with her when she come to his pa. Said he had other horses, too, that was all his. Not belongin' to his pa."

Bridie nodded. "Now, lass, that's a thing to think on. That'd mean that young man had himself a pa that sets a value on keepin' things. Like animals. It'd be likely that some'a that likin' has spread to the young man. It happens in families, like the way you're ready to learn what I know about plants. Likely, he'd be the first one to think on."

"How'd you mean?"

"Wouldn't you think he'd need a place to keep them horses?"

"I don't know, Gran. He seems to…" She tried to think of what he had said about where he kept him animals, but she could think of nothing.

"I mean, while he's doin' his runnin' around. Seems he uses up a lot'a time goin all the way back to the…? Where is it he goes?"

Emma picked up on the thought. "The Sac and Fox, Gran. Yeah, he does. You think he might be interested in stayin' all the time in our barn?"

"Oh, I'd think he'd find a better place than the barn, a young man with ideas, the way he has."

"Better place…?

Gran knew it was time to move on. There was an art to knowing when the seed was planted, when it had been fertilized and watered, and when it just needed time to sprout. "Child, look at the new crop'a grass comin' up in amongst the chickweed and it bein' big enough to pull for the table. Come on in here and spread your apron. We can pick it full'a greens and wash 'em up for supper. Greens of a spring are good for the blood, and chickweed, it's got things in it that's especially good for people. The Good Lord knew we'd be needin' somethin' in the spring, so He made chickweed. "

Emma spread her apron, and because of the many plants, the garment was full in minutes. When the chickweed was cleaned in the stream and the grass blades removed, it would go well with fresh spring onions.

Gran talked about this plant and then that one, filling in the time and separating her words from Emma's thought. When Emma's mind returned to their conversation, she must think the idea had been her own, so she could present it to the young man as a thing she had just decided.

Emma was a girl who did not have to be struck by lightning to have a good idea. She also recognized a good idea when it had been slipped to her under the cover of other words.

Six

Emma stood before the woodstove and stirred the clabber milk in the steel kettle. She dipped the wooden spoon to the bottom of the container to keep the milk from scorching and moved the spoon around and around, her thoughts chasing after the curds of milk swimming in the yellow whey.

Gran was not going to leave here, and Emma, herself, had instinctively offered to stay, and now a way must be made so that her words would be true. It was a fact that pa could have done more than he did to the place, but still, a lot had been done. Gran thought it would be valuable to someone, and she was likely right.

There was Ben and the way he made her heart flutter when he looked at her and smiled. And the way he brought little things, showing how he thought about her when he was not with her. And the way he stayed over and talked with the family, seeming to enjoy it.

There were a lot of things to think of, and stirring the clabber to make cottage cheese gave her a good time to think.

But now, the curds were sticking together, and it was time to strain them out of the liquid. Fastening the cheesecloth to the top of the tall crock, she poured the whey and clabber chunks through the strainer.

The whey drained through into the crock to be fed to the pigs, and the white ball of cheese hung above it. It was now time to leave the cheese to drain down the last bit of whey. Covering it, she went on to her next duty.

Whirling around in her mind was the urgency of getting her thoughts together. She would talk with Ben, and she would say... what? How could she tell him that she and Gran needed him, without scaring him away, or maybe making him think they were both crazy?

That night she lay sleeplessly on her pillow, planning what she would say. Then he had come, and she had said her words. He had walked away after the promise to bring his stock to put behind the Bertrand fences. She must have been successful.

What was left, now, was to tell her pa. She found him in the barnyard looking over the wagon that had brought them to this land. Squatting down beside him, she began.

"Pa, I ain't a'wantin' you to go, but if you got'a do it, I'll not be the holdup any longer. I got a promise out'a Ben to bring his stock on over here, and he'll see after Gran and me."

"You did? For a fact? Well, daughter, that'd be the best I'd ask for short'a you comin' on back with us. When do you allow it'll happen?"

"Soon, Pa. It was a new idea to him, and chances are it'll take a week or two to settle in. When he comes back, I'll say to 'im the place is ready. Is that all right, Pa?"

"Yep. I reckon the place's ready as it'll ever be."

Old Bridie Scott rested better that she had in some time. Emma had told her that Ben had accepted their offer, and Pa had said he could bring his stock anytime. Ben had not yet talked with Maurice, but there would be no problem there. Her son-in-law's interest was no longer on the red land.

In addition, these actions eased the pressure of filling Emma's book with information. If Emma was not leaving, there would be time, but it must not be put off.

Over east in the Sac and Fox country, Lem listened to his son's account of what had happened at the Bertrand's and was puzzled, to some extent, but his son was of age, and what he did was his business. It was true that he was not needed at home, particularly, as his next son was coming into his teens.

Ben, himself, went about the transfer in a businesslike way. He had a job at a ranch near the Bertrand's. He'd just take his stock, or some of it, at least, and drop them off on the way when he returned to work.

Or maybe he should talk with her pa before he took animals. It might be presumptive on his part… however… Emma had said…? His mind sought to make sense of it all.

But in the end, he set out on the spotted horse, determined to conduct this business the way it should be done.

As he neared the spread, it seemed he was expected.

"Didn't bring no hoof stock, I see," Maurice noted.

"No, sir. Thought there ought'a be talk, first, so's I'd know where I stood."

"Not a bad thought. The girl tells me you two had a talk, and you made promises. Don't mind sayin' it was a relief to me. I was hatin' to go off and leave her all alone, 'cept for the old woman, and she wasn't takin' to bein' moved. Is it true that you made promises?"

"Yes, sir. I figure it's time to get out on my own. I'll be here to keep the fences up and tend to the stock. Workin' around here like I do, the women folk ought'a be safe."

Maurice nodded, agreeably. "Well, bein' you ain't got your stock here and had a chance to get set up, we'll hold up leavin' for a few days. When is it you think you can get it done?"

Ben raced his thoughts. *Did the man not believe he'd do what he said he'd do? Surely he'd know Ben's pa had raised him better than that… to go back on his word? But if that was the problem, he could go on over to the FLAT "O" Ranch and get the job started, to keep his promise to the foreman. Then he could get on back to his pa's and get his stock.*

Surely, that'd ease the mind of the man at the ranch, so's he could get on off back to where he came from. That'd waste the total of four or five days, but if that was what it took… well, what could a fellow do?

Under considerable pressure, he had begun the job of breaking a string of ponies, and the foreman was not pleased that he had to take time off. He finally agreed on releasing him for a week, because of Ben's skill, and Ben headed back to the Sac and Fox lands.

Gathering his own horses in a string, eight animals long, was really not what he'd rather do, but Emma's pa was antsy to get it done, and likely this'd calm 'im down. He shook his head at the strangeness of some folk's ideas, but, still and all, it was true that if his animals were closer to where he worked, he could take care of them much more easily.

When he arrived at the Bertrand spread once more, Maurice greeted him pleasantly, helping him position his animals inside the fence, and giving last minute advice here and there.

Being pressed for time, Ben bade him farewell, and Maurice said, yes, he'd be glad to be on his way. So if Ben could hurry and get it done and show him the paper, he'd be off.

Ben was reasonably quick in his thinking, but he stopped dead in his thoughts when he heard the word "paper." What was this? Was he wanting a contract? And if he was, what would it be about?

"The paper, sir?"

"Yeah, the paper. Didn't reckon there'd be a preacher you could bring all the way over here. Figured you'd just show me to paper after it was done."

"Preacher? I ain't seemin' to follow, sir?"

Maurice seemed startled and tilted his head to better examine the stupidity of the young man before him. Behind her father, Emma stood with wide, horrified eyes as she saw the turn of events. Her hands were clamped firmly over her mouth and nose.

Suddenly, she broke away from where she stood and rushed up to her father. "It's all right, Pa! We ain't talked nothin' about that! He's just gonna stop over now and again, like he's been a'doin.'"

Whereupon, Maurice turned his puzzled gaze toward his daughter. "What kind of a crazy thing are you a'sayin'? You sayin' you was thinkin'a lettin' this fellow move in, and you not seein' the preacher? You thinkin' I'd go off and leave you in a mess like that? What kind of a pa'd that be? I'm hatin' bad enough to leave you, but I was thinkin' you made plans."

"No, Pa. We didn't...."

Maurice sighed, wearily. "Well, now, Emma...?"

Ben looked from father to daughter and to the concerned faces gathered behind them. He was a realist and had always been a realist. He expected to have only what he had earned and expected to receive nothing from anyone that had not been earned. He took nothing for granted.

But what was the problem here?

Therefore, when it finally penetrated his thinking that a great and unbelievably magical scene was acting itself out before his eyes, the force of it caused an involuntary flinch.

He had never thought he would have a handful of stars to call his own, but that did not mean he wouldn't like to. He had never touched a rainbow, either, but....

So all the times he had talked with the lovely Emma it had never occurred to him that he might actually have her for himself, but that did not mean he didn't want her. And here they stood before him, watching and waiting. It was time for him to say something, but what would it be? Should his words be to her pa? Or to her, with everyone around... or what?

His eyes pled with Emma for a sign, and she burst into tears. "Don't pay 'im no mind, Ben. You don't need to say no more. I'll go on with Pa."

The sound of her words cut away his indecision. "Mr. Bertrand, sir, it's true I ain't asked Emma to... to get... to see the preacher. I mean, I didn't say nothin', yet. It wasn't 'cause I didn't want her. It was 'cause I didn't figure myself to be good enough for the likes'a her. I was aimin' to stay here and keep her and her Gran safe, and that was all. But it don't have to be like that."

He drew in a deep breath and opened his mouth. "Now, Emma, this here's not the best way I'd like to say this, but I can say it. Emma, I love you, and I want to marry you. Will you marry me?"

"No, Ben, you don't got'a do that!" Emma wailed in anguish.

Maurice intervened. "Girl, you sayin' you don't love this man?"

"Oh, no, Pa, it's just that I …well, he didn't…."

Ben summoned his courage and began again. "Emma, I got'a say that it was a mistake on my part. There wasn't a time I didn't love you, ever since the minute I first saw you. Will you marry me?"

Emma knew when it was time to act. "Yes, Ben. I'll marry you."

Maurice nodded. "Now we got that took care of, when'll it be?"

Ben raked his brain. There was a preacher over at the FLAT "O" that put up his shingle for weddings and funerals and did some work on the ranch in between. He would certainly be the closest one.

"Well, sir, I got a problem on time. I was always one to want'a keep my word. I took a week off'a my horse breakin, promisin' to be back, and that'd be tomorrow. I know where there's a preacher. Thing is, I can't get 'im over here and get back, and I can't take her over there and get back. It's gonna take some fast thought…." He glanced around, inviting any ideas that might come to anyone of the assembled group.

Bridie had discreetly kept to the back, but that didn't mean she hadn't been listening. Waiting a modest half-minute, she stepped forward.

"Seems simple to me. Maurice, you get on your horse and go over to the ranch and see the weddin' gets done. Then you bring Emma back here, and the boy gets on with his work, to keep 'is promise. When he can, he'll come on home."

"Well, I could…."

"Would you do that, Pa?" Emma's eyes pled in desperation.

"Get yer bonnet on, girl. I'll saddle us up a couple'a horses."

The Bertrand horses followed the spotted pony, single file, down the narrow trail between the trees. The only sounds were those of the horses' hoofs on the ground. Maurice felt relief that the ordeal would be over, and he could get on his way. Emma's heart beat against her chest with a pounding that practically took her breath away.

Married! Within hours, she would be married! Wasn't that something that should have been thought about and planned for? But before the sun went down, she would be married…!

Ben was not much better off than Emma. He always figured it was something he'd do sometime. Girls were pleasant things to look at and think about, especially Emma. She was just about perfect. When he brought her a set of fancy buttons, they had appeared on one of her dresses. The red ribbon he brought tied up her hair at this very minute. Yessirree, Emma…! She was…! Words failed him as he tried to comprehend his own good fortune.

Then, with a boom into the center of his heart like a charge from a double-barreled shotgun, the knowledge crashed in on him. By sundown, Emma would be his wife…! wife…! wife! The word sounded so foreign and strange as he grappled with the reality of it. Emma would be his wife!

As he led the way between the trees toward the FLAT "O," he seemed to be stuck in one of those dreams where he knew that what was going on was not real, yet he was unable to stop it. Surely, just before she said the right words, the dream would be gone in a puff of smoke. And there he'd be left, sitting up in his sleeping bag, rubbing his eyes. It was a dream, of course, but what could he do about it?

Dreams like this had to be lived out.

The foreman at the FLAT "O" was pleased to see Ben but puzzled at his following.

"The preacher? Her old man's makin' you marry her? What's goin' on, man?" The foreman frowned in sympathy at the mess Ben had obviously gotten himself into.

"I can tell you later. The thing is, if you could spare the preacher for a few minutes, we can say our words, and her pa'll take her on home. I know I got four days left on them ponies."

"That's right. I'm not undertandin' this, but I can bring the preacher, if that'll get you back to breakin' them ponies."

The preacher had been cleaning the chicken house for the FLAT "O" Ranch and had been raking the droppings into a pile to transfer to the melon patch. Small inner feathers floated about, settling on his hair and clothing. His gumboots were pasted with manure and feathers, and dust had settled on his face above the bandana over his nose.

Pulling down the bandana as he listened to the foreman, he replied, "You want me to WHAT?"

"Ain't got time for questions. Come on out and go get your book. I want'a get this done."

"What's the big hurry? Is she…?"

"Don't seem to be, but her pa's with her. I ain't heard the particulars, and I ain't carin.' Just get a move on. I got horses to break."

The preacher sprinted to the bunkhouse and came back with a small blue book, creased from use.

He looked from Ben, whom he knew rather well, to the bonneted girl, then to the obviously impatient father. The foreman was right. This needed to be gotten over with.

"Dearly beloved…wait, what's the girl's name?"

Ben furnished, "It's Emma."

"Dearly beloved, we are gathered here today to join this man and this woman in holy matrimony. Miss Emma, do you take Ben…"

And a few minutes later, in the corral of the FLAT "O," the ceremony was completed.

A sigh escaped from the mouth of Maurice. "Is it all over? She gonna get a paper?"

"Paper?"

"Yeah, the one that says she's married."

"Oh, sure. I got 'em in the bunkhouse. I'll be right back."

In minutes he returned and filled out the proper blanks. Handing the paper to Emma, he pocketed his wedding book, picked up the rake, and returned to the chicken house.

Ben looked from his bride to her father. What should he say? He thought it might be proper to kiss the bride, but, as he had never done it yet, he sensed this was not the time to start.

"Sir, I thank you for comin.' I'll take care'a her the best I can."

Maurice nodded. "I know you will. You promised, and I see what you do to keep a promise. I can feel good about goin' and leavin' 'er, now."

Emma was helped into the saddle, seated modestly sideways because of her skirts.

"Son, I 'speck I'll be goin' on and not see you no more. Anything you find at the place, consider it yours. So, good luck to you."

Ben nodded, watching the two horses turn to follow the path through the trees.

"Wait, sir!"

The horses stopped.

Ben dug into his pockets bringing out several coins in his hand. "Sir, this here ain't much, but it's what I got on me. I want you to take it for what you're leavin' for me. I know it don't half pay for it all, but...."

Maurice looked at the handful of coins. He could certainly make use of them. Extending his hand, he accepted the money that Ben poured into them.

"Thank you, Son."

And they were gone.

Then, that night in the bunkhouse, he could only explain. "I always wanted to ask her, it's just that I hadn't got around to it."

A lot of laughing and joking followed his admission, but they all agreed, on one thing. "Well, anyway, you got yourself a looker. Best I could see around that bonnet, seems like you may'a got your money's worth."

After that, Ben ignored them all. He was having trouble enough with his own thoughts. At the end of the fourth day, he swung into the saddle of his spotted horse and headed through the trees.

What now? What would he be walking into? It was clearly time for the dream to burst into nothingness.

Seven

Ben came through the gate to the smell of beans cooked with cured ham. Taking the horse to the barn, he brushed him and fed him and did this and that to use up the time, but finally it was necessary to go into the house.

Emma was at the stove. She turned to look at him, and the eyes that could be flashing with laughter or sultry with seriousness, were wide with...? What? Fear, maybe? Apprehension?

Ben washed his face at the washstand and combed his hair, dampening it down to keep it neat. He saw the food being put on the table, but he hesitated.

"Cornbread's comin.' Just sit where you want to, Ben."

He took the nearest chair.

It was a silent meal. The old Gran tried a few words, but they died out on the air. Ben decided something had to be said, and it should be said in front of the old woman as well.

"This here's good food, like I ain't had for days. The FLAT "O" ain't especially known for its good grub. Now, I'm goin' out to the barn and get some things done. I think it'd be fair to say to you this.

That paper Emma's got, it don't mean nothin' till she wants it to. I ain't expectin' to stay inside here, so...."

The old woman pulled herself up from the chair, hobbling from the room, and Emma looked at Ben with her frightened eyes. "No, Ben. You ain't gonna do that. This here's your house. You done been put through enough for it to be yours, dead to rights."

Ben objected. "Oh, it wasn't nothin.' Like I told your pa, it wasn't that I didn't want to say... well, it was mostly that I didn't know I was supposed to."

"Me, neither. I thought we was gonna have time...."

"We got time. We got all the time we want. It's just you and me, here, and there ain't no one to tell us what we got'a do nor when."

"And it ain't like I don't like you. I do. I just never thought about... so soon..."

"Me, neither. I'd thought we'd be friends a while."

"And maybe take walks in the woods... together?"

"Or sit on the porch and watch the stars..."

"And talk..."

Ben nodded. "Or take us a ride in a buggy, just for fun."

"Oh, I like a buggy! Pa didn't never get one. Said there was too many'a us to get in a buggy."

"Well, there ain't too many'a us no more. There's buggies built that's just the right size for three." Ben smiled with pleasure that he had finally gotten the words flowing. They came easily, now.

"I'd like that! Where'd we go?" Emma's eyes sparkled with enthusiasm.

"The tradin' post, maybe? And there's new places bein' put up...."

"New folks movin' in? Close, like?"

"Not too far."

"Well, we could..."

"The buggy. There's a place where they make 'em. I can...."

"Won't it take money?"

Ben nodded. "I got money."

"But you gave Pa...?"

"I gave 'im what was in my pocket. Should'a give 'im more for the favor he done me."

"Favor?"

"Yeah. Could'a been a considerable while, yet, for me to get the sense to ask you to…." He hesitated for the reality to sink in. "For me to say to you…."

"I know, Ben."

The eyes. They were now a soft gray-green, and they lowered, a small smile softening her mouth. Ben was surprised, but if he was finally saying the right thing, now was the time to say more of it.

"Yeah, me and my slowness. I could'a waited around for months not sayin' nothin,' and then let some other fellow come in here and…."

"Now, Ben! There weren't no other fellow, and you know it!"

"I don't neither know it. Pretty girl like you, it's a good thing to have your pa bein' with you, bringin' you back home safe."

"Oh, Ben! You say the silliest things!"

Food forgotten, Ben stood and extended his hand. After a moment of hesitation, she reached out to him. Together they left the kitchen.

"You want'a see the garden Gran's helpin' me with?"

"Sure do."

Within the brush fence of the herb garden, Ben looked at the plants, bushy and green. Many of them he recognized.

"You sayin' these plants all got names! Now, if that ain't the beatinest thing I ever heard."

"They all got names, and they all got somethin' they do. Sometimes Gran says they're working plants."

A ferny bush beside him had several black and yellow caterpillars working around in the leaves.

"Believe you got worms on this'n."

"Butterflies."

"Huh? Look more like worms."

"Oh, they're gonna be orange butterflies. That's a dill plant and them butterflies like it. It don't hurt the plant, none. Besides, we got lots'a the plants."

And the evening passed. Eventually they returned to the cabin.

"Ben, you come on in with me. This here's the only good bed in the house, 'cept for Gran's. Mine was good, but they took it along so that if ma's time was to come… you know? It was littler, and pa said it'd fit in the tent."

"Well, I…"

"Come on in. This here's your bedroom, too."

Eight

It was a year later that little Andrew Jackson Green was born. He was named after an eastern president that had once had charge of the country. A lot was said about that president in the papers that made their way into the territory. Some things good and some things bad, but a lot of words had been written. It seemed like a good, strong name.

A postal route was established through the territory from an eastern Oklahoma town called Vinita up into Abilene, Kansas. It brought mail and supplies to the big working ranches and the trading posts. A freighting route was set up, which irregularly brought heavier merchandise.

As Ben had expected, the need for horses was constant and lucrative. He put some of his pastures into native grain plants, those that needed only the amount of moisture the Oklahoma weather provided, and his animals grew sleek and fit on it.

His horses increased. They roamed the pastures, foaled, and grew rounded with fat and flesh, and they brought good prices. It became known, in the way that news gets around, that young horses, properly broke to the saddle or harness, could be bought at the Green spread.

When young Andrew was past three, he was joined by a sister they named Mary Elizabeth, after Emma's mother, and they called her Lizzie. Two years later, their children had a little brother they called Clayton. Andrew was now a big boy of six.

By this time, Andrew was taking his place on the farm, handling the horses as well as many other chores and was eagerly looking forward to helping saddle-break young ponies the minute he became old enough.

By age eight, he was proficient with his rifle and often provided game meat for the table. He found fish by following creek to the spot where it emptied into the Deep Fork, into the gouged-out pool of reddish water painted by the minerals and ores in the red dirt. Catfish and perch were abundant in the pool.

Ben continued to build up the land staked out by his wife's father. He was still fascinated by the words filtering down to them from the eastern government. Words were said that the new territory of Oklahoma should, indeed, all be settled.

Certain portions had been assigned to native tribes, but the central nugget of land was still referred to as Unassigned, even though

Ben and number of other settlers occupied it. It all sounded strange. Why would land that was occupied be referred to as "unassigned"?

These words, however, were nothing new. It was because of them that Maurice Bertrand had been persuaded to move into the land, and though he and many others did not stay, there were tougher, hardier souls who came later, and they did stay.

In the new Oklahoma territory, a good living could be made by anyone who was not afraid of work. Even now, small settlements clustered around trading posts, and letters could be posted out on mail routes circling through the territory every few weeks.

Catalogs were brought into the territory, and fancy goods could be had. Orders could be sent away, and goods received back, sometimes as soon as a month. The catalog, itself, made a good picture book to see what was going on back east. Trading posts with catalogs became very popular.

Andrew, Mary Elizabeth (Lizzie), and young Clay learned their letters and numbers from the few books brought from Missouri by their grandparents so many years ago and from the catalog and various pamphlets.

Old Bridie Scott, now the great grandmother of three, pulled herself along from day to day by the strength of her own determination and a pair of stout walking sticks. The brush-fenced garden had been expanded, little by little, as plants reproduced, and others were added.

On one side of the garden, there were the medicine plants. Perhaps the backbone of them was the rosemary, roots of which Bridie had brought west with her. Being a heat loving plant, it had taken off quickly in the Oklahoma sun and set forth its needle leaves, thick and aromatic with oils.

The leaves were to be harvested on a sunny morning, just after the dew had dried. Hung upsidedown in deep shade, they released their moisture slowly, becoming stiff and brittle. When the stiffness set in, the remaining oils were kept safely inside to be released in the heat of the soup kettle or in the teapot.

Added to soup, a few needles brought up the flavor. Steeped in hot water, they made a tea that warmed the body from the inside, extending comfort to aches and chills. Yes, it was necessary to have many rosemary plants to drive the winter "no see 'em" from the blood and to provide comfort to those weary of the cold.

Another valuable plant was the boneset. Its tall stiff stem and green-white buds and flowers were attractive, but its best value was in the strength it gave to bones. It was good for the healing of a broken arm but even better if it was used regularly, giving strength to the bones, so they would not be broken.

Also loving the Oklahoma sun was the lavender. One might think it was grown for the beauty of its purple flowers, and truly, that would be enough, but that was not true. The precious seeds had come with her father's family from the craggy mountains of the old country across the ocean, and it was a plant to be cherished in all its forms. The delicate-smelling blossoms could be tied in a bundle of cloth and hidden in stored clothing. The smell permeated the cloth, and chewing insects were discouraged.

The fine pointed, silvery leaves of the plant made a tea that was soothing and calming when one had the jitters. It was a cup of tea that was nerve healing, and sleep inducing. It calmed the blood from flowing too rapidly, and blossoms of lavender perfumed water to make a relaxing bath.

And peppermint. Such a wonderful flavoring for the candy made from honey, and who could be expected to live a pleasant life without peppermint to settle stomach upsets? Peppermint tea, tasting so pleasant, was readily taken by small children, and it was valuable for complaints of overeating, or too much activity. Also, peppermint mixed well with other plants for a new and different taste.

One of these other plants might be the bramble. Blackberries, dewberries, and raspberries grew clusters of fuzzy leaves in the spring. Those leaves could be eaten fried in the skillet or could be dried for a rich and full-bodied drink. Berries, picked at their peak of ripeness and dried, added a zest and an attractive color to the tea.

Then there was wormwood, with its lovely aroma and bitter taste. The dried leaves assisted lavender to keep insects from the linens, but stood alone in their ability to clean parasites from the bodies of small children. A child who failed to thrive could often find a good use for a dose of wormwood tea within their bodies.

There was goldenrod for the kidneys, horsetail for healing, and stinging nettle for the aches of old age. The yarrow with its umbrella of tiny white blossoms was so good for cramps in the gut.

The clumped and spreading trees of the creek sheltered the delicate yellow cowslips with their lovely taste and color. A tea made of cowslips would bring the easily high-strung woman back to her natural equilibrium.

The lovely pink coneflower was an aid in combating pains of a winter cold.

Also, hibiscus blossoms, rose petals, blue cornflowers, lady's mantle, shepherd's purse, as well as dill and fennel had their place and their own special uses.

Bridie Scott walked the rows of her garden, snipping here and pruning there, keeping her plants in perfect condition. Gardening with herbs was a constant duty, but it was also a constant pleasure. The texture of the leaves had a satisfying effect on the skin of her old fingers and the scent of the sun-drenched fragrant oils on their leaves... these were an everlasting pleasure. Capping it all was that her Emma seemed to have the same feeling. Yes, Bridie had done herself proud by managing to stay on this red dirt and see her Emma settled and happy. Thank you, God.

Activity went on all around them.

There began to be talk of a rail line to cut the territory in half from the north to the south. Granted, a lot of the talk was initiated by the boomers, still eager to settle the territory. For those in charge, good money could be made in the new cities, if they could just be placed along the rail line.

Newspapers from Arkansas, Texas and Kansas sent reporters into the territory and articles were printed, proclaiming the wonders of the new land, watered so well by the rivers from the Salt Fork in the north, through the Cimarron, to the Canadian Rivers, both north and south. In addition, smaller streams such as the Cottonwood and the Deep Fork, as well as Crutcho and Soldier Creek, did their share.

Old Bridie, now walking with canes, took the toddler, Lizzie, to the garden with her, talking in simple words, pointing to this and that. Perhaps she would take after her mother.

And Emma tended her garden plants.

There were the potatoes, peas, and beans of various kinds. They were the backbone of her meals. Added to these were the native plants used by her grandmother's people for their taste and nutrition.

There was the native amaranth with its thick, succulent leaves to be steamed and served with butter, but if the wealth of greens was more than could be cooked during the season, the tiny pepper-sized seeds of the plant were stripped off in the late summer, and dried to add flavor to baked goods. When ground, they also extended the milled flour, so expensive and hard to get.

The root of the arrowhead plant that grew in creek was dug and added to many dishes. It was good for energy when a lot of work was to be done.

Bittercress and wild onions added zest to summer meals, but dried and crumbled, they put flavor in winter soups and stews as well.

The roots of the cattail were dug and peeled and sliced into a skillet of hot grease to add texture and depth to a meat dish.

Chickweed, the winter salad green, popped up, mildly spicy and pale green in the fall, and it lasted until spring, making a tasty relish for the heavier winter dishes.

Chicory could be grown for its lovely blue flowers alone, but its dried roots made a sharply stimulating drink for winter. By adding a few green pine needles, it became a bracing brew for a dull winter afternoon.

Clover and dandelion blossoms gave a lightness and variety to cornbread and other baked products, and the leaves of the dandelion spiced up the mildness of other greens, such as the lamb's quarter, often called "goosefoot" because of the shape of their leaves. Wild mustard even sprouted in the winter, adding a change of flavor to the chickweed.

The tiny fat seeds of the peppergrass were stripped and ground for their sharp taste, good when sprinkled over the stewed leaves of poke greens, and served with boiled eggs.

And there was the prickly pear cactus. Its thick paddle-like leaves were scraped of spines and cut in strips to prepare like green beans, and they could be had fresh at all times of the year. In the late summer, however, the leaves formed buds around the edges. These buds often reached the size of a small egg, and they could be rolled in batter and fried, or they could be left to bloom and form fruit... a small sugary globe that made excellent jelly with the addition of a little salt.

Another winter sweet fruit was the persimmon. All summer they remained as small green globes of puckery sourness, but in the fall they turned orange and softened, waiting for the first frost. The freezing weather pulled the moisture from the globes, leaving a super-sweet mush within a delicate, wrinkled skin. These tiny fruits could be eaten as candy, straight from the tree, or the seeds could be removed and the highly-sweet mush made into pies and cakes.

Going a bit farther with the uses of the persimmon, the mush could be dried, ground into powder, and used as a sugar for other baked products, or made into candy.

It took a little effort, of course, and doing these things was not as pleasant for Emma, now, as the times when she went with her Gran, but it was a thing to be done if she wished to feed her family well.

Food preparation took a lot of Emma's time.

Nine

It was in the year of 1888 that the simmering caldron of conversation about the opening of the territory finally began to come to a boil. Like a flock of crows descending on a freshly planted cornfield, so a frenzied activity built around the perimeter of the Unassigned Lands.

A favored site had been in the center of the territory at a place called the Oklahoma Station. For the last eight years, it had been targeted by numerous groups of boomers due to its desirability, namely a Star Mail Route that now extended from the Oklahoma town of Vinita in the east, all the way to Albuquerque in the far west.

The desirability of this site was further enhanced by the Arbuckle Trail coming up from the south and crossing the river nearby, linking Texas, on the south, to Kansas on the north.

Due to one thing or another, all of these settlements failed. Many of the settlers were not accustomed to being so far from comforts and amenities, but this problem was corrected by the coming of the Santa Fe Railroad.

It was in 1886 that the clearing for the railroad had began, and mule-drawn graders had scraped out a roadbed.

For the convenience of the workers, a Post Office building was erected at the Oklahoma Station, and the Santa Fe Railroad Company shortened the name of the place to the simple "Oklahoma." Later, to differentiate the territory from the town, "City" was added to the name and it became Oklahoma City.

Actual rail placing began in the spring of 1887, and a section house and pump house were built. A well was dug for the use of the employees, and they were joined on the site by the Quartermaster Department of the US Army, and a house was built for their forwarding agent.

Work continued, and by April of that year, the Santa Fe line was open all the way down from Arkansas City, Kansas, and it was ready to receive freight and passengers. It was then that an attempt was made by the authorities to clear out the boomer settlements before the official opening of the land. It was necessary that the land be open and cleared of inhabitants for what was to come. The Fifth U.S. Cavalry moved in to accomplish this task.

Other business establishments blossomed along the Santa Fe route, and lumber and grain could now be had, as well as other items necessary for homesteading. The grading and clearing operation of the railroad and other excavated roads required a lot of mules and men to drive them. These "mule skinners" also required services.

This was where Ben and the now eighteen-year-old Andrew became involved. In their pastures they kept horses that they broke to the saddle, and alongside of them were the mules, great gray-brown beasts with drooping heads and massive bones, bred for strength in pulling, and also for their endurance.

Many mules were produced at the Green spread, being the neutered product of a horse and a jenny. Good prices were paid for them, and the Green hoof stock became well known.

Ten

The land around Oklahoma City provided such a natural townsite that those who came to work prepared to stay. Soldiers, construction workers, railroad employees, and the owners of the businesses, which supplied them with goods, began to settle in the surrounding area, building themselves everything from dugouts, to squatter's huts, to lumber-built houses.

These "boomers," the first vanguard of the population, had come, planning to stay, assuming the improvements they made on their land would make them owners, in fact.

The older city of Purcell, on the southern edge of the territory, kept a running account of the activities of the boomers, writing about them in their paper, the Purcell Register. It made good copy.

At one point, a reporter wangled an invitation to a boomer camp and was escorted into the trees and treated to a meal created from prairie chicken and quail, topped off with a desert made from bee tree honey. After the meal, he went back to the station.

His hosts, who had entertained him, soon heard of a company of soldiers coming from Fort Reno to "clear them out." Coincidence? Whether or not the reporter had anything to do with it, the boomers fled their houses and hid in the thickets of oak trees.

Bands of soldiers were not the ultimate law, however. Often news of a raid led the soldiers to a noisy "welcoming committee" of several hundred gun-bearing boomers, who just "happened" to be there. The soldiers often found a reason to retreat gracefully and rapidly.

Words were circulated as to what was done to soldiers who interfered with the lives of the squatters, and these stories, true or false, dampened much of the eagerness of the Cavalry.

Gathering together in meetings and talk-groups to encourage themselves, the boomers vowed they would stick together and stay on their land, no matter what. They promised that no military detachment had the legal right to throw them off their claims.

They had worked their land and had food enough to keep them through the winter, and if they were run off, they would only hide in the trees and return to their homes when the coast was clear. It became a badge of their hardiness to be forced to "take to the oaks" and still have the guts to return.

Ben Green, who had added fencing and tilled land to the spread left him by Emma's father, knew that none of this affected him. It seemed unfair that the settlers were being badgered by the law, but he, himself, was not involved.

In the course of his employment, he heard a lot of things. There were many kinds of settlers. There were the bands that came into the territory together, helping each other, and there were lone families of resilient souls who went it alone. It was all good, and he agreed that the land they conquered should be theirs. Certainly.

Ben, however, knew that the land beneath his home was his. His mother's people had been generations on the land to the south, and when he and his father had moved north to the Sac and Fox, they had been free to build where they pleased. Even here in the territory, hadn't the Bertrand's been brought here and promised the land?

There had been no resistance then, and the ownership of the land had not been in question. Why should its ownership belong to the eastern government who had never seen it, rather than to the people who had always lived there?

Clearly, it should belong to the people who had hunted its woodlands, fished its steams, built houses on its land, and grew their crops. This was very clear to him, so he went about his business, causing trouble to no one and giving very little thought to it all.

Young Andrew grew strong and skillful, taught by his father that he should be able to do anything that needed doing, so he did it. When a sawmill began to operate in the vicinity of Oklahoma City, he made the trek, with wagon and mules, through the trees to bring dimension lumber to the Green spread beside the creek.

It took several trips to bring in enough lumber, and he and his father put up a building, larger more suitable, to house the growing family.

Two girls were born to Ben and Emma after Clayton, bringing the family up to five children in addition to their parents.

And Emma, her days busy with the care of her family of seven, hardly had a moment to stop. Like others in the territory, she was never caught up, but always had time to stop for tea, should someone drop by.

The population of the area had increased to the point that she might expect to have company as often as once a week. If a newcomer or a stranger happened by, they were often hailed and enticed into her kitchen for a fresh drink of water, or a cup of tea. Or perhaps a bite to eat.

Old Bridie Scott had managed to survive to the amazing age seventy-two. She wearily passed the days in her garden that she still reached with the aid of the two canes. Balancing herself and inching forward, she looked at the thriving plants and stretched her brain to remember every bit of information that she needed to pass on.

It was a worry to Emma that Gran was losing strength, but the old woman was still able to get to her favorite place, and the busy Emma passed it from her mind. Then came the time when she did not appear for the evening meal.

"Lizzie?" Emma called to her oldest daughter. "Lizzie, go see if you can find Gran. It ain't like her to keep us waitin'."

Lizzie found her.

Gran had settled onto her stone bench, built for her by young Andrew when she could no longer lower herself to her favorite rock. He had fashioned a backrest of strips of wood, so she could rest more easily. The late afternoon sun had warmed her, and a chorus of birds had flocked in the trees over her head, chattering noisily.

As it so often was in her garden, Bridie was alone, so it seemed only natural to converse with her Maker. "You give me a good life, Lord. I can't see how a body'd be able to think of a thing he'd need that he couldn't get here in this here red land."

She looked down the rows of plants, the increase of those so carefully dug, and brought here by herself and young Emma.

"And that Emma, Lord, she was one'a the good things You give to me. I get happy bumps all over me, just thinkin'a that brave girl sayin' she'd stay here with me. I knew then it was the place for her and me. I still know it."

The time had passed by, that afternoon, and Andrew a big boy of twelve years old at that time, had whistled through his teeth for the dogs he had trained to bring in the milk cows. It would soon be time to eat, and old Bridie Scott knew she should begin to make her way to the house.

Her two canes lay across her lap over her clean apron. She gazed at them and sighed with recriminations over her laziness. How shameful to spend all afternoon in the garden and still have a clean apron, but she had been forbidden to kneel in the rows and pull weeds. Emma had told her it would be too worrisome for her to think Gran might need help to get up, and no one would be there to give it. She did not wish to worry her precious Emma.

Bridie smiled to herself with the knowledge that her sweet Emma had told her she must just sit on the bench and rest, because she had earned it.

Had she? How could one ever earn the wonders of the life she had been given? How, indeed!

"Lord, how much does a person need to do 'afore You take 'em home? I done got to the point I ain't a help to no one no more. Now, I ain't wantin' to be one to tell You what to do, but when You're ready for me, I'll be waitin'."

The thought of what heaven would look like, according to the Good Book, put a smile on Bridie's face. The Book said there'd be a river, and it would be so clear, it would look like crystal glass. That would be strange, after the murky red water of this land. She'd get used to it, though.

Then she thought of the trees. Twelve different kinds of fruit would grow there, and it wouldn't even have to be canned or dried. There would be a fresh new kind of fruit every month, and long before anyone got tired of it, there'd be a new kind. Using her shaky old fingers, she tried to name twelve kinds of fruit, but she kept forgetting the first ones before she got finished.

"I reckon it'll just have to be a surprise."

Wouldn't need any kerosene, either. Brightness would be everywhere, and there wouldn't be any night. That's what the Good Book said.

She leaned forward, and fumbling for the handle of one of her canes, she sighed. Moving about was so hard to do, she'd just wait and that sweet little Mary Elizabeth would come and help her. She, herself, had plenty of time to sit and wait, and the little girl had chores, so she'd just sit here and wait with her thoughts.

There was so much to think on about heaven. When she got there, she wouldn't be tired anymore.

The lowering sun shone warmly on her shoulders, neck and the back of her head. Smiling, she leaned her head against the solid boards of the back of her bench. With a relaxed sigh, she made the comfortable transfer from her bench in the garden to her new home on the distant golden shore. Her old lips still held the smile of pleasure at what she saw when she got there.

Young Lizzie ran to the garden where she was sure her Gran could be, and she found her with her eyes closed. Asleep.

"Gran? Gran, it's time to eat and Ma says bring you."

But Gran did not open her eyes.

"Gran…? Wake up, Gran?"

Patting her young and smooth hands on the wrinkled ones resting on the clean apron, the little girl knew Gran would not wake up. With wet eyes and a trembling chin, she ran to the house.

"Ma…! Pa..! Come and see Gran…!"

Eleven

They had found a place in the edge of the trees beside a large oak, a place where they were able to dig past the network of tree roots. With love and tears, the wrinkled body of old Bridget McMahan Scott was put to rest.

"Wait!" commanded young Andrew, and he had run to the garden and struggled back with the resting stone, smooth and flat, and certainly Gran's favorite place.

"We could put the stone… maybe… right here? I know she ain't gonna need it no more, but maybe one of us…? We might…well, we could…?"

Ben nodded. "Very good idea, Son. Someone might need to stop here and rest, sometime. It'd be a good place to rest, here in the shade. Let's put it right up here at the end."

Andrew scooted the stone into place and dusted his hands on his overalls, and then the family returned to their chores. There was always something to do. Later there would be an occasion to shed private tears and rest a moment on the smooth, flat stone.

Emma had reason, many times, to be glad of the stone. For weeks and months, tears welled up in her eyes, and she was obliged to walk out past the garden and sit on the stone. It drew her with an invisible cord and the tears that seemed to drown her soul were shed, streaming down her face.

She wept for the loneliness that only Gran had been able to fill, and she wept for gratefulness that the courage of Gran had made her present life possible.

Of course, that had happened years ago, and now Emma often sat on the stone without weeping, but the small corner of loneliness remained, and nothing in her life could fill it. Truly, each person has his special place that no one else could fill.

The years had then passed quickly, and Andrew was a young man of eighteen, as tall and strong as his father, and very nearly as skillful.

It was about this time that the government surveyors came by.

In their wagons and with their fancy instruments, they came, and they marched forward, sighting through the trees. Crews of workmen came with them, and when a tree blocked the sights of the surveyors, that tree was cut away.

Ben and Andrew spared a short time from their work to try to make sense of it all. It seemed a good thing to mark the land up in regular pieces so no two people would claim the same piece of land, and so there would be no argument as to whom it belonged to, but there seemed to be more to it than that.

When they came near to the Green's property, the surveyors sighted right through a fenced horse pasture, cutting their trees where they would, without a please or a thank you.

What was going on? What would the rules be, concerning the opening of the land? Did the surveyors know?

Well, no, the surveyors said, they weren't sure what the rules would be, except that no one could have more than a quarter section, 160 acres, total.

Well, Ben reasoned, that should be enough for anyone. Shouldn't it?

Changing the fence line to keep it within the surveyor's boundaries, Ben chose the section where the house had been built, and it luckily took in the crystal spring and a corner of the free-flowing creek, so handy for the horses to drink.

The settling would be a good thing for everyone. Wouldn't it?

It would be good to have neighbors so close. Imagine the wonder of it all, if they could have friends so close that they could come over of an evening to sit and talk?

There were a lot of small homesteads around the FLAT "O" Ranch, and they began to be hassled by soldiers from the Fifth Cavalry stationed in the territory. The hassling became so great that the owners of the FLAT "O" made the decision to shut down and take their stock into the Chickasaw lands to the south. Some of those who had homesteads also left, but others remained.

Where more than two or three gathered, the conversation invariably turned to the opening of the land and to the soldiers with their orders to clear out the boomers.

Ben knew the problem did not involve him, and he felt bad for those others who were involved. But that was all before the soldiers came to his house.

The two men rode up, and Ben left his chores in the barn and went to meet them. Neighborliness demanded as much.

"Evenin,' friends. What can I do for you?"

The corporal dropped nimbly off his horse and approached Ben.

"Corporal McKelvey, here. What's your name?"

"Name's Ben Green. Got troubles somewhere, that I can help out with?"

"Nope. I reckon the help's comin' the other way."

"Huh?"

"I come to make sure you folks was a'clearin' out. Time's gettin' close, and we got'a make sure there's no one still inside'a the lines."

"Inside the lines?"

"Yeah, inside the Unassigned Lands."

"'Fraid I don't follow you, sir."

The corporal seemed surprised. "I figured everyone knew. These here quarter section claims are gonna be up for grabs in the land run that'll be held in April. If you're wantin' land, you'll have to clear out and line up at the border, just like everyone else."

Ben nodded, agreeable. "That's what I hear, officer. But this here land, I been on it for nigh onto twenty years, buildin' it up from the log cabin you see out yonder, with one-strand wire fences, that was put up by my wife's pa. It was my understandin' that the land settled by the new people was to be theirs if they put on improvements like I put on mine. I got a good spring, but I got a dug well, too, for the waterin' of the stock."

The corporal listened with expressionless eyes. "I can see all that, and you're not the only one like you. But that don't make no difference to the rules, and you're on land that ain't yours."

Ben felt he must disagree. "The way I see it, it don't belong to the government, neither. My ma, she was born on the land here about and all her people before her. I'd be of the mind it was more hers than the government's."

"Where is your ma?"

"Died, when I was a little fellow."

"What was her tribe?"

"Tribe?"

The corporal rephrased the question. "What were your Ma's people called? Were they Sac and Fox?"

"Oh. My Pa said he married her in the Wichita country. Reckon you'd say she was Wichita."

The corporal nodded. "Well, Wichita land's be down south. It's already been took. This here is a different land. Where is your pa? Is he Indian?"

"No, he ain't Indian, but he's married to a Sac and Fox woman."

"She ain't your ma, though."

"No."

"Then you're right back where you were. This here visit is a friendly passin',' just to tell you the rules. I got'a see you gettin' your stuff together to get off. Me and the private, here, we've got the job'a clearin' the land, whether we agree with it or not. If we can't do it, they'll send enough others to get it done."

"I got'a move? But I got stock and…"

"You'll have to decide what to do with it. You got a while yet, but I got'a see you tryin' to get it done. 'Course, you got the right to enter the run, and if you was the first to stake a claim on this land, you'd get it back."

"But the animals…? Corporal, that's what we do, me and my son. We raise animals. There's been times you people bought my horses."

"I know, mister. But that's the rules. We just stopped by tell you. We'll be off, now."

"So long, Officer."

Ben watched as the two uniformed men rode away. Andrew came in from the horse lot, puzzled.

"What's wrong, Pa?"

Ben drew in a breath and sighed, long and loud, seeming to pull himself farther within his body and to wilt, just like a tender plant in the sun.

"He's got'a be wrong. It can't be the way he said."

"What's that way, Pa?"

"That soldier, he says we ain't got our land, and it don't matter what all we done to it, we

"But the horses, Pa…?"

"I know, and that's what I said. He said that was our business, and we'd just have to deal with it."

"This bein' your ma's land… that don't count for nothin'?'

"Don't seem to. Might'a if she'd been alive. I'm thinkin' there wasn't no paper on their marriage, and pa wasn't even for sure if they was married by a preacher that got papers sent in. He wasn't for sure what her actual name was. Called 'er Rose."

"But your pa, he could come and say…."

Ben shook his head. "Nothin' he could say'd change it. He wasn't born here."

The very thought of it drained away his strength, and Ben leaned against the hard rail fence he had built from the split sections of tough blackjack oak. He had built the fence, carefully notching the rails to make it solid. Scarce money had bought the strands of fence wire that enclosed the pastures.

Twenty-six horses and half that many mules were contained within the fences.

"Ma know?"

"Huh?"

"You had a chance to tell ma what the man said?"

Ben shook his head, slowly. "Gonna wait a few days. Could be, I'll have a idea on what to do. No need to have the both'a us worryin' about the same thing." Then he added, "Till we have to."

Father and son dragged themselves back to their work, their thoughts far away from what they did.

Nagging at the back of Ben's mind was the thought of something he should be thinking... something that would help him make sense of it all. His Pa had certain words he read in the Book that had seemed to help him when he was puzzled. If he could just remember what it was.

He had learned his first words in the Bible his grandmother had given to his Pa, and it must have been a good book to learn from, or his Pa had been an uncommonly good teacher, because Ben could read and understand just about any printed material he came across. The word he wanted to remember seemed to sound like "trust," and that was one commonly used in his everyday speech, but how was it used in the Book?

The evening meal was lively with chatter from the little girls, and other things that needed to be said, and it was not noticed that Ben and Andrew had little to say.

Over desert, Ben announced that he had a little business on west, and he'd go take care of it in the morning. It was not an unusual thing, and nothing more was said when Ben added, "I'll be needin' you to go along, son."

Andrew had sighed and nodded, knowingly, woodenly spooning blackberry cobbler into his mouth.

What had to be done, just had to be done. But it might help if he understood just a little more.

That night he lay in the dark his eyes hopelessly open and wide awake. Could he maybe find that word his father liked in the huge book full of so many words? Trying to remember it seemed the word might have been said by the wisest man, or maybe that man's father.

They had both written part of the Book, and their stories were side by side.

Slipping quietly from the bed, he lit a lamp and took his worn copy of the Bible from its place, still wrapped in the tattered lace shawl that had belonged to his grandmother. When he had left his father's house with his horses, his father had handed it to him, apologizing that he had nothing else to pass on. Ben had taken it, knowing it was a valued possession, but he had just put it away. That could have been a mistake. It had given help to his Pa, and maybe it could help him. He began to read.

As the hours passed by, he began to be caught up into the words. He backed up and re-read passages forgetting the word that had placed him there. There remained, however, a nagging itch at the back of his mind.

Then he read about those who obeyed God and what God would do for them. He read, "Ten thousand shall fall at thy side, and ten thousand at thy right hand, and it shall not come nigh thee." After the third reading, he decided that perhaps this was more comforting than whatever he had been looking for. Right now, it was interesting to think that he could fell "a thousand" and with his son's help, it would make it "ten thousand."

With that reasoning, his own family could perhaps hold off the whole of the Oklahoma Territory. He read no farther because the idea of "ten thousand" was so heavily on his mind, he needed to think. Going back to his bed, he stared up in the darkness seeking to make sense of it all.

Sometime before daylight he drifted into sleep, but awoke with the firm determination to see what it was that he must do to acquire the strength he would need. There would be a way. Tomorrow he would find it and he would be able to protect his land and his family. He would find the strength to hold for his own children what he had considered to be his already. His father had started with nothing and had brought him here, and could he do less for his own family?

Encouraged, he ate a hearty breakfast and kept his decision to himself. He would know much more by nightfall, and he could make better decisions. He had decided, however, to keep the Book handy and give it a little more attention. It was clear to him that it contained answers.

If anyone was in need of answers, it was certainly Ben for the whole world had begun of seem backwards.

Twelve

Ben and Andrew left early, and young Clay shouldered his gun and headed for the woods. Lizzie had permission to make cookies, but first, the nuts must be cracked and the kernels picked out.

Younger than Clayton, in fact, only seven years old, was Sarah Bridget, called Sally, and two years younger was Annie Lee. Eagerly waiting with a hammer for cracking and a crochet hook out picking out the kernels, the two girls encouraged their sister along. Sacks of nuts gathered in the fall now hung from the ceiling of the feed room of the barn. Suspending them from the ceiling was the only way to keep the squirrels from carrying them off.

As Liz and the little girls left the house taking their noisy racket with them, a silence descended that drug down on Emma's shoulders. Like a weight, the quietness crowded around and pushed against her with its sadness. But what was there to be sad about?

It had been months, maybe years, since she had been forced by loneliness to visit the stone at Gran's grave. The pain of her passing had dissolved into emptiness, and it left its own uneasiness. She looked around at the things that she should be doing and turned her back on them, walking out to the enclosure around the plants.

The garden was a constant pleasure to Emma, and as she gathered herbs for tea… or for the stomachache… or for jittery nerves, she could hear the way Gran's voice sounded and the way she said her words. It was only in the garden that the clear memory of her words passed through Emma's mind.

Walking past the garden, she went on to the headstone and lowered herself down on it, leaning back against the rough bark of the oak. The tree had grown large in the years since Gran had gone. Why, the branches were so thick and dark, it was almost impossible to see up into it. That made it a favorite place for bird nests.

Emma slumped wearily, puzzled over her tiredness. The girls had taken over a lot of the garden work, and the canning and drying season had not yet come on. It was only March, but many of the garden things were already planted.

A bang sounded in the timber, followed closely by another one. The familiar sound meant that meat for supper was assured, but no one would know what it was until Clay brought it in. He was a crack shot and had taken over most of the hunting.

Liz, barely sixteen, was equally as good with the gun, but she did not enjoy hunting. Emma, herself, had never shot any of the guns, feeling there were enough others to do it.

Ben was already talking of buying guns for the little girls and getting them started. He had a thing about guns. He was firm. Everyone he loved needed to be able to shoot, either to feed himself or defend himself as the occasion demanded.

It would be good when the dreaded land run was finally over, and the woodlands would be filled with people. From where she sat, she could see the line made by the surveyors as they had cut the trees and trimmed limbs to make their straight lines and had pounded their marking stakes. A small smile played about her lips at the thought of someone living just past her front gate.

Well, the run was weeks away, and she had a lot to do, so she left the stone and went slowly to the house. Such a good house! Room for everyone, and not crowded like the log cabin had been when she lived there with her parents.

Ben and Andrew rode side by side when possible, otherwise single file through the trees. The straight lines made by the surveyors made good trails, and father and son headed toward the headquarters of the Fifth Cavalry.

"You got any ideas yet, pa?"

Ben jogged along. He had been awake the whole night, thinking. He had no ideas of value. "Not yet, son."

As they reached Taylor Springs, they saw the Cavalry uniforms everywhere. At the headquarters, he explained his way through three men and finally was in front of the captain in charge.

No, there had been no mistake. The rules were that NOBODY be inside the boundaries of the territory on the weeks before the run. That meant absolutely nobody.

Perhaps he was a native, entitled to special consideration, but could he prove it?

Well, if he couldn't prove it, he was just like everyone else. He was to move out of the territory and join the run. Perhaps he could get land if he had a horse that was fast enough. There would be a way.

Thirteen

With a discouraged sigh, father and son left the camp and headed down toward Oklahoma City and its activity. Clouds of dust boiled up behind the horse-drawn graders. The air was thick with the yells of the muleskinners as they drove the beasts, pulling the red dirt into shapes suitable for making roadbeds.

The railroad had brought stacks of lumber and piles of brick, and even now, the kiln-baked blocks were being placed in their herringbone pattern to pave the marked-out street.

Ben found the foreman.

Sure, man, they could use more mules. Only thing was, they couldn't pay for them. The boss man said they had enough animals, so they'd just get their work done with what they had.

"Well," Ben began. "I got a plan on how we can conduct a little business."

"Got'a be fast with it. I got'a get back to the job."

"Won't take long. I got a reason I can't keep my mules at my place for a while. So I was…."

"You got a disease goin' on? 'Cause if you do…."

"Naw, it ain't nothin' like that. It's just that I'll not be in a position to take care'a the mules."

"Told you I didn't have no money to spend."

"Didn't ask for none."

"You givin' away your mules?" The foreman chuckled, wiping a dusty hand over his sweaty face.

Ben explained, "Not the whole mule, just his time."

"What'd'ya mean, it's time?"

"What I got'a do is find a place for the beasts for a month, maybe six weeks. Here with you, I know they'd be fed and took care of. They're all young yet, but they been broke to the reins, and…."

"You'd make us the loan of some mules… sure enough?"

"Yep."

"You ain't expectin' no money for the loan of 'em?"

"Nope, but they got'a be fed good."

"No trick there. I got lots'a money for mule feed… just none for the mules, themselves."

"Then I'll bring 'em."

"When?"

"Week, maybe ten days."

"Sure thing, fellow. We'll be glad to get 'em. It's a pair? Two pair?"

"Naw, man. It's thirteen."

"Thirteen? Did I hear you right?"

"You must'a, 'cause that's what I said."

"Thirteen mules! YIPPIIEE! Could be I can get caught up to my schedule. Could you bring 'em tomorrow?"

Ben shook his head. "Nope. Got things to do tomorrow."

The foreman looked longingly toward Andrew. "Maybe him...?"

"Naw. I need him, too."

"Well, bring 'em when you can...."

"Sure, and we'll be seein' you."

As they rode off, Andrew commented, "Pa, I could bring some'a them mules on down here if...."

"No, son. We said a week. If we brought 'em sooner, it'd start lookin' like we was over anxious, and he might get the idea he was doin' us a favor. As it is, he's lookin' forward to getting' 'em, and come time we need us a favor he could do for us, he'll be open to doin' it."

"I see what you mean. So that'll take care'a the mules."

Ben nodded. That left twenty-six horses. If the FLAT "O" was just still there... but it wasn't. And besides, there was another matter.

"Son, judgin' the horses like you know 'em, which'n would be the fastest, do you think?"

"Fastest? Like long haul or sprint?"

"Sprint. More like one able to zigzag and duck under trees."

"Hmmm, I hadn't thought on it like that."

"Reckon we better."

"The run?"

"Gonna have to think on it."

"I could sort out some, and you could try 'em, makin' up your mind."

"It'd not be my mind to be made up. It'd be yours."

"Mine? But wouldn't you...?" His heart pounded as he began to see the direction of the conversation and the importance of his part in it.

His father explained, "I could look 'im over, but the choosin' and the runnin', that'd be up to you."

"Me? You'd want me to make the run?" He needed to be sure that what he thought was said, was actually said.

"There'd be none better. You pretty nearly spent half your life with your backside in a saddle! Don't see how we could do no better'n you."

"Well, sure, pa. I could...." His voice trailed off as the dread of its seriousness settled onto him. "Pa, couldn't we both saddle up? Likely one of us...."

Ben shook his head. "You're the best we got, son. I got other things to do."

Andrew rode on in silence, not bothering to ask what other things there were to be done. That was pa's business.

It had been a long day for the two men, and springtime dusk had settled in, making a dark box-shape of the house, the lighted windows of the kitchen shining like welcoming eyes, watching for them to come in.

The sweet spice of nut cookies met them at the door, and leftover baked ham with sweet potatoes was on the table, along with a kettle of spring greens, stewed and flavored with seasoning from the garden.

Father and son hardly had a mind to appreciate the sight and smell of it all.

Fourteen

It was on the second of April, twenty days before the advertised land run, that Ben called his family together. It was time to make plans.

"I want'a say to you, I been wrong. Knowin' this here was the land that belonged to my ma's people, gave me the idea it'd be mine. Bein' a good land, I was glad to have others comin' in to get a share. Seems I was mistakened in my thinkin'."

Emma had noticed a preoccupation in Ben, but he often had periods of semi-silence when there was a thing to be planned or figured out. It was her way to let him have his time and space, knowing it would pass. And so, for the last couple of weeks he had been going through one of those times.

"You was wrong in your thinkin'? How'd that be?"

"I'm a'fixin' to tell you. This here land that's to be opened up to settlers...? That the surveyors marked off? Well, our land is bein' stirred in the mix."

"Our land?" Emma's forehead creased with puzzlement.

Young Clayton leaned forward with concern. "No, pa. You said we was…."

"Hush, Clayton. I was wrong. Seems the government in the east, that ain't never been here nor seen the land, seems they think they know more'n us, that's been here forever. Seems folks that never set a foot on it think it'd be theirs to decide what to do with."

Liz leaned forward, studying her father with her smokey blue eyes. Her sixteen years of life, protected though she was, had taught her that things can change rapidly. Storms from the northwest can turn into whirling masses of air that can pull the mighty oaks from their roots. The dying down of a strong south breeze in the fall can bring frost before morning, covering the world with white furry crystals. She knew how quickly things could change.

"Pa, how're we gonna keep 'em from takin' our land?"

"Good question, Lizzie. I been givin' it a lot'a thought. Me and Andrew, we checked on what the soldier said, and it's true. We got'a clear ourselves out'a here or get ourselves in trouble with the law."

Clayton, again. "With the law, Pa? We ain't never done a thing wrong! You always told us…."

"And I was wrong," he repeated, wearily. "Now, listen to what I got planned. In three days, Andrew and me, we're gonna take the mules over to the road-buildin' in the City. Clay is a'goin' along. Thirteen'a them pesky stubborn animals could be handful for two."

Clayton's eyes brightened. It wasn't all bad if he was to finally get to help in a delivery. "You got 'em all sold, Pa?"

"No, Son. Just a loan."

Quick to see a profit, Clayton suggested, "We gettin' money for the loan."

"Not this time. We just got'a hide 'em for a while."

"Hide 'em! But, Pa…"

"I know, Son. You got'a lot'a questions. I want you to wait and listen, and then you can say all you want to."

Clayton nodded and looked down, studying his palm, calloused from using the saw, the hammer, and other tools

"Now, what it is we got'a do, is this. We're takin' the mules down to the work site. Foreman down there'll take care of 'em in exchange for the use of 'em. Then the horses, they all got'a go over to Pa's place."

Emma again. "All the way over to the Sac and Fox? But…"

"Emma, honey, I said to you, we got'a clear out'a here. We got the two hogs I was fixin' to butcher, and we'll get that done and the meat took care of, but the boar and them two other sows, they'll be took down to the canyon. The little canyon with the spring in it."

Then Lizzie. "Pa, the wolves! At night time, you think…?"

"We'll lock 'em in a cave with wire and brush. Daytime they'll be safe, but come dark, someone with a gun'll be down there with 'em."

"Down there all night?"

"All night," Ben pronounced with finality. "Then the little girls, they got'a go over with the horses, and Emma, you'll be goin', too."

"Me? But I need to be here…."

"Wait, Emma. I got'a explain. The little girls need you, and…."

"But Lizzie could go."

"I need Lizzie here. I'm hatin' to say it, but there ain't no away around it. I need her on a gun."

"GUN! But, Ben…."

"It's the only way, Emma, honey. You ain't been taught to handle the gun like she has. Could be, you'd get excited and shoot, and hit somebody. Liz, now, she can pop a twig out of a tree top and land it on somebody's head. She's got 'er a steady hand, and that'll be what we need."

Clayton's eyes, shoebutton black, widened with excitement. "Me, Pa! What'll I do?"

"Plenty. Part'a the time, you'll be in the canyon with the hogs."

"Aw, Pa…"

"They's lots'a jobs. Now, this here's the second'a April, and we got twenty days. In a week, we'll all go east with the horses. Emma, you put what you'll need in the wagon. Then me'n Andrew, Liz, and Clay, we'll come back, and then our horses, them that we rode back, they got'a be put in the canyon."

He looked around at the ring of faces, silent, finally, each with their own racing thoughts.

"Then there'll be ten days left. If'n I don't miss my guess, that soldier'll make regular rounds to see for sure we cleared out like he warned us. I'm thinkin' there's no reason to blame him, havin' to take orders like he does, so we'll make it easier for 'em. We'll be gone."

Clayton edged closer to his father. "Really gone?"

"Yeah, far as he knows. Me and you boys, we'll be in the barn, and we'll not be able to be found. There's hay a'plenty to hide under.

And Liz, she'll be in the old log house. They's that sleepin' loft down at the end that old Maurice made for the boys. Partly it's closed off, and if Liz was to be in that part, there's be no way for her to be seen, less'n she sneezed at the wrong time. That's why I want her to go down there with soap and water and a brush. That cubby hole's got'a be cleaned out'a dust and spider webs, so's she don't get no ticklin' in 'er nose.'

Ben paused, sipping from the tea mug beside him.

"Now, there'll be that last ten days, and we still got'a eat. The way I got it figured, the soldiers'll not be out searchin' at night. So if we use a candle on the floor for light, so's not to put light through the windows, we can cook a little food."

Liz had been following closely. "The smoke, Pa. Wouldn't a body be able to smell the smoke, us cookin' at night?"

"Could be, but not likely. We'll keep it low and get it done early. Bein' spring'a the year, they's smells a'plenty out there. Green things growin' and flowers bloomin,' they all make smells. I'll leave it to you and your ma to say what'd be the best to cook. We can figure on eatin' cold beans and taters and a few flapjack sandwiches. I figure we still got jars full'a berries and corn. "

His eyes settled on Emma, who ran a quick inventory of her pantry, and nodded. "Reckon I ought'a take the jars out'a the pantry and hide 'em. No person'd leave food, if they was to for sure clear out. It'll look more natural."

"Good idea. And the clothes, too. Your's can go with you, and ours can be hid under the hay in the loft. So, anybody got any ideas?"

Clayton did. "You gonna let me shoot, Pa?"

"You ain't gonna shoot less'n you have to. We don't need to go wastin' shot. Between now and then, it'll be up to you and your brother to work out who takes care'a the animals in the canyon, but that last day, the day'a the run, you'll be in the hayloft at that little window. We'll hang up a thin curtain that you can see through, and you'll stay there and keep your trigger finger in your pocket, less'n you hear from me."

"What'll I hear?"

"I'll tell you later. Now, Liz, she'll be in the big oak by the grave. That tree's got limbs bigger'n a lot'a trees, and she can move around to keep out'a sight of anyone lookin' up from the ground."

"Who'd it be, Pa? Soldiers?"

"No, Son. I figure it'd be a runner wantin' to take our land.'

Liz's eyes narrowed. "And I got'a shoot 'im?"

"No, Liz. If it's a person that's got'a be shot, it'll be me that does the shootin.'"

"But Ben!" wailed Emma.

"Emma, honey, there ain't nobody gonna take our land. Your pa brought you here, and your Gran kept you here. You and the land was give to me in one package, and it was the best thing ever done for me. I ain't lettin' it get away."

Clayton pulled the talk back to the subject of defense. "Pa?"

"Huh?"

"Andrew. What's he gonna do? You ain't said where he'll be?"

"I'm fixin' to. Andrew, he's gonna be over on the line four miles to the east. He'll be on whatever horse he thinks is the fastest, and he'll be waitin' for the gunshot."

"He'll be in the run?"

"He's the best we got. I figure he's got a better'n even chance'a makin' it. Him, knowin' right where he needs to go, and us here holdin' it for 'im. That'll give him a good boost."

Silence. Each grownup in the room scanned his mind for an idea that could possible help. The little girls had become bored and had lapsed into a game of their own behind the cook stove. Their soft voices made a background sound for the thoughts of those around the table.

Liz quietly left the table and took a tin of fresh baked cookies from the cupboard. She set them on the table, and then refilled the tea mugs with steaming brew.

Ben nodded approval. Picking up a spicy, delicately browned cookie, he wondered, "These here… they keep over a good while, don't they?"

Emma nodded. "They do if I can keep hands out'a the tin."

"I'd be thinkin', then, if a lot'a these was made… a body'd be able to make a meal out'a these and a mug'a milk… and that cow's got'a be milked anyway."

Emma left the table and came back with a pencil and a scrap of paper. She wrote: "Hide clothes, food and dishes. Bake cookies."

"The dog, Pa? What'll we do with old Barker?"

"He'll go east. Likely he'll have to be tied up the whole time or he'll be back here just when we don't need to be havin' 'im around."

Ben to Andrew. "Son, I'm figurin' you just about settled your mind on a horse?"

"Almost. There's the black stallion we was keepin' for stud. There was a time that he'd be the fastest, but now I'm thinkin' a that roan, the one that just wandered in, and we thought somebody'd be here to claim 'im? It's been over two months, and… well, I really like the way he moves through the woods."

Ben nodded encouragement, and all eyes centered on Andrew for more words of comfort.

"So I been takin' 'im out. Walkin' 'im over to the line and runnin' 'im back. Sort'a teachin' 'im what'll be like. You know what, Pa? There's been a wagon pulled up to the Deep Fork for the last two days. Folks just settin' there, waitin'."

"You didn't say nothin' to 'em, did you?"

"No, Pa. Figured you didn't want me to."

"Figured right. You thinkin' the roan is faster than the black stud?"

"Younger, is all. If it'd been five years ago…." But it wasn't five years ago. It was this month.

"Yeah. Could be faster, and you'll need to stay away from the Deep Fork with 'im."

"But that's the closest place."

"Could be, but it won't make too much difference. The way I figure it, me and Liz and Clay, we'll hold this place till you get here."

Clay smiled slightly to himself and again studied his hands in his lap. With a quick reflex, he tested his trigger finger. It seemed to be working well.

"Pa, if a body'd come in at the gate, a shot from the barn loft window'd not reach 'im."

Ben nodded. "That's what I'm countin' on. I don't want you bein' over eager and hurtin' somebody."

"But, Pa…"

"You heard me. Now, Liz, you and me, we're gonna climb up the big oak and sight through the trees to the cottonwood by the gate. Come time somebody looks at the gate like he's fixin' to stake a claim on what we got, you'll take a bead on a twig limb. Come time he steps through the gate, that'll be when you pull the trigger, droppin' the twig down in front'a the person. The noise and that twig, I figure they'll stop most folks."

Liz thoughtfully nibbled the cookie and nodded.

"But then, happen he don't stop, you'll aim again at a rock. We'll decide where that rock'll be, and you'll shoot to ricochet in the air. If he don't step back and leave, you'll shoot in the air, and that'll be the signal for Clay to aim at 'im. A pepperin'a shot from that far off, it'll not hurt 'im less'n it gets in his eye, which I don't expect to happen."

Clay's eyes sparkled, and he re-tested his trigger finger. It still worked well.

"What next, Pa?"

"If the danged fool keeps on a'comin' toward the house, or if he makes out to pound in a claim stake, we'll all three make air shots. Hearin' shot from three ways, that'll make 'im take off."

"What if it don't, Pa?"

"Then one of us'll need to be lookin' for a doctor to take care'a some poor traveler's busted kneecap. There's been times when one fellow stepped in the front'a of a hunter with a gun aimed at a rabbit. That's about the level to loose a knee. It'd be a bad thing, loosin' a knee in this country, with so much work and walkin' to be done. We'd be doin' the best we could for 'im if such of a thing happened to somebody goin' past our house."

Emma frowned with concern. "Ben, you'd really...?"

"You heard me say to your pa that I'd be takin' care'a you and this place he left me, and there ain't been no change since then. So you plan on takin' yourself and the little ones and tryin' not to worry. Come three days after the run, we'll be comin' after you. By then, the garden'll be a mess'a weeds, and you'll be needin' to get at it."

This touch of humor brought a smile to Emma's concerned face. She added one final annotation to her list. "Hide everything."

Then calling to the seven year old hiding behind the stove, "Sally, come on out of there and rinse the cups. Then I got things for you and Annie to do."

They were certainly big enough to start picking the kernels from the nuts for the cookies. If they ate most of them, what did it matter? The woods had been full of nuts, and they had only to beat the squirrels to them. Next fall there would be another crop... for hadn't Ben said he would take care of their red dirt farm? Hadn't he said that no one would take it from him?

Fifteen

It was decided that Clayton would be left to care for the stock when the horses were taken away. Ben watched as the string of animals walked past, a team pulling the wagon with his wife and two little girls aboard. Behind it were tied twelve animals. It was really too many, and they would likely tangle their tethers, but it had to be.

Andrew was next, leading three, followed by Liz, leading three more. What was left was the big stallion and his own following of the last three. Twenty-six animals.

They made an impressive sight as they disappeared through the trees, following along the winding creek toward Deep Fork.

Bringing up the rear, Ben moved into position. Four miles to the east they reached the Deep Fork, planning to follow it through the Sac and Fox land to the village where old Lem lived.

Even above the sound of the animals, Ben was aware of other sounds. A muted nicker of a strange horse drifted past, and he looked sidelong, without turning his head.

Through the trees he saw the corporal, flanked by the private, and they were standing still, watching. What wonderful luck, Ben thought. He couldn't have asked for better timing. Perhaps things were beginning to work in his favor. The soldiers were undoubtedly on their way to see if their orders had been obeyed.

Ben did not allude to their presence. Ignoring them instead, he followed the path made by the wagon, turning to walk along the edge of the Deep Fork. Sure enough, where Andrew had seen a wagon and team waiting, there were two others. Those planning to be part of the run were already gathering at the eastern line.

Still a week to go, and they were gathered there already. Who could resist free land?

The corporal, Amos McKelvey, turned to the private. "Look Jonathan. That's a sight I'm glad to see. That settler decided to clear out. I was afraid he'd decide to fight for it, and we'd be forced to bring in help to clear 'im out."

"Help? We could…"

"Not this time. A man like that one, with grown youngens…? We'd be facin' up agin a arsenal. Easier that we come up agin a whole detachment of the Fifth Cavalry than that fellow wantin' to keep a farm what he's worked for and built up like that'n."

The private nodded. "Don't hardly seem fair, though. It's a good place he's built up. He ought'n to have to lose it."

"No, it don't seem right. But the army'll think of 'im as a "boomer," and he's got'a go. Still, he's got a chance with the run. That oldest son'a his, I'd not want to come up agin him as a horseman. Neither that nor a gunfighter."

"Reckon we'll not have to, with them clearin' out like you told 'em to."

The two soldiers waited in the trees until the parade had passed, and then they moved along behind them to the Deep Fork that marked the north edge of their responsibility. From there, they followed the eastern border a mile south and cut back through the timber.

"Good land here."

"Sure is."

Walking east leading a string of horses provided a good time to think. Ben pulled his thoughts through his mind, searching for some small thing he might have forgotten.

Andrew's active mind planned and re-planned his run with the roan. The nearest route was rough with tree roots and it had shallow tunnels under the grass made by gophers and armadillos. The longer route was smoother, with much less likelihood of the roan stepping in a hole and straining (or breaking!) a foot. Which way would it be? The enormity of the outcome of his decision weighted heavily on his young mind.

Liz moved along, allowing her body to sway to the movement of the steady spotted mare. The horse was getting old, but she still produced fine foals, and pa was sentimental about her, likely because she was the daughter of the horse he had ridden when he used to stop over at her ma's house. He had named her Firebird because of the reddish brown spot shaped roughly like a bird in flight. Mainly she was called Fire.

Her surefooted gait moved Liz along with a rocking motion, and the girl closed her eyes and relaxed. Surely, there were times when her pa's mother would have been moving along on her special paint pony, shutting her eyes to conserve her strength for the next camp. And pa's grandmother, before her… she likely moved along in the same way.

Liz nodded. Yes, there were things to do at the end of this trail, but it would not be making camp or setting up a shelter. A tiny smile played at the corner of her mouth as she wondered what her Grandmother Rose would think about the oak tree and the rifle.

An even larger smile spread on her lips as she thought of Grandmother Bridie. From what she had heard of the younger Bridget McMahan Scott, and what she had known of her when she was a small girl, Grandmother Bridie would have insisted on being given a gun. It would be unthinkable to lose her beloved red lands.

Emma held the reins, encouraging her team forward. Racing through her mind was the fact that whatever she needed that she had forgotten, it was something that she would do without. She'd manage.

Sally and Annie were nestled in the bedding in the rear of the wagon. Their family of rag dolls was spread out along a quilt. The dolls must be fed and cleaned up, and occasionally, they must be disciplined. After that, the dolls must be wrapped comfortably and put to sleep.

Three miles along the bank of the Deep Fork, the dolls were all asleep lined up between two little girls, themselves also asleep.

It was fully dark before the entourage reached the village, but at first light Ben, on the stallion, Andrew on the roan he called Smokey, and Liz on Firebird were headed back west. By late afternoon, they reached the farm and herded all of the animals into the canyon. It was a shame to take them there so soon, as grass on the small canyon floor was limited, but it seemed necessary.

Clayton, with his bedroll and rifle had made his camp on a rock ledge. Containers of food were kept in a small cave near the tiny spring. Ben stood before the stream and watched the small trickle of water flow from it, then he turned to gaze at the animals.

Three horses, two cows and three hogs, and the two young calves. That was a fair amount of stock to be watered by that tiny flow.

"Clay, come on back with me and get buckets. You'll be needin' to save the runoff if we aim to keep these animals watered."

"Sure, pa."

Liz had cleaned and wiped down the hidey-hole in the low balcony of the old cabin where her mother had lived. She carried up quilts and a pillow, and spread them out. At least, she should get a lot of rest in the next week. She wouldn't have to hide unless someone was close, but she would have to stay in the cabin. What could she do to pass the time?

The few books, the ones from which she had learned to read, had long since been memorized. There was her mother's notebook, the

85

one that described the plants. It was practically memorized, as well. It would be so good to have another book, one she had not ever read.

As she sat up to the old table, the one they had used before Andrew had brought in the wagonloads of smooth lumber, she thought. Elbows on the table, and chin in her hands, she had a lot of time to think.

If she had a book, which she didn't, what would she want it to be about? Not animals and plants. Not weather. Maybe people. A lot of people. She had never been around a lot of people, but that day might come.

Her smokey blue eyes became misty as she dreamed. When everything was over, people would live on both sides of her, in front and in back, and all around. Why, it could be that she would be able to see someone's house from their own front gate! What a wonderful thing!

There would be girls to talk with. She had never had a friend her age. Her little sisters were too young, and they had each other. Clay and Andrew had the things boys do, and if that was not enough for them, they never let it show.

But she, Mary Elizabeth Green, she had never had anyone. Until Gran died, she had Gran, and the age difference had not mattered. But now…? Nothing.

If she had a book, it would be about people, and it would be almost like a friend. Girls…and, boys…?

A boy, now, that would be interesting. What would a boy think of her? Searching her mind, she could remember no time that a boy of her age had been near enough to look at her, let alone give her a thought. Well, that could change.

Late in the evening, Liz set the soaked beans on the stove and built a fire of dry wood. It made a fair amount of smoke, but it burned hotter than green wood and would get the beans started faster. Then she'd add the small green sticks to hold a smolder of flame into the night. The beans should be done by morning.

She set a skillet on the stove and stirred pancake batter. A lot of small cakes would be best, they had decided. They would be easier to handle, and they could be used as sliced bread.

Andrew came in and ate what was ready, and then he headed into the woods toward the canyon. A half an hour later, Clayton arrived, stating he was starving. Liz was not impressed. Clayton starved at least once each day, often twice.

Pa gathered the leftover food and the cooking pots and carried them to the hayloft. If the soldiers came, they would likely search the houses for signs of occupancy.

From the last of the milk Clayton had brought from the canyon, Ben poured a small amount into the dish for the barn cat. The bulging sides of the cat indicated that it was not underfed. The grain in the barn attracted families of mice. The cat, however, enjoyed the milk, and it helped to keep him on the premises.

As daylight broke, Ben and Clayton climbed into the loft and the cat lapped contentedly at the milk.

Sixteen

It was on the 19th of April that the two soldiers from the Fifth Cavalry detachment stationed at Taylor Springs were sent out to make a check of their assignment. It had been a relief when the FLAT "O" Ranch had pulled out and moved onto assigned land outside their area. It would have been a major battle to clean them out.

Amos McKelvey, the corporal in charge of the pair, turned his horse toward the old site of the FLAT "O." The buildings and dugouts used by the men of the ranch would be a temptation for those wanting to sneak in to the territory before the set time.

"Sooners," they had begun to be called, because they came in too soon.

One of the Kansas reporter had written in his paper that everyone wanted to be first, and a lot of the newcomers came too soon, and some were even sooner. That seemed a good thing to call them. Sooners.

That differentiated them from the boomers, who openly lived on the land and resisted being moved out.

Now, that family by the name of Green, they didn't really fit either the boomers or the sooners. This land had always been their home, and it seemed cruel to drive them out. But soldiers were soldiers, however, and they did not make the decisions. Decisions were made by those far away and sent to them to be carried out.

It was a relief to see the Green family leave.

Nearing the site of the FLAT "O," the soldiers reined their mounts to a tree and cased the buildings. The structures seemed empty, but it was necessary to check them individually. And they heard a sound from one dugout.

Moving soundlessly on the green grass, they neared the building, and the private stood aside as the corporal kicked his foot against the partially opened door.

"COME OUT!" he yelled, and in an instant he was flat on his back, and a ghostly form flew over him and disappeared in the woods.

The private rushed forward, "You all right?"

"Yeah. What was it? Gray wolf?"

"Looked like it. Went too fast to get a shot at it."

"Yeah. Well, if a wolf was brave enough to come in here, likely the other buildings'll be empty."

"You look inside?"

"Not yet."

"Could be usin' it for a den."

Pulling the door back, they peered inside. Empty. Or… what was that in the corner?

Leaning closer, they bent down to look into the makeshift cabinet. The sound of mewling came out of it.

"Cats?"

"More likely wolf pups."

Reaching bravely into the dimness, the private brought out a furry ball not four inches long.

"New born. Not more'n maybe a day old."

"What'll we do with 'em?"

"They got'a be killed."

"Yeah, well…" He hesitated at the thought of this tiny, soft innocent thing being killed. Didn't seem right, somehow.

"We got orders to clear out these buildings. The pups got'a go."

The private still hesitated.

"On top'a that, you and me, we're aimin' to live hereabouts. You want them wolves to be our neighbors?"

"We let the ma get away."

"And if we let these grow up, we got more mama wolves. I'll head on back to the horses, and you see to killin' 'em."

"Sure thing." The private hated killing a living thing, but such duties fell the lot of the underling, this time himself, and they must be killed.

Then they moved toward the Green place.

Corporal McKelvey voiced a concern. "I'm hopin' that fellow got all his plunder out. That'll take a concern off'a us."

"That'd be good."

As they neared, they were both relieved to see no signs of life around the house or the corral. Entering the front gate, they walked up the path.

"Hello, the house!"

No answer.

Corporal McKelvey came closer and turned the handle of the door, stepping behind it just in case a bullet came barreling out. It was part of what he had been trained to do.

No bullet.

Inside the house, they moved cautiously from room to room. "Got a good house, here. I'd like to have one like it."

"It'll take a while for us. We got'a get discharged, first."

"Before that, we got'a have someone make the run for us. My brother's supposed to be here, but I ain't heard nothin.' You heard back from your girl friend's brother?"

"Not yet. Likely I won't. Either he'll get here or he won't," was the sad prediction.

"Cupboards all empty. Looks like they sure enough cleared out."

"Got a cabin out back. We gonna check it out, too?"

"Need to."

Liz heard the door creak open. That door had creaked as long as she could remember. She had been in the hidey-hole occupied by her thoughts. Hearing the door open, she lay back on the quilt, trying to breathe silently. It wouldn't be pa downstairs, because it was still broad daylight.

She heard voices.

"No food. Cool stove. You check the balcony."

Footsteps on the ladder, and then a voice very close to Liz's ear. "Nothin' up here. Spiders and old quilts."

"Good. Let's get on out to the barn."

The gate to the corral had been fitted with hinges, but they had never worked smoothly. A whistling squeal sounded out as it was swung open.

Ben and Clayton remained motionless under the hay.

"Looks empty. Step up the ladder and check out the hay pile."

The private climbed high enough to see into the loft.

"Nothin' here."

The corporal looked in around the feed barrels, startling the cat into scampering across the floor and leaping into the open corral. Amos McKelvey leaned over and looked behind the barrel. There on the floor was a container with a small amount of milk.

Old milk? Clabbered, maybe? He touched it with his foot and it rippled. Fresh. Someone was feeding the cat. Thoughts raced through his mind. This fellow, Ben Green, he was the kind of a man Amos would like as a neighbor. If he continued to poke around... who knew?

He wished he hadn't been so thorough in his looking. He didn't need to have looked behind that barrel. But now that he had, he didn't need to tell anyone.

"See anything up there, Jonathan?"

The private looked around. What he saw was a huge pile of hay, but the tiniest corner of a quilt was visible at the edge of it. He could go on up the ladder and check it out... or he could come back down the ladder.

As he turned to descend, he saw the glass fruit jar, about half full of water. So, who was it that needed a drink of water in the hayloft?

Stepping down, he answered, "Didn't see nothin' up there that wasn't 'sposed to be there."

"Good. Let's get on out."

Seventeen

Then it was late afternoon.

All was quiet down the trail at the FLAT "O" compound. Spring grass had sprouted in the arena where stubborn colts had been broke to the saddle. The shed that had been used as a bunkhouse was empty, with swinging doors and open windows.

Dirt dobber wasps busily worked in the mud of a nearby spring, rolling their pea-sized ball of fresh mud. Clasping the mud ball, the golden-orange insects struggled on papery wings to lift off into the air. Zooming through an open window, the dobbers landed on their newly built adobe structure, expertly tapping the soft mud into place and drying the application with a buzz of their wings.

When the mud tunnels of the dirt dobber reached the correct length… and when the mud was sufficiently dry… the females inserted themselves into the tunnel, depositing an egg inside. Other winged builders brought paralyzed spiders to poke into the tunnel to nourish the larva that would soon hatch from the egg.

Then other mud balls were brought and the tunnel was closed. With a final tap-dance of feet and a last check with sensitive feelers, the dirt dobbers flew away, the fate of the next generation having been properly assured.

A female red fox nosed aside the door to the cook shack, pushing her lithe body into the room. Quiet as a whisper, she stood, cocking her head this way and that.

Hardly audible came the scuff and shuffle of tiny feet, and the faintest of squeak of pink babes in the nest. The fox moved ahead. Slinking toward the cabinet door that had been left ajar, the fox waited patiently.

Inside the cabinet, the small gray rodent twitched her pink nose, apprehensive of whatever it might be that waited by the door, but her maternal instinct held her fast. She could run and save herself, but there were her pink babies in the nest… and … well?

Those few seconds of indecision were her undoing. With a crash through the doorway, the red fox closed her jaws on the female rat, cracking her spine. With a mighty gulp, the rodent slid down her throat. The next snap of her jaws took the pink babies from the nest, sending them after their mother.

Turning quickly, the fox darted through the door and disappeared into the weeds sprouting up by the cookhouse. A short run brought her to the rock shelter of her den where she opened her mouth, gagged and deposited her catch before her kits.

Yipping and tumbling about, the round-bodied kits pounced on the rat, growling and tearing at it with their tiny, sharp teeth. The female fox settled onto her stomach and watched. The kits were doing nicely. Now, if her mate was lucky in his hunting and was as successful as she…

But the mate had come onto a nest of copperhead snakes. They were still tangled in their birth ball, but the female serpent, after giving birth, had gone on her way.

Biting through their heads, the male fox had quieted four of the wad before the rest began to crawl away. Scurrying after them, he caught two more. Gathering the six serpents in his mouth, their heads and tails hanging away from his jaws like a writhing beard, he proudly lifted his head and ran toward the rock ledge.

The female saw him coming, and lolled out her tongue in an elaborate greeting. The kits had consumed the nestling rodents and were attacking the adult with their sharp but ineffective teeth.

The male deposited the young copperheads, with their tails still twitching, into the midst of the kits. With yips of delight, the furry balls left the lifeless rodent for the writhing bodies of the snakes. The male watched with pleasure and then lifted the dead rat with his teeth and placed it carefully in front of his mate.

She lolled her tongue in appreciation and ate it with great relish. It was necessary that she eat well, because the kits still needed her milk.

The shiny feathers of the black bird in the tree glistened in the sunlight as it had watched the scene below. The bird saw the female copperhead crawl away, but before he could descend onto the ball of young ones, the fox had intervened.

So now the fox had run away, and two of the young copperheads remained, thinking they were hidden. Darting from the tree with a squawk, he swooped down, closing his powerful orange beak on the necks of the snakes, breaking one after the other. Then gathering them both in his beak, he rose up on strong wings and flew toward the nest.

It would be interesting to see which of his three chicks would finally get the two snakes. Contests such as this went far to determine which chicks would live well and which would become food for a larger, hungrier winged creature.

From under the eaves of the bunkhouse, a bird of great size emerged. It was covered with feathers of soft tan, roughly the color of cooked oatmeal, and it had a sunburst of feathers around each bright yellow eye.

Pausing, with a powerful taloned foot clamped to the edge of a board, the bird critically panned the woodland with a complete circle of its head. It was sunny daylight and not its favorite time to hunt.

However, the emptiness of its stomach dictated that it at least look about.

After the sweep of its gaze, it turned back and focused its black-slit pupils onto the movement in the grass.

Then, pushing off with its taloned foot, it dropped on feather-silent wings and scooped up the full-grown female copperhead snake. Beating its wings more rapidly to compensate for the weight of the serpent, the barn owl flapped its way back to the bunkhouse.

Flipping the snake into the air, it caught the fanged head in its mouth and in an instant, broke its neck vertebrae with a powerful, hooked beak.

Crawling back into its nest shelf, the owl began to swallow the snake, head first. It took upward of 15 minutes, but each gulping swallow drew in another two or three inches of the snake. When the tip of the snake tail slid down the throat, the owl lowered its yellow eyes and settled its head down into a collar of neck feathers.

A warm sunny day was for sleeping, and he intended to do just that.

A female gray wolf slunk carefully back to the swinging door of a dugout dwelling and disappeared inside. There was no greeting of squeaks and squeals, and though some of the smell was right, there were no babies in the place where she had left them.

This was the third time she had returned, as it was past time for feeding the pups, and they were still not here. There was, however, the strong smell of the other animal. Convinced, finally, that her babies were gone, the wolf turned and followed the tell-tail trail of the human.

Across the paddock she followed the scent. Then, where it became stronger, she saw the lifeless bodies of her pups. Nuzzling them tenderly, she turned each one over, making certain no life remained. Finally, she turned away.

But as she turned, she caught a faint twitch of a tail. Instantly, she turned and grabbed up the infant, holding him softly in her powerful teeth. Dashing away from the hated place of the human smell, she hid in a thicket of brambles.

Depositing the limp ball of fur on a bed of dry leaves, she cleaned him thoroughly, ridding him of the hated human smell. Stroking a warm, insistent tongue across his face and ears, she was rewarded with the faintest of squeaks. Encouraged, she turned him over with her nose and continued the stimulation.

Finally, pushing him to his feet, she whined encouragement until he rocked forward and took a small step. With a soft bark of triumph, she curled her body around him and pushed him toward her bursting nipples. Resting her head on her paws, she watched with pleasure as he nursed.

Eighteen

Sitting on a rock in a dense part of the timber, the man watched as the two cavalry officers came into the abandoned corral. He watched them slide off their horses and tie them to a torn fence, and then walk about from building to building

They were thorough, certainly, and went into every building. He knew, of course, that they were under orders to clear out every human being in the territory, in preparation for the land run that would happen in two days.

From his perch, he saw the female wolf flee the dugout home of one of the ranch workers, and he saw the private remove the pups and take them away. He waited and watched as they finally mounted and rode into the trees.

He had been very careful not to be seen. He had even sold his horse so he would have more freedom to move about. He did not need the horse, as he had no intention of entering the run. Where he was going, he could walk... or perhaps trot.

The FLAT "O" corral, itself, was not his goal. It was much too large, and he was sure the hands who worked at the ranch would be running for it, and who was he to stand up against a dozen guns? Besides, what would he do with it if he had it?

The ranch was not what he wanted, but it made a good waiting place. Three times he had seen the officers come to check the place. If they had brought a dog, he might have had something to be concerned about, but they did not, so all he had to do was be careful not to leave footprints.

He avoided the dusty paths and did not walk through tall weeds that would bend and show that someone had gone that way. Mostly, he stayed in the woods, hiding in the dense parts and staying where he had a good view of the buildings. Though he didn't want them, the buildings made a convenient place to sleep at night.

Now that the officers had come by once more, he was probably safe. Likely they would not make another check, and he could relax. He would get a good night's sleep on the night before the run and wake up early and be on his way. It would be easy to hide in the trees and be ready to plant his claim stake, and he could head out for Guthrie to the land office.

Just yesterday, he had gone once more to look at the place. Instead of a patch of trees and grass, it had a house and barn, fences, and started crops. In fact, it had everything he wanted. In addition, he knew, for a fact, that the boomer who lived there had been forced to clear out.

Also, yesterday, he had been tempted to pull the stake and put in his own, but he had restrained himself. Hiding out and becoming what they called a "sooner" was enough.

He had timed the run, and if he came early and staked his claim, he had time to make the fourteen miles to the land office, and be there at a reasonable time… not too early and not too late.

He smiled to himself in anticipation. It was a good place, and it would be his. It was very tempting to go back today and look at it… just admire it from afar, but it was too risky. Too many trips could create a path, and one couldn't be too careful when the stakes were as high as this.

So the man lay back on his stony perch and napped. He was not disturbed by the scream of the eagle overhead or the rustle of rabbits moving through the dry leaves around him. All he had to do was rest and wait.

Nineteen

Then the time came. The 22nd of April, 1889, dawned, a picture-perfect day.

Clayton had come to the log cabin before daylight, bringing a pail of milk. No longer fearing the return of the soldiers who would be busy at the border, Liz had created a fire in the old stove, frying pancakes on the griddle, then dropping the last of the eggs into the skillet. Most of the chickens had been eaten during the last two weeks. It would take a while to rebuild their flock.

The chickens they had left had been chased into the timber, and perhaps they could be rounded up and enticed back with the promise of grain once more. That, however, was a small matter. What was necessary just now, was to make sure everyone had plenty to eat, because today was an important day.

Liz had laid out a piece of old dark overall material to take into the tree with her. On their test run, she had become painfully aware of how rough and hard the bark of an old oak could be. It had been decided that she and her father and brother would be in their places before ten o'clock.

At best, they would be three hours in position.

Between bites, Ben gave repeated instructions to Clay.

"Now, Son, I know I told you this before, but it'll not hurt you to listen one more time. That old ragged curtain we hung on the window to the loft, you make sure you hold the gun just like we said. Don't have that barrel no more'n a couple inches through, and you get where you can see through that hole we made, and get a good sight on the front gate. You got that?"

"Yeah, Pa. You showed me what you wanted done."

"I know. It's just that you got a job that's important, and we'd not want your shot to be wasted. Time a body gets close to that surveyor stake, they'll be close enough to feel the sting'a your shot. Don't be shootin' no sooner."

"Sure, Pa." Clay had buttered a pancake and rolled it up, eating it from his fingers. "I know I got'a wait."

Ben turned to his daughter, looking pretty as a spring daisy, even though she wore one of Clay's shirts, and Andrew's overalls, with the pant legs rolled up. The snow-white apron played up her pale skin and deep-set eyes, so like Emma's.

Emma. Two more days and he could go after her. It seemed she had been gone for years, but… Enough of that thinking!

"Andrew?"

"I'm ready, Pa. Fixin' to head on down to the canyon and get the roan. He's been jittery, locked up in there like he is. He'll be glad to get out."

"Which way'll you be comin' from?"

"I'm keepin' a open mind, Pa, not knowin' how it'll be. I'm thinkin,' though, that I'll be comin' back up from behind the garden. I'll be here quick as I can."

"I know you will, Son."

The door closed behind Andrew, and the three were left alone. Ben looked at Clay.

"Now, Son, you got'a...."

"I know, Pa. You told me and told me. I know what I got'a do."

"And you, Liz?"

"I'm ready, Pa. I'm just not wantin' to climb up till I have to. Them limbs are harder'n rocks and rougher'n cobs."

"That's fine. Remember, the first shots, if we got'a shoot, they'll be comin' from you."

"I'll remember, Pa."

Ben looked at the gun on the table beside him. With his finger, he flicked an imaginary speck of dust from the shiny barrel. Nerves could be hard to control.

Andrew's long strides carried him to the canyon, and he pulled the brush aside just enough to slip through. When the roan horse saw the bridle, he came running toward Andrew, whinnying joyfully.

At first, Andrew cringed at the sound, and then realized it was too late to be worried. Slipping the straps over the horse's ears, Andrew adjusted the metal bit in its mouth. Leaping on his back, he trotted to the mouth of the canyon.

Pulling aside a bit more of the brush, Andrew led the horse through the gap and closed it behind him. Back in the saddle, he moved through the trees, keeping to the dense parts. Wading through the creek, he trotted down a lane that had been surveyed. The cream color of the stakes stood out against the green of the grass.

His only concern, now, was to slip past the cavalry officers, and he had scouted out several places where that could be done. They would, of course, be patrolling the border, but two men could not be every place on the one-mile stretch of land.

Waiting in the shadows, he saw the private walk past, going south. He held still, willing with all his might, to keep the roan from whinnying a greeting to the horse. The roan was silent.

Fearing to wait for the corporal to pass by, going north, he softly clicked the horse into a walk, and the animal's sure-footed steps carried man and animal across the cleared path and into the brush again. Fearing to be too close to the line, Andrew took the horse farther into the trees outside the Unassigned Land.

Safe. A long breath escaped from his lungs, and his hands began to tremble and perspire. He had not realized he had been so tense. So, now he must wait for the two hours before the signal would be given.

Back at the house, Clayton excitedly positioned himself at the window to the barn loft. It was a good place to see from, but he must not move the curtain the slightest bit. He must not even breathe on it, he told himself.

Ben stayed in the house. Raising a window, he stationed himself far enough back that he could not be seen.

In the oak tree, Liz had spread the pad of denim cloth and seated herself on it. Resting the barrel of her gun on a solid limb, she trained the sight toward the front gate. Now, all she had to do was wait, and be careful not to let her thoughts drift away. All her attention must be on the front gate until Andrew rode in.

The family depended on her, and she could do it.

Twenty

Off to the south, not far away, a man stepped from the abandoned bunkhouse carrying a short sign bearing his name and a number. Hurrying through the trees, he came in sight of the place with the good house and solid barn.

He paused, involuntarily, as his greedy eyes took in the scene. His! When the sun went down tonight, it would be his!

Stepping through the gate, he looked quickly toward the surveyor stake. It was still there. No other sign was in sight. Another step and he was under the massive cottonwood tree.

BANG! A blast came from nowhere, startling him amid step, and a foot-long piece of limb came floating down in front of him.

Someone shooting at him? Surely not! Just a squirrel, but when he looked up, he knew it was not a squirrel in a cottonwood tree. Maybe in an oak or a pecan, but not a cottonwood....

But which direction had the shot come from? With the echoes in the trees, it was impossible to tell. He transferred his sign to his left hand and slipped his gun from its holster. This prize was too valuable not to defend. He took a few careful steps forward.

Another BANG! An air shot? No... because there followed the ping of a ricochet from a stone. Hunters? Hardly....

Another step and a BANG. Clearly it was an air shot. Was it the start of the run? Who would have thought the starting gun could be heard from here? …and wasn't it a bit too soon? It was not yet noon.

Another step. Now, where should he put his sign? If it was too plain, someone would just pull it and put in his own and maybe beat him to the land office. Now, if he put the sign over in the shadow of the barn…. Yes, that would be the place.

He turned and took a few tentative steps in that direction.

Clayton leveled his shotgun and licked his lips. Pa said to wait until he was closer. Forcing his finger to be stiff, he waited, not breathing. Another step… one more step. There!

Squinting into his sights, Clayton's strong hands held the barrel firmly, and his finger squeezed. The blast echoed in the barnloft and in every other direction as the shot sprayed out.

The crouching man jerked upright and flung his sign in the air. Grabbing for it as it hit the ground, he ran for the gate and was last seen disappearing through the trees, running past another claim which he could have legally staked.

Clay felt a joyful whoopee build up within his chest, but he forced himself to be silent as he reloaded and settled in to wait. Somebody else might come, and he might get a chance to do it again!

He could enjoy hoping.

Twenty-One

As the time neared noon, the perimeter of the Unassigned Lands of the Oklahoma territory was ringed with tense and anxious runners. From the Cherokee Outlet on the north to the Chickasaw on the south, wagons, buggies, and saddle horses waited for the signal.

A group of hopefuls had arrived on the train from Illinois, the women providently carrying baskets of food and belongings. The men rode horses ranging from $500.00 thoroughbreds to swaybacked nags, breathless to be on their way.

What they hoped for were not the 160 acre tracts but town lots where they could carry on the businesses they had walked away from. Among them were butchers and blacksmiths, tailors with the tools of their trade waiting behind with their womenfolk, and pharmacists, with their chemicals and mixtures to be shipped in on the Santa Fee at a date previously set.

Miners, sick of their dark jobs underground, had left Pennsylvania and headed to the new land. They were determined to find work as farmers in God's sunlight, and as proof, they carried long sheaf knives, ready for the harvest that would certainly be theirs.

A train at the southern border was dedicated for the use of reporters from papers in the north as far as Chicago, west to the Pacific, and east through New York. Reporters came from San Francisco, from towns in Texas, and even from London, across the ocean.

This was the literary scoop of a lifetime, not to be missed, and the dusty hardships were gladly endured.

As the train pulled out of the station, eager hands grabbed at the windows, and some were able to pull themselves to the roof, where they flattened against the force of the wind and held on as best they could. The danger to be risked was overbalanced by the possibility of success. If they could just hold on until they were past the crowded borders, they could expect to be near to a claim stake that had not been taken. If they happened to break a leg as they jumped from the moving train, so be it. Some even succeeded in holding on.

Many were already within the perimeter of the Unassigned Lands, having posed as construction workers on the railroad or other buildings. They needed to pretend to use their hammers just long enough to avoid being shipped away as frauds.

Some made it, and others did not. The lawmen who enforced the sending away of the "sooners," often became sooners themselves just as soon as they could sneak away from their duties.

Towns had been planned, but due to the inefficiency of the faraway government, the final platting of the lots had not begun until days before the scheduled run. One surveyor company began platting over the plans of a previous survey, creating a hodge-podge of shapes, with the same plot of land being claimed by two or more runners.

Some plots of land were still in the courts months later, even years, with the rightful owner still in dispute.

From the town of Purcell, in the south, the eating houses were packed with those looking for a last meal, and those seeking write about them. Men ate with camping gear on their backs, ready to pour down the bluff and into the river that must be crossed.

The livery stables, packed and overflowing for the last few days, were suddenly emptied as animals were harnessed. The animal that would hopefully carry its rider to a choice piece of the magical land was groomed, fed, and harnessed with great care.

On the sand at the edge of the river, the horses finally stood, switching flies and rippling their skins in anticipation. Their riders tense, holding the reins with sweaty hands, waiting… waiting…

At the signal, they plunged into the water, splashing and swimming their way into the territory.

New partnerships and bonds of necessity were forged within the crowds gathered at the borders.

Nellie Black, from Topeka, had worked as a domestic ever since her husband had died. To provide for her three children, boys 12 and 10, and a girl seven, she had secured employment in the only occupation she knew. In order to procure room and board for the children, her salary was negligible, and her work hours were impossibly long.

Stretched out before her were years of not being able to better herself, and she had poured over the flyers and brochures long into the night. Could she? Likely not, but if she could… Free land… 160 acres, if one was lucky enough…

Nellie had never been particularly lucky, but she also had never lacked courage. Gathering her family around her, she told of her plans and of the hardships they must go through. Her boys excitedly pushed her on, encouraging her and telling her they would help, and they would all have a part of the new land.

Nellie, herself, being practical, decided to take a chance, and the worse that could happen would be that she would, again, be in domestic service. So, gathering their meager possessions together, they boarded a train to take them to Arkansas City.

When she reached the border, the price of horses had gone so impossibly high, due to the tremendous demand, that purchasing one was out of the question, much less the purchase of a wagon. Trying to bolster her courage, she camped among those waiting at the border. Something could happen.

Her sons, as outgoing as their mother, moved about among the men, offering to do small jobs and generally seeking to be useful, to perhaps earn a few pennies.

The older one, twelve-year-old, James, sought to curry down the horse belonging to a man with a good looking team and a solid wagon. Two small girls peeked shyly around the curtains.

To the boys, the man seemed to be a prosperous person, possibly a businessman who would be able to afford a few services.

"Mister, that's a good team you got. I always fancied bays like the ones you got. Time come I ever get to have me a horse, that'd be what I'd like. Chance you'd like 'em curried while you're waitin' and me and my brother, we'd do a good job."

Edward Goldberg, beset with his own concerns, passed off their comments. "I reckon not right now, boys."

It would take more conviction than that to discourage James and Billy Black. Small but expert hands caressed the velvet noses of the horses, being rewarded with mumbles and huffs of appreciation from the animals.

"I sure like them horses, Mister. We got nothin' to do right now, and we'd brush 'em down for nothin'."

"You'd... ?"

"Yeah. Back in Topeka where my ma worked, they had horses, and they let me'n Billy take care of 'em. Said we helped to earn our livin' that'a'way. Ma did their cookin' and cleanin'."

The boys were beginning to be a bother. "Where's your pa, boys?"

A short hesitation, and James explained. "He passed on from a sickness. He was left back in Topeka. Ma and us, we came on out here on the train."

No pa and certainly no horses. How did they expect to get down to the land, let alone join in the run? He asked the boys if they had a plan.

"No. Ma was wantin' to maybe buy a horse and a cart... or somethin.' We got here and everything cost too much money."

Hmmmm. So he wasn't the only one with troubles. The boys' ma was in just about as bad a fix as he was, thinkin' he had a chance in the run driving a wagon with two small girls in it. He could do much better on horseback, but where could he leave the girls, both of them under six? What in the world was he thinking, coming down here like this?

Behind him stretched years of sharecropping. He had tended the fields of others and was given a portion, a very small portion, of the yield. His lovely wife helped with the work, but it was too heavy for her. During the past year, she weakened and did not gain her strength, and then life became too much for her. She, also, had been left behind.

Edward began to feel an empathy for this unknown and unseen woman, but at least, if she actually got some land, she had these two strong-looking boys, just coming into sprout-grubbing age. Now if he had a couple of boys like these… And his thoughts turned into ideas.

"Boys, whereat is you ma stayin'?"

"Over yonder. We got us a tent, but it ain't big enough for Billy and me. Our little sister…."

"Take me to her, will you?"

Surprised, the boys readily agreed.

Nellie Black sat despondently in the tiny tent and the bored seven-year-old girl slept on the ground beside her. Surely there was a way. When one tried hard enough…?

The man stood before the tent door, and Nellie crawled out.

James explained. "Ma, this man wanted to be brung to see you."

Edward stood, hat in hand, to be polite. "Ma'am, these here two boys come by admirin' my horses and told me somethin' about you. Now, if I'm bein' a bother, you just say so…"

He was certainly not being a bother. It was almost a relief, just to have an adult actually want to see her.

"No, Mister. What'd it be you wanted to say?"

"I'm thinkin' you got no horse."

"No. We was wantin' to, but…"

Time being a factor, he interrupted her explanation. "What I wanted to say was, I got two horses, and I'd have a chance in the run if it was just me, but I got two little girls, and they got'a have a wagon to stay in. Now, I was thinkin', if we could…you know, 160 acres is a big place, and there be room… I mean, if we was to…" How should he put it and be polite?

"You wantin' that we should keep your girls? Well, we ain't got much but…."

"Not exactly, ma'am…."

"Call me Nellie."

"Sure, Miss Nellie. I was thinkin' if my girls wasn't with me, I'd have a chance, and if you'd be willin' to do that, I'd share whatever I got with you and yours. Your boys'd be a big help to the both'a us, chance we got us a piece'a land."

Nellie's mind sought to comprehend his meaning. "You'd leave your wagon and your girls, with me…?"

"And a horse, chance you needed one while I was gone."

"Well, we'd not...."

James, with eyes sparkling, begged, "Say yes, Ma! Please say yes! I'd take care'a the horse!"

Nellie looked from the boy to the man her mind racing on ahead of either of them. "Sit down, will you Mister...."

"Call me Edward."

"Edward. This idea'a yours could use some thought. Now, I don't need no horse left here for me to take care of, but a wagon... now, that'd be good. If you was to leave me your wagon, and your little girls, and you ride one horse and let my boys team up on the other'n..."

"Well, that'd be a idea. They ride good?"

Nellie allowed herself a slight smile of pride. "Back where I worked, it was the duty of them boys to ride horses, givin' 'em the exercise the rich folks didn't have the time to do. They ride real good."

"Well, now we could... Let's see..." Edward sat down on the ground, somewhat weak from relief. "I got a good waitin' place in the line, over by a big tree. We could take your tent over there, and you could see to my girls."

"That'd be good."

So it was that Edward Goldberg and James and Billy Black were on the strong bays when the signal came. They finally settled on a prime tract somewhat north of the new city of Guthrie.

As soon as it was convenient, the families legally joined their forces, and continued to add members to their family. The former share-cropper grew his own crops for his own family, and Nellie still slaved at domestic duties from dawn till dark, but it was her own duties, and that made all the difference in the world, and the share-cropped was forced to share no more.

Twenty-Two

Three brothers who had gone west to seek their fortunes had returned, disappointed and disillusioned, just in time to join the run. Circling around to the closest border to the town of Kingfisher, they lined up with the rest.

One rusher, overly eager and crazed from excitement, ran his horse out across the boundary before the signal sounded. A uniformed member of the Cavalry attempted to push him back, and the man began to fire his pistol, indiscriminately, in all directions.

A stray bullet shot the horse out from under one of the brothers. As the horse fell, the signal gun sounded. The horseless brother leaped on behind another brother and they galloped away.

The brothers settled just outside of the town and had a crop to harvest in their own fields before the year was out.

A barber from Kansas City had suffered a bout of the wanderlust as he studied the brochures. New towns… new people… a new life!

He packed up his cutting equipment dividing it between his two saddlebags. He outfitted his wife in men's clothing and packed the rest of their worldly goods in two other saddlebags. Putting his other equipment in crates, and entrusting it to the Santa Fe rail lines, he was ready.

Heading out toward the territory, the couple spent their nights in farmhouses, barn lofts, and boarding houses in small towns, until they reached Arkansas City.

Late one evening, they climbed on their mounts and ambled nonchalantly over the border into the Cherokee Outlet. Leisurely moving south, they crossed the rivers, swimming when necessary, and guiding the horses across the muddy water with a rope line.

On the Easter Sunday before the run, the couple was comfortably camped on a rounded hill overlooking the new city of Guthrie. They were near enough that they could get a good night's sleep and still stroll on down in the morning.

The barber put his claim on a lot on Harrison Street, a good central location for a business, and his wife put her claim on the lot next to it. When the land office opened, the couple were fourth and fifth in line to register their claims.

Their barber chairs and the waiting bench were collected from the Santa Fe depot and set up in a tent. At night, the tent flaps were closed, and the two barber chairs became suitably comfortable beds.

The location was such a good one, and business was so brisk, the barber taught his wife the particulars of the craft, and she continued to dress in men's clothing. As she worked, shaving and cutting hair, from dawn to dark, her smooth face was disguised by a moustache made from her own hair, the bulk of which she kept neatly tucked up under a black derby. In six months time, they made enough to pay to have a shop put up and let her revert once more to being a woman.

Twenty-Three

Possibly the largest accumulation of rushes were congregated at the 7C Ranch, located on the eastern border by the Canadian River. The terrain was slightly less tree-covered, and therefore it had a certain advantage. This advantage was offset, however, by the crowds.

Wagons were ten to twenty deep in places, and several occasions of weariness and temper, along with ample gunpowder, created skirmishes, which ended in blood and anger.

A caravan of five wagons brought the families of two brother and their aged parents to the border. Every available inch in the wagons was loaded with soaked burlap bags containing cuttings taken from apple, peach and plum trees. Over ten thousand cuttings, total, had been trekked across Arkansas from the land beside the Mississippi River.

It was the plan of the family that a fruit orchard of many acres would be set, and in due time, there would be fruit to sell, and it would support every member of their large families. It was an exciting idea, and the Stratford's waited nervously as all male members over 21 joined in the run.

Success happened, and two tracts side by side were registered at the land office in Guthrie. Decades later, peaches still grew in the small community which was named after the family.

It was incredible and magical that, at the shot of a gun, ownership of the coveted red land became possible.

Farther north from the 7C Ranch, rushers were sprinkled along the border, waiting for the gunshot that would signal the official opening of the Unassigned Lands.

A sizeable crowd had congregated at the Deep Fork River where a young man had slipped outside the line that others were wishing to be inside of, and he was jiggled by the dancing feet of the roan beneath his saddle.

Andrew Green had been successful in staying unseen until he joined the gathering at Deep Fork. His pounding heart finally settled down within his chest, now that he was on safe ground. Moving farther north toward the Deep Fork River, he heard the waiting crowd. Human and animal's sounds, the smoke of cooking fires, and the smell of food floated out on the April air. The occasional nickering of a horse, and here and there, a commanding shout to hold back the crowd.

And what a crowd it was! It was positively scary how many people were gathered here, and any one of them could take his land from him! A stumble and fall of his horse could do it… a hoof in a gopher run… anything! It was too terrible to think on.

The soldiers were still patrolling. First the corporal rode to the riverbank and turned. After a pause, he headed south. Minutes later, the private did the same thing. A good plan of coverage they had. He was lucky to have gotten safely through.

Then the waiting men in the milling crowd began to fill their saddles. Andrew had no timepiece, but the position of the sun told him it was almost noon. The nervous animals were moved into line.

Andrew held back. He did not want to be part of the first pack, and the distance of fifty feet made no difference in time, once his swift roan got started.

Race horses, plow horses, mules, some teams pulling buggies. Here and there were men on foot. Behind him was a boy. He was clearly not more than fourteen. Surely he was not to be in the run! He was much too young to file a claim, but there he was, twitching nervously and looking from side to side.

Andrew turned away. The boy was not his concern.

The private walked by and reached the bank of the Deep Fork but he did not walk back south. This must be it!

Within minutes, the corporal came by and halted. All conversation stopped, and the milling crowd was quiet, except for the snort and stomp of the horses.

Twenty-Four

The cavalry man called out, "Stay where you are until you hear MY gun. You may hear a number of shots, but MINE is your signal."

Silence. Breath came in ragged, short bursts. Then from the far south came the report of a gun. Immediately after the shot came another one, somewhat closer. The men on horseback dried their sweaty hands on their pants legs and took a firmer grip on the reins, looping them around their hands, already sweaty once more.

In the distance was another shot and another one. All eyes were on the shiny gun in the hand of the officer. Then they saw it rise into the air. One more shot, sounding much closer, and then the officer pulled the trigger of his gun.

A plume of smoke curled up from the nozzle of the gun, and the corporal yelled, "GO!"

The first wave of men and beasts leaped across the border into the new land. In an instant they were fanned out, and the way was clear. As he had planned, Andrew joined the second wave, being much less closely packed, and he had the advantage of knowing exactly where he was going. This was practically his own back pasture.

Pa had made his plan, and it was a good plan. There was much less danger of his horse being run against, or becoming frightened or overly excited if he hung back.

The roan plunged forward, knowing exactly what was expected of him. He had done exactly this several times over the last few days. Tearing down a straightaway of claim markers, he plunged into a thicket of low limbs. Andrew leaned forward, laying flat against the saddle to avoid being dragged off by low limbs. Diving into a cluster of heavily leafed redbuds, he totally disappeared. As was his plan.

Glancing behind him, Andrew saw runners in all directions, and he saw one that seemed to be following him. The boy! Surely, he was not...? But, yes...!

Then Andrew forced his mind away from the boy and back onto his own plan. His only competition was the boy on the pinto pony. The fellow's hat had blown back, and his red hair flew out in all directions, but he gouged his heels unmercifully into the ribs of the pony. The little horse, sensing desperation, flattened out in his run and almost kept up with the roan.

Splashing through the creek, Andrew scrambled the horse up the bank and heard the pinto behind him. Whoever the kid was, he sure knew how to ride!

Changing his plan slightly, Andrew dove into a thicket toward the canyon, the pinto close behind, and then made a sudden turn calculated to bring him up beside the barn. Momentum carried the pinto past the turn, but the boy quickly brought him around.

Clay heard the sound and instinct told him to re-aim his gun, but Pa has said NOT TO! Trembling and torn with excitement, he held his gun barrel to the window.

Liz, not under such orders, leveled the rifle toward the corral, positioning her finger on the trigger. She had never shot in the direction of a person, but she might have to now. Clenching her teeth and ignoring the ripples of tension playing along her arms, she held the barrel steady, pointing it toward the sound.

As the roan's head broke through the scrubby brush, she tingled with relief and relaxed her finger. It was Andrew! He was here and it was all over!

But it wasn't. Immediately behind him came another rider, crashing through the trees like a bear from a honey bee tree. Forcing her mind to think, she again fingered the trigger as she looked for a gun in the hand of the rider.

There was no gun that she could see. Andrew was slowing down, and the second horse also slowed raising dust clouds. Sliding down from the tree, she moved from cover to cover, closing in on the two persons in the corral.

From his perch, Clay had also seen Andrew ride up and had leaped down from the loft and now had his shotgun braced on a saddle tree. He lined his sights on the second rider, and gasped.

He was only a kid! Why, he couldn't be no older than Clay, himself! Lowering the gun, Clay walked on out of the barn.

The pinto had lowered his head and heaved for breath as the boy looked from one to the other of the gun bearers.

In a voice changing from a deeper base to a youthful squeak, the boy yelled, "Don't shoot at me, please. I didn't mean nothin' wrong."

Andrew demanded, "Who are you and why were you followin' me?"

By now Ben had entered the corral.

The boy with the red hair gushed out his explanation. "I didn't mean nothin, really. I didn't hardly know what to do, and that roan, there, he looked like he knew where he was a'goin,' so we took off. Then we couldn't hardly get stopped."

Ben stepped in. "Were you in the run?"

"Yep. Well...."

"You ain't even...? How old are you?"

"Fourteen, sir."

"Well, you know you can't stake no claim."

"I know, but I'm all we had. My ma, she's back there, and if I got somethin,' I was to go and get 'er, and...."

"Well, Son, this here claim's been staked. But now, you look out there through the gate. I can see a claim that's got no name on it. You got a name stake on you?"

He did. Tied to the saddle and banging against the shoulder of the pinto was the pointed stake.

"Well, now, I'd say you ought'a get on over there and get that in the ground."

"Yes, sir!"

"But, Pa, he can't file and...."

"I know. Let me think. I got'a get on over to Guthrie to the land office."

"Yeah, Pa, but...."

The kid with the tousle of red hair came tearing back, breathless with excitement.

"Mister, I got'a go get my ma, and... You think someone'll try to jump my claim...?"

"Quiet, everybody. I got'a idea. Son, what's your ma's name?"

"Maggie Duncan. You think I could...?"

"Wait, now. You ma, did she go to school?"

"Some."

"You ever see 'er write her name?"

"Yeah, some."

"Come 'ere, Liz. Let's go to house."

The puzzled young people followed him.

"Liz, get you a piece'a paper and write 'Maggie Duncan.'"

Even more puzzled, she obeyed. Ben showed the paper to the boy. "That look anything like your ma'd write?"

"Uh, well, it seems a mite plainer'n she'd write."

"Try agin, Liz."

Liz loosened her grip and let the pencil wobble a bit.

"That better?"

The boy tilted his head and studied the name. "Pretty much, sir."

"All right. What's your name?"

"Jeremiah, sir."

"Can you shoot, Jeremiah?"

"Some."

"Give 'em a gun, Andrew. You three boys, you're gonna keep the claim jumpers away from this place and that place over there, and me and Maggie Duncan, here, we're goin' to Guthrie."

Liz wheeled around with surprise. "Me, Pa?"

"Yes, you. Get you the best bonnet you got that hides your face and a neck scarf for your chin."

"A shawl, too? And a dress?"

"No dress. Just get the shawl. You got'a sit a saddle. You be ready when I bring the stallion up. We're gonna make a fast ride."

Turning to the boy, "Now, Jeremiah, your ma's gonna be a mite worried, I figure, but you're gonna get your land, and she'll forgive you for not comin' right back. You stay here for a few hours and help guard. Come late afternoon, you go back after her. Danger'll mostly be passed by then. My girl, here, she's gonna go sign for your ma. I figure there'll be so many folks there, no one'll look to see how old she is."

Twenty-Five

Within minutes, the black stallion followed the roan through the trees and the three boys were left alone. Andrew took charge.

"All right, Jeremiah, I want you to go back over to your land, and Clay, you go with 'im. I want ya to keep back out'a sight and watch. Don't be takin' a shot or comin' out'a the trees, less'n I call you."

Clay wondered. "What'll you do here at our house, you all alone?"

"I'll stay right here and say these claims is both took. I'm thinkin' most folks'll take on off and find somethin' that's not been claimed."

Following the line of surveyor stakes, father and daughter headed west. Many of the claims had already been staked, and loaded guns defended them. As they went along, Ben would shout, "Just passin' through. Ain't even armed."

Guns were lowered, and arms were raised in salute.

"Pa, what we're doin'…? Me signin' a name that ain't mine…?"

"Yeah?"

"You thinkin' that's really right? Should we ought'a be doin' this?" Her voice was hesitant. It was unthinkable that her father would knowingly do something that was not right.

They rode along to the sound of the horse's hooves on the ground. Finally, "Well, Lizzie, honey, there could be two ways'a sayin' it. I could see how you might wonder if it was right, but that boy, he won that land, fair and square and by the rules that was give to him. Wasn't his fault he was too young. Like to'a done his pony in while he was at it. Don't know where his pa was, but we know he wasn't here. Likely the boy was a better rider than his ma, and he couldn't help bein' only fourteen. Seemed to me that land ought'a been his."

"So what we're doin' ain't wrong?"

After a pause, "It ain't no more wrong than what was done to us. We took care'a our land since 'afore you was born, and your Grannie Rose, she lived on it from away back. Then folks comes that says it ain't ours and we got'a run for it. Well, we did, and so did Jeremiah Duncan. I'm allowin' him and his ma'll be good neighbors."

Liz smiled and sighed with relief. "I'm glad it ain't wrong."

"Now, Liz, I didn't actual say that. What I said was...."

"I know, Pa. And I said I'm glad it ain't wrong."

Ben had a good idea where the land office was. Guthrie was only a handful of buildings around the railroad track. But as they neared the city, the noise of it and the rolling clouds of rising dust came to meet them.

The tracks were overflowing with people, a milling mass of dusty, thirsty humanity that seemed to cover every inch of the hill that had been staked out as the town. The flow of people drifted into the valley, and the shouting of tired, angry mob was deafening.

Excited horses reared, and wagon wheels ground past angry crowds.

"Liz, I wisht I hadn't brought you to this."

"I can make it, Pa. Let's find the place."

"Well, standin' here, I can't rightly tell where it is. Now there's a street that crossed the tracks... about here...? Well, if we followed the tracks, we'd...."

They found the land office, accidentally, and the line in front of it wound, snakelike, within itself, a coil of tired, hungry, thirsty humanity. Following the line to the end of it, Ben and Liz took their place, holding the bridles of the horses.

They inched forward, hardly making a showing as the sun sank lower in the sky, and then, finally, they could see the door. It was practically dark, and they were certain the office would close before everyone could register. If that happened, it would be an all night wait.

But the serpentine line crawled along, and another group was taken into the tiny building. The next group would be theirs. If it would only stay open...!

Then they were inside. Liz did not have to fake a wobbly hand as she signed "Maggie Duncan." Weariness had taken its toll, and total darkness had fallen around them.

"Seems we'll be stayin... the night...?"

"Where'd it be, Pa?"

"Well, we could…."

"Pa, could you get home in the dark if it wasn't for me?"

"Oh, I… Well, pretty near… but…?"

"Then let's go." She spoke with more bravery than she felt.

"But that'd be two, maybe three hours."

"That'd be better'n here."

"You're right on that. Only thing I think of is goin' back through them new claims in the dark and them not seein' who it is. Could be, we'd get a gun leveled at us."

"We could talk. Or sing. Or somethin.'"

"For three hours?"

"Let's go, Pa. If we got on out'a this crowd, could be someone'd let us stay over on their land."

As they headed east, the timber on each side of the surveyor's section lines was dotted with cook fires as the new owners of the claims were poised, gun over knees, ready to defend their property.

"Just a passin' through. We ain't armed."

Over and over they repeated the words, and finally they were home. The welcome shape of the barn arose black against the moonlit sky, and a light shone in the windows.

"You go on in, Liz. I'll see to the horses."

Liz wearily stumbled toward the door of her house. The kitchen was full of people, and most of them were crowned with hair in every shade of red.

Jeremiah separated himself from the crowd. "That's her, Ma. She got back!"

A woman came toward Liz, enveloping her, and pulling her close. "Oh, you sweet, darlin' angel. Likely you ain't real, but even if you ain't, I'll never agin doubt the Good Lord."

"Real? Me?"

Her hands clamped Liz's shoulders and held her at arm's length. "I got'a look in the face'a someone who'd do what you done! Who'd think there'd be such'a person…?" She suddenly became at loss for words and wiped her knuckles into her moist eyes.

Andrew felt the need to explain to his sister. "This here's Maggie Duncan. First off, she wouldn't believe what we told her, and then she thought likely somethin' happened when you didn't get back."

Ben came in and, looking neither right or left, headed straight for the Book. Laying his hand on its soft tatters, he looked up. "Thank You. I reckon ten thousand fell by our right hands."

Looking around at the strangers in his house, he decided, "You must be the Duncan's. Did my boy fix you somethin' to drink? Good!"

Liz sank wearily into an offered chair.

Ben, again. "Now, for the last mile, I been thinkin.' My wife ain't here, and she'd be the one to say. But for tonight, you folks need to go out to the little cabin we got in the back and get yerselves some rest. Tomorrow, we'll sort things out."

"But, Mr. Ben? Shouldn't I be spendin' the night over on the place?"

Ben shook his head. "Wouldn't think there'd be somethin' happenin' tonight. Clay, you take the folks over to the cabin and come straight back."

Liz stumbled into her room and fell into the bed. Tomorrow would be soon enough to pull herself out of Andrew's overalls and Clayton's shirt. After a night's sleep she might be able to make sense of the happenings of the day.

Twenty-Six

It was on first light of the 24th of April that Emma and her two young daughters excitedly climbed aboard the wagon to head west. It had been a long week, but it was finally over and they could return.

Ben's pa and his pa's wife had been good to them and had helped with the care of the horses, but Emma's heart was not there. She hardly allowed Ben a word with his pa, so impatient she was to be on her way home.

They were headed west into the afternoon sun, and she could wait no longer. "Tell me quick, Ben. We got neighbors?"

Ben nodded his head, but then was irritatingly quiet.

"Well, tell me…." She demanded.

"Didn't figure you to be anxious to hear about a neighbor that was a crabby old bachelor. You got'a recall, we didn't have no say over who was first to get to the land."

"Bachelor? Not a family? A body'd'a thought…" Her voice trailed off with disappointment.

They rode along in silence, the tethered horses spread out behind them, amiably plodding along. The dog they had tied to the wagon bed on the trip east, and who had to be kept on a rope to keep from attempting to return to his home, was now set free. He leaped and frisked, lolling and waggling, knowing somehow that he was returning home.

Emma again, anxious to make the best of the situation. "Well, leastways, he'd be a person, and he'll have to build some kind of a house. Reckon he'd have folks comin' on later?"

Silence.

Emma countered shyly, "Didn't think to ask 'im if he had folks?"

Liz rode the black stallion beside the wagon, leading several other horses. She listened with interest to the conversation of her parents. A slight smile at her father's cruelty.

Emma. "How old of a man?"

"Now, Emma, how'd it be to march over to the new neighbor, tired and dusty, and demand to know how old they was? Would that be a neighborly thing to do?"

"I reckon not. It was just that I was thinkin…."

Liz could stand it no longer. "Pa! You hadn't ought'a treat her like that! She's had a bad time… worse than us."

Emma again. "Like what? You mean there ain't no fellow…?"

Ben, restraining a grin. "Yeah, there was a fellow. He's fourteen years old!"

"That all?"

"No, there was another fellow, and he's twelve."

"Two boys?"

"That's what I saw."

"Well, they can't file a claim. They ain't old enough."

"Well, their claim's filed."

Another silence.

"PA!" yelled Liz, exasperatedly. "TELL HER, PA!"

"Tell me what?"

Ben decided he'd strung this out long enough. "All right. You got a woman neighbor."

"A woman? How old?"

"Didn't ask her. She's got boys 12 and 14. Got'a be close to your age."

"Two boys! Friends for Clay!"

Ben added, "And some girls. Five or six or seven or somethin'."

"How many?"

"Didn't count 'em. You'll see 'em by dark."

"Really? You're not teasin' me about a woman…?"

"Nope. Got no man, though."

"Alone? She made the run, and went to Guthrie… and took care'a youngens… and everything?"

"She didn't do the signin.'"

"Then how'd she…?"

Liz could stand it no longer. "I signed for 'er, Ma."

"You? No, you're teasin' me agin."

"No, Ma. I promise."

"But you got'a be twenty-one, and you ain't but sixteen! Ben, is she tellin' the truth about signin'? She ain't twenty one!"

"Didn't figure that'd matter. She ain't Maggie Duncan, neither, and that's the name she signed. So now, the way I figure it, Maggie Duncan's obligated to be your friend. We put her in debt to you." A mischievous grin played about Ben's mouth.

"Aw, Ben!"

"Nuther thing. I got 'er even more obligated by lettin' 'er sleep her youngens in the log cabin."

"Our cabin?"

"Only one out there that I know of," Ben said, with exasperating honesty.

By late afternoon, the wagon and the strings of horses came through the front gate and pulled past the house into the corral. The late afternoon sun reflected off the plate glass windows of the house, picking up the colors of the spring flowers in the yard, descendants of those brought to the red land by Bridie Scott.

Within sight of her windows, not hardly a hundred yards away, a wagon was parked under the trees. Moving around in the trees was a woman and several children. They looked up, and then hurried toward Emma.

Neighbors! Wonderful things, neighbors! At least Emma was sure they would be wonderful. She had never had neighbors, before.

Weariness evaporated like the morning mist.

Maggie approached. "You must be Emma! We been waitin' and watchin.' We had the idea you'd be tired and hungry, so we made up a stew from the venison we got. We was hopin' you'd…?" Her voice begged to be assured that what she had done was all right.

"We'd love to eat with you. I'm starved."

They gathered around the old table in the log cabin and filled their bowls with the rich broth.

Quickly filling in the gaps of information, Maggie told them, "My man, Amos, he sold the place when his old pa died. That was back in Arkansas, near the river. We set out, hopin' to make the run and get us a place, but if we didn't, we'd go to a town and him, and the boys'd go to work.

"Well, it was down in the bottoms… we was camped out on the ground, and a snake got in the beddin,' and he got a bite. We didn't have nothin' to treat it with, and time we got to where somethin' was, it was too bad gone." Maggie paused, swallowed hard, and continued.

"We left 'im there, under the headstone, and they's times I would'a turned back, 'cept there wasn't nothin' to turn back to. My boys here, Jeremiah and Michael, they said to go on, and they'd do what their pa was aimin' to do. So we come on.

"Time and agin, I was tempted to stop off in some town that was all set up and use the money we had to buy us a place, but these boys, they thought their pa'd want us to come on.

"Then we got over to the startin' line a week early and waited around, tryin' to decide what'd be the best. Not knowin' nothin,' we finally figured out we'd have to lay the problem off onto the Good Lord.

"Jeremiah, bein' the oldest, figured it was up to him to make the run. If we didn't get nothin,' and that was what we was thinkin' might happen, then we'd go on to the nearest town. Likely the boys could find somethin' there to do.

"Turned out that pony'a ours took off a'runnin' just like the devil, hisself, was after 'im and followed after your boy, a'thrashin' and crashin' through the trees, and splashin' up the creek bank. The other youngens and me, there wasn't nothin' for us to do but watch, and keep remindin' the Good Lord that we needed help. Turned out, we got help!

"That man'a yours, he put us onto what to do when the boy got here, your girl signed for us, and your boys helped us to guard the land. All them good things couldn't'a come from nobody but the Good Lord. So what we figured next was, we still got the little bit'a money we had. I'm knowin' it'll not buy a place like you got built, but this here little cabin…? We'd be right happy to have one like it.

"So, if we ain't used up our favors from you, maybe you could put us onto someone who'd tell these boys how to put up a cabin like this'n? They're strong and could likely do all the work, but they'd need help knowin' what to do, and we'd expect to pay full price for the teachin.'" She hesitated and looked full into Emma's face, and then in Ben's. "Was just wantin' you to know that."

It was a long speech. Maggie and her two sons trained their eager eyes on Ben.

Ben responded. "Ain't nothin' to the puttin' up of a log house. All you need is trees, time, a choppin' ax, and a strong back. Could take three weeks to be in the dry. Maybe, two weeks, if me and my boys was to help."

Twenty-Seven

Liz, the lonely, had never seen so much activity.

A steady stream of people, horses, wagons, buggies and equipment made their way down the surveyor's right of way, directly in front of her door. A road was quickly forming under the continuous passage of wagon wheels, and it was only a hundred yards in front of her front gate.

It was becoming hard to remember her duties with so much to think about, but it was spring, and duties still had to be done. One sunny afternoon, however, she slipped on her bonnet and struck out down the road to see where everyone was going. She had been hearing words. A lot of people, a whole town's worth of them, were living not two miles away from her.

Just three weeks ago, she had seen a huge machine of some sort being hauled past her house in two wagons. Then, early the next morning, an ear splitting screech had torn through the trees, echoing back, and seeming to come from everywhere.

A sawmill, pa had said. The machine that made the kind of lumber he had used on their own house. The noise had lasted all day, screeching, ripping, and tearing through tree trunks of oak, cottonwood and sycamore. Wagons passed on the section line loaded with lengths of logs headed for the sawmill.

And such noise!

The noise was a good noise… the sound of people. Not the lonely drone of the cicada crickets, or the trill of the tree frogs. It was the noisy shout of a machine… a machine that was doing something… something that would change her life.

After Maggie's cabin had been set together, Andrew had gone to the mill to see if he could get a job. He had stayed all day, and the next day he had taken Clayton with him. The Duncan boys wanted to go too, but they had to put in a garden before they could think of doing anything else.

Walking down the trail, that was so fast becoming a road, Liz's heart pounded with anticipation. Bravely she went on. The town had people, and they were just ahead. Dozens of wagons had rolled down this road and had continually gone back and forth. She was beginning to recognize some of them.

There were at least two, maybe three, green wagons painted on the side with large letters, 'KENDALL BROTHERS, We Haul.' And sure enough, they were always hauling something.

Buggies had gone this way and that.

She walked along for a mile, and through the trees just ahead, she could see the sawmill, belching its black smoke, ripping and tearing, spitting streams of yellow sawdust. Above the noise of the machine, she heard voices yelling to each other, shouting this and that. All around about there were horses and wagons, some loaded with tree trunks and others with stacks of cream colored planks of wood, cut in all sizes and lengths.

She walked past the sawmill. At first, it was hard to believe her brothers when they told her a town existed less than two miles to the east. Then it became hard not to believe, especially after she had seen the train of wagons that had taken the better part of an hour, just to pass in front of her house.

She had been busy with the darning needle and the sock egg, and beside her was a basket of accumulated socks with holes in the toe or heel, or both. The carved wooden ball of the egg was inserted into the toe or heel of the worn sock, and with the thick needle, she bound the hole together with wide stitches side by side. When the hole was covered, she stitched across the darn, weaving her needle under and over, creating new fabric. Darning socks was a senseless chore, leaving a lot of time to think.

That day, Liz had sat at the table, thinking her own thoughts, when her little sisters had come running into the house.

"Come look! Millions'a wagons a'comin' by!"

Even with Sally's habit of exaggerating, it seemed to be a thing to watch. She had moved her darning operation out into the yard, and it seemed Sally had been telling the truth.

Wagon after wagon had rolled past, interspersed at intervals with carts and buggies. It had been very late in the evening, and the sun was already down, still some of the drivers waved in her direction, and the little girls had waved back, laughing and dancing around. It had been a puzzle as to where all these people would go, as the run for the free land had been over a month ago.

There were several carts pulled by mules in the wagon train and one or two wagons filled with what looked like some kind of machinery. Several of the wagons were driven by girls, seeming to be no older than herself.

It had intrigued her with the strangeness of it all, but it made more sense when Andrew told them of the town. It seemed town from somewhere up north had moved all together, occupying their own quarter section. The town had its own name. They called it Prosper. Hmmm.

Andrew had learned about it later from two young men who had come with the town, and currently operated the sawmill.

Then, late one evening, one of the young men had come to the house with Andrew and had eaten supper with them. Dave was his name. Dave Hill.

He was not quite so tall as Andrew, but then, most men weren't. His hair was light, sun bleached almost to the color of the sunshine, itself. His eyes were blue as a summer sky... so light against the deep tan of his skin that she seemed to be able to see into his very mind.

How had she noticed so many details? Well, he had sat directly across the table from her, and every time she glanced in his direction, he seemed to have been watching her, but then he looked away. And when she knew he was looking at her, she turned her attention to the food on her plate.

After the meal, he had gone out to the barn with Andrew, and she was left with the cleaning up and with her thoughts. They were strange thoughts. A few times, a man, or possibly a couple, had taken a meal with them, and the talk had been free among the visitors and her parents.

This time, the talk had been sprinkled with silences, and the young man would try to revive the talk by asking a question.

How long had they lived here? All their life? How interesting.

How deep was the winter snow, and when did it come? Was it true that the snow didn't stay on the ground all winter? Wasn't it hard to hunt, if there was no snow?

Andrew had assured him that hunting was no problem. In fact, he'd take him hunting as soon as they had a little time off at the mill.

Liz had watched when she could, and as he smiled, small creases formed on each side of his wide mouth. A strong nose. She had noticed that as he turned to one side to speak to Andrew, or to Pa.

There were questions she would have liked to ask, but she didn't know enough to ask them. When someone was from some place so far away, a lot of things would have been very different, so one needed to know something about things, or they might ask stupid questions.

Besides, Dave was Andrew's friend. What would he think of her butting in on their conversation?

But the next time he came, he had lingered, separating himself from Andrew. She had found the courage to ask him if he had a family. Yes, but they were still up north. Did he have sisters? No, just three brothers, all younger than himself. Did he get lonely for his family?

No, not yet, he had said. He hadn't had the time!

His light blue eyes looked directly at her, and he had admitted that he did not expect to be lonely. He was, after all, past twenty, and he had paid down on one of the lots in the town. If the work in the sawmill held out, he'd have it paid for by Christmas, and he didn't see how the sawmill work would not hold out. Everyone needed lumber, and so many of the claims had trees that needed to come down and cash money that needed to be in their pockets.

Liz had been gathering the dishes together, scraping the leftovers into the dog's dish when that last fascinating bit of news reached her ears. He was buying his own land! He would be living in the town. As her mind processed the information, she had paused with the knife in her hand. She felt his eyes on her, and her cheeks burned.

Quickly and noisily, she scraped the next dish. What must he think! But he was not in a hurry to leave, and he thought of something to break the silence.

Andrew, he told her, was going to help him put up a one room log cabin for the winter, and was going to give him the logs from the land back of the canyon. (Liz remembered the conversation between Andrew and her pa, that they wanted that land cleared, so the grass would grow better.)

Dave continued. He already had a well, but he needed to order some fence wire to keep his horses at home.

A week later, Dave had left Andrew to his chores and had followed her to the garden. There were green beans to can tomorrow, and if she picked them in the evening while it was cool, she and her ma could have them in the canner before the kitchen got hot.

Dave had just walked up as she was bent over the vines. Without a word, he had knelt down on the other side of the row and began to help. The way he selected only the mature beans, carefully leaving the smaller ones, she knew this was not the first time he had picked beans. It seemed strange, though, to have him so close. Their hands were almost touching.

Searching for something to say, she stupidly uttered, "You don't have to help me. I'm about through."

He had just smiled that wide smile that made creases in his lower cheek. "Sure I do. I'm good at picking beans. I told you, all my ma had was boys, so one of us had to be all the time helpin' her. I was the one she picked to do it."

"You were...?" How did one respond to such a confession?

"Why, I can even make biscuits. Livin' alone like I do, I'd get a mite hungry if I didn't know how to cook."

Well, that made sense. If Pa and Andrew didn't have Ma and herself, well, it only made sense, didn't it?

And when the bushel basket was full, he had picked it up without a word, and leaning it against his hip, he had carried it to the house. Setting it down, he asked, "Do we need to start snapping?"

Startled, she had replied, "Oh, no. Ma and me, we'll...."

But he had insisted. "I got a few more minutes before I need to leave. Let's get 'em started." So they had.

It gave her such a strange feeling, thinking of Dave. She had asked him about who lived in the town, maybe girls her age? He had told her, yes, there were several, maybe eight or ten, but they were really busy and probably wouldn't have time to come to see her for a few months.

That was when she had begun to think of going visiting all by herself. It was a very scary thought. What if they didn't like her? And, certainly, they would be busy. She, herself, was busy, and she already had a house and barn and a good garden and animals, and all they had to start with was a piece of ground under the trees. Well, sometime things would be different.

Twenty-Eight

So, today, all these feelings had built up into a mountain of curiosity, and she managed to steal an afternoon to go exploring.

She passed the sawmill, and several other homesteads in the process of building shelters. Older children were busy with shovels and hoes, working small gardens. Grownups tended fires under wash pots, hung clothes on the line, pounded shingles on the roofs, and strung fence wire among the trees to restrain their animals.

When someone glanced her way, Lizzie waved but kept on walking. She didn't want to disturb anyone who was busy.

This was finally her chance to see what was going on in the town, and that would be the best thing to do today. If the town was actually real, it would still be there tomorrow, and she could savor the anticipation of the friends she might find. Liz walked on, filling her eyes with the newness of it all.

On a wooded tract of land adjacent to the town site, a woman was bent over the small plants in her garden, picking out small weeds. Her wide brimmed bonnet hid her wavy hair, at one time a rich chestnut, but now bordered with silvery white. Covering her arm was a loose, cotton shirt the type any woman would wear to protect their arms from the sun.

Beside her on the ground was a basket filled with last year's dead leaves, moist and pungent, smelling strongly of the earth.

When she had pulled all the small weeds, and the ground around the plant was bare, she dipped into the basket of decaying leaves. She built up a protective collar around each flowering plant, patting it firmly to retain moisture in the ground.

She did not hurry, but moved slowly and continuously.

The late June sun beat down on the bonnet shading her face and on her shoulders, flowing its warmth through the fabric of her dress. The warmth of the sun on her back was comforting, even as it produced a moist band of perspiration across her forehead.

It was totally pleasant to sit on the warm ground and care for the rooted rosemary plants she had brought here from her former life in Illinois. She had no reason to hurry. She had a good life and plenty of time to live it.

Her good life had not happened, accidentally. Truly good things seldom do. Neither had the good things in her life come to her gradually as she matured. At her time of life it would seem that she should have reached this stage in easy increments as situations in her life dictated. But this was not so.

In actuality, it has been very different. It was almost as though she had come alive in her mid fifties and decided to take charge of the rest of her life.

Circumstances from her childhood had pushed her this way and that, and she had adapted well, reacting but never acting. Adapting is a skill and a talent but taking charge...? For that, bravery was necessary.

She had been forced from her Tennessee home at an early age and had received an accidental education, much more thorough than her station in life would have afforded.

She had studied first with the children of the family her mother served, and then at the gracious hand of an old minister, whose home and library she, herself, dusted and cared for. It was because of the old man that she was encouraged to gain a certificate to teach school. Then other things had happened.

Sadie McClure had spent her years looking down toward the earth, working with her hands and with her mind. She worked with those around her and with their children. What her hand found to do, she did to the best of her ability. For more than fifty years, that had been her life, and then, when past fifty-five years old, she had looked up.

Suddenly and actually, she had looked up.

It was then, in the course of a few minutes, that her life had changed. Many times she had thought back on that day, and as she pulled the small spring weeds, she passed those thoughts through her mind once more.

Children's kites had flown overhead in the high winds of spring. They dipped and soared, seeming to be alive, but each of them was tethered to the earth by a string in the hands of a person. The kites were flown at the pleasure of the string holder and taken down and put away when the playing was over.

In one moment, that particular moment, she saw that she had allowed herself to be a kite to be flown at the pleasure of others. She had adapted to the circumstances life had given her, fitting herself into the families she worked for as a governess and into the communities she had worked as a teacher.

She had never been herself. She had been a part of her mother's family, her brother's family, and then her nephew's family. She had always been treated lovingly and gently, but, nevertheless, her life had been tied to theirs.

Then it was on that fateful day, as she watched the kites, a skein of birds had flown past, migrating south. High in the sky they flew, each with its own wings, beating with great effort as it moved ahead. No string tied them to the earth. They moved on their own in the way they wanted to move.

The birds settled onto the waterways, fed on seeds and insect life, and then they returned to the sky, making their own way with the beat of their own wings. Riding on the waves of air caused by the flock, they were, nevertheless, each an individual.

What a wonderful concept! Within the suddenness of a thought, a new life was born.

That was the day Sadie's life had changed. Like a cocoon, motionless, breaks open to release the flitting butterfly, Sadie McClure became a new person.

It was also on that day she decided she would go to the new land, the place the flyers and brochures described. She made her plans and she would go, welcoming others to go with her, but whether or not, she would go.

It had been a long trip to the Oklahoma territory, almost two months, but she had led her nephew's family across two states, and now they were settled in the town.

And even now, the energy she had thought she would never have, aroused her each morning with new eagerness. The very trees around her seemed to give her strength. When she had thought she would be alone the rest of her life, she had met and married an old childhood friend, who, by another route, had reached the same destination as she.

So here she sat on the warm ground, mulching her plants with mineral rich leaf mold. She was here by her own choice, not brought by another. A bird chose its own direction. Right or wrong, its choices were its own, and it was a wonderful thing to take control.

As so often happened, these days, Sadie's thoughts wandered through parts of the past few months. She had been deep in thinking, now, and at that moment Sadie's thoughts were interrupted.

She sensed someone nearby and turned toward the pair of neat, but dusty, shoes. She lifted her eyes to view the flowered skirt, dark blue shirtwaist and white bonnet. The face under the bonnet was pale and protected under the shade of the ruffled bonnet brim.

Tendrils of dark hair curled around the edge of the bonnet and lay flat on her high forehead. Young, she was… and she stood quietly not four yards away, just watching.

As Sadie turned to look at her, the girl smiled, dimpling low on each cheek.

Sadie spoke first. "Well, hello, young lady."

"Hello," came the response. "I hope you didn't mind me watchin'. I was thinkin' how you put the leaves around your rosemary plants."

"Do you like to garden?" It would be a good thing to talk with this young lady. The new town was full of young people, but, like their parents, the days were too short to accomplish what had to be done. This young lady seemingly had time to come calling on an afternoon… such a civilized and sociable thing to do!

"Sometimes," the girl responded. "I like gardenin' better'n some other things. It was just that you reminded me of my Gran, the way you put the old dead leaves around your plants. She did the same thing, and I helped her."

"You speak like your Gran isn't with you?"

"No, she died. I was nine, and she was really old. She wasn't my Gran, really. She was my mother's Gran, who was brought here from Missouri."

"Oh, you came from Missouri, did you?"

"Oh, no, ma'am. I was always here. My ma was my age when she was brought here. Gran taught her about plants, and my ma wrote a book, drawin' pictures of the plants, and everything."

"A book, huh? I'd enjoy seeing it sometimes. Now, young lady, I was just goin' to fix myself a cup'a tea. I don't suppose you'd have time to join me?"

"Yes, thank you."

"Well, I'll just…"

Though the new land had poured strength into her, and the breeze of the territory had cleared her mind, her knees were still past fifty-five years old. Reaching out toward the handle of the shovel to assist her to stand, her hand was, instead, clasped by a firm, strong young hand.

"Let me help you, ma'am. Time to time, my Gran had a mite'a trouble getting' her balance after sittin' down, a'weedin.'"

Just look at that, Sadie told herself! Such a thoughtful young lady as this one must surely have had very good training. What young person would even think of the weakness of old knees, much less consider offering a helping hand?

"Now, honey, just call me Sadie. We'll just go in the cabin, here, and I'll make us some tea."

"My name's Mary Elizabeth Green, Miss Sadie. My family calls me Liz."

Sadie detected a hesitation at the use of the nickname. "Do you like to be called Liz?"

The girl was not quick to answer. "Maybe. It's all right. I thought that sometime I'd like to be called Mary Elizabeth. That was my real grandmother's name. The one that went back to Missouri. I didn't ever know her."

Sadie smiled in her direction. "Then, Mary Elizabeth, that shall be your name."

At the door of the tiny log house, Sadie stepped aside and invited the girl to enter.

As Liz's eyes accustomed themselves to the softer light, she stopped, amid step, and stared at the unusual piece of furniture occupying a wall of the cabin. Only large enough for a bed, a stove and a tiny table, room was found for a set of shelves maybe two feet wide, and as tall as her shoulder.

"Ah! Miss Sadie, is that…?"

Sadie turned to see the girl staring at the new bookshelf that she had insisted she must have and at the brightly colored spines of her precious horde of books. More than sixty of them, there were now, and they stood proudly on the shelves, their colorful bindings brightening the tiny cabin better than any canvas painted by a famous artist.

Looking from the girl to the books and back to the girl, she saw a reflection of her own self at a young age, and time flew backward.

It was at her own age of sixteen that she had been put into service, caring for an old couple. The man, a minister, had an extensive library.

At first it had seemed a pleasure just to dust the books and handle the expensive, embossed covers, but the old man had seen her longing looks, and perhaps heard her unconscious sighs.

For the next wonderful, unforgettable year, she had read for hours and talked with the old man, discussing the classics, reading the poetry, trying to reach the hidden meaning in the essays. A glorious year to be often remembered.

In the smoky blue of the girl's eyes, Sadie saw what she had been sure had been in her own eyes. When it was necessary to leave the employ of the old man, he had generously given her the start of her own library. The same library that the girl now stared at in rapt attention.

The old man had given her a choice of twenty-five books to be taken from his shelves that had created within her a wonderful and tormenting mixture of gratefulness for the wonderful gift and sorrow at leaving so many other books behind.

The seconds dragged on as the bonneted girl stared at the books. Sadie and the tea were forgotten. Stepping forward, the girl reached a tentative finger toward the nearest book.

"Real," she stated softly to herself, hardly believing her own words.

"Sure enough are."

"I was thinkin' they might be just pictures or somethin,' like maybe a new thing I hadn't ever seen, made up just to make a room look pretty. I never even saw more'n five books together at one time, ever before."

"They're all real," Sadie assured her. "Do you like books, Mary Elizabeth?"

"I think I would if I had any. What we got at our house is little books for learnin' to read, ones that my Gran used when she taught her girl that I was named after, and then she taught my ma. Then I was taught. Ma and Pa both taught me."

"What a fortunate young lady you are."

Liz nodded and sighed. "Yeah, but them books are about to come apart from bein' read, and they're little stories. There's times, though, that Pa brings home papers he got somewhere, tellin' about things happenin' back east. I read them."

Then she added, "Ma's thinkin' on startin' to teach my two little sisters to read. She's sayin' I could help 'er."

"How old are your sisters?"

"Annie's five, and Sally's seven."

"Such a good age to begin." Sadie set a steaming cup of tea on the tiny table.

Liz sat on the edge of the stool, still looking at the books.

"Do you like poetry, Mary Elizabeth?"

Liz smiled appreciatively at the use of her name. "I think I would, Miss Sadie. I don't rightly remember any except the little verses in the book. I've thought it'd be fun to write some down, if I was to learn how."

"Dear, would you like to look at a book?"

"Oh, yes, ma'am!"

Twenty-Nine

With cups of cooling tea on the table, a book of poems written by old English authors was examined. When an hour had gone by, Liz suddenly rejoined reality.

"Oh, Miss Sadie, I got'a be getting' back. Ma said for me not to be in the way'a folks with work to do. I told her I'd not be long, and she'll be wonderin' what happened to me. But I sure do appreciate you lettin' me look at the book."

"Mary Elizabeth, honey, I can do more than that. Next time you come to see me, tell your mother you'll be gone a bit longer, and you can stay and read whatever you like. You just come on anytime. I don't have a lot to do like some of the other folks."

"Could I? Oh, thank you, ma'am. I mean, Miss Sadie! I could do that!"

Sadie watched from her cabin door as the girl hurried away, but turned to wave just before disappearing into the trees.

Reheating the tea, Sadie sat on the stool beside the shelf table, and she stared out the tiny window. Thoughts flowed into her mind, filling every nook and cranny with ideas, already full fledged and ready to be put into place. She saw before her the next experience of her life.

It was not a idea to be built upon gradually and continuously, but a full fledged and totally formed plan. Left to her was only the finding of a way to bring it to pass.

With her life's savings from her years of teaching school, she had planned to finance a school building for the new town of Prosper. She also planned to teach, only to span the time until a teacher could be found. Perhaps the teacher was already here!

With great foresight, she had brought with her the teaching books she would need to teach her nephew's children, a responsibility she considered to be only her family duty. But now she would wait and see.

If the girl came to the house regularly to read in the classics, as Sadie was certain she would have, perhaps it would interest her to...? Sadie was afraid to allow her mind to hope.

Well, it was much too soon to know, but plans must be made, just in case. A girl with a very strong want-to could earn a teaching certificate in two years. Maybe a lot less.

Liz, herself, walked back down the surveyor's trail toward her home. She must, somehow, have covered the ground between Prosper and the farm, but she did not remember it. Her feet must have made the steps, because she now walked through the door.

"Ma, I saw..."

With breathless excitement, Liz related the events of her afternoon.

Emma listened. "Who is this person that's got time of a afternoon to sit and talk for an hour with a girl she don't even know?"

"She's...well, she's older, I think. But not like Gran, except she tends her garden the same way. She's from somewhere? Illinois...? I think."

"Hmmm, she sounds nice. Did you see any girls your age?"

"Sure, ma, lot's of 'em, but I didn't stop to talk. Everyone of 'em busy. Them girls got more to do than a pup with five youngens to follow. But Miss Sadie... well, she had time. And, Ma, she said I could come to see her anytime."

During the month of July, Liz found herself at the tiny cabin several times a week. After the first visit, she was permitted to take one of the precious books to her home to read in the evenings and at spare minutes.

Sally and Annie were graduated from doll playing to certain grown-up chores. House cleaning, gardening, and washing clothes over the rub board were first, then sewing and ironing. This gave Liz more time with the books.

It was the first week in August that building lumber was delivered beside the tiny log cabin belonging to Sadie and her new husband. A much bigger house was to be built. Liz was there when the boards were delivered in the big green wagon.

"My brothers, Andrew and Clayton, they'd'a helped cut this up," she commented, nodding toward the pile of lumbar.

"Your brothers work at the sawmill?"

"Sure do. Them and pa built us a house out'a boards they hauled in from a mill somewhere a long time ago."

"Your pa's a builder?"

"Law, yeah. My Pa can do anything."

Sadie's mind was working fast. Thank the Good Lord for answers to prayer. "Does he work for other people?"

Lizzie nodded. "When he can. He built a cabin for our neighbor, and he helped on buildin' another one for a family that moved in back'a us."

"Is he…? Does he have somethin' he's workin' on right now?"

"Only the corn patch and the hay meadow."

So it was, that Miss Sadie and Mr. Eben, her husband, made a trip out to the home of Mary Elizabeth. When the buggy pulled into the yard, Emma nervously checked the temperature of the tea and the appearance of the raisin and honey cookies.

Just imagine! They were entertaining company! Real company! Not someone who just dropped in to rest his feet or to get a drink of water.

When the buggy pulled out onto the road two hours later, arrangements had been made. Ben would start to work on the house, and Andrew and Clayton would help when they could.

When the house was in the dry, he would begin to work on the schoolhouse. Thank you, Lord, for guiding us to meet Ben Green.

Bouncing along on the rough road, Sadie was almost dizzy and lightheaded from excitement. She… Sadie (McClure) Carlile… was no longer a kite, to be guided by others. She was a bird in flight… and she knew where she was going! Had she not just arranged to have the schoolhouse built? Not waiting around for others to make the decision for her?

Not only that, there was that wonderful young lady who seemed so interested. It was hard to be patient. It would be bad to get her own hopes up too soon. Well, she'd just have to see how it went.

It went well.

When September arrived and when the heat of the Oklahoma sun was not so powerful, school started. The school building was not yet complete, but the hammering and sawing simply served to enliven the schoolyard. Ben Green, and anyone who could help, were putting up the walls and ceiling of the new schoolhouse, pounding the fragrant, cream-colored boards into place.

Thirty

Young Andrew Green's strong arm pulled the saw back and forth, cutting the boards to the correct length. He kept his eye on the cutting mark, difficult as it was, as he felt himself being watched. Others had come to volunteer their time and do what they could, and among them were girls.

Caroline Kendall, almost fifteen, was interested in the scenery before her as Andrew's saw spit streams of sawdust with each thrust of his arm.

Gwendolyn Martin noticed the way his eyes, shoebutton black, crinkled in his face when he smiled in her direction. She found his darker skin fascinating. Gwendolyn was sixteen already, and it was certainly time to start looking around her. The scenery had become very attractive.

Pretty, red-haired Isabel Crowley had noticed how strong Andrew seemed to be as he lifted the heavy planks into place, holding them with one hand while the other pounded in the nails. Isabel was almost seventeen, and a strong young man would fit well within her plans. If he happened to look the way Andrew Green looked, well, so much the better. After what she had been through, she had become wary and wise.

For weeks the pounding continued. It was to be a large building. Forty feet long and twenty feet wide, and that was a very good size.

And benches. Finally, Sadie's husband had split enough cedar shingles for the roof and had now begun to work on the benches. Later, there could be desks and chairs, but for now it would be benches and tables.

And slates. Paper was expensive, and so were slates, but paper was eventually used up, and slates could be erased and used over and over. Sadie had put in an order for slates, and they had been delivered by the Kendall Brothers.

And chalk. Chalk was cheap and could be furnished by the child's family. Each of the children could bring his own chalk and a cloth to be used as an eraser. Every parent could afford chalk.

Sadie had told the girl, "Mary Elizabeth, honey, we can order all the books you missed by not gettin' to go to school. There's a place back in St. Louis…. Well, we'll get 'em. Oklahoma's too new, right now, but soon there'll be schoolhouses every two or three miles, and there'll be tests to take to get a certificate to teach. When that happens, you'll be ready. Fast as you learn, you'll see it'll be no trick at all to have yourself ready."

Liz certainly hoped that was true.

The textbooks came in with the slates, brought to their door by the driver of KENDALL BROTHERS, We Haul. Sadie was eager to have Liz look at them. There was always a chance, and Sadie kept herself ready that she was asking too much of this young lady and it might be best to back off a bit… until…?

Liz thumbed through one of the books. "You think, really, that I could…?"

"I know. For sure."

More pages were examined.

Sadie continued. "In the meantime, honey, you take this McGuffey primer home with you and read how they tell you to teach letters and numbers. It's important for new readers to get a good start on the way letters sound when they're turned into words."

"Oh, thank you!"

On the second week of September, the schoolhouse still had not been finished, but classes began for the younger children. Older children still had fall work to do and would not be released for a few weeks, and by then the first room of the schoolhouse would be finished.

Sadie, herself, would teach older grades until Mary Elizabeth was ready.

Under the shade of an oak tree, the benches were set up. Little Ruthie, grandniece of Miss Sadie's, and Alecia, granddaughter of Eden, climbed onto the benches beside Sophie Kendall, Marcie Banner and others who had come down from the north with the town.

Other five and six year olds were among the settlers, and they came dressed in clean overalls and dresses and with their hair slickly combed. They eagerly climbed up onto the benches. Liz's own two little sisters were among them. The teacher, "Miss Mary Elizabeth," stood before the class. Miss Sadie took her place nearby so she would be handy to help, if needed.

Liz began, "Students, you may call me 'teacher' or 'Miss Mary Elizabeth.'"

All that had been Miss Sadie's idea. She said students must learn to respect their teacher, even if it was a big sister. Liz continued.

"We'll start with the first part of the alphabet. 'A' is a sound we make when we talk. We use the sound to say apron, ashes, ask, and all."

A little hand shot up.

"Would you like to say something, Alecia?"

"Yes, ma'am. I mean, teacher. I know what 'A' is for."

"What is it for?"

Loudly and clearly, her voice rang out through the trees of the new territory. On the second line of the verse, she was joined by others who had seen her book ABC Book, the one she had brought from Tennessee.

"A is for apple, that grows on a tree.

Some are for piggy, and some are for me."

Other voices joined in.

"B is for ball for baby to play with.

B is for ball, the dog runs away with.

C is for chicken, with flappity wings.

She scratches for worms and wiggley things.

D is for dog, with a waggley tail...."

Thirty-One

It had been a magical summer. During August there had been the afternoons Liz was excused from her regular work to spend extra time with Miss Sadie. Emma realized the time was soon coming that Liz would leave her, going on to her own life. It was time to prepare to let her go.

As she thought about it, Emma had fleeting thought of her own parents leaving her in the territory when they went back to Missouri. How had they felt? Her father's main concern seemed to be for her safety and reputation and that she be kept from shame. That was a good thing... from a father.

But her mother? What she remembered was the tears and the resigned acceptance that her life would absorb this upset as it had absorbed so many before it. So now she faced another move that she did not want. And how did she feel about the loss of her daughter? Was that horror drowned among the other horrors of her life? Was it a continual nagging pain that she had lost her daughter, or was the feeling pushed away and an empty feeling allowed to take its place? Either way, she knew her mother would survive, changing her life to adapt to whatever shape the survival required.

So, back to her original thought. She knew when she lost Liz, as she soon would, it would not only like losing a right arm, for the work Liz did, that she was able to do. Rather, it would be like losing a piece of her heart. How can one live with a damaged heart?

Certainly her mother did not do well.

Then, on the heels of that thought, she had reason, once more, to be grateful for the small Nebraska town, the one she had so recently learned had even existed. Because of it, Liz would, without doubt, make her selection of a life mate and live close by. If the town had not happened, her precious daughter could have been forced to live miles away. So Emma was comforted with the thought.

Liz, herself, rode on a crest of excitement, seeing new opportunities open up before her. Her quiet and lonely life was now a daily adventure.

Dave had told her about the church, and she and Andrew went one Sunday. They saw benches filled with people in their best Sunday clothes. There were other young men like Dave, and a lot of girls who had smiled at her and at Andrew. Mainly Andrew?

Isabel Crowley had come to Liz, smiling and friendly. The next week, Liz had stopped in for a minute at Isabel's house, and had helped her hang the wash on the line before going on to Miss Sadie's. Isabel had a lot of work to do. She and a slightly younger cousin had made the run, bringing along younger siblings. Such bravery was unusual, even if it was born of necessity. Isabel had been faced with no other way to go.

Also, there had been the next visit by Miss Sadie and Mr. Eben. After the tea and cookies, there had been serious talk. It was time to bring Mary Elizabeth's parents into Sadie's ideas.

Emma had nervously twisted her handkerchief in her fingers as she listened to Miss Sadie. "Could be I'm not hearin' you right, Miss

Sadie. It seems like you're sayin' our Liz could get schoolin' and be a real, honest to goodness teacher that get's paid to teach. I'm thinkin' that'd not be... what you...?" Emma seldom had reason to misjudge her own understanding, but this was possibly one occasion when that happened.

Miss Sadie's head nodded. "Mrs. Green...."

"Call me Emma... please?"

"Emma, you heard right. I been workin' with your girl, and she's sharp as a whip. I lay it onto the educational foundation you and her pa gave her. She has a determination most girls don't have, and she wants to try. If she changes her mind, nothin'll be lost. Any learnin' a body gets, it's a good thing."

Emma sought for words. "But you... all that time..." It was such a new thing to Emma for someone to be so interested in a girl not her own that she found difficulty in grasping the words of Miss Sadie. The people she knew in the territory had more than enough on their own plate that to make such an offer to a stranger. She and her neighbors were accustomed to taking care of their own.

But this Miss Sadie assured her in a soft and kindly voice. "Emma, honey, I spent the most years of my life teachin' youngens. That's the one thing I know best how to do. A girl who learns to teach... well, she's got a thing she can do all her life. A thing that'll take care'a her and make enough money to keep 'er, no matter what else may happen to her. That's what it did for me."

There was a small silence as Liz's ma and pa looked at each other, then at Liz, herself. It had seemed strange to Liz, sitting there with the people she loved and knew best talking about her as though maybe she wasn't even there. Deciding her future. Making plans for her. Discussing what was best for her. It was a very flattering position to be in. She turned her attention from one to the other.

Ben wondered. "Supposin' you'd put in all that time. It ain't that I'm agin it, but I'd need to know how much money'd you'd need for helpin' her so's I could plan on it. If it's somethin' our Liz wants... somethin' that we can get for her, well... her ma and me, we'd... want..." He paused to select the right word.

"Oh, no, Mr. Green! The only money she'd ever need would be if she wanted to buy a book to keep! She's got the use'a my books and my time for free. Then, there'll be a time, likely next year, that there'll be a cost put on the parents with children in the school. That'll go to her. Your girl knows enough right now to start with the little ones. The experience she'll get right here in Prosper will the best education she could get at this time. I'll be there to help, and later she can do more, and she won't need me."

Emma stared into space, focusing on the white ruffled curtain decorating the window. Her girl… a teacher! The thought of it was too much, tightening her throat and requiring that she swallow before she could speak. She bowed her face into her hands, resting her elbows on her snow white, freshly ironed apron. A tear slid down her tanned cheeks.

Ben nodded, slowly, trying to comprehend. "You thinkin' two years, then…?"

"Two years, easy. Sooner than that if she has the time to work. Could be, she'll have a little trouble with English grammar, you know? The way words are used and the order they're put together. Spellin' may take some time, but the other things, they'll be easy. Now, Mary Elizabeth and I, we've talked, but we knew it'd be you and her ma that'd decide what was best for her."

Ben had nodded, reaching absently for another cookie.

Then Sadie had concluded, "So if there's nothin' more you need to say or no questions to ask, we'll be goin' off and let you think it over." She had smiled and reached for her handbag, but Ben had stopped her.

"Wait. I'm thinkin' the talkin's done. Liz, is this a thing you want to do?"

Liz startled at the sudden calling of her name. She had watched, as in a dream, as Miss Sadie and her parents had talked. "Sure, Pa. It seems like it's somethin' I've always wanted to do, only I didn't know what it was. Seems like if I got that there'd be nothin' else I need to ask for."

Thirty-Two

So Mary Elizabeth Green began to seriously attend a class of one. After the little ones had their session, Liz and Miss Sadie sat at the shelf table in her cabin and worked on numbers, fractions, decimals, and Roman Numerals.

They worked on nouns, verbs, prepositions, and diagrammed sentences. They worked on documents written by the government in the east and articles in the newspapers written in Kansas, Texas, Arkansas, and even in their own Oklahoma City.

Liz read her assignments by the light of the kerosene lamp in her room.

For Liz, the lonely, life had taken a whirlwind turn. It was as if she was one of the cocoons her old Gran had showed her. She was like the one they had put in the glass jar and tied a cloth over the lid. Each day it looked the same, and then one day it was gone. In the bottom of the jar lay a dry wrinkled old husk, and fluttering to be free was a butterfly, golden-yellow, and trimmed in black.

They had opened the jar, and out flew the butterfly, fully-grown and strong. It was as though it had always known what it should do, and when its wings had hardened, it went about the life it was meant to have.

Was this what she had always been meant to have? Did she need to look at the last years as the husk that had protected her wings? If so, what would have happened if Miss Sadie had not appeared to remove the lid and let her go free?

Liz, the lonely, now had Isabel for a friend, Miss Sadie for a teacher, and she had Dave. What was Dave? At first he was Andrew's friend, and then Andrew began to look at Isabel, and Dave wanted time with Liz alone. So that made him her friend. Boy friend? Such a strange term, and such an odd description for this person who could seemingly do everything.

For years, she had wanted something, and now she had two things, and they both needed the same space of time. Miss Sadie and the books and Dave and... well, her heart?

Dave was now working 12 hours a day at the mill, but still he came to see her every evening, though he was sometimes so tired he could hardly stay awake.

Liz was happy to see him, though she knew each minute she spent with him must be made up later, studying by the light of the lamp. She would be forced to struggle to keep her eyes open, or she would not have her assignments ready for Miss Sadie to correct, and that would be unthinkable. Her teacher set a fast and heavy schedule.

By the first week in October, the school building had walls and a roof, and a deep pile of sawdust on the floor. Dave and his partner had caught the fresh yellow sawdust in boxes as it spun away from the saw, and they had brought it to the school to cover the dirt floor. The sawdust helped a lot to keep down the dust from shuffling feet and the sneezed the dust made.

By the second week in October, the older children came. That made a total of thirty-one children from five to twelve, and Liz continued to teach the five and six year olds. They were seated behind a curtain stretched across one corner.

Miss Sadie taught the rest of the children. When she could, Liz peeked out and watched Miss Sadie, telling herself, *So that's how to do it!'*

It was on the first week in December and the first snow of the year, that Dave had come to see her. In the coziness of her parent's parlor, he had become serious.

"Liz, there's somethin' I got'a say. I know you got lot's to do, and so do I, but I want you to know somethin.' I been seein' a lot'a you, and the more I see, the better I like you. The thing is, I'm wantin' to marry you."

"You… but…?" Such a surprise, but then, it really wasn't.

"Yeah, I know it can't be right away, much as I'd like. I ain't got no place to live that's big enough, and you got that schoolin' with Miss Sadie, but I'm wantin' you to know where I'm aimin.' If you think I'm aimin' in the wrong direction… like if you wasn't thinkin' in the same way, well…"

Liz's heart pounded. Marry! Of course, she knew that she would sometime… and it would be to Dave, of course, but… "Dave, I…"

Dave put a calloused finger gently against her lips. "Don't say nothin,' yet. I ain't expectin' a answer. Just wanted you to know what was in my mind."

It was in January that Liz began to teach numbers to the next higher class… addition, subtraction, and multiplication.

It was in March that a late snow powdered down onto the territory. Spring flowers had already popped through the ground, and trees had sprouted tufts of green leaves. The bare, black branches and twigs of the redbud trees were sprouting rosy knobs that would be their red-purple blooms, the ones that appeared long before the leaves.

Truly, it looked like an early spring, but the fickle weather had one more trick to play. Andrew and Dave took advantage of the powdering of snow to go rabbit hunting on a Sunday afternoon.

Andrew first. "Liz says you and her set a date."

Dave nodded. "It'll be May. By then, I ought'a have the other room on my cabin. Say, Andrew, there's a thing I'd like to ask. When we get married, I'd like you to be my best man."

"Best man? What's that?"

"You don't know? Well, it could be that it's somethin' that just happened to folks up north, or maybe it's a old custom that hasn't made it to the territory. It's been done back up in Nebraska before I left. The best man is the best friend of the fellow gettin' married. He stands by 'im, while the preacher talks."

"What for?"

"I ain't sure, but I think it was needed back in the days when a fellow stole a girl away from her family, and there was a fear the family'd be tryin' to get 'er back before she made promises. When that happened, he'd need the friend to help 'im fight off her family, till the words got said." Dave chuckled at the absurdity of the story.

Andrew agreed with a grin. "Silly thing to do, don't you think? My Ma and Pa'll not be givin' you no trouble."

"I know, but you're my best friend, and it's a thing I'd like to do. Nuther thing, the girl mostly always brings a friend, too."

"What for?"

"I think it's to help 'er get into the fancy dress she wears. Could be, she's supposed to help fight off the family, too. We been talkin,' and Liz wants Isabel to stand with her."

"Isabel?"

"Yeah, you know, Isabel...? The girl you been seein' about seven times a week!"

"Yeah, sure."

It was during the first week of April that Liz began to hear the ten and eleven-year-olds recite their sums. They gathered on the recitation bench and wrote their spelling words on their slates as Liz pronounced them. After spelling, she listened as they took turns reading in the fifth grade McGuffey Reader.

It was the second week of April that the new dress came in the mail. Dave had taken Liz to the city of Guthrie to the catalog store, where she had ordered the beautiful white linen dress for her wedding. So impractical for life in the territory!

While she was there, she bought white yarn to knit a fringed shawl to wear over it. When the wedding was over, it would be useful to wear over other dresses. The white linen dress, while terribly impractical, would be wonderful to save for special occasions.

So, on the second week of April, the new dress came and was delivered by the Kendall Brothers as they came home for the weekend.

Emma stared at Liz, dressed in the new dress. "Liz, honey, I almost think I see a tall white candle a'standin' there. You look so beautiful, it's fair to make me cry. I didn't get to have no weddin' dress, the way it happened that I was married almost 'afore I knew it, but I'm glad you got one.

The wedding was set for the third week in May.

Ben, as he worked with the crops and the horses, felt his thoughts returning to the picture in his mind, the picture of Liz, dressed in white with her dark hair piled on her head the way her mother's used to be. In his mind, Ben more clearly saw Emma wearing the red ribbon he had brought her.

He stared at his daughter in wonderment. Could it possibly be that this unbelievable image was really his own little girl, or was it a vision? What a wonderful thing a white dress could do for a beautiful girl! Worth every penny it cost!

The more he thought about it, the more he thought of old Lem, his pa. Getting up in years Lem was and he kept pretty much to his home, allowing the sons of his second family to care for him. Lem, of course, had not seen Ben's own hasty wedding, and now Ben's daughter was ready for the alter.

The old man had experienced a hard life, but he had the courage to walk away from an impossibly situation. He had done what he had to do, and now he should be able to see some of the fruit of his struggle.

Then the decision was made. Ben would make a trip to the Sac and Fox and tell him about Liz. Perhaps the old man would be able to make the journey. At the sacrifice of two days in the spring busy season, Ben traveled east to see his father.

Lem was up and around and was pleased to see the son he had not seen since the time of the land run. The girl was getting married, huh? Well, it'd be a thing he'd really like to see. Come the time it was to happen, he'd see if he couldn't get out the buggy and head on over. Yessiirree, he'd see if he couldn't do that. It'd be thing he'd really like to do.

Riding back, Ben tried to understand the seeming eagerness in his pa's voice as he promised to come to the wedding. The aches and pains of age and hard work caused him such misery, it would be hard trip even in the easy-riding spring buggy he had. Of course, there was a chance the old man didn't really understand what it was all about. He knew the old ones sometimes had trouble… well, anyway, he'd see how it went.

The second week in May, Isabel Crowley had washed and pressed her blue dotted-swiss best dress and also pressed the matching blue ribbon, with the well-used sadiron she heated on the wood stove. She had oiled and shined her black button shoes, even though she knew the sawdust floor of the church would ruin the shine with the first steps.

Isabel told Liz, "You got'a bring your dress to my house, bein' close to the church, and we'll walk over there when the time comes."

Andrew had shook out his brown dress pants and buttoned the starched collar to his white shirt. His ma had snipped away the ragged edges of his hair, and he had laid out a clean handkerchief for his shirt pocket.

A small grin played about his mouth as the thought of the duties of a best man. Imagine, him helping Dave to fight off Pa and Ma, till Liz said her promises! The whole thing of standing there wasn't such a bad idea, though. If he didn't have anything else to do, he could always spend the time looking at Isabel. Looking at her had never given him any trouble, and seemed a good use of his time.

Dave was relieved that the second room had finally been added to his cabin, and that the furniture he had ordered had finally been delivered by the Kendall Brothers, and now he found that he had time to be nervous.

With a tremor in his voice, he practiced his vows. "I do." "I do." What if he forgot and said the wrong thing? What if the answering words just wouldn't come out of her mouth? Would the preacher give him a second chance?

For the dozenth time, he brushed imaginary lint from his black dress pants. He had ordered a new shirt, and it was a good fit, even if the collar was not as stiff as he would have liked. He seldom wore a tie, and so he had practiced the tying of the new one with a length of rope until he got the circles, bends and pulls to work right.

Early on the day before the wedding, old Lem Green (born Lemuel LaGrone) climbed into his spring buggy and set off, his wife seated along side him. Once again, Lem patted the pocket of his shirt to make sure he had everything he needed.

After a day of travel, he arrived at his son's house and was put up comfortably in the old log cabin. Long after his wife was asleep beside him, old Lem lay with wide open eyes, staring at the darkness of the ceiling.

Finally, he slipped his legs over the edge of the bed, cringing from the aches of the day's trip. Quietly, he slipped through the door, hoping the squeak did not disturb the sleeper.

Once outside, he sat on a convenient rock and looked about him in the moonlight. His life had taken so many twists and turns, he could hardly remember them all. A few of them, though, stood out from the rest. He had given his treasured Book to his son, to whom it naturally belonged and had acquired another. It was the book that had had taught him to trust and that had saved him a lot of doubt and uncertainty. He just gave his problems to One who could better handle them better.

Thought of the Book naturally brought on thought of his ma. Quiet and sweet she had been and her life had been hardly anything but pain. He wished she could see how well his own life had turned out. Two good women had loved him and given him children, and what more could a man ask of life?

Healthy children and grandchildren grew up around him, and they were all good people. Not one had ever caused trouble with the law.

His life had been like a tall mountain. Climb a while, rest a while, but there was always another climb. Get tired... find a place to rest. Get thirsty... find a sparkling stream. Get lonely... find someone who was also lonely.

And one more thing. Hold a beautiful item for a lifetime... then find the right person to give it to. The giving of this last precious gift would be a completeness to his life, and it would happen tomorrow.

The lanky hunting hound belonging to his son had found him in the dark, and after sniffing him carefully, had stretched out beside him. Barker. This dog must be about the fourth Barker since the one he had gotten when Ben was two... or was it three?

Old Red had been his first best friend, leaving the lowlands with him, and caring for him as long as he had the strength. Yes, Barker was a good dog, but Red had been a friend. A man had time in his life for both of those things, if he was lucky.

All in all, he had been a lucky man. He dosed against a tree, but the hoot of an owl had aroused him, and he went back into the cabin to the soft bed beside his good wife.

Thirty-Three

Then it was Saturday. Liz had trouble remembering what she was doing most of the time. Had it been selfish of her to plan a wedding on a day when so much work needed to be done by so many? Perhaps… but Liz had done it anyway. She came early to Isabel's house, and her friend was ready with a bracing pot of tea.

Liz's nervous hands had forgotten how to brush her hair, and Isabel insisted she sit and calm herself, and that she would do it. Brushing the long dark strands soothed Liz somewhat, and the sausage curls were finally shaped and pinned in place. The silky ribbon was wound about them in a shining halo, and the curled ends of it hung over Liz's shoulder beside the one curl that was allowed to escape the pins. She looked just like the fancy ladies in storybooks.

Then the dress. White linen, with a wide portrait collar. Tiny looped lace edged the collar and the sleeve cuffs, and a row of tiny pearl buttons marched down the front. More pearl buttons fastened the cuffs of the sleeves. It was the buttons that had made the dress so expensive, but, as her mother had told her, buttons were an investment.

Good buttons always lasted longer than the dress and could be reused many times.

Pa worked hard for his money, but even he had thought the buttons were a good buy and worth what was paid for them.

Isabel's dress of blue and white perfectly set off her shining red curls. It was a wonderful idea of Dave's that her special day could be shared with a special friend. Having Isabel with her would help chase away the butterflies flitting around in her stomach.

Then it was time to start toward the church. They saw the preacher arrive. Brother Hap Palmer wore his black pinstriped suit and black tie. What a special thing that everyone, even the preacher, was dressing up just for her!

Such a gift! She was overwhelmed.

As they came closer, they heard the music of the accordion being played by Lydia Palmer, the preacher's sister. Like a chorus of bird songs on a spring morning, the notes filtered through the trees. Trills and runs were made by Liddy's talented fingers.

Then they were in the yard of the church. Fears beset her! What if Dave changed his mind and would not come? Would Andrew make him come? A brother would have the right… wouldn't he? She paused on the step and sighed, nervously. She looked quickly at Isabel.

Isabel's green eyes crinkled as she smiled. "You're beautiful, you know! I don't think I ever saw nothin' prettier'n you are."

Liz pushed her fist against her chest to ease her pounding heart and then bravely stepped through the door. The building was full, and the only sound was that of the accordion, its notes now just a soft whisper.

Together through the quiet sawdust they walked, Liz and Isabel. Ahead of them stood the preacher, holding a book and smiling. Beside him stood Dave and Andrew.

The notes of the accordion floated away, and the room was quiet. "Dearly beloved, we are…."

From the back of the church came a voice, deep and graveled with age, and very insistent. "Wait a minute, preacher. I got somethin' to say."

Horrified, Ben reached out to restrain his father, but Lem shook away his son's hand. The preacher hesitated, frowning with concern.

Ben, scouring his brain for what to do next, decided the best thing to do was to follow his father, who was determinedly marching toward the front of the church. Ben walked closely behind him up the aisle.

Liz, as in a dream, had turned and watched as her grandfather came toward her, his face a study in soberness. Time seemed to stand still, requiring no breathing, and then he stood in front of her. Ben stood beside him in a state of nervous tension.

The old man turned to his granddaughter. "Mary Elizabeth, I got somethin' needin' to be done. Time you was a baby, I looked in your eyes, and I thought I saw my ma, your great grandma, a'lookin' out at me. That white skin's yours, and them blue eyes, seemin' maybe strange and out'a place, still and all they was my ma's eyes, fer sure. I loved my ma, and I loved you.

145

"Time went on, and I saw you wasn't like her. Sweet and gentle, my ma was, and weak. My ma was weak in the way to make a man think more of a kitten than a woman, and it gave her a hard life. She was mostly pushed around. There is them as likes to see kittens get kicked around. I was glad when I looked in your eyes and saw you wasn't like her."

Ben began to be even more nervous. What was his pa trying to say, and why was he saying it here? Why was he disturbing Liz's special day with his ramblings?

He really must do something. "Pa, don't you think...."

Lem put his hand on his son's arm. "I ain't through, Son. Don't be hurryin' me. These here folks can spare a old man time for his words."

Ben stepped back, and Lem turned to Liz and continued. "Then you got bigger, and I watched them eyes. Them eyes could get hard when they needed to, and they could sight down a gun barrel. You could shoot a coon at fifty paces, and you kept your family's land with your good aim. That was somethin' my ma could never do."

The old man paused and drew in a deep breath, so he could go on. "They say to me that you'll be a teacher on account'a the learnin' you got. It's a good thing. That's another thing my ma couldn't a done, and I'm proud for you.

"Now, what I come here for, I got'a do. Time was when I needed a friend, and then your grandma Rose, she come to me. It was just her and me, ready to make a life. There wasn't a thing my Rose couldn't do.

"Now, my ma, she gave me a thing that was precious to me, and I handed it over to my Rose. It was these here beads."

From the pocket of his shirt, Lem's slightly shaky hands drew forth a strand of creamy pearls. Holding the strand curled in the palm of his hand, he went on.

"I gave these to her, but it was not what she wanted. They were too white, maybe, and what she wanted was color. I could see the way the colors looked on her skin, and I knowd she was right to feel the way she did. So when I saw that, I got her the colors she wanted and she gave these back to me. For a while, I was hurt that she wouldn't take my gift, but I put 'em away.

"Then I lost my Rose. But the Good Lord felt sorry for me and sent me someone else to love. We have a good life and many children.

"Mary Elizabeth, I watched how you grew up, and I kept watchin' them eyes, knowin' there was a thing I ought'a think of but I wasn't thinkin' of it.

"Finally, it come to me. You got that white skin, and them blue eyes, but down inside you, you got your grandma Rose. I see her a'lookin' out'a your eyes, strong and quick, knowin' what she wanted and settin' out to get it. It was a look that made me feel strong, and my insides felt like they 'bout died when I lost 'er.

"Then, I was given someone to love, but one person don't take the place of another, and my lovin' wife back there on that bench, she'd be the first one to tell you. There ain't no way I can fill in for the man she lost to a stray arrow.

"But here I am, still lookin' at this string'a white beads my ma gave me. She said to me they was valuable, and I should use 'em to buy myself another chance. I kept waiting, and there didn't never seem to be no need to get rid of 'em."

He closed both hands protectively over the string of beads and paused. A quiet fell over those gathered on the crowded benches, and the quiet was so great that the birds in the trees outside the church could be heard calling to each other.

"So, what I want to do is this. I want'a give these here beads to my Rose one more time. I know she's gone, but there's a part'a her in the look'a them eyes'a yours, and I know now why she gave 'em back to me. They didn't match her. Shiny bright colors matched Grandma Rose, and she knew it. These here, they wouldn't'a looked good on her....maybe like blue feathers on a bird supposed to be all red.

"I had thoughts about what to do, wonderin' this way and that, and then I saw the white beads all over your white dress, and I said to myself I was doin' the right thing. So I got a present here for you, and it's from your Grandma Rose and from me."

A tear trickled down the dark, leathery cheek as he fumbled for the tiny catch that closed the strand of pearls. Liz, still in her dream, watched him, her own eyes filling.

Isabel reached toward the old man and smiled, holding out her hand for the necklace. Relieved, he dropped the pearls into her palm.

Then Liz reached out and held the shaky old hands in her own as Isabel's capable fingers fastened the clasp at the nape of her neck, under the flowing ends of satin ribbon and that one dark curl.

The creamy white pearls lay softly against her neck, exactly matching the color of her skin. They might have been invisible if it had not been for the translucent glow that came from came from the depth of each bead.

Lem extracted a hand from Liz's and reached out to touch the pearls one last time, whispering softly, "My Rose. Goodbye, Rose."

Turning to face the waiting people, he explained. "That was all I wanted to say."

Ben reached out, and Lem now took the offered arm and walked back to his seat, sitting down beside his smiling wife.

Liz pressed one hand against the pearls, and touched the fingers of the other hand to her eyes. She swallowed hard, and sniffed softly.

Rev. Palmer startled slightly as though reviving from a trance and again lifted his marriage book.

"Dearly Beloved, we are gathered here before God and all these people to join this man and this woman…"

The service was short, but there was much to talk about it as they ate the cake and drank tea under the shade of the yard trees.

Andrew looked at Isabel, dressed in her wide skirt of soft blue, with her hair gathered in the loops of a blue satin ribbon. "Isabel, I got the buggy here, and I thought…"

At her smile and nod, they left together.

Liz was hugged and cried over, and the pearls were admired, but old Lem was nowhere to be seen. With his wife beside him, he was headed east, back to the land of the Sac and Fox… his home. He had done what he came for. He had finally sent to rest, his thoughts of his beloved Rose.

Goodbye, Rose, and hello, Mary Elizabeth. He had done what needed to be done, and life goes on

Thirty-Four

The sun had passed overhead and had begun to sink as Dave finally claimed his bride from among the admiring crowd of girls. His cabin was less than a quarter of a mile away, too close to use a buggy. He took the white knit shawl and draped it over the shoulders of the white linen dress, being careful not to crush the streamers of ribbon.

He smiled at the crowd and held out his arm. Liz accepted it, and they walked together toward Dave's cabin. Those still in the churchyard watched until the white of her dress disappeared into the trees.

Emma touched Ben's arm, a touch light as a butterfly wing. Without looking down, he reached over and closed his hand over her fingers. She nodded, and he led her toward the buggy.

Clayton would make sure the Sally and Annie Lee got home all right.

The Journey

One

T he girl, now sixteen, was sitting on the splintery wood of the wagon tongue stared toward the west. The bank of dark clouds had piled themselves above the horizon but they were edged in brightness.

If it was true, as the old saying went, that every cloud had a silver lining, it was now time to turn some of those clouds wrong side out. Indeed, it was past time. Minerva Isabelle Crowley could use a bit of brightness just now.

Of the many rugged ups and downs in her sixteen and a half years of life, this was certainly the roughest. There were five people who lived in the two covered wagons, and she was the oldest. Here they sat at the starting line for the great land rush, and they had nothing. They had no more now than they had had 400 miles ago. Truly, they had nothing but hope.

She looked around at the almost empty campground, at the dust on the ground and the remnants of last night's big party, and wondered how it would all work out. The rush for the land was over, and they had no land. It was now time for some decisions to be made. Even if they had made the run and been successful, there was no one among them who was old enough to sign for it.

How she had reached this predicament would have been unbelievable if it had not true. Sometimes she still didn't believe it, but when she woke up in the mornings, there it was, staring her in the face. Looking back across her life, she did not see how she could have done any differently.

It had started 13 years ago. Little Minerva was four years old when she lived down by the big river with her mother, father, and baby brother. Her little brother couldn't walk, but could he spit his cereal down his chin and make her mama laugh and hug him. Then mama would laugh and hug her and sing a song about how she was mama's little Minnie Belle.

Then mama didn't get up one morning, and the baby cried all day. Papa looked anxious and worried, and then the baby didn't cry anymore, and they put him in a box. Later, they put mama in a box, and papa didn't get out of bed. Strangers came and walked around in her house, and then they put papa in a box and took everyone away.

They even took her away.

A lot of people came to look at the boxes, and they sang a song. Little Minnie Belle just wanted to go home. She looked around and didn't see anyone she knew. Finally, she curled up in a tiny ball of misery and wedged herself into a corner in a strange house. If she said the right magic words, she might disappear.

A nice lady found her and hugged her, and said, "You poor little dear! What's to become of you?" Minnie didn't know the answer so she didn't say anything.

Then the nice lady looked around at the people, and it seemed like she was mad and she shouted, "You mean there ain't been no talk on who's to take the girl? Don't you dare say to me she's to go to the home!"

Minnie brightened at the word "home." She really wanted to go home with mama and papa. She looked from one to the other of the big people, but then they said loud words she didn't understand, and they didn't seem to be talking to her.

After that, the nice lady got really mad and shouted, "I know I ain't nothin' but a second cousin, but that little thing ain't a'goin' to strangers long as I got breath. You just tell me where I can get her things, and I'm leavin'."

And she did. She hugged Minnie up to her and snuggled her in the buggy beside her. Then the buggy wheels rolled and rolled, and they came to the house where the nice lady lived.

"Now, darlin,' you're mama and daddy had to go to heaven, and you're gonna stay with me for a while. I have a little boy almost as big as you, and you'll have fun playing with him. His name's Denny."

Minnie had thought it over, and said, "I think I'll just go on to heaven with mama."

The lady had looked sad, and had hugged her again. "God love you, little nubbin,' seems like that'd be a good thing, only you can't do that. Seems like you got stuck with stayin' with me and my little Denny. Now, honey, you can call me Aunt Addie."

Denny had been almost a year younger, and was eager to show Minnie his toys. Minnie thought it was only fair to show him her doll, and somehow, they found a way to play together.

Truth be told, Denny was more fun than her own little brother had been, but she would still have gone on to heaven if they had let her. A time or two, she had walked out of the yard and looked round to see if heaven was very close, but someone always found her and brought her back. It must be very hard to get to heaven.

Not long after that, Denny had a little sister. That's what they said it was, but it looked like her own little brother…red, with crooked legs and it cried a lot. It even spit cereal down its chin. Its name was Amy Yvonne, but it was called Vonnie.

The days went by and the red thing turned into a little girl, just like the big people had said it would. She was kind of fun to play with. Almost like having a great big doll that could do things besides just lay in the doll bed.

A man named Harley lived at the house, and sometimes it seemed like he was Denny's papa, but that couldn't be. He didn't hug Denny or sing to him or take him any place.

No one told her what to call the man, so she didn't call him anything. In fact, she stayed as far away from him as she could. He said scary things when he looked at her. Sometimes he said things about bringing in stray cats and feeding them. Minnie Belle didn't see any cats around anywhere, stray or otherwise, and if they were there, what did it have to do with her? But he had a mean face when he looked at her and said it.

The man made Aunt Addie mad, and sometimes she shouted at him, and other times she just looked sad and walked away.

When Minnie Belle was seven, she and Denny got to go to school. They had biscuits and sausage in a tin bucket for their lunch.

Sometimes they had an apple or some cookies. At the school there were a lot of children to play with and a teacher who read stories to them and taught them how to read stories to themselves. School was a good place. It had a good smell.

Then, when she was nine, there was another baby. At first they called him Arthur, and then they called him Artie.

It was after Artie was born that Minnie no longer got to go to school on Mondays. That was the day Aunt Addie went to the big house down the road and washed sheets and pillowcases and other stuff for all the people who lived there. Before Artie came, Aunt Addie took Vonnie with her, and she played around while her mama worked, but she couldn't take the baby. That meant Minnie must stay at home and look after the two of them. Every Monday.

Aunt Addie came home at lunchtime and fed the baby, but then she had to go back. It was such a long day that Minnie dreaded for Mondays to come, and she tried not to think of all the fun they were having at the schoolhouse without her.

It was about this time that Minnie noticed a strange thing her aunt did. Every night, after the man went to sleep, Aunt Addie would creep carefully out of bed and pick up his pants that he usually threw in the floor. She would take the pants to the kitchen and carefully look in each pocket. The reason Minnie knew this was that she had seen a light in the kitchen and thought she'd get up and get a drink and see what was going on.

There at the table was Aunt Addie, spreading a few coins out on the table. Minnie had opened her mouth to say something, but her aunt looked up, startled, and put her finger to her mouth to shush her. So Minnie had just stared, quietly.

It was the next day that she had been taken aside and told what was going on.

"Minnie Belle, honey, you're gettin' big enough to know. That job I got a'washin' for the boardin' house, it don't near make the money we got'a have, and Harley, he don't never give me much. I got'a do this, so's we can get by."

"Oh."

Then Aunt Addie has said, "Don't worry, honey. It ain't so bad. Harley, he plays money games and sometimes he wins, and sometimes he loses. When he loses, I can't take much money, but when he wins, he forgets how much he's got, so I can take more."

Minnie tried to process this information.

Her aunt went on. "Harley, he don't know how much I get paid. He thinks what I earn is enough for us, but it ain't. That means I still got'a work. If I didn't work, then he'd know I didn't have no money comin' in, then he'd wonder where I got what I got'a spend on us. After a while, he'd figure out I was takin' from his pockets."

Aunt Addie had sighed a long sigh and gazed toward the window. "It didn't turn out the way I thought it would. Now there ain't no way out."

Young Adelaide (later Aunt Addie) Spencer had been attracted to the flashing dark eyes and the wildness of Harley Baldwin, and she had run off and married him against her parent's wishes. Very soon, he began to treat her so badly that her parents tried to get her to leave him. That was when he had taken her a very long way away from them.

Addie had soon seen her mistake and made plans to leave him and go home, but by then she was pregnant with Denny. So she stayed.

The owners of the boarding house had not really needed a washwoman but had agreed to pay her a pittance to make a cover for her story. They paid her a few coins, got the bedding washed, and they kept their mouths shut. When Vonnie was a baby, Addie had taken the three of them, Minnie, Denny and the baby, and kept them in the washroom. It had been Minnie's duty to keep the baby quiet while the washing got done. So she missed school that year.

Now she must stay at home with them on Mondays.

When Minnie was eleven, her freckles disappeared. She had hardly noticed it, but when she looked in the washstand mirror to poke her unruly red hair back in place, she had looked into the face of a stranger. The tan blotchy freckles were gone and underneath had been smooth, pale skin and rosy pink cheeks. A touch of pink decorated her chin and ear lobes. Who was that girl?

It became harder and harder to comb her hair, and one day she bravely brandished the scissors into the midst of it, and red curls soon lay in a heap on the stand beside the wash pan.

The whole event had been easy. She had just pulled the comb through the tangles until they were smooth, and then grabbed a handful and held it out from her head. About six inches was enough. She snipped with the scissors and held a handful of red-gold corkscrew curls in her hand. The rest of the hair had snapped back against her head.

It hadn't taken very long until all her hair was short, and a fluffy pile of red lay on the washstand. Scrubbing the bar of soap against her head, she had worked her fingers into the lather, and then rinsed.

Success! The comb had pulled through the mess smoothly and easily, and in minutes it was dry. Bouncy curls popped up all over her head, falling over her forehead. Grabbing up a handful from the top of her head, she tied a scrap of blue cloth around it. Much better. The tips of the ribbon peeked up out of the curls. She shook her head from side to side, and it felt so deliciously light and cool! She grinned from pleasure at her first success.

But when she saw the way ten-year-old Denny had stared at her and the way six year old Vonnie had asked her to lean down so she could touch it, she began to be scared. She hadn't even asked permission to do it. What would Aunt Addie say?

It wasn't so much what Aunt Addie said, as what she did. She had come in from outside and glanced her way. Then, with an armload of clean clothes from the line, she had stopped still and stared. She stared so long Minnie felt something should be said.

"Aunt Addie, I...? Did I do somethin' wrong?"

Her aunt had slowly shaken her head, and had put the clean clothes on a chair. She came to Minnie and hugged her, and said "Oh, honey, honey..." like she was very sad about something.

Then she had added, "It could be trouble, but we'll deal with it. It'd'a happened sooner or later anyway."

Minnie felt fright bumps pop up on her arms and neck. The last thing she wanted to do was cause trouble to the only person in the world who loved her. "Hadn't I ought'a done it?"

"It's all right, honey. You had the right to cut off your hair if you wanted to and, anyway, there wasn't no way for you to keep from growin' up. The thing is, you and me, we got some talkin' to do."

It was after that talk that Minnie knew there was, indeed, a new problem, but she was not clear in her mind what it was. The main thing to remember was to never be in the same room with Harley if no one else was there. Well, if that was all there was to it, then that would be easy. Who wanted to be around him, anyway?

But when he called to her and wanted something brought, what could she do? She'd just deal with it… as her aunt had said they would have to do.

When Minnie was thirteen, baby Esther Elaine was born. Such a pretty baby! They called her Laney. When the baby-red of her skin went away, she turned a creamy tan with dark eyes and hair. She began to look like her sister and her brothers, so different from Minnie's red hair and green eyes.

Minnie loved the baby and did much of the caring for her, but her birth brought about another change. Minnie still did not get to go to school on Mondays. She had to take Aunt Addie's place. She bent over the washboard and rubbed the lye soap into the sheets, dreaming of what was going on in school.

Denny had a job, too. He came to the boarding house with her each Monday and spent the day in the stable, forking hay, cleaning stalls and exercising the fancy carriage horses. He loved horses and thought it was a good deal, and the few coins they paid him was just the cream on the oatmeal for him!

Baby Laney laughed and patty caked and pulled up to the furniture as she tried to stand. Laney was healthy and strong, but not so well was her mother.

Aunt Addie grew pale and listless and always seemed sad. She seemed uninterested in the garden vegetables and did not care if they grew well or not or if they got put in jars for the winter.

It was scary to Minnie, and she tried to do everything herself. She and Vonnie picked the beans and dug the potatoes. They canned jar after jar of tomatoes.

The winter Minnie was fourteen, Aunt Addie seemed hardly able to drag herself from the bed to eat meals, and she paid almost no attention to Laney. When the little girl wanted something, she came to Minnie.

Addie developed a cough that didn't seem to get any better. At night, Minnie could hear her hacking at the cough that did not seem to respond to the warm menthol pads on her chest or the cough syrup they bought from the Watkins route man.

Worry nagged at Minnie, often waking her up at night. She had dreams that she was lying on the ground with a heavy weight (a rock?) on her chest, making it difficult to breath. Something had to be done for Aunt Addie.

It was then that another change came about.

One day, Addie called her into the room and had her shut the door. "Now, Minnie Belle, honey, there's something got'a be done, and you're the one to do it."

Minnie's heart had quickened at the words. Anything! She'd do absolutely anything to make Aunt Addie better.

"Now, here's what it is. You 'member back when you seen me take money from Harley's pockets? Well, with this cough and my weakness, I ain't been able to do it."

Now, fear clutched at her chest! No money except what she and Denny earned, and that would not be enough.

"So what you got'a do is come in here and get his pants and carry 'em to the kitchen. You got'a do it, so's you'll have what rightly belongs to you and the other youngens."

"Me? But...?" Surely she had heard wrong.

"Minnie Belle, you got'a. I got no one else. It'll be all right."

"But, he don't... Aunt Addie, I..." There were no words that fit her thoughts.

"Now, honey, don't be scairt. He'll not know it. You'll be able to tell by the breathin' when he's sound and gone."

"But how'll I know what to take?"

"Honey, I got this kind of a rule. If he don't have much, I take a third. If'n he's got a lot, I take half. Sometimes I take more'n half. Most times he ain't got no memory for what he's got." A coughing spell took her breath and her strength, and she covered her mouth with a cloth. Minnie stared in horror as she caught a glimpse of the flecks of blood on the cloth.

"Oh, Aunt Addie, I got'a get you a doctor! I got'a....'

But Addie's hand held to Minnie's sleeve. "It ain't nothin', honey. Just a skinned throat from the coughin.' Now, I got more to say. Come the chance you get to take morn'n you got to spend right then, you put the rest away. I got a pint jar in the hen house, under the second nest box. Put it in there. 'Nuther thing, that'll mean you got'a start gettin' the eggs, like I done."

"Sure, Aunt Addie, but...?"

"Don't be sayin' this to the others. They ain't needin' to know. Likely, they'd slip and say somethin.' Promise me, will you?" And another coughing spell cut off any further conversation.

Finally, she could talk again. "Now that jar, it's got a little money in it. Come a time you need it, you'll know where it is."

"Oh, I wouldn't take nothin' from the jar. I'd not never...."

"Hush, honey. You'll have to. Come time I ain't here, there's things you got'a do. I know you ain't nothin' but a girl, but weak as I am, I'm what's standin' here 'tween you and a bigger trouble. Now, if I can hang on for just a year or two...."

"Sure you can. I'll.... Well, I can... There'll be somethin' that'll give you strength. I could kill a chicken and stew the broth... well, if you'd drink it, warm on your throat...?"

Minnie heard her own voice beg for encouragement, but she got none.

"There's them young roosters you could kill. Now, if you do that, the best'd be to make a pan'a dressin' out of it or a kettle'a noodles to stretch it out. The youngens, they'd get good out'a the broth and you too."

"But you! I was wantin' it for you!"

The head of her beloved aunt slowly moved back and forth. "It'd be a waste, honey. It'd not be good food that'll help me."

Minnie Belle swallowed with a dry throat. "Then what?"

"Likely nothin'. I been restin' and that ain't helped. I just feel the strength goin' out'a me, like air a'squishin' out of a feather pillow when you lay your head on it. Feels like it got started and likely won't ever get stopped."

Minnie reached out and took the cool, bony hand.

A tear rolled out of Addie's eye and slid down into her hair. "Minnie, honey, one'a the best days'a my life was the day I went to your ma's funeral and brung you home with me. Your ma and pa and little brother, they went so fast from the influenza there wasn't no time for last words for you, and I know it's been a burdensome thought all your life on how you was left the way you was. I tried to make up what I could, but I know it ain't the same."

Minnie still had no words, so she just stroked the cool skin under her hands.

Addie continued, "Still and all, you was a truly a gift to me from the Good Lord, as much as the ones I gave birth to. Maybe more. Happen I get the chance to see your ma, that'll be what I'll say to her."

Minnie's hand stopped as the meaning of Addie's words seeped into her mind. Addie was telling her to be ready because she was going to be left alone once more. Now, she truly had no words. She swallowed a hard, painful lump in her throat and waited.

Addie again. "It's in my mind to tell you what to do, but I got no thoughts, and I'm thinkin' you'll make the best plans when the time comes. I'm sayin' this to you now, so's it'll not be such of a scary surprise. You'll know how to stay out'a the reach'a Harley, and you'll need to be watchin' out for Vonnie. Don't say nothin' to 'er till you got'a. You'll know when."

The deep coughs racked through the frail body on the bed, and Minnie held her in her arms until the spell was over. The cough had sapped her aunt's small strength, and she slept.

It was that spring that Denny was thirteen and began to look for a better job. The thing easiest at hand was day labor behind a plow, preparing ground for spring planting and clearing weeds from the plants that were up. It was a good thing, really, as it used up his energy, and he brought coins home to put with Minnie's.

She wanted to tell him about the jar in the hen's nest, but she didn't. Sometimes a burden of knowledge must be born alone, and she was used to it. So far, Denny was still able to put up with being around his pa, and things must be held together as long as possible.

Then the summer was over and Vonnie and Artie went back to school, leaving Laney with Minnie. Addie made no further attempt to leave her bed, gratefully accepting a tray brought by Minnie.

"It's good food you bring, honey. I don't see how you do it, and you such a slip of a girl. Me not eatin' much, that don't mean it ain't good."

"I'm fourteen, Aunt Addie," she reminded her.

"Really? It don't seem possible!"

Minnie again. "I'm wonderin,' we got a good sun shinin' in at the west window. Happen you sat in the big chair with a quilt around you... maybe you'd...?" Her voice trailed away.

"I know what you want, honey. I'd be glad to give it to you if I could. But me, I don't feel the cold, and my throat don't hurt no more."

She continued, "Course, me not havin' pain, that don't mean nothin's changed. I ain't seein' how you could do it, but it'd be good if you was to be able to get out'a here. I know I left you with four others to look out for, but that wasn't my plannin', neither. That Denny, now..."

"Oh, Aunt Addie, Denny's doin' good! Works all day, he does and brings in his pay. Only thing, Harley keeps askin' how much... he...?" The sentence was too painful to complete.

Finally, "The thing is, Denny, he don't say much, or he pulls some out'a his pocket to show his pa, and Harley says lookin' at the backside'a the horse ain't no way to make a livin,' and he's thinkin'a takin' Denny with him when he goes tradin'. To teach 'im how to do it, he says."

"And Denny, what does he say?"

"Not too much. Says, maybe later."

"You got much in the jar? Case somethin' happened?"

"Pretty much. Wouldn't last long, though, with the five of us."

Addie nodded and sighed. "Wisht I could'a done better by you."

"Don't you worry. Denny ain't like his pa."

The chill of winter came and seeped through the windowpanes. Most nights Harley finally came home, but he was usually very late. He must be fed and allowed to get to sleep so she could check his pockets.

She must stay awake until it was done, and the fear of it never left her. Quietly opening the door and crawling along the floor was such a humbling act, that she spent precious energy trying to figure out another way to live.

The pants must be taken into the kitchen, and then brought back. There was a chance she would drop a coin, or that they would jingle together, and he would wake up, but she did what she had to do.

Then, back in her bed with Vonnie and Laney, she lay awake, staring at the dark ceiling. If she was alone, being almost fifteen now, she would pack a bag, take the money and walk away. By morning she would be so far she would never be found.

But she was not alone.

She could talk with Denny, and they could leave together, somehow managing with the others, except for two reasons. Denny did not yet know how bad things were, and if they left, his plowing money and her washing money would be stopped until they could find new jobs. And there was very little call for day plowing in the late fall and winter.

Like the dust in the summer dirt-devils, whirling around and around and getting nowhere, so her thoughts went. One after another they chased themselves. Morning came, and she dragged herself from the bed to put sticks into the cold cook stove. Vonnie and Artie had to be sent off to school. It was important, as this was Vonnie's last year.

Harley came in so late, sometimes, that he did not get up until the others were gone, and only Minnie and little Laney would be in the kitchen. Then, Minnie would have to hurriedly put the food on the table and wrap up herself and the little girl, and go to the barn… or the chicken house. Somewhere. Anywhere!

"Where you think you're goin,' girl? You ain't got no business out there this time'a the day. Them chickens can wait."

But Minnie quickly made up a few words and slipped through the door, finding something to do in the cold barn until he finally left. Sometimes the weariness was so great that she crawled back in her bed, but Laney was ready to play, and she laughed and beat her fists against Minnie so that sleep was impossible.

Two

Fall moved on into winter, and Christmas was just ahead. There was to be a program at the schoolhouse, and the children wanted to go.

"There'll be toys and oranges give out to all of us," Artie had insisted.

Vonnie had agreed. "They got costumes and everything, and some of us girls are gonna sing. We got white dresses like we're angels, and there's songs we been singin.' You thinkin' maybe we could go, Minnie?"

"You're in the program?"

Vonnie had nodded, hopefully, her dark eyes sparkling with excitement. "Laney'll get somethin,' too, if we was to take her along."

Minnie had spent so many dreary days in the house that the program at the school sounded like a precious gift, especially sent to her to make her life livable. There would be people, a hot crackling fire, laughter, strings of popcorn. She remembered these things from when she was in school.

And the program. There'd be poems and songs, and spiced tea in steaming mugs. Maybe apples as well as oranges. It happened, sometimes. Taking Laney would be a chore, but between herself and Denny, and maybe with Vonnie's help… well, they'd find a way.

She talked with Addie. "The youngens, they got their heads set. They're thinkin'a the candy and singin,' and there's talk there'll be toys.

I'm thinkin' it'll not be the best to leave you, but if Harley was to come in early, well, maybe we could…"

"Honey, don't you think on me. It don't matter if Harley ain't here. He ain't a lot'a help anyway. You get the youngens and go. It'll do you good."

One of the rare snows of southern Arkansas fell the day of the Christmas program. Who would have thought it.

Lighted lanterns decorated the walls, flooding the room with golden light. The huge potbelly stove radiated heat and good smells from the spiced cider and the peppermint tea that simmered on the top of it. Fresh cut pine and cedar limbs outlined the windows and red candles gave their wavering light through the frosted panes. Laughing people in bright colors milled about, sampling the popcorn.

White sheets had been strung across the front of the room to hide the preparations for the entertainment. When they were finally ready, all chairs were filled, and others stood around the walls of the little building.

Minnie had been careful to get herself a front seat, and she held Laney in her lap. The excited two year old pounded her fists on the desk and laughed, staring around at the bright pictures on the wall and the cedar tree decorated with colored paper chains. The minty smell of school paste permeated the whole room, filling Minnie with melancholy and nostalgia. School!

The curtains were pulled, and costumed shepherds tended "sheep," marked with elastic headbands and paper ears. Across the back of the scene were the girls in their white dresses. Vonnie's creamy tan skin stood out against the white of the costume. She smiled a recognition, as little Laney squealed and waved.

Song after song was sung, and Minnie was pulled into the past by the choir of little girl voices. Dreamily, she allowed her mind to absorb the songs, the happy words, the delightful smells and the whole, wonderful night. The sounds carried her into a magical place filled with forgetfulness.

When the singing was over, there were presents. Artie got a tiny metal wagon with wheels that really turned. It was painted a bright red, and his eyes shone as he examined it. Vonnie and the other older girls got hairbrushes and mirrors. Such an astonishingly wonderful present! A rag doll with yarn hair was handed to Laney, and her happy

163

laugh rang out in the room. She hugged the doll and danced around, entertaining everyone.

Then the candy. Store-bought ribbon candy, broken into manageable chunks. Dipped chocolates with a sweet, white mushy filling. Red and white peppermint canes, twisted red and black licorice, mint pillows, and slices of gummy orange jell covered with sugar. And jellybeans.

Sacks of candy were handed to all children as they left. The full moon shone on the white snow so that the lantern was not even necessary. Laney drooped into sleep and rode home of the shoulders of Minnie and then Denny, taking turns because of the weight of her chunky little body.

A light waited up for them. The soft gold rays shone through the window. In the dim light, she could see the horse Harley liked to ride. It was mouthing on the stack of hay in the corral. Good. He was home, and Addie had not had to be alone.

The children went quickly to bed, and Minnie gratefully blew out the light and followed. All was quiet behind the door of Addie's bedroom, and Minnie was grateful her aunt had been able to get some quiet rest. Morning came.

Almost rested, she crawled from the warm bed when the roosters started to crow, and she began to put a fire in the stove. Earlier than she expected, Harley came stumbling out of the door.

"Reckon you better go see about her. Could be, she ain't doin' so good."

Fear clutching at her throat, Minnie hurried to Addie's bed, quickly laying back the quilts. Her aunt was quiet, peaceful, and her hair fanned out on the pillow. Asleep?

Placing her fingers gently against the skin of Addie's neck, Minnie knew that the thing she feared actually was true. Adelaide Spencer was no longer in pain. Slowly, she stood and went into the kitchen. The man sat in a chair holding his feet toward the warming stove. He looked up as she came in.

Dazed, she made herself speak. "She's gone."

"Gone?" he said with faked innocence.

"Dead. I'll go…. Reckon I ought'a go tell someone?"

"Go ahead."

"You think… maybe the preacher?"

"Whoever you want. You was the one that let her die, now you get her buried."

Minnie refused to let the sting of his words wound her. Her capacity for pain had been filled and any further agony only slid away. The preacher. She'd go get the preacher. Behind that thought, came the concern, should she leave the others? Chiding herself to be sensible, she reminded herself that he was their pa, so what could happen?

She slipped out the door and ran across the powdered snow to the church house. A twitch of strangeness flicked over her as she passed the church door and went up to the house next to it, the house where the preacher lived. It seemed to have been years since she had come to the service, at least not since Addie had taken to the bed.

Preacher Jim answered her knock. "Come on in, Miss. You wantin' to see me?"

"Uh, yes...I, well...we got...." Words tore at her throat but she finally managed to push them out. "My Aunt Addie, she..."

"Sick?"

She shook her head and opened her mouth. Nothing came out.

Preacher Jim supplied, "Not dead, is she?"

Grateful, Minnie managed to nod.

"Did he...? I mean, what was the cause?"

"The coughin' I reckon. Can you...?"

"We sure can. Now you got'a sit here a minute and drink some'a this tea. Seems like you ran all the way over here. You rest, and I'll go get things started."

Minnie sank into the indicated chair and picked up the tea mug. The hot sweet liquid slid comfortingly down her dry throat, and she turned toward the preacher's wife when she spoke.

"Honey, you..." the preacher's wife began.

At this point her tears began to flow. Minnie lowered her head onto her arm and wept tears that scalded her eyes and soaked the sleeve of her coat. When her mama had gone, there was Aunt Addie to fill in. Now she was gone, and there was no one. Worse than that, there would be TROUBLE! Hadn't Aunt Addie said there would be?

"Honey..." the preacher's wife began again. "Is there some things you need to say?"

Maybe. Minnie looked up into the kind face and opened her mouth to speak. But the kind look of the sweet lady told her there would be no way she would understand the misery, the man, the small children, and the lack of money. No way. "Ma'am, it's just that I'll miss her likely more'n I can stand. She was…."

"I know, honey. Now you know where to get help, come time you need it. We'll be right here."

Minnie gratefully nodded. "Thank you, Ma'am. I got'a get back to the youngens. Thank you for the tea." And she slipped through the door.

She was past the churchyard before the preacher's wife thought to wonder why the girl was in a fever to get back, when the children's own father was there with them.

People came. The house was full of strangers who brought food and comfort. The men went to the barn with Harley, talking about this and that to keep his mind off his grief. It seemed they did it very well.

Women bathed and dressed the remains of what had been Aunt Addie. Blackened spots had formed on her arms in groups of four, easily matching a man's fingerprints. A bruise was on her forehead. The women looked at each other, and then looked back down at their work. It couldn't have been. No! No one wanted to think about it.

Minnie crept away into the chicken house and slipped her fingers under the hay of the nest. The hard coldness of the jar reassured her. It was not the jar that Addie had put there. That one was buried in the corner of the chicken house, with feathers and chicken manure covering the scarred earth where she had dug. It was full.

If she dug it up and simply put on her coat and walked away, who would know? She was fifteen and past, tall enough to look older. She was experienced in cooking, and certainly in washing, and she could get a job very quickly. She could take care of herself well, and she would never have to look at the man again.

She crossed the chicken pen and looked down. It would be easy. She would be walking away from Denny, who had worked as hard as she had. From Vonnie, barely thirteen, and Addie had made her promise to keep Vonnie away from her 'pa.' Frightful and horrifying word!

And Artie. Smart, lively and sweet, for a boy. What would happen to him? And most of all there was Laney. Darling little Esther Elaine who was almost Minnie's own baby, from the tending she had done.

Minnie stood still as the needs of the children paraded through her mind, and she knew she could not do it. At least, not yet.

Then they were at the church and a pine box occupied the front of the aisle. Preacher Jim said words, and Minnie sat woodenly hugging Laney close for the comfort the small body gave her.

Harley sat on the other end of the bench, wiping his eyes with his handkerchief. Later, he stood beside the grave staring down into it. Denny stood solidly beside him with his arm over Artie's shoulder, and Vonnie held to Minnie's arm, the one that was wrapped around the little girl. What a family picture they must have made, all standing there together. Such pretense!

For the next few weeks, life went on, little changed. There was not the food tray to take to Addie and not the loving looks and words of thanks from her. There were, however, all the words of warning she had given. Those words circled themselves in Minnie's mind. Watch out for Vonnie, and watch out for yourself. Get away if you can.

Yes, that was best. But where would she go?

In the late spring, they had a round of birthdays. Denny turned fifteen, Vonnie was past thirteen, Artie was nine, and Laney was four. A roly-poly laughing four years old. Minnie would be sixteen in the early fall, but she felt as though she was a hundred.

Obeying Aunt Addie, Minnie had kept as far away from Harley as possible. Then, in mid-spring, he had made her sit and listen.

"You're getting' some size on you, girl. I been aimin' to say, since I'm keepin' you, anyway, it'd be time we could make it legal."

"Legal?" She hoped she had not heard him correctly.

"Sure, legal. I'd be willin,' and you'd not ever have to think on leavin' here. You do a fair job'a runnin' the house, the youngens like you, and Addie weren't no older'n you when we run off together."

Horrified, Minnie had backed away. "Oh, I couldn't really…!"

"Sure you could. It's been months, now, and no one'd have the right to say nothin'."

'But…"

"Now you think about it, girl. I ain't a'wantin' to send you away, but that's what I'd do to any stray cat, 'stead'a feedin' it." With that, he went out, banging the door behind him.

The rattling of the closed door scraped away the indecision from her brain, leaving the raw, painful truth. Something would have to be thought of, and soon. She might as well leave, as he was going to turn her out if she didn't marry him. She gagged at the thought. He had made his meaning clear.

She got nothing done that day as she moved from room to room, and back again, her mind in a whirl. Where would she go? And the little ones? So if she took them, how could she manage? One thought chased after another with no decision being made.

The days passed, and the house was taken care of, and Minnie scraped her brain for an idea.

The nightly pocket searching continued. She never ceased to be afraid, and she put it off as long as possible. Sometime before morning it must be done. If she was caught, what would she say?

One day slipped into the next, and she began to see flyers and brochures that he left around. They were about a place called the Oklahoma territory. There was something called Unassigned Lands that were going to be given away to the people. Big patches of land. Ever one of them was 160 acres. Knowing Harley as she did, Minnie knew something was up.

"Denny, you been seein' these sheets?" Minnie handed one to Denny.

He took it and nodded. "I been hearin' about it. Some folks is plannin' on goin' and tryin' out for the land."

"Do you think he's aimin' to go?"

"Could be, but we don't have to. Minnie, you think there'd be a way we could… well, you know… take the youngen and go… somewhere? I've thought and thought, but I got no idea. With what we got saved, you and me, happen we could find a place where he couldn't find us. Do you think?"

"I been thinkin' on it, too. Didn't have no good idea, so I let it go."

Concern (fear?) showed in Denny's eyes. "But I get scared…."

"He hurtin' you, Denny?"

"No, not me, but…"

"But what?"

"I ain't wantin' to say it, but it seems like he looks strange at you, and he don't look away. Could be he's got somethin' in mind."

Minnie sighed. Was it that obvious? "Reckon we'll have to think harder. Five of us, you know, that'd be a fair trick for the two of us to pull off."

"I know." And the matter slipped away as the days went by.

Another Christmas passed, and Harley called the family together. "I'm givin' fair warnin'. We're pullin' out'a here. Got us a better place to go. I want you to look around and find what'll fill two wagons, and be ready. Two, maybe three days, and I'll bring in the teams and wagons, and we'll head out."

"But, Pa, its winter time!" Denny had objected.

Harley nodded, exasperatingly. "That'd mean we'd have to take our coats, wouldn't you think?"

"What'll happen to the house?"

"Be no worry's mine. Folks that bought it, it'll be their worry."

Minnie heard herself gasp. "Sold! The house is… sold?"

"Yep. It was too big to get on the wagons." He laughed loudly at his joke.

"We got'a leave in two days?"

"That's what I said. Wasn't you listenin'?"

Denny cringed at the rebuke. "We goin' to the Oklahoma territory?"

"Yep. Ain't in no hurry to get there. Got things to do till then. There'll be places with good pickins' all along the way. Dennis, its past time you left the fields and come alongside' a me. I can learn you how to make a good livin'."

Denny did not respond.

"All you got'a do is be ready. Now you," and he pointed to Minnie, "get yourself ready to be put into two wagons. Could'a just got one, but I'm bein' good to ya. You and the girls, you got one to yourselves. So be ready."

If a change was made, now was the time to do it. Minnie looked at each in turn. Solid, hardworking Denny, pretty, agreeable Vonnie, wiry, quicksilver Artie, and the sweet little doll, Laney.

Looking in their faces, she knew that it if had not been for Laney, she would have been ready to try it that minute, and when Harley came home, he would be greeted by an empty house. As it was, with the shortness of time, there was too much to do to be idly wasting thought.

"Vonnie, you and me, we got'a start packin' clothes. Denny, I reckon you'll be wantin' to look after the lanterns, 'n if you could bring in the pressure canner… Artie, you take Laney and play with her outside. Vonnie, you go get started on the clothes."

Denny and Minnie were alone.

"The money?"

"I'm fixin' to get it. I know where to put it, and it'll not be found. Then you and me, we got talkin' to do."

Denny nodded. "I got work to do today, and I'll tell 'em I can't be back. I'll be helpin' quick as I get home."

"Denny, how big is a wagon?"

"I figure it'll be two and half, maybe three, feet deep, four feet wide and either eight or ten feet long. Ain't much space. I got'a go, now."

Denny was gone, and Minnie slipped past the playing children, out to the hen house. Pushing the spade fork into the ground, she turned out the three pint jars, heavy with coins. The one in the nest also had some coins in it. They were heavy. It was going to take some thought.

The first project was the rag doll Laney had been given at the Christmas party last year. When she was not playing outside, Laney and the doll were inseparable. Carefully slipping a seam, Minnie inserted eight quarters into the cotton. She would have liked to put in more, but they mustn't make lumps.

Next came the winter coats, hers and Vonnie's. Ten quarters were spaced along the hem of hers, and eight in Vonnie's.

Dimes. They were lighter but not so valuable. Artie's school coat absorbed three dollars worth.

Two days, and the morning of one was about half over. By noon, twenty-four dollars was scattered into the clothing, and she had a list of what she had put where. Such a dither as her brain was in, she was sure to forget something.

She looked at the food in the kitchen. Flour, meal and sugar must be packed. Salt, pepper, spices, and it all took up room. Potatoes and beans, dried peas, kettles, skillets and pans. Dishes? They were so heavy, but there were the thin metal pie plates. They'd use them for dishes, and they could still be baked in. Under the dishes, she placed a cardboard and pasted dimes solidly. Twenty dollars worth.

The rest she left in the jars to be counted with Denny. As yet, she had not had been forced to tell him about the pants pocket source of money. What was left in the jar was near to what she and Denny had been able to save.

When Laney was put to bed, the coins were spread on the table. Vonnie and Artie stared with round eyes at what seemed to be a fortune. It was actually thirty-seven dollars.

Denny stared his siblings in the eye. "We don't tell pa."

"How come?"

"Cause we might need it, and it wouldn't be there. Times he has money, its gets lost in card games, or somethin.' What we got here is what me and Minnie earned. It's got nothin' to do with him."

"Oh."

Two days later he kept his promise. The two wagons, ten feet long, waited in the yard, looking pitifully small against the size of the house and what needed to go into them.

Harley announced, "You got tomorrow and the rest'a today to put in what you got'a take. Dennis, you can make a place to hook stuff on the sides, if you want. And you," pointing at Minnie, "see you get in everything we need."

Braving the strength of her voice, she asked, "What'll food be cooked on?"

"Whatever you can figure out. Cookin' ain't a thing I ever bothered with." With that, he was gone.

Denny let out a long breath. "First money's got'a be spent, now. I know where to buy a three-legged thing to cook on, and it's got a shelf for kettles. Cost us three dollars." He looked questioningly at Minnie, who nodded.

Denny started to pick up quarters, but Minnie stopped him. "Take pennies. They're heavier."

"Three hundred pennies? Start countin', Artie. Then you can come with me."

Excitedly, the pennies were stacked in piles of ten and poured in a sack. Denny and Artie disappeared out the door. Minnie and Vonnie began to pile things aboard. Bedding came last.

Minnie cooked the last meal on the kitchen cook stove, and they ate, but Harley was late. Very late. They finally went to bed in the wagons.

Hours later Harley came, leading four horses with harnesses on. By the light of a lantern, he hitched the animals to the wagon tongue, and yelled to Denny.

"Get up and grab a line. We're on the way."

"Now? Tonight?"

"Right now. Time's a wastin'."

Denny rubbed his sleepy eyes and climbed onto the buckboard. His father moved the team into the road, and Denny followed in the second wagon. The animals followed along with little direction. Pa must have gotten good horses, anyway.

They rode all night. Minnie half-woke up occasionally, but allowed herself to be pulled back to sleep, lulled by the rocking motion of the wagon, the grind of the wheels against the gravel and her own exhaustion. Tomorrow was soon enough to face the troubles of life.

By dawn, they were miles down the road leaving the old farmhouse far behind them. As daylight filtered through the trees that tunneled the road, Denny began to study the rounded rumps of the horses. Something was familiar about these animals. Had he seen them somewhere?

When darkness was pushed away by the daylight, he had no doubts. They were the ones from the stable behind the boarding house. Hmmmmm.

The sun was high before Harley allowed them to stop.

"Them horses, Pa. They're the ones from the boardin' house, ain't they?

"Sure as shootin.' Bought 'em off the boardin' house. Knowd they was good animals and we'd be needin' the best. Figured to make you happy to have 'em, the way you took care of 'em."

Denny mulled the matter over in his mind. He hadn't known the animals were for sale, and if so, how would pa have the money to buy four of them? And why did he bring them home in the dark of the night? Of course, there could be reasons. If pa had money from the sale of the house, and if he had a job to work late…? But why didn't they wait till morning to leave? It didn't add up.

Artie and Vonnie looked for twigs and dry sticks while Denny and Minnie struggled to learn the oddities of the outdoor cooker. The legs had to be just right or the platform would not level.

Breakfast turned out to be pancakes with butter and honey. Minnie set a dozen and a half eggs on to boil for lunch. That and the leftover pancakes would have to do it.

Minnie sat beside Denny, speaking low under the sound of the wheels on the gravel. In quick words, she told him of the nightly raids on the pants pockets. She explained how she had distributed coins in various places.

Denny listened, nodding occasionally. "Well, it's in my mind we got'a do it again."

"Again?"

"You thought about the money he likely got for sellin' the farmhouse? Buyin' the wagons didn't take it all."

"The horses? Maybe?"

Denny shook his head. "I'm thinkin' not. These here horses come from the boardin' house, and if he paid money for 'em, then I'm watchin' for birds to fly upsidedown. I figure he walked off with the horses, and if he did, he's likely got a wad'a money still on 'im. Don't know where."

"Pocket? Wouldn't it be too much for a pocket?"

"That's what I got'a learn. He's got it somewhere."

"What can I do? Could be, you could hand his pants out'a the wagon, to let me look?"

"Yeah, could be. First thing, let's not do nothin' the first night. Let's see how it gets on, and could be there'll be ideas come to us."

Three

The weather stayed damp and cold in the lowlands. The girls couldn't bear to strip down to put on sleeping gowns, and even if they did, the gowns would not be warm enough. So, snuggled in their heaviest coats, they crawled under the pile of blankets, lying as close together as possible.

The change from her busy life to a day of sitting with nothing to do but think put Minnie is a state of nervous jitters. That, and the fact that Harley did not go off somewhere during the afternoon and evening. After the evening meal, he tinkered around with the wagons, checking wheels and brakes. A toolbox by the wheel brake held the wrenches, bolts, a rubber mallet and the axel grease. It was just a small wooden box with a flap lid, but it now had a shiny new hasp and a heavy padlock.

The horses recognized Denny and whickered their rubbery lips, huffing their breath conversationally. He rubbed their velvety faces and curried their rounded sides with the scratchy currycomb. They were in excellent shape and were beautiful animals. He tried not to think about how they must have been acquired.

It was while caring for them that he noticed the new hasp and lock on the tool box. Now, why would there be a need to lock up the tools? There was no lock on the box on the other wagon. That must be the answer. When he could, he examined the hasp. It had been put on with new screws, turned tight into the wood. The lock appeared to be a good one. That left only one thing to do, he must get the key.

It was in the dark of the night that a movement aroused him, and Denny remained motionless, hardly daring to breathe as his father silently stepped down from the wagon bed and moved to the toolbox. Carefully, quietly, the lock was opened and the lid was lifted. So, now Denny knew where the money was.

After breakfast, Harley handed Denny some coins. "Next farm we come onto, you go and see if they'll sell us eggs and milk."

Good! So he was going to fork over money to eat on. That was good. It would be difficult to spend any of their hidden money without him wondering where they got it and how much more they had.

And then, as they traveled through a wooded area, he turned the reins over to Minnie, and stepped out of the wagon. Three rifle shots later, he was back with three squirrels. They would mean a kettle of squirrel dumplings could be eaten cold for dinner, or the broth heated to pour over biscuits for supper.

To block the wind, the wagons had been lined up, so the fire under the cooking tripod would be protected. Minnie huddled into her coat, stamping her feet to keep the circulation in her toes and occasionally stirring the meat with the long handled spoon. Harley and Denny were inspecting a far-side wheel, talking between themselves.

Walking this way and that in a futile effort to keep warm, she walked by the toolbox. The lid was laid back, and the padlock was on the buckboard seat. On an impulse, she darted a look toward the men, and then rammed her hand into the toolbox. There was a lot of paper money, and coins were in the bottom of the box.

Gently and firmly, her fingers closed on some of the coins, and she drew them out, slipping them into the pocket of her apron.

Smelling the rich broth, she thought of Aunt Addie and the times she had tried to cook something nourishing to make her well. She felt the familiar tightening in her throat, and tears began to flow down her face, leaving streaks of coldness from the night wind.

Vonnie had been trying to amuse Laney, but the little girl became droopy with sleep, and she had been put to bed. Vonnie came near the blaze and held out her hands to warm them, and then glanced toward Minnie's face.

"Thinkin' a ma, ain't you?"

Minnie had managed to nod.

Vonnie added, "The smell'a broth a'cookin' always makes me think'a her. You was always tryin' to make 'er well." The girl sniffed and wiped her eyes.

Minnie reached out and put her arms around Vonnie, drawing her close, and the tenderness brought more tears to their eyes. Sobbing quietly, they held each other close.

The men came back, talking together, and Harley glanced toward the open lid and then toward Minnie. The girls were still sniffing and wiping their eyes, so he closed the lid and snapped the lock into place. Stupid, blubbering girls had not noticed the open lid, but he chided himself to be more careful. What he had in the box would stand him in good stead when he got to Little Rock. He could park the family somewhere and find a game.

Watching Minnie stir the broth, he dreamed of the new people with money who would be flocking to the new land. He would be there waiting. There were towns planned, places called Guthrie, Edmond and Oklahoma Station. All he had to do was decide which place would be the best, or he could try all three. The very thought of it brought a small smile to his lips.

Not only that, he promised himself, the red haired girl at the cook fire would also be his. He wasn't sure just how or when, but it would happen. He had made her a civil offer of marriage, and before he was through with her, she would be glad to take him up on it.

She wasn't the only woman in the world, of course, but she was the closest and the children liked her. See there how Vonnie stood with her arm around her? If it was her that he took, it would work out well. On top of all that, she was a picnic to look at, with her pink and white skin, and that hair when she didn't hide it under a bonnet.

Leaning against the wagon, he dreamed of the day she would… well, it should be soon. One way or the other, he'd have her. She owed it to him for taking care of her all these years, and when it was over, she'd be glad. Every girl wants to be married. Anyway, the time would come.

Minnie drained the broth into another kettle and worked with the meat, picking out the tiny bones. The bones were put in a bit of broth to stew over the coals during the night. Extra flavor, dark and rich, could be stewed out of the bones.

"Vonnie, put on a stick or two, will you? I'm wantin' to get this ready to put away so we can get some sleep."

The girl poked sticks into the blaze, stirring it with the poker while Minnie mixed the flour and baking powder into dumplings. With a spoon, she dropped the lumps of dough into the simmering broth, watching them sink to the bottom, then rise to the top, fluffy and light. A few more minutes and she could put on the lid and leave it till morning.

A chill wind whipped through the camp, and Minnie slipped carefully out of her apron, wrapping it securely around the heaviness in the pocket. Slipping it under the buckboard seat, she snuggled under the quilts with Vonnie and Laney. She didn't even remove her shoes. Her last thought as sleep claimed her was on how wonderful it would be to have a bath.

They were somewhere down the road when Minnie found the opportunity to talk to Denny. Up ahead, Harley called to his team. Artie was sitting in the back, playing with his toy wagon and his few other toys, and the girls were beside him. Laney was hugging the doll that contained the eight quarters. Following from behind Harley's wagon, Minnie could see that everyone was occupied.

"Denny, your idea was right. The box is where the money is."

"It is? Did you…?"

"Didn't get the key. He left the lid up, and I reached in, grabbin' what I could get. There was a lot more. Then you and him came on back, and I got back over to the fire."

"How much did ya get?"

"We'll see." Carefully, she unrolled the apron from the handful of heaviness in the pocket. Reaching in, she drew out a pool of coins of various denominations. Staring down at her hand, she squealed involuntarily, immediately clamping her hand over her mouth.

Denny's eyes had spied the small silver key at the same instant and, in his excitement, had thrown his powerful arm around her and squeezed.

"Oh, I'm sorry! Did I hurt you?"

"No, well, maybe. But look! We got a key! its got'a be the right one!"

"Sure. There'd be two keys to come with the new lock. He's got one in his pocket, and that'd be the other'n."

"And the money. Look, here's three, three fifty, almost four dollars. Where'll we put it?"

"Maybe, wrapped in a tea towel in the cook box? That'd be a place he'd never look?"

The coins made a comforting little bulge tucked between the meal and the flour barrels.

"Denny, how long to you reckon it'll be before Little Rock?"

"Don't really know. Likely a week, no better time than we're makin'."

"It'd be good to have a room, for maybe just one night? The girls and me, we could use a bath."

"Yeah, maybe he'll… could be he'll want to stop a day or two. Rememberin' how it is that he likes his games, and he ain't had a chance for a week." Nodding his head, he agreed with himself. "Sure, and that'd be it. Time we get to Little Rock, he'll be itchin' to get in a game. Could be I could say the little 'ens was needin' a rest and a clean up, and could we wait over a day? He'd likely be glad'a the excuse, and it'd be a way to not tell us what he was doin'."

Minnie nodded. Clever plan.

"But then, what if he lost the money?"

"We'll just have to get some of it before we get there. I been thinkin,' and I got a good idea."

"Yeah?"

"Come evenin,' you could need to talk to him about somethin,' the horses or such, givin' me a chance to see if the key works. Then, if somethin' went wrong and you had to come back, you could cough real loud like you got somethin' in your throat."

Denny thought the matter through. "Should work. I could do that. Tonight?"

"Let's see how it goes. We got several days."

The pair of wagons crawled along the back roads, under the canopy of trees, and along the valleys. Small streams were forded, hills were climbed, and Little Rock was surely very close.

The night camp was beside a rushing stream. The rush of the water could be heard some distance away.

Denny and Minnie looked at each other, each excited with the same thought.

"Good thing, the sound of the water! That'll cover noise!"

"And I can ask pa to come look, to see if maybe we could catch some perch for supper. How'd that be?"

Harley checked the wheels, as he did each evening. Denny took the horses downstream for water. He left them in a protected spot where winter grass was green, and he spent some time walking along the small creek.

Minnie waited and watched, setting a blaze under the stove. The silver key made a tiny weight in the pocket of her thin apron. Finally, Denny was back.

Nodding in her direction, he walked past her. "Pa, I could use you a'lookin' at the water downstream. Seems like there's fish of a size to fry. I got the net laid out, and I'd need you to walk it up the other side."

Harley looked at the water, thoughtfully. "Could do that. Need to take Artie down there to see how it's done. Happen we come on to other places to fish, he'd be the one to help. It'd give 'im a thing to do."

Even better, thought Denny.

The men walked away, and Minnie watched from the corner of her eye until they were well into the trees. She could hear Denny's voice, somewhat unnaturally loud, giving directions and making comments. That would be his way of telling her how things were going.

Stepping up to the toolbox, she slipped the shiny key into the lock and popped it apart. Easing it from the hasp, she lifted the lid and reached in. Feeling the wad of bills critically, she separated out about a third of the money and quietly closed and locked the box. The bills were quickly tucked in her apron pocket.

As prearranged, she walked toward the fishermen and called out, "Havin' any luck down there? I was wonderin' if I was to heat up the skillet."

Denny's voice called back, "Looks good. Hush puppy's go good. I'm about to starve."

Minnie pushed against her chest to steady her pounding heart. Taking several long breaths, she dipped lard into huge iron skillet used mainly for frying fish and chicken. The flames licked up from the dry sticks, melting the lard into a sizzling liquid.

Then Denny came to the camp with the first of the catch. "Gonna clean these, and Pa and Artie'll bring some more."

His raised eyebrows questioned Minnie, and she nodded, as she continued to beat the batter for the hush puppies.

The cornmeal coated the fish filets, and they spit and sputtered deliciously in the hot lard. The globs of batter turned into golden hush puppies. The tantalizing smell drew everyone close as though by a magnet.

Minnie, however, was so jittery she hardly tasted her food, and when it was time to go to bed, she took off her apron and wadded it into her pillowcase, keeping it firmly under her head until morning.

In the dim morning light, before anyone else was up, she counted it. Twenty-four bills of five dollars each. One hundred and twenty dollars! It was more money than she had ever seen, much less held in her hand.

Setting the flour, meal, and sugar out of the wooden food box, she tucked the bills between the pasteboards with the dimes. There! Now, if they got away with it, their future was secured. If they could just figure a way to get away from him!

At the next night camp, Harley announced. "Figure to be in Little Rock by tomorrow night. Gonna treat you women to a room in a boardin' house, givin' you a chance to get gussied up or whatever you do. Could be there two nights. Maybe three. 'Afore we pull out'a town, we'll stock up on flour'n stuff."

He watched the relieved expression pass over Minnie's face. See there? He'd win her over. Maybe get her a present. Could be he'd find a good game, and it'd be more days than that before they left. One way or the other, though, he'd have her.

It took the first day in the boarding house to wash up all the dirty clothes. In the laundry room, Minnie heated the flatirons and pressed the clothes as well as she could. Vonnie folded and repacked them into the wagons and cleaned out the accumulated dirt from the bedding, shaking the sheets and quilts. Artie tagged after Denny, caring for the animals in the stable.

Meals came with the room at the boarding house. It was a wonderful treat to slide a chair up to a real table, and eat from a china plate. Not only that, she ate food that she had not had to cook while kneeling on the ground beside the road. The stay extended to four days.

When evening came, Harley left, taking Denny with him. It was not hard to find the green tablecloth people where dice and cards were the game pieces.

On the way, Denny was admonished, "Now there's a thing that happens. When there's gamblin' games and a new fellow comes in, they feel 'im out to see what he's got. If he's got a roll on 'im, could be they'll let 'im win for a night or two, makin' 'im greedy to go up to high stakes. Then when he gets to thinkin' he's better'n them, he bets a wad, and he looses it. I know that's the way it is, 'cause I've done it, myself.

"So here's the way it'll be. You're gonna watch and see how it's done. I got a roll on me, and I'll let it be seen. Could get a big winnin' tonight, maybe tomorrow night, too. You're gonna watch close. The next night, it'll be you at the table. I'm telling you this so's you'll be ready and not get scared. It's high and past time I was makin' use'a you."

"Me? But, Pa, I don't…?"

"I know you don't know your hat from a hole in the ground. I done let you go too long. Now, we'll have words made up, and I'll be lookin' like I'm helpin' you. I'll tell you to play one thing, and you'll act like you're stubborn and you'll play somethin' else, whatever we got set up for you to do.

"That'a'way, we'll see if they'll let you win, bein' a beginner and one that don't take advice. We'll have you bettin' little wagers, and then you'll get mad at me and quit doin' what I say."

"You always know you'll win?"

"Sure. Well, not every time, but pretty much. You just see you watch close. Be no time till you catch on."

They walked toward the river and along the narrow sidewalk, stopping now and again to look in a door. Then they walked down a half stair and opened into a dimly lit room. There were a lot of tables, every one with a dark green tablecloth. Harley walked around here and there, and a place was made for him at a table.

"Pull up a chair, friend."

Harley sat down.

"You, too, boy."

Harley spoke for him. "Naw, I reckon not. The boy ain't never played. He just come along to watch and see how it's done."

180

The games went on until long after midnight, and Harley pocketed his winnings. "Sure want'a thank you boys. I'm invitin' you back tomorrow, and we'll do it again."

"Not likely! I won't be losin' two nights in a row."

"See that yer back!" he insisted, generously.

Walking back to the boarding house, Harley confided, "Reckon I'm what they'd call a pidgin, or a easy mark. They're settin' me up."

Denny offered, "Well, you got winnin's. You could walk away."

Harley shook his head. "Don't work that'a'way. There's more to be had. A real player don't quit after the first win, less'n he ain't got 'im a strategy. That's what we got."

Denny passed the news along.

One more day and they would be on the road again, headed for Fort Smith on the western border of Arkansas. It was time to get prepared.

The piles of freshly laundered dresses and overalls, of sheets and underthings that Minnie and Vonnie had washed in the laundry room of the boarding house had been folded and sorted, and taken aboard. Harley had handed Minnie two five-dollar bills to restock the food box.

Minnie had been rearranging the laundry, but from the corner of her eye, she saw him unlock the toolbox, set out the axel grease, and then spend a fair amount of time quietly examining something within. Minnie tried to force the fear from her pounding heart by trying to think of something else. Surely he could tell that some money had been taken.

She had been against it, but Denny had insisted she take more after the winning of the first night, and she had taken an additional sixty dollars. How could he possibly help but miss it? However, he had closed the lid and re-clasped the lock before bringing the two bills to her.

She had thanked him and tried not to appear alarmed as he moved around the wagons, checking this and that. Finally, he had climbed into quilts and had gone to sleep. Taking the younger children, she had walked to the grocery store for the new provisions.

The girls had chattered happily, feeling sure there would be a peppermint stick before they left the store, but Artie lagged along, wearily dragging his feet.

"What with you?" Minnie had asked, cheerfully. "To too much playin' with them street boys back there?"

No answer.

"You ain't ailin' are you? I wasn't expectin' to see you foot draggin' on the way to a store that sold candy."

Still no answer.

A quick glance in his direction did not indicate much change. His smooth tan cheeks were touched with a healthy glow of pink. The dark, heavily fringed eyelids were lowered as he watched his feet. Hmmmmm. His shoulders hunched forward a bit, not really in the way that Artie would walk.

As she placed her order, she judged the weight of the items that must be carried back to the wagon. Likely there'd have to be two trips, especially when it came to the potatoes, but she intended to spend all the money.

When the basics were taken care of, there should be money for peanut butter and maybe raisins. So much could be done with them. Oatmeal mixed with butter and sugar, and studded with raisins made cookies that did not have to be baked. Same with peanut butter. It was so hard to think up what would make stomach-filling snacks when the camp stove was so limited in what it would do.

Artie dropped behind, and Minnie chided him, "Try and keep up, Artie. We got a lot to do to be ready to cut out in the mornin.'"

Artie sped up momentarily, and dropped behind again before they reached the door of the grocery store.

"Listen, now. No peppermint till we get everything to the wagon. I'm thinkin' it'll be three trips, and that'll likely take up the mornin.'"

The first trip brought in the flour, meal, and sugar, filled in with salt, cocoa and a few small items. The second trip brought in three pecks of potatoes. On the third trip, Artie was really lagging behind.

At the door of the store, Minnie began to be concerned and waited for the boy to catch up. "What's in you, Artie? You shouldn't be runnin' down already. We're almost to the peppermint sticks. Come here! You got a fever?"

The brush of pink on his cheeks was brighter. Minnie slid an experienced hand along his neck and around the back of his ears. Warm. Too warm. Not good at all!

"Where you been at, boy? You feel like you're comin' down with somethin.' Seems to me like you're needin' to be put down for the day quick as we get back."

Artie heard the dreaded words and made no objection. If Minnie had been concerned before, she was now doubly concerned. Being put to bed was the ultimate test of feeling, and Artie had so greatly enjoyed playing with the boys who lived around the boarding house. He should be yelling a protest! What could possibly be wrong with him?

Loading everyone with parcels, even assigning five pounds of raisins to Laney's small arms, they set out. Minnie packed the parcels here and there as she found room among the stuff, and she passed out the peppermint sticks, saving one for Denny and three for the younger children for the trip tomorrow.

Artie looked at his candy and sighed and then slipped it into his pocket. Something was definitely wrong with him.

Again in the room of the boarding house, she put Artie in the bed, first sponging his hot face. All the walking had made Laney so tired, Minnie was tempted to tuck her in the bed with him, but what if Artie had the influenza...? Or something? It could be catching. So the little girl was bedded down on the floor.

Sucking the candy sticks, Minnie and Vonnie moved around the room, packing the few things they had taken from the wagon. It was a good bet that Harley would expect to have an early start in the morning. Could be they'd be runnin' from danger.

The weather seemed to be fairly mild, so Minnie rooted around in the packed items for her light jacket. That and a thinner bonnet might be more comfortable than the heavy coat.

Smoothing the jacket on the bed, she felt a crackle of paper in the pocket. Now what would that be? Feeling inside, it seemed to be a whole sheet of school tablet paper, folded small. Strange...!

Warily glancing to see that Vonnie was occupied, she quietly unfolded the sheet, noticing at once the familiar handwriting of Aunt Addie. Doubling it again, she mentioned nonchalantly, "Vonnie, I feel the need to go to the outhouse. Be back in a minute."

Down the hall and out the door she went to the only place where she could be assured of a bit of privacy. Seated behind a swinging door, she opened the sheet of paper and read.

"Darling Minnie Belle." The writing was a little shaky, like she was having trouble holding the pencil or maybe that she was in a hurry.

When you read this, I might be gone. Harvey's come in mad at me because I ain't well like I used to be to take care of him. He hit me hard, and I fell down. If he does it again, I might not get up. Listen to me. I want you to go away and take all the children. All of them. Don't feel bad for me. I only wanted to live for you and them, but you will be better off without me and gone. You been a good girl and I love you just like my other ones but you got to get gone. Don't be waiting. Don't you ever feel bad for me, because I won't hurt no more after he kills me. Don't say this to the others if you don't have to. He is their pa. But you got to go. I love you, Aunt Adelaide.

Staring at the letter with a mixture of knowing and unbelief, she read the words again. Tears oozed from her eyes and splashed down on the paper. Tears of anger, of hot, livid anger and hatred! She raised her head and stared at the rough wood of the privy stall door. The tears flowed, unchecked, down her face and onto her neck. Sobs dredged themselves up from the sea of memory where she had hidden the hurts of her life.

A broken dam of feeling swept over her, stirring up the torrential tide of bitterness in her stomach, gagging her. Turning to face the stinking hole of the outhouse, she heaved up her sickness, shivering in the strangle hold of her anger.

Someone came into the outhouse and went into one of the other stalls. Minnie forced her nausea back into her stomach and wiped her eyes on her sleeve. Carefully folding the paper, she tucked it in her pocket. She wanted to keep it forever as proof that her anger had not been just her imagination.

Looking in the dusty, cracked mirror, she saw the redness of her nose and eyes. Running cold water from the faucet, she splashed her face. Vonnie didn't need to be getting worried.

Back in the room, Minnie saw only the girl on the pallet and the boy in the bed. Vonnie must be gone to take some things to the wagon. Kneeling beside the bed she pressed her knuckles against Artie's neck. Hot! Slipping her fingers under the covers, she felt his armpits. Hot and dry. It was clearly time to bring that fever down.

Pouring water from the pitcher into the bowl, she wrung out her handkerchief. She patted the wet cloth against his forehead and pulled away the covers to sponge his neck, and then she saw the spots. She gasped involuntarily, from relief. Measles! Not influenza!

She leaned weakly over the bed, trying to assimilate what she was sure was good news. Children got over measles. She was still leaning over the bed when Vonnie returned.

"Minnie? What's wrong, Minnie? Is he worse?"

Running to her, Vonnie dropped to her knees beside Minnie? "Oh, you been cryin'! He's…? Is he gonna die? Tell me what to do! Let me do somethin'! What's wrong with 'im?"

Rubbing a damp hand over her own distraught face, Minnie managed a smile. "Rest yourself, Vonnie, honey. We got lucky, I think. It's only measles. I was scart it was worse, but now I can smell 'em. You was too little to remember how measles stink, but at least you had 'em. We only got Laney to think of."

"Measles? But he's so sick, we can't…."

"I reckon not. We'll…."

Well, that changed some plans. There would be a few things they'd need from the wagons. Leaving Vonnie in charge, she slipped on her coat and walked to the livery stable beside the boarding house.

Climbing wearily into the wagon, she sat on the buckboard seat trying to collect her wits and decide what to do. A doctor? That would mean an expense, but worse, it would tip off the boarding house that measles was in the room. But what if it wasn't measles? Maybe something worse.

With her thoughts chasing each other, she stared sightlessly ahead. From nowhere, Denny appeared, his hair tousled and his eyes staring wildly. Focusing immediately, she stared at him, opening her mouth to ask?

His loud whisper stopped her. "Pa lost bad! He's mad, and he's come for the gun and more money. You got'a run and hide!"

Minnie paused, trying to process his words. She could hear Harvey at the other wagon, fumbling with the key and the padlock.

Denny again, in a louder whisper. "RUN! HURRY!"

Minnie tried to move her legs, but they were just stumps of wood. Her hands refused to pick themselves up from her lap. She sat motionless on the seat of the wagon, her eyes turned toward Harley.

185

From the corner of her eye, she saw Denny leave and hurry around the other wagon, toward his father.

With a bang of the toolbox lid, Harvey snorted loudly. Stomping toward her, he demanded, "All right, whereat is the money?"

Her tongue as stiff as an icicle, she stared at him. Words were an impossibility. From the corner of her eye, she saw Denny step into the other wagon behind his father, holding his finger to his lips. She did not look straight at him.

"Hand over the money, you stray cat! That's the thanks I get, feedin' you and puttin' a roof over your head! Ain't gonna happen no more. Don't know how you done it, but I know you did. Now, you're gonna give me the money."

"Money?" she heard her lips ask, dumbly.

"The money! Hand it over."

Finally able to lift her wooden arms, she turned palms up. "What money?"

Face red with anger, he reached out and slapped Minnie across the cheek, causing her to fall forward in the wagon bed.

"WOMEN!" he shouted. "ALL ALIKE! Can't do nothin', can't never understand nothin,' can't hear nothin' less'n it's been slapped into 'em."

Minnie's mind raced, trying to decide which was best to do, rise up and face the man or huddle inside the wagon. Then the sight of the letter flashed before her eyes, and an avalanche of bitter hatred flowed over her seeping into every pore. Eyes streaming tears of anger, she suddenly stood and faced him.

"DON'T YOU NEVER HIT ME AGAIN! I HATE YOU!"

With a loud nervous laugh, Harley shouted back, "I'll show you who hates who! You're gonna get me that money." Raising his right hand, he brandished the gun, finally aiming at the ceiling of the stable. The shot echoed loudly in the large barn.

"NOW, YOU SHE-CAT, MAKE LIKE YOU'RE AFTER THAT MONEY OR THE NEXT SHOT'S FOR YOU!"

Minnie watched the gun hand lower and the barrel of it line up with her face.

"MOVE, NOW!"

With her eye, she measured the distance from his hand against the length of her leg. If it was not for her skirts in the way, she could likely kick the gun away from her face. Sliding her hand down her side with the idea of pulling her skirt aside, she heard a war whoop yell and a crash of bodies against boards.

There on the sawdust floor of the stable lay Harley with Denny on his back. The next instant, a cloud of dust flew as they twisted and writhed in the narrow space between the wagon wheels.

Then the next gunshot echoed in the stable. The writhing stopped, and slowly Denny pulled his arms and legs from the heap and stood shakily to his feet. Staring down, he swayed against the wagon wheel, holding the rim of it for support.

Then the loud whisper, "Minnie, get the money! ALL OF IT!"

Woodenly, Minnie stepped out of the wagon, walking down the tongue. Slipping around the other wagon, she saw the padlock lying on the wagon seat. Closing it and locking it, she pitched it out the door as far as she could throw it, into the barrels that collected the garbage.

Reaching into the box she closed her hand around all the bills and drew them out. Unmindful of modesty, she lifted her skirt and stuffed the money into the top of her stocking, pressing it firmly against her leg. She was adjusting her skirts when two men came running.

"Heard shots! You hurt?"

Minnie's tears, still close to the surface, began to flow once more, drowning her words. Leaning against the canvas cover of the wagon, she hid her face in her sleeve and sobbed.

Denny came toward her and faced the men. "Been a shootin.' Better somebody call the police. The fellow over there hurt hisself, and could be dead."

The two men glanced at each other. "You go. I'll stay with 'em."

The man who elected to stay rounded the wagon and looked down. "You know this fella?"

Denny nodded. "He's my pa."

"Pa? He's your pa? You shoot 'im?"

Denny shook his head. "Reckon he must'a shot hisself."

"Suicide?"

"Don't think he aimed to do it. He was a'aimin' the gun at my sister."

"Sister? That girl your sister?" The man's eyes took in the tan, weathered skin and dark straight hair of the boy, and then the pale skin and red curls of the girl. "Well, if you say so."

Minnie's sobs quieted, and they waited for what seemed an eternity until the two uniformed men stepped into the dimness of the stable.

"Don't nobody move! You," and he pointed toward Denny, tousled hair and with dirt and sawdust on his clothes, "come over here and stand facin' that wagon."

Denny meekly submitted to the metal handcuffs slipped over his wrists, and the snap of the lock seemed to echo as loud as the shot.

"Now, you stand there! What're you seein,' John? Is he dead?"

"Stone dead. Bullet clean through 'im. Ya can see here, how he's got 'is arm doubled under. Gun hid underneath. Come help me roll 'im over."

Together they straightened the body from its crumbled heap and the gun fell away, trigger finger still in position.

"Suicide?"

The bystander offered his own knowledge. "Boy here says the man's his pa, and was shootin' at his sister."

The officer turned to Denny. "That right?"

Denny nodded.

"How come 'im to fall?"

"I pushed 'im."

"Pushed 'im, huh?"

"Yes, sir."

"You right sure you didn't have no part in the shootin'?"

Denny stared at the officer in unbelief. "You thinkin' I could get that gun back in 'is hand and underneath 'im with this fellow standin' here?"

The officer turned to the man. "How long you been here?"

"Heard the shot, sir. I was out back with the horses, and I come straight on. Couldn't'a been morn'n a minute."

The officer looked back at Denny. "You're gonna have to come on in to the station with me."

Denny's eyes flashed. "How come? I told ya what happened! I never touched that gun!"

The other officer lifted Denny's hand and sniffed. "Don't smell no lead," he announced.

The first officer nodded. "Still got'a take 'im in. Papers to be filled out."

"But...?" Denny looked from the policemen to Minnie.

"Do we need her?"

"Might's well."

"But we got three more little 'ens in the boardin' house. I need to be there."

"Well, we'll be back before dark. You go on in, Miss. Come along, boy."

Minnie, now dry-eyed and terrified, watched as the body was loaded aboard a closed-in wagon, and Denny was forced, still handcuffed, in beside it.

"Go on in the house, Miss."

Not knowing what else to do, she went. Now she had the task of telling the others. And Artie... oh, my... what in the world was she to do? Maybe she could wait until Denny came to tell them what happened.

It would soon be time for supper to be served, and she'd take the girls and go to the dining room. No one would notice Artie was not with them. She could bring back a bread and butter sandwich. If it was the measles, he'd likely not be very hungry.

Taking several deep breaths, she stepped out into the courtyard and put one foot after the other, determinedly moving herself forward. After another deep breath in the hall, she grasped the doorknob and turned it. Stepping inside, she took in the scene. The boy in the bed, Laney on the pallet, and Vonnie on her knees before the window, the curtains pulled slightly aside.

"Oh, Vonnie, you...?"

"Did Denny kill Pa?"

"What did you see? You been there all the time?"

"You didn't come back, and I thought I'd see. Then I heard shots. Did he?"

"Huh?" Minnie stalled, not knowing how to say it.

Vonnie insisted, "Pa. He's dead, ain't he? Did Denny kill 'im?"

"He's... well, yeah, I reckon... it seemed he was dead. You seen Denny bein' took off?"

"What about Denny! Tell me, did Denny kill 'im?"

"No. Denny never touched the gun."

"Then how come they took 'im?"

"He had to answer questions."

"But he had handcuffs on. Why did they do that? Was he a'tryin' to get away?"

"I don't know why they put handcuffs on 'im. They say he'll be back before night."

Vonnie looked doubtful. "They promised?"

Minnie nodded. "Now, Vonnie, your pa... he..." She had hoped to have a little time to think of how to tell her.

Vonnie stood and pulled the curtain closed. "Minnie, I don't care about Pa. Been times I wanted him to go away, for the way he looked at me. Made me scairt."

"But, Vonnie, honey! You never said nothin' to me!"

Vonnie sighed, wearily. "Figured you had enough on you, 'thout me a'whinin.'

Minnie crossed the room and put her arms around the girl. "There wasn't never a time that you whined. You should'a said somethin.'"

"There wasn't nothin' you could'a done." But Vonnie held to Minnie, her arms in a desperate hug. She sniffed delicately and leaned her head on Minnie's arm.

"Vonnie, honey, it don't matter now what he done. You just lost your pa, and you got a right to cry. Bein' mad at 'im don't take that away."

A sob, then another. In a few minutes it was over. "You sure Denny didn't do it?"

"Real sure. How come you keep askin'?"

"'Cause there's been times I thought he would... the way he looked at Pa when he was..." Her words were gone.

"I know, honey, but it won't happen no more. Denny'll be here, and you can talk to 'im yourself."

Laney sighed and turned over, opening her eyes. She sat up and rubbed her eyes. "I got hungry."

Minnie smiled at her. "Me, too. Seems like I smell food a'cookin,' and there ought'a be a dinner bell right soon. We got'a wash up and be ready."

It was a good boarding house dinner. Fried chicken, one piece each. All the potatoes and gravy they wanted. Buttered corn, and cabbage fried in bacon grease. Cornbread and apple cobbler. Cornbread would be good to take back to the room for Artie.

While she was deciding, a uniformed policeman appeared. "Miss Minnie Crowley? Follow me."

Startled, Minnie stood and followed him, and Vonnie and Laney were on her heels

Back in the room, Denny stood with another officer. He was no longer in handcuffs, but weariness looked out of his eyes. "Minnie, I just…"

He was cut off by the officer. "We'll handle this. Miss Crowley, you get the children's belongings together so's we can take 'em to the home."

"Home!"

"Yes, Miss. Underage children, left without no pa. They got'a be took care of."

"But my brother and I, we can…."

"We know he ain't your brother. Don't even got the same names. Now, do what you're told."

"Where at's the home you're takin' 'em to?"

"We'll tell you where. Fact is, you two can come along and see. They'll be took good care of, and when you got grownup kin that can take 'em, we'll be glad to let 'em go."

"Grownups! But I'm…. I been takin' care…."

"You're sixteen, and he ain't even that old. Now move it on, and get them things ready. We ain't got all night."

"Well, I… my little brother, here, he's sick, and I think it's the measles. I think he hadn't ought'a be moved."

"You can quit thinkin.' The State'a Arkansas'll do your thinkin' for you, concernin' these youngens. They'll know what to do for 'em at the home. Won't be the first case'a measles they had over there."

Minnie forced herself to gather the few things that were in the room. Any argument seemed to be futile, so she may as well go along with it.

"Mister, we was plannin' to leave in the mornin' till all this happened, and he got sick. Most'a what they got is in the wagon, packed. Could you wait till in the mornin,' and we could bring 'em on over and have all their clothes with 'em?"

"Yeah, and you'd be miles up the road by mornin' and with a sick youngen. Tell you what I'll do, though. I'll take 'em on, and you can bring their things tomorrow."

Artie was now awake and was watching with a look of unreality as though he was in a dream. Minnie knelt down by the bed.

"Artie, a lot'a bad things happened, and we got'a get you in a bed for a few days. You got the measles, and we can't stay here in the room. These fellows, they'll take you where you can be took care of, and…."

"You goin'…?"

"No, but Vonnie and Laney, they'll be there. I think you ain't well enough to be talked to right now, so they'll just go on and get you to bed. Here, let me pull back the covers and help you."

They were herded into the double-seated buggy and bounced away down the brick street like an action in a fairy tale book. Surely this couldn't be happening. By morning, she and Denny would have something figured out, and the two of them could find a place to stay until Artie was better. They'd be on their way, and it would be a pure relief.

"Measles? Just what we needed," was the welcome they received at the children's home.

Minnie and Denny were stopped in the reception room, and Artie was taken one way, and Vonnie marched the other, following after a white uniformed matron, her arm protectively around Laney. As the corner, she turned and waved, smiling bravely. Minnie and Denny were taken back to the boarding house. Their troubles of the day did not seem to be over. The manager was waiting for them.

"I'm here to tell you two to pack up your plunder and get out."

"Out? But it's…?"

"I don't hold no truk with shootin's and handcuffs. I run a decent place here, and you got'a hit the road."

Denny wearily raised himself to his almost six feet of height, looking down his nose at the plump manager.

"If I could say a word. We ain't a'stayin' here no longer'n we can help, but we got tonight paid for. You thinkin' you want to give back the money? If you ain't, then leave us be, and we'll clear out in the mornin.'"

"Well, if you'll truly…."

"Nuther thing. I was held up against my will and didn't get no food that I paid for. Now I expect to be given somethin' to eat."

"But it's late, and…."

"I know you got somethin' left, so let's go get it." Whereupon he began to march stolidly toward the manager, and she was obliged to start walking, move out of the way or get stepped on.

Denny found himself at the table with three pieces of chicken and two pieces of cornbread. Beside his plate was a bowl of apple cobber.

"And we got breakfast due us, 'afore we leave," he announced to the attendant.

Finally, back in the room, Denny settled himself in the armchair by the window and Minnie sat down on the bed.

"First off, Artie sure enough just got the measles? It ain't nothin' worse?"

"Seems that way to me. 'Member, he wasn't born when we had 'em, and Vonnie wasn't as big as Laney."

"I ain't had time to think it through, all that's happened."

"I know. Denny, I'm sorry about your pa. I was afraid he'd notice the money bein gone, and …"

"That wasn't all of it. You and me, we done the right thing, takin' it. If it was left, he'd'a lost it for sure. Things didn't go the way he wanted, and fellows here were onto his kind'a dealin.' They set 'im up, and got 'im so mad he couldn't think what he was a'doin.' He'd'a lost every cent he got his hands on."

"Well, we…"

"Top'a'that, he was mad at you."

"At me?"

"Yeah, for turnin' away from 'im. You got to lookin' good to 'im, and he thought he could knock you around and get you scairt so's you'd give in… I mean, so's he'd… well…" Denny hesitated at the word.

Minnie cut in. "Denny, he's gone. If you ain't a'hurtin' with him bein' gone, then we got other things to do. We got'a clear out'a here and get some place else. Boardin' houses are easy, but they cost a lot. Could be we could get a room somewhere."

"Have to be a place where we could keep the horses."

"That's right. I forgot."

"Could be I could work out their keep. I'm a good hand with horses, and if the place's got room that's not bein' used…"

"And it ought'n be more'n a week and…."

"I don't know. That home… it didn't look good to me. It looked like some big old monster that sucked little'ns in and ain't gonna spit 'em out."

They counted the wad of bills still riding in Minnie's stocking. Twenty-two fives. One hundred and ten dollars. It totaled two hundred and thirty dollars plus the coins. Money, it seemed, was not to be one of their problems.

"And we got a big order'a groceries, fixin' to be on the road."

"Good, and the thing we got'a do now is find a place to stay till we get the youngens sprung loose from the home."

"Then there's the funeral."

"Yeah. The police, they said we didn't...."

"Denny, I'm thinkin' you need to go. He's your pa, and happen there'd be a time you'd regret not goin'."

"No, that time wouldn't come. But I'll go, or it'll seem strange to the police. You're comin', too."

"But I..."

"You're comin'. We ain't riskin' getting' separated."

Four

The two massive white limestone buildings stood side by side, and totally dominated the block just south of the business district. They had just recently replaced the dilapidated wood frame structure that had housed the state juvenile home.

When the old frame building had been in use, Miss Lola Cantrell had ruled with a will of iron, and Mrs. Mary Scruggs had been her second in command.

Mary Scruggs, widow, had worked faithfully under her command, but when the new buildings had been completed, the children in the home had been divided by age, with ages 6 to 12 and above being in one building under the direction of Miss Cantrell and birth to 6 years were assigned to the other building under the supervision of Mrs. Mary Scruggs.

Lola Cantrell had been somewhat torn by the reduction of responsibility, though it had been offset by a lighter workload. She had been assigned a new assistant, Miss Mamie Rush, a plain spinster just out of her thirties.

Miss Rush's main duty would be to prepare the older children for placement in homes and businesses so they could learn a trade, or at least, work for their keep. The state had responsibility for them until age 14, at which time they were expected to be earning their own way.

When the police brought the Baldwin children to the home, they had been brought to Miss Cantrell to be processed. Vonnie, Artie, and Laney were to be left there to be taken care of, as the older brother and sister were underage and had no visible means of support.

Artie, fully broken out with the measles, was put to bed, and Vonnie and Laney assigned to a dormitory room. Papers were filled out assigning the responsibility of the children to the State of Arkansas until such time as a blood relative with an income came to claim them or until they were of an age to be released, which was 14 years.

"But we can take 'em," Minnie had insisted, but she was ignored and turned away.

"You can come to see 'im at visitin' time. Just see you don't come too often. We find they adjust better, not seein' the ones that remind 'em of where they come from."

So Minnie and Denny left the building, vowing to each other they would get them out. Somehow.

When they had left the building, Miss Cantrell conferred with Mamie Rush on the disposition of the children

"Got us a handful with these. That'n with the measles, he'll spread it to all the others who didn't git it last year. Won't be no trouble, though, and we'll get it over with for a while. Now that girl, bein' thirteen already, we got'a git on with her. Likely she's had no trainin' a'tall, and she'll need to be trained for the easiest thing we got."

Mamie Rush lifted her chin with indignation. "That'd be for me to decide. Cook's helper for a place that's got a full time cook, that's always needed. A month, maybe six weeks, and she'll be ready to send out."

Miss Cantrell nodded, ignoring the slight rebuke. There were always requests for girls, especially the prettier ones, to hire out as cook's helper to a wealthy household. If the girl worked out, and looked nice in a uniform, she had a chance to work up to parlor maid.

But there was another problem. "That little sister, she ain't six yet. When was she five?" Possibly there would be a way to keep her, and not send her to the other building to Mrs. Mary Scruggs. Miss Mamie Rush dashed all hopes.

"Just turned five. Looks more'n that, though. Could be we could…?"

Miss Cantrell nodded. "Could be a mistake, and she could be just turned six. If there ain't no birth certificate on record…."

But there was, and Laney was moved next door with the younger children, ages birth to six. Five-year-old Laney had never in her life been out of the company of one of her family, and she took exception to the separation.

Vonnie had hugged her and said it would be all right, but she had kicked and screamed as she was pulled away from her sister and practically dragged down the hall and out the door. Vonnie was left sniffing and wiping her eyes. Not good.

Facing Mrs. Scruggs, Miss Cantrell attempted to intervene. "The older brother and sister talked like there'd be someone to take her. Happen we kept the girls together for a few days to see, it'd be easier on you."

Mrs. Scruggs, who had taken orders from Miss Cantrell as long as she thought she must, had insisted, "The girl ain't six. I follow the rules. She'll simmer down and play with the other little 'ens, just like every other girl that the state's got'a take care of."

Besides that, the state paid the home a set amount for each child under its roof, and every dollar was needed. A five-year-old was less trouble than a baby, and babies were most of what they got. When the new building had been built, it had been equipped with a baby deposit drawer, and a steady stream of them entered the home by that method. A girl, finding herself with an unwanted baby, no longer had to go to the banks of the Arkansas River with it. She could come, always at night, it seemed, to the drawer. She could pull the outside handle and the drawer pulled out, revealing a bed with soft blankets just the right size for a newborn. Then, she had only to quietly deposit the baby, close the drawer and slip away.

The drawer was checked every hour, by the clock, though generally the crying of the baby brought the attendant sooner than that. Some of the babies were kept and cared for, but many were adopted. A couple wanting a baby could go to the home and look over the latest deposits, and if they saw one that suited them and if they had visible means of support, an adoption happened. It seemed a good deal for everyone.

So little Esther Elaine Baldwin was brought to the younger home, and assigned to a room with five other girls, four and five years old. The first night she exhibited her endurance by crying and sniffling all night long. The room mother was so exhausted that Laney was moved to another room with two house mothers, and seven other children, ages three and four.

Finally, totally exhausted herself, the little girl slept for ten straight hours and woke up with a fever. She was immediately moved to the sick room and sponged down to reduce the fever. She had not eaten for a whole day, and when she finally ate, she returned it, posthaste, all over the quilt on her bed.

While cleaning the bed and the child, the nurse noticed the spots peppered along the girl's neck and chest. Within hours, she was totally broke out with the measles.

When the news reached the ears of Miss Cantrell, she allowed herself a small smile of sarcasm. "She should'a let me keep the child here where we mostly all had the measles. She's gonna have fun with it goin' through all them young ones that ain't been exposed."

Mrs. Scruggs would never have admitted it, but she sincerely wished she had done that very thing.

Vonnie was assigned to a room with several girls of thirteen or late twelve, who were being "trained." There was not a lot of choice of training. Some few were trained to be "nurses", meaning they were taught to apply a bandage, take a temperature, and give a bath.

Then there was "factory" work, which meant they were put on the few old treadle sewing machines and set about patching clothing and sewing up rips in bed linen.

The other occupation, and by far the largest, was cook's helper. This meant they were taken into the kitchen, which prepared the meals for both homes and were set about peeling potatoes, snapping beans, stirring soup and washing dishes. General drudgework.

Vonnie was given a gray dress of course material, and a heavy dust cap from which her resistant hair kept sliding, uncontrollably.

The kitchen was a large room apart from the two homes. It was larger than the house where Vonnie had been born. Massive cast iron stoves lined one wall with roomy boxes between them to hold the sticks of wood that fueled the fireboxes.

The first question asked her was whether she knew how to build a fire, one of the first duties of a cook's helper. Miss Mamie Rush stood behind her and watched as Vonnie laid the fire and transferred coals from a neighboring stove to ignite the well-placed handful of wood shavings.

Nodding approval, she moved Vonnie to the food preparation table. Potatoes were a good start. Vonnie's experienced hand grasped the paring knife and scooped out the eyes of the potato. Rinsing it thoroughly, she began to slice away the skin in a thin strip that held together in a curly string until the potato was peeled. Vonnie put the peeled potato in the pot and picked up another one.

Miss Rush smiled with pleasure. This one was going to learn fast.

"Now, Amy, have you ever made pies?"

Vonnie continued to peel the potatoes.

Miss Rush raised her voice. "AMY?"

No answer.

At close range, she asked. "Girl, are you deaf?"

"Huh? Me? Uh, no, ma'am."

"I was talkin' to you. Now, Amy, you got'a practice listenin.'"

"Oh, ma'am. You said Amy, and I ain't ever been called that. I was always called Vonnie."

"Well, your name is not Vonnie. It's Amy, so you must get used to it. Like I was askin,' you got a hand for pastry?"

"For what?"

"Pastry. Pie crust and the like."

"Yes, ma'am. I can make a pie. And cookies and cake."

"All right, today we try you out. We got peach cobbler bein' served for dinner, and we'll need twelve of the big pans baked and out'a the oven in time for the bread and the baked potatoes to be put on. Now, we got the flour and bakin' powder, here, and the pans. Let's see how you'd go about it."

Vonnie was taken to another table and shown the pans, twice the size of the ones used by her not-so-small family. Bags of flour and cans of lard and baking powder were setting on the table. A large mixing bowl was in front of her.

Vonnie looked around and saw what she was looking for and began to walk away.

"Amy, come back here. Don't be walkin' away when you got a job to do."

Vonnie came back. "You got a place here where I can wash? I was goin' over to the tub'a dish water to wash my hands to make the pie dough."

"Oh, uh… Well, go ahead."

With clean hands, Vonnie measured the ingredients and stirred, finally folding the dough and putting it on the table. With the giant rolling pin she flattened the dough and, doubling it carefully, lifted it in one piece and, one by one, lined all twelve pans.

"Ma'am, where'd I find the peaches?"

Miss Rush turned to a smaller girl nearby, "Mary?"

"Yes, Miss?"

"Bring twelve jars of peaches to the table."

"Yes, Miss."

Vonnie opened the jars and emptied them into the crusts.

"Ma'am, we get to use cinnamon?"

"Uh, well, whatever you want. Mary, get the cinnamon."

"Yes, Miss."

The tall spice can appeared, and Vonnie mixed flour, sugar and cinnamon and sprinkled it over the golden peaches. Then, back to the flour and the top crusts began to appear. When the pies were all covered, she pinched the sides thoroughly to prevent overflow of juice, jabbed a few escape holes for the steam and trimmed off the excess dough.

"Ma'am, at our house we always made cookies out'a the leftover dough."

"Cookies?"

"Yeah, see, I got dough strips and sugar and cinnamon, and we'd sprinkle the strips. We'd lay 'em in a pie tin and bake 'em while the stove was heatin' or after the pie came out. We always liked pie dough cookies."

"Well, I can see... I mean, sure, go ahead and make them. Likely the younger children... Mary, bring a few pie tins."

"Yes, Miss." And the pans appeared.

In twenty minutes, the strips were lightly browned, and the cobblers were safely in the ovens.

"Very good, Amy. Now, while the cobblers are baking, you can help Ellen sort the beans and get them to soak. Now mind, you look careful for little rocks that look like beans."

"Yes, ma'am." Did Miss Rush really think she couldn't tell a bean from a rock?

Vonnie and Ellen were examining the beans when Miss Cottrell came in the kitchen. Motioning to Miss Rush, she sat down at a table. Miss Rush filled two cups from the steaming teakettle and joined her.

"I see you got Amy started. How's she doing?"

It was difficult for Miss Rush to restrain her pleasure. "She's doin' good. She can lay a fire, peel potatoes without cuttin' slabs off, and she's made the pastry for twelve cobblers. They're cookin,' and then she made what she calls 'cookies' out'a the scraps."

Offering the platter of warm strips to her superior, she took one, herself.

The rich, spicy taste of the crisp, flaky strips was very good. Miss Cottrell took another strip.

"Very good. Now's let's consider this. She's got a problem with her hair, the way it slips out'a her cap. Can't have that. We can cut it and give her a short bob. You can do it. It'll be hid under her cap. Now, picture her in a white dress with a lace dust cap." The picture was pleasing.

Miss Rush looked at Vonnie, tilting her head for a better angle. Vonnie continued to sort the beans, feeling a bit self-conscious. Did they not know she could hear them? They talked over her like she was a piece of furniture, and what was this about cutting her hair?

"Well, now we got the Nester's wantin' to take on another young one. Mrs. Nester sent her girl over to see what we had about ready, and I put 'er off, us not havin' anyone close to bein' ready. My next thought was of Amy. She's got the look I think Mrs. Nester'd take to."

"But she's just got here and...?"

"I know, but she's already thirteen, and that means we need to get her on out."

"But the Nester's, they're picky, and I haven't had no chance to see...."

"I know that. That's why I came here. Put her on everything you think she'll need, rememberin' if we don't send her, we'll be sendin' someone. Either her or one of the other girls. Now, about Mary, what do you think?"

Miss Rush sighed. "She'll never be nothin' but a helper. She's clean and polite, but she's got'a be told everything she does. She don't seem to remember one day to the next how things go."

Miss Cottrell nodded. "Then who else is there?"

Another sigh. "Miss Cottrell, you thought on bringin' in some eleven year olds? That'd give us extra time with 'em."

A moment of thought. "Could be necessary. But right now, who's the most ready?"

200

Miss Rush's eyes scanned the room, settling again on Vonnie. She really hated to let this girl go. There seemed to be so much potential with her.

"Well, I…" she stalled. "How soon'd it have to be?"

"Anytime between now and a couple'a weeks. I see you not wantin' to let this girl go right now, but you got'a think on what it'd mean to her. Mrs. Nester's is one'a the best places. All her girls move up, and Amy'd likely get a chance at parlor maid in a few years."

Vonnie forced her eyes to look at the brown speckled beans passing through her fingers. Parlor maid? A few years? YEARS? What was all this talk? She was certain she was to be here a couple of weeks at the longest, just till Minnie and Denny got the business with pa settled and Artie got well. They must be very busy or they'd have been to see her.

Another handful of beans. Skillful fingers slid the beans off her palm, picking out the occasional small stone the size and color of a bean.

Miss Cottrell again. "Now I could likely hold Mrs. Nester off for two weeks, especially on account'a havin' the measles to contend with. She'd want that business all over, for a fact."

Finally Miss Rush agreed. "Well, in two weeks. I know it'd be a good thing for her. Sort'a like steppin' in a lucky spot."

"I have to go, now, so if you'll test her in a lot of ways, quick like, we'll talk again to see how she's doin.'" Miss Cottrell picked up her pencil and notebook and another fragrant strip of spiced pie dough.

Miss Rush watched as the crisp, white uniform disappeared through the door and down the hall connecting the cookhouse to the home. She was right. It really was a lucky break for the girl. And the thing was, she seemed to have been trained well in her home. It was a pure shame when something happened to make the girls land up here.

Vonnie sat with bowed head, eyes trained on the beans but her thoughts racing. She lined up the facts. It appeared she was mistaken on why she was here. It had seemed a good thing. Artie was taken care of, and likely Laney had finally settled down. She would have expected to work, to earn their keep, so she had done the best she could.

But on the other side of the picture, these people were planning to send her to someone's house to work. How would Minnie know where she was? And they were glad she knew her way around in a kitchen, so what did that mean?

And why didn't Minnie and Denny come to see her and tell her what was going on? They didn't even bring her extra things, and the home had to furnish underthings that did not fit very well. And this dress, the fabric was so thick it chaffed the skin under her arms and on her wrists.

Also, what made the women talk in front of her like she was a piece of furniture? With no ears? Something was going on, and it was going to take some thought.

"Amy?"

No answer.

Miss Rush came to her. "Girl, listen when I speak to you. It don't matter that you ain't been called by your name. That's changed. When I say Amy, you'll say 'Yes, Miss.' Do you understand?"

Returning her beans to the sack, she stood and faced Miss Rush.

"Yes, Miss."

Vonnie felt the anger boil up in her chest, but this was not the time to let it go. She knew how to be silent and take abuse, for hadn't she been well taught by her father?

"Amy, I want you to prepare the chickens to fricassee. They'll be needin' extra time bein' older birds and likely tough."

Fricassee. The recipe rolled itself across her mind. Cut up chicken. Roll in flour, salt, and a lot of pepper. Brown in lard. Drain. Add spices, cover with water and herbs. Simmer or bake for at least two hours.

"Miss?"

"Yes, Amy?"

"The fricassee, that'd be for dinner or supper?"

"I can't see that it matters, but it's planned for dinner. Twelve o'clock."

"Yes, Miss."

"Now, you may begin."

Vonnie was taken to the wet prep table, with its pans of water and six fat hens lying on the counter, still in their feathers. Hot water simmered on the iron stove. A pan of scalding water would loosen the feathers and make short work on the plucking, so Vonnie turned her back on the whistling kettles, and began to pull feathers from the breast of the chicken closest to her hand. Pinches of feathers were tugged from the carcass and piled in a heap on the table.

"Amy! Don't put the feathers on the counter! Now, if you'd dip them in hot water, the feathers…."

"Huh?"

"Amy!"

"I mean, yes, Miss."

"The hot water… now pour it in the pan and dip the chicken…."

"In the hot water, Miss?" Vonnie asked the question with wide, innocent eyes.

"Yes… in the water. That's what we're talking about."

"Yes, Miss."

Leaving the counter, she went to the nearest stove and lifted the heavy tea kettle of hot water. Her thoughts raced. Was this the right time? …or should she wait? The next thought through her mind reminded her that two weeks was a very short time.

Between the stove and the counter, she hesitated, allowing the handle of the steaming kettle to slide through her fingers. With a crash and a splash, it landed on the stone floor of the cook room, bouncing and slinging a stream of water across the room.

Horrified, Miss Rush fled backward. Vonnie stood as though in a trance, staring at the kettle and the dented edge where it had struck the floor. It would take a lot of repair before that old kettle held water again. The kettle, however, was not first in her thought.

The first instant after the crash, she felt nothing, but she knew the pain would come. The force of the stream had flung her skirt against her leg, and the heavy, water-soaked fabric plastered itself painfully against her knee and calf, the excess water flowing down into her heavy, high-topped laced shoes.

The searing pain stabbed her leg and foot with grinding agony. Biting her lip, she tasted blood as she stood and stared silently at her foot. Whether or not she had done the right thing, it had now been done.

"AMY! You clumsy…! Didn't you know to lift that heavy kettle with both hands? Now look what you did!"

Ellen and Mary had left their duties and stood staring. Two other girls joined them.

"GIRLS! Get back to work. Mary, you mop up the water. Amy, come with me."

Vonnie followed Miss Rush down the long hall. The sound of her heels clicked angrily on the stone floor. Vonnie's every step sent new waves of searing pain undulating up her leg as the fabric of her skirt rubbed against her skin. How bad was it? She really hadn't intended to make permanent scars, but if she had, then so be it.

In the dispensary, the nurse took over. "Got us a burn, did we? Well, let's see how bad it is."

With tenderness, the nurse drew the skirt aside, and clicked her tongue in sympathy. She loosened the laces of the shoes and gently drew them off.

"Only one foot, huh? Well, that's better than both," she observed, sympathetically.

Expressionless, Vonnie answered. "Yes, Miss."

Miss Rush looked at the nurse, and then at Vonnie. Something was going on here. What was it?

"Well, I'll leave you two alone. I'll be back after Amy. Just keep 'er here till I come."

When the click of her heels died away, the nurse commented. "Got a pretty deep burn here on your calf and ankle. We've got this wet pack, and it'll stop part'a the pain, but you're gonna hurt for a considerable time. Now, I'm wantin' you to come and lay down on this cot, and it'll hurt worse for a minute, but I got'a... do it!" She looked into Vonnie's silent face.

Vonnie nodded. "Yes, Miss."

The cold pack was placed on Vonnie's leg, and she was suddenly attacked with a hundred flaming knives, gouging and boring through the flesh to her very bones. She was so filled with pain that her throat closed, gagging her with its tightness. All the air was sucked from her lungs, and she felt her arms trembling. Her clenched teeth made her jaws ache, but when she relaxed them, her teeth chattered noisily, so she clenched them again.

The nurse stood beside her, taking one hand and tenderly holding it while watching her face. The first white-hot pain passed over, and a numbness began to settle in. Waves of non-feeling replaced the pain, and Vonnie felt her muscles ease and her teeth no longer chatter.

"Honey, you're very brave, but the worst is over now. You'll lay here for a while, then I got zinc ointment that'll help with the healin'. It'll be a while before you put on that shoe again."

Vonnie lay motionless. Blocking the pain from her mind, she set her thought into motion. A body had to use what they had, and she had a kettle of water. She had used it. What could she do now?

If only Minnie would come. Something terrible must have happened to keep her away… and Denny? She, who had always been surrounded with family, was now totally alone. Artie was in the next room, but no one could go in except the girls from the laundry to pick up the stinking bedding.

"Miss?"

"Yes, honey?"

"My brother, he's in there with the measles. Is he…?"

"Which one is your brother?"

"He's Artie Baldwin."

"Oh, Arthur. Uh, honey, he had a bad time."

"Is he dead?"

"Oh, no, Sweetheart. He's doin' fine, now. It's just that he had a bad case, and we're bein' careful. Sometimes, boys… Well, we're wantin' to be sure he gets well."

"Could I see 'im?"

"You can't go in, but there's a window, here.…"

Vonnie sat up and attempted to stand. The knives were back, stabbing her with their sharp points.

"Wait, honey. We got a crutch here that'd keep the weight off that foot. It'll be sore for a while. Now, let me help you. Just put this under your arm, and put your hand on here. There. Very good. Now I'll hold onto you."

At the big window, Vonnie leaned against the wall and stared. There were at least twelve beds in the room. Some of the children sat up on the beds and played with this or that, but Artie was still lying back on his pillow.

"Miss? Are you sure he'll…?"

The nurse's arm hugged Vonnie's shoulders. "Don't you worry, honey. We'll have him well and up playing."

"How soon?" There'd be no way to get out of here until Artie was up.

"Maybe a week. Could be a little longer, but he'll be good as new."

She leaned against the wall and watched the room. Some plan had to be made. If only Minnie.…

"Honey, I want you back on the cot. Standin,' that'll cause the blood to settle in your leg, and it'll hurt more. You'll need to have that leg up for a while."

"How long?"

"A day… maybe two days."

Hmmmm. That'd likely keep her out of the kitchen. This would take a new set of plans.

Lying on the cot, Vonnie watched the nurse as she folded the white bandage strips and put the folds on a short ironing board. From the stove, she took a flat iron and pressed the bandage flat, lingering a moment, then turning the fold to press it on the other side.

"Miss?"

"Yes, honey?"

"Could I ask how come you're ironin' the bandages, that'll just get messed up agin?"

"Why? Because of germs."

"Germs…?"

The nurse smiled, understandingly, then nodded. "Yes, they're little things, too tiny to see. Seems like it was discovered that it takes germs to be sick. They're sayin' this'd be the way to kill the germs."

"Hmmmm. You pressin' on 'em smashes 'em?"

"Uh, no, it's the heat. It burns 'em and kills 'em, and then the bandage is so clean that it's more than clean, and it don't get germs in the sores."

"Oh. Heat kills 'em. I can see how that'd happen."

"I suspect you can. Now, I'm wantin' to look at your leg again. Could be we'll need another herb pack."

The nurse turned her foot this way and that, closely examining the wound. "No, I think we're ready for the zinc ointment."

"Zinc. Word sounds strange."

"It's new. Seems like it's better for healin' than medicated salve."

"New, huh? Can it be bought by anyone?"

"Bought?"

"I mean, if a person on the outside wanted to buy it. Could it be bought with money?"

"Maybe. If not, it soon will be. Could cost a lot of money, though."

The nurse squeezed the fluffy white crème onto her fingers, gently touching it to the flaming red blotch on Vonnie leg. She saw the girl tighten her jaws, but she did not utter a whimper.

"Now you can sit up, if you're tired'a layin'. Only thing, your leg's got'a be helt up high."

"Thank you, Miss."

The nurse returned to her bandage folding and ironing.

"Miss?"

"Yes, honey?"

"If you had other things to be doin,' me havin' to sit here, I could do that for you."

"You could?"

"I know how to use a iron, Miss. I got brothers and sisters. I was little when I learned."

"Well…." The thought was tempting. It seemed she never had a chance to catch up on little duties. "Well, honey, sure and it'd give you something to do, instead'a starin' at the walls. I'll just bring the board over here so's you can reach it. Now, you see…."

"I been watchin,' and I know what you were doin.' Could be, I could just start right in."

The nurse left her and sat down at her desk to make notes and catch up on some paperwork. From the corner of her eye, she watched for a minute. At the same moment, an idea struck her head with marvelous force. She could use that girl!

It was noon, and the nurse was helping Vonnie onto the crutch preparatory to going to the dining room when Miss Rush returned. She stared at the girl, then at the nurse.

"I need to talk to you."

The nurse patted Vonnie's shoulder. "You know how to find the dining room. The thing is, watch where you put the crutch leg, so it don't slip on the rocks of the floor." At an attempt to add a bit of lightness, she added, "We don't need a broke leg on top'a the burn!"

Vonnie stumped away, leaving the two women.

"How is she?"

"Got a bad burn. Gonna be a while healin' up."

"I'd'a never thought she was that clumsy after the way she mixed the pie dough. Seemed like she just poured that water, ruined a kettle, she did. Didn't hardly make sense."

"Poured water? Now, why'd she do that?"

"Don't know that she did. It's just… well, are you ready to go eat?"

"Could be. I got a thing to ask you. That girl, she's been helpin' me make bandages, and I thought, I really need help, and you remember I used to get a girl, now and again. If that girl was one that I could have, I'd sure find a use for her."

"She's thirteen."

"I figured that."

Miss Rush continued, "And thirteen is when she should be out'a here and in service somewhere. We got 'er a good place, and then she got burned, so…."

"You're sendin' her out? Already?"

"Seems capable. Just had a clumsy spell. 'Course, we'll be obliged to wait till her leg heals, now."

"Couldn't talk you into my gettin' her? She seems quick, and there's times, like right now, when I really need help."

Miss Rush shook her head. "Miss Cottrell got a call from Mrs. Nester. It'd be the best place Amy could hope to get."

"Oh. Mrs. Nester, I see. Well, I'd'a liked to'a got her."

Small Esther Elaine Baldwin sat on the little chair and stared at the children playing all around her. There were toys in the room, but her doll was gone, and how could she play if she didn't have her doll?

Not only that, where was Artie and Vonnie? And Minnie and Denny and Pa? Nobody liked her anymore, and they gave her away to people who didn't even know her name. Esther? Who was that? She told them she was Laney, but nobody heard her.

The playroom had a very big window that opened into a hall, and behind the window, two women stood watching.

"The new five year old, Esther, how's she getting' on?"

"See for yourself. There she sits, watchin' the others play. Says she don't want any… or somethin.' She doesn't speak very plain. We don't hardly know what she says, half the time. Cries at night, keepin' the others awake."

"All night?"

"Mostly. Finally moved her in the night room. Maggie has to watch that drawer all the time and don't get much sleep. Figured she could put up with the whimperin' and whinin'."

"Well, the youngen'll get used to it. They all do. It's just that some takes longer'n others."

Laney sat on the little chair. She had milk for breakfast, and she drank it down because she was thirsty. Then she sat still on the bench looking at the oatmeal until they took it away. Finally, they lined up and walked to the playroom, and she sat down on the little chair.

She really needed to go to the outhouse, but she didn't know where it was. Someone took her to a room with a strange thing in the corner and sat her on it. The coldness seeped into her legs, and the bigness of it was scary. She might fall in it and not be able to get out, so she had screamed. Finally they let her stand down.

Now, as her bladder filled, her discomfort grew. She looked at her empty hands, lying there in her lap. If she had her doll, maybe…?"

Then her bladder gave away, and she watched in fascination as a pool formed around the legs of the chair. Her soggy dress pressed warmly against her legs, and her shoes were full and overflowing. Well, anyway, they wouldn't have to take her in that room again.

The women chatted, watching the children.

"As I live and breathe! Look at that Esther! She's done and soiled her clothes!"

"Did she know where the room was?"

"She's been took, and she screams and won't go. Nuther thing, she always wets her bed. She's got'a be changed every night. Can't put her with another girl till she gets over that."

"Hmmmm."

"Somethin' else. She don't eat nothin.'"

"Nothin' at all?"

"Only her milk."

"Hmmmm. Well, she'll get used to it. She'll be too hungry, and she'll want to play with the toys. Some are just more trouble than others."

Laney Baldwin sat on the wet chair in her soggy clothes until someone came and changed her. Her shoes were set on the steam radiator to dry, and when the person walked away, she padded across the floor in her sock feet to the chair, now dry again. Sitting on it, she folded her hands in her lap and waited.

Minnie and Denny went once more to the lobby of the home. No, it was best that they not see their brother and sister for a while. It hindered their adjustment.

What did they mean, sister? There should be two sisters!

Oh, the little one was taken to the other building because she was not yet six.

Alone! She was taken away from her sister, and she was alone?

It's best. We found it's best for the little ones to be by themselves. So if you'll just not worry, and let them be....

But what would it hurt just to see them a minute?

"Rules. Over the years, certain things worked better than others. So, if you'll just go away…"

Seeing the children was not the only problem of Minnie and Denny. Most pressing was finding a place to stay. Finally deciding they couldn't get into the home, they might as well make some long-range plans.

There were a few rooming houses, and a few people with rooms to let. A room in a private house seemed to be the best thing, and they'd count on renting it for a month. With Artie getting over the measles, and it being the dead of the winter, it seemed foolish to start out any sooner than that.

For a period of warmth, they went into a small café and ordered hot tea and a sandwich. Tongue loosened by the warmth of the tea, Denny began, "The horses. We got 'em out there on the street and we got'a get 'em in somewhere. We can't be sleepin' parked along the street, and we got'a get the animals out'a the harness and inside. There'll be rain, and…."

"Yeah. That'd be first."

"So I thought. Livery stables cost a lot, but I got time, and if I was to find one that had space and could use help, I could maybe work out their keep."

"That'd be a plan. Then they'd be in good shape when we leave."

"So I could start out on foot, a'lookin.' You could stay with the wagons and explain, happen the police come by and wonder. Then we'd get a room."

Minnie huddled into her coat and winter bonnet, her mind too dull to think. People walked by, people with a place to go. The horses hung their heads dejectedly, rippling their flesh under the leather strips of the harness. Denny was right. They had to get inside. There was no grass, and they needed care.

Artie. He was so sick, surely they were taking good care of him. She was sincerely glad he was not in the wagon, but she should be able to see him and Vonnie, maybe for a minute. Surely Vonnie was able to see Laney....

But first, the room. She had shivered in the same clothes for three days and had not taken off her coat and bonnet the whole time. They had parked the wagons behind a big warehouse, and had slept in them for the last two nights, but then they had been run off. They were now on the street.

A room. It would cost a lot, but they had money.

Then Denny was back. "I found a place. Not the best place, but there's room. Best part is I do the mornin' feedin,' and I can see our horses get fed. Then I got'a muck out the stalls, and I done plenty'a that. You follow along after me, and we'll get 'em on over there."

Minnie aroused her wooden body and held the reins. When the wagon ahead of her moved into the street, she clicked her team in behind them. Clomping down the brick streets, the weary, hungry horses obeyed the command of the leather lines and put one foot before the others.

Denny turned toward a small side street and on into an open shed made of sheets of metal bolted together for a roof. The sides were scraps of tar paper and lumber. Inside, it was dry and dimly lit, and, side by side, the wagons were parked.

The animals were loosed from their harnesses and turned into dry stalls, out of the cutting wind, with fresh hay pitched into the feed bins and they settled themselves into serious chewing.

On the sidewalk, Denny and Minnie looked this way and that and chose a direction. The wind arose and was blowing icy drops of moisture in their faces, permeating their clothes with dampness. Minnie slogged along in her soggy shoes. Her frozen toes squished in the dampness of her unwashed stockings.

The first four houses with rooms to let, took a look at the two of them and slammed the door in their faces. Surprised, they went on. Then at one rundown house, they walked to the house over broken chips of sidewalk through a trash-strewn yard. What a mess!

The door was opened by a woman in a soiled dust cap, who looked them over, critically.

"Brother'n sister, huh? I've heard some good ones in my time, but that'n takes the cake. If you're brother and sister, I'll eat my apron. Now, if you think just 'cause I don't have no fancy mansion that I'll let trash rent my rooms, you can think again. Sure, I need money, but

I don't need your money. Just get on away from my door, before I sic my dog on you."

The mention of a dog did not seem to be an idle threat. The scruffy beast snarled and growled from behind the woman's soiled apron.

Minnie, her mind so dulled by weariness, had only the strength to wonder if the woman would wash her apron before she ate it. Likely not.

The crash of the door in their faces totally coincided with the crash of thunder. The stinging specks of moisture became large, icy drops soaking into their clothing. Darkness was closing in, and lamps were being lit in the houses.

Looking down the street, they could see no more signs.

"We got'a go on back, Minnie."

"Back where?"

"The wagon. I was told we couldn't stay in them, but we got no choice. We're soaked, and you look like you ain't doin' too good."

So they turned and slogged in their wet shoes back to the livery. The stable was dark and empty, the night man having retired to his room. Denny crawled in under the canvass canopy and fell, exhausted onto the quilts. Pulling the edge of one over his wet clothes, he fell asleep.

Minnie sorted among her clothes for her heaviest dress. Tossing a quilt over her head, she stripped off the wet clothes and pulled on the dry ones, icy cold against her wet skin. Wrapping in a quilt, she worked her stockings off her numb feet, massaging her toes in an attempt to restore feeling. Dry stockings… two pairs, and then her light Sunday shoes. Buckling them tightly, she burrowed into the depth of the quilts, and, ignoring her growling stomach, dropped into sleep.

It was still dark when Denny crawled into the wagon.

"Minnie? You got'a wake up. We got'a make a plan. Have we got anything we could eat?"

Minnie rubbed her eyes. "Eat? We got raisins. Just lift the lid on that box."

Sharing the raisins with her, Denny continued. "Now, me bein' here ain't no big thing. I got'a start to work, anyway. Now you… If you was to be able to stay under the quilt and still breathe, you could sleep a bit longer. We got'a find a room, somehow, but first we're gonna do somethin'."

"What'd that be?"

"We're goin' to the five and dime and buy you a ring."

"A ring! Have you gone daft?" Minnie was now fully awake.

"Yeah, it come to me in the night. We got'a put a ring on your finger, and when we go to ask for a room, we'll hold hands. We'll be married."

"Married! Are you crazy? What's our name?"

"You pick it! Your name or mine, or we can be the Smiths. It ain't a thing I want to do, but we got'a get inside somewhere. This cold rain ain't a thing to be sneezed at." And at that moment, he sneezed loudly.

The irony of it brought a smile to them both. "That'll wake the night man. I got'a get busy, and you get under the covers. That'll give you a couple'a hours."

Minnie was too tired to argue. Burrowing under, she sighed and dropped back into sleep.

Denny sneezed again, and again. Sleeping in the wet clothing was likely not a good thing to have done. He poured grain in the feed bins and took the currycomb off its peg on the wall. There were five horses in the livery, and added to his own four, made a total of nine. It would take a while to curry nine animals, but it was too early to go to the five and dime anyway.

As he drew the sharp bristles over the backs and sides of his horses, they rippled their skin with the pleasure of it and looked around at him, snorting and huffing conversationally. Wisps of hay hung from their chewing mouths as they watched him move around them, finishing the currying by combing their manes and tails.

When his two hours were finished, he was free to go until the evening when he would remove stall manure with the pitchfork. Climbing into the wagon with Minnie, he whispered.

"Wake up, Minnie."

"Yeah."

"You be ready, and when there ain't no one here, you got'a get on outside. I'll be there. You got'a put on your coat…. It's blowed up cold."

"Coat's wet."

"Mine is, too, but it'll be better'n nothin.'"

A small corner café had its doors open. Pushing Minnie through the door, Denny followed. The stove in the café had the small room toasty and dry, and the air felt good in their noses after the heavy dampness. Sliding into a booth, they sniffed appreciatively at the warm coffee and food smells.

"Denny, I'm so hungry I could eat a horse."

"Me, too, but let's eat food, instead. We'll need the horses."

Coffee, eggs, biscuits and a large bowl of thick oatmeal with milk and a lot of sugar. It almost made them feel that their luck would turn.

Then in the five and dime, also warm, they looked around.

"We want'a see the rings."

"What kind'a rings?"

"Wedding rings, maybe. How much are they?"

The clerk smiled. She loved to sell wedding rings. Such happy people bought them.

"They're right back here."

The couple followed her, but they seemed strangely glum. There was a smell of wet wool around them, and the girl had dark circles under her eyes. Then it struck her… the wedding ring was a have-to case. Looking at her face, with dark rings under her eyes, it would be easy to believe she was two months past. Oh, well….

A nice ring was five dollars, but they settled on another that was three dollars. It was pretty. It had a big center stone and two smaller ones, clear and sparkly as a mountain waterfall.

"You want I should wrap it up?"

"No, thanks. I'll just wear it." And she unceremoniously slipped it on her finger, and the couple left. The clerk watched. Well, now, that wasn't much fun.

Back on the street, they went a block closer to the river. Maybe rooms would be cheaper there. Yesterday's rain had gone, but the cold dampness hung just above the ground in a thick cloud, and mist filled the bed of the Arkansas River.

They came to a small, hole-in-the-wall grocery store with a sign beside it. "Room to let, upstairs." They looked up. Above the store was a pair of dark windows under the steep gable of the roof. The room, no doubt.

They went in the store. Approaching the counter, Denny reached for Minnie's hand, affectionately catching her fingertips, allowing the sparkling newness of the ring to be seen.

"Mister, we saw your sign. My missus and I, we'll be needin' a room. For a month, anyway. Can we…?" Denny was not used to asking for a room.

The man turned and called into the room behind him. "Louisa, a couple about the room."

Louisa came, spreading her thick shawl around her shoulders. "Come on up. There ain't no heat up there right now, but it's got a oil burner that'll heat it up good." Sniffing, she observed, "Seems like you got caught in the rain. Wet wool does have a whang to it."

Minnie agreed. It sure did.

A dresser, a bed, two chairs and a washstand. "Now, I don't allow no cookin' up here. I was figurin' to rent it to a single man who'd be eatin' in the café. It's yours if you want it."

Denny looked at Minnie, who nodded. "How much?"

"Five dollars a month if you don't use the stove. Six dollars if you do, and I got'a have two month's rent. Sorry to do that, but some folks… Well, you know how it is."

Minnie did not know how it was, but it didn't matter. They had a room, and it was dry and warm. She opened her purse and took out two fives and two ones.

"Thank you, kindly."

Minnie nodded. "Well, we got'a go get some of our things we left up the road. You got a key?"

Back on the street, Minnie shook her head, sadly. "Twelve dollars for that dump, and we can't even cook there."

"But it'll be warm and dry, and we might not get sick from the weather." With that, Denny sneezed loudly. "Sleepin' in the wet likely didn't do me no good. We're lookin' at two trips to get quilts enough down there to make me a pallet? Looked like there wasn't too many on the bed, neither."

That day they got settled in. While Denny worked in the livery, Minnie heated water and took a sponge bath. Wonderful! The clamminess of her feet was dried out, and she leaned over the stove to let her hair dry. The humidity had pulled her red curls so close to her head, she seemed to be wearing a cap. The dryness of the stove separated the strands of it, and the bristles of the brush stroked life back into her head. The dull mirror did not show the full extent of the dark circles under her eyes, and that was a blessing.

While Minnie hung the wet clothes on the line strung in the room, Denny washed and put on dry clothes. It might even be worth the money to have the dryness of the room to count on. The closeness of the river assured them of mists and fog, but the tacky little room was at least a comfortable place to be.

In the late afternoon, they put on their almost dry coats and headed out. It would be necessary to go back to the café and then try to see the youngens. Twice, they had been turned away.

Again they were turned away. Crestfallen, Minnie begged, "Can you tell me how my little brother is? Seemed like the measles...."

"Arthur? Well, Arthur is still in the infirmary. He's recovering, though, and when he's well, perhaps...."

"We can't see 'im till after he's well? How about Vonnie?"

"We have no one registered by that name."

Fear clutched at her heart as she stared in horror. Not there! Then, "Oh, you might have her name bein' Amy."

"It is my understanding that Amy is her name."

"Yes, well, we... Could we see her?"

"Not today. She's not available."

"Where is she?"

"She hurt her foot. She's in the infirmary having it dressed."

"Hurt her foot? How bad?"

"She'll be fine."

"How did she hurt it?"

"Seems she spilled some hot water...."

"Burned it? Is it burned bad?"

"I wouldn't know. I didn't see it."

"Well, when can we...?"

"Try next week. We find it's not good for...."

"We know. You told us. How about Laney? I mean, Esther?"

"You say you're her sister? And you don't even know her name? So, what is it, Laney or Esther?"

"I'd think you'd have her as Esther," Minnie supplied, humbly.

"Well, I can say this. You don't look like no sister to any of 'em. Him, maybe, but not you."

Minnie became desperate. "Ma'am, if I go away, can he see 'em?"

"No, not today. But the little'n, she's not here. Not bein' six yet, we had to send her next door."

"Oh. We could go over there...."

"No. All visitors come through here. Good bye, now."

The receptionist stood meaningfully beside her desk, and there was nothing for them to do but stand and go out the door.

They went to the street and stood, staring back at the two buildings. The receptionist watched from behind the curtains. "If them two are brother and sister, then, for certain, birds fly upsidedown."

Back in the room, they lit the lamp and the small oil burner. The smallness of the attic room made it heat quickly, the delicious warmth soaked into their bones. They had brought a box of raisins back with them, and they munched on them while watching the flame of the oil burner.

Minnie began. "I'm thinkin.' It seems like it's too much for folks to think of us as brother and sister, so I'm thinkin' next time we go, you go alone. Could be they'll let you see one of them."

"Could be. I keep thinkin,' and it seems it'll be harder'n we thought to get 'em out'a there. How long is the measles?"

"Well, for a boy… I don't rightly know, but I heard he'd ought'a be in for two weeks. Girl, a week to ten days. That's just what I heard."

"So Artie, he come down on a Thursday. This here's Sunday, and tomorrow's Monday. By my figurin,' he's got ten days to go. We can't take 'im out 'afore then."

Minnie nodded, reaching for another handful of raisins. The sweetness of them seemed to pump a bit of energy into her veins.

"Then Laney. I got a idea."

"What'd that be?"

"Places like them homes, they're always short'a people to work, at least, I heard tell. Now, if I was to go over to the one where she is, I'd see if they'd put me on. Washin,' that's one thing I can do. They're sure to have a heap'a washin' all the time, with babies and such."

"Well, and then…?"

"If I was in the buildin,' chance I'd know where she was and at least peek in on her."

"You think you could get hired?"

"I could try. Now, if we was to say ten days from now, we could set plans. I'll know a lot more after they hire me."

"If they hire you."

They blew out the light, and Denny flattened himself on the warm, dry pallet under a pile of quilts, and Minnie stretched her exhausted body between the quilts on the bed. It wasn't much of a prize for a bed, but it was warm and dry, such as they had not had for three days.

"A-choo!"

"Denny, you're gonna catch your death! I told you it ought'a be you in the bed and me on the floor."

"It ain't the floor that's bad. It's the nights we spent in the damp. I'll be fine."

Five

Laney Baldwin watched the big people move the little bed into another room where there was a big bed. Something told her it had a lot to do with her. Sure enough.

"Now, Esther…?"

They still thought she was Esther. Well, it seemed to do no good to try to straighten them out.

"Now, Esther, we're gonna let you sleep in this room tonight. It's too far to the bathroom, so you'll have to use the potty." The woman pointed to the little white bowl with the handle. Laney stared at it. A potty! Now, that would be nice, and she wouldn't have to lay in a wet bed till someone came to see her.

"Do you understand?"

Laney nodded.

"Now, we'll put on your nightgown, and you can go to sleep."

Dressed in cozy flannel, she sat on the little potty for a minute, and then climbed into the bed.

After a while, a strange sound happened, and Laney opened her eyes. The room was still brightly lit, and the person on the big bed sat up and rubbed her eyes.

In a minute, she heard a baby cry. Or was it a baby cat? No, it was a baby. So they were going to let a baby sleep in this bright room, too. Maybe they would put it in her bed.

But they didn't. The person picked up a blanket and went to a little bed by the wall. The baby was in the little bed, and she picked it up. It cried louder, and the person wrapped the baby and took it away, her slippers scuffing along the floor.

Then she was back, and she slipped between the covers of her bed. Laney felt the urge again, and slipped down from her bed to the potty, then back under the warm covers. This was a better room, and she drifted into sleep, again.

Before morning, she was again awake. They must have brought the baby back, because there it was.

And it was morning, and she opened her eyes. Two people were in the room.

"Busy night, huh? Not too often we get two babies in the same night. Must'a been a full moon nine months back."

"Yeah, two in one night."

"Did you get any sleep from the whinin' of that little girl?"

"She didn't make no noise. 'Cept when she climbed down to use the potty, and she was quiet about that."

"She used the potty? I just came into change the bedding. She's been wettin' the bed every night. Hmmmmm."

Later, when Laney again enthroned herself on the chair in the playroom, she folded her hands in her lap. They looked funny. She still had a few red speckles on both arms, and they itched. She scratched each one individually with her fingernail. It gave her something to do, and it felt so good to scratch them.

Vonnie had hardly been able to sleep from the throbbing of her burned foot. She had a lot of time to consider whether she had done the best thing. It had gotten her out of the kitchen but was she any better off?

She had spent the day in the infirmary, dusting the lower shelves of the medicine chest and lining the bottles so the labels could be seen. It would be fun to know what they were all used for, but the nurse was busy, and Vonnie did not want to disturb her. Later, a boy came in with a skinned knee, and a girl who got a splinter under her fingernail, and it must have really hurt to get it out. She screamed a lot.

Then, just before supper, Vonnie was told she would be in the infirmary again tomorrow, and she could dust and arrange the bottles in the upper shelf. The nurse had whispered to her that if things went well, she would be permitted to slip into the quarantine room and speak to Artie.

She asked the nurse if she knew anything about her older brother and sister, but the nurse had sadly shook her head. Maybe Minnie didn't know the truth about the shooting, and Denny had been put in jail for killing pa. If he was in jail, well, but he wouldn't...? Would he?

Her thoughts went back and forth. When her foot got well, she would again be put in the kitchen until it was time to go to someone called Mrs. Nester, who would want her to wear a white lace dustcap and have hair so short it could be hidden.

Minnie wouldn't know where Mrs. Nester was, and couldn't come and get her out. When she had to go back to the kitchen, what else could she do to delay being moved out? Too much salt in the soup? No, it had to be something that was clearly her fault. She had to be a person Mrs. Nester wouldn't want.

Finally she went to sleep.

Miss Cantrell had a late meeting with Miss Mamie Rush.

"How's that girl, Amy? That burn gonna cause trouble?"

Miss Rush nodded. "The burn's pretty deep. Can't get her shoe on, and Nurse Brannon wants her foot to be kept up. Didn't take her back to the kitchen, 'cause she'd be more trouble than help. Nurse has her dustin' and makin' bandages."

"Well, at least she's doin' somethin.' If she doesn't start getting' better, it'll have to be someone else to go to Mrs. Nester. Ellen? She's been in trainin' the longest, hasn't she?"

A pause. "Well, there's times it's not how long they been in trainin,' but how much trainin's gone into them. Ellen, well it ain't her fault, really, but she's slower'n molasses in January. She don't hardly make mistakes, but she don't get much done, neither."

Miss Rush was glad it was not up to her to sell Ellen to the upper crust woman in the mansion. Truth be told, though, Mrs. Nester had been a big help to a lot of girls.

Now if Ellen was sent, she would probably stay in the kitchen, but she likely wouldn't mind at all. Even Mrs. Nester's kitchen was a good place to be. Ellen could do worse.

Miss Rush waited for Miss Cantrell to dismiss her.

"Go check on Amy. If she can stand at all, she can go back to the kitchen."

"With a crutch?"

"With a crutch." The words were spoken with finality. "Nurse Brannon says it'd not be safe on the stone floors, otherwise."

With a weary sigh, Miss Cantrell waved her hand, and Miss Rush fled down the hall.

On Monday, Minnie asked Louisa, her landlady, where she could find a store that sold to domestics. She had need of a uniform dress and cap.

Louisa smiled, brightly. "Thinkin' you and your husband'll stay around with us for a while, huh?"

Minnie forced a smile. "Well, it's a good place, and I'm needin' to work."

Louisa nodded, understandingly. "Them times come. Well, now, you'll find that store…"

It was a fair distance, but Minnie was able to buy a dress made of the heavy gray fabric of the low servant, such as kitchen and laundry help. She bought a dust cap with a heavy ruffle that fell low on her forehead.

It cost four dollars for both pieces. It was scary how fast the money flew when there was none coming in. Well, nine more days and maybe they'd be ready to go.

Back at the room, she dressed in the new clothes, amazed at how professional she looked. The floppy brim of the hat covered so much of her face that Denny swore he would not recognize her on the street.

Reaching the home, she stood looking at the buildings for a while. What, really, would be the best to do? Laundry was more believable. She wanted to be thought of as experienced, and she was not sure what kind of work went on in a home like this one, except washings.

Laundry, it would be. Walking around to the back of the building, she hesitated, breathed deeply, and went to the back door. Knocking gently, she stepped back. A young girl opened the door.

"Could you take me to the person that hires on?"

"Wait here, miss."

Minnie waited. In due time, the girl returned. "Miss Scruggs says she'll see you."

Minnie followed the girl down the long hall with a stone floor. Mary Scruggs, a fleshy, comfortable looking woman sat in her easy chair. She turned to greet Minnie.

"Lookin' to be took on? Likely you'll not like what we got open. 'Course, there's a chance to work up, in time."

Minnie bowed her head slightly. "I'll take what you got, ma'am."

Mrs. Scruggs nodded. "What we got is a case'a the measles, and half of the youngens we got are broke out and sick. We took in a little girl that was comin' down, and now it's all over."

Measles. Little girl. Laney. It added up.

Mrs. Scruggs continued. "It ain't bad, really. It's best for the youngens to be exposed when they're little and get it over with. Then, happen we get a chance to adopt one of 'em out, we can say they done had the measles. So, what we got is the bedding laundry."

Minnie looked up and nodded encouragingly.

"So if I was to hire you, it'd not be a regular job. We'd need you till we get over the measles, but with the turn over here, could be somethin' else'd turn up by then."

It was time for Minnie to speak up. "Ma'am, its laundry that I do best. I started at a boardin' house, washin' the beddin' when I was thirteen. I'm really needin' the job. I'm guessin' meals come with it?"

"Meals? Oh, of course, there'll be food in the kitchen. Now the pay. What the job'd pay, bein' an extra, like I explained, is two dollars a week. Eight hours."

"I'll take it. I just got'a go tell someone I got a job, and I'll be right back, ready to work."

"All right, Miss… uh…?"

"Minnie Belle Crowley, ma'am. Thank you! Thank you! I'll be right back." And she was gone. Such good luck!

"…and I work till seven o'clock. I'm thinkin Laney has the measles. They said it was brought by a little girl."

Denny nodded. "I'll be here for you at seven. This here ain't a part'a town to be walkin' in, a girl alone."

Back in the laundry room, Minnie rolled up her sleeves and attacked the mountain of stinking sheets and pillowcases. A rub and a rub, and a splash in the water. Another rub and….

At noon, she was invited into the kitchen and allowed to fill her plate from whatever looked good. She looked around her at several young girls near the age of Vonnie, but Vonnie was clearly not there.

After dinner, she returned to the laundry room. With the up and down of the rubbing, her thoughts worked on how she would be able to find the room where Laney was. The building was so terribly big. How far could she get from the laundry room, appearing as she did, in the clothes of a laundry person? Then her break came.

Mrs. Scruggs came for her, and she followed the woman down the hall. "We got this pile in the infirmary where they changed out the sheets. We got 'em in a cart you can take back with you. First, though, come on to the drawer room. We got one little girl that has trouble sleepin', and we moved her bed in here. She's the little one that brought us the measles."

Minnie struggled to keep her face expressionless. "Yes, ma'am."

In the tiny room at the end of the hall, she gathered up the sheet from the small bed, and tossed it in the cart. So Laney gave them some trouble, and they put her in a room by herself. Well, that might help for what she needed to do. What, actually, was a drawer room?

Back by the infirmary, she paused to pick up the rest of the load, and saw, sitting on a chair with her leg elevated, a girl with a bandaged foot. The girl carefully cleaned each bottle and set it back, in the precise way that Vonnie had.

Coming close enough, she touched the girl on the shoulder. Vonnie turned, and her mouth popped open, but Minnie quickly put her finger to her lips. In a faint whisper, she mouthed, "I work here. I'll talk later."

Vonnie quickly turned back to the dusting, but watched from the corner of her eye as Minnie gathered the stained sheets. Vonnie's hands were poised and steady, but her heart pounded with relief. Minnie knew where she was!

And that wasn't all. Finally, Denny came, and she was allowed to hobble to the reception room on her crutch and talk with him for fifteen minutes. She whispered, "I got to see Artie. The nurse let me sneak in. He's pretty sick.

"Ten days," Denny had told her. That was the plan, and if she had any ideas, she could tell him next time they let him visit.

Six

Back at the café, Minnie watched as Denny ate. It seemed supper also came with her job, and she had filled her plate with stew and cornbread and topped it off with a generous bowl of canned peaches for desert.

Once more in the room, they compared notes. Ten days still looked good. Artie would be better, and Laney...? If she was first in the other home to come down, she would be well by then.

After five days, Vonnie was deemed well enough to return to the kitchen.

"Now, Amy, we've got the ground meat and the spices, and we're gonna make a meatloaf. We'll be makin' a hundred servings, and we got meat enough for sixty. How much oatmeal will it take to stretch it out? What would you do first?"

"Yes, Miss. I'd take a pan and put in the meat to see how full it got. Then I'd put in oatmeal and pour in milk or water and stir it till it got almost as full."

"Milk or water? Why?"

"Yes, Miss. It'd be 'cause dry oatmeal takes up more room, and when it got wet, there'd not be enough."

A pause. "Very good, Amy. So now, I'm going to let you stir the mixture while I watch you."

Vonnie began. How could she mess up the meatloaf? Of course, she might not need to. Minnie and Denny were going to get her out in nine days. She needed to help them figure out how.

She mixed the meatloaf, and packed it in the pans. Tomato sauce was spread over the top, and the many pans were slipped into the oven.

"Very good, Amy."

"Yes, Miss."

"I have good news for you, Amy. It seems you've been selected to take training in the kitchen of a very lovely and generous woman. She is very good to her servants and promotes them well. You are a very lucky girl."

"Thank you, Miss."

"She's even willing to take you with your burned foot. She says accidents happen. Of course, we don't want any more accidents, do we? They can be quite painful, I'm sure."

"Yes, Miss."

"Now, Amy, when the meatloaf is ready to take out of the oven, you let Ellen do it. I don't think you would be steady enough, with your crutch."

"Yes, Miss."

Later, when the meatloaf was ready, Vonnie stood aside as Ellen, armed with oven mitts, slid the giant pans from the oven and took them to the table.

Looking toward the door that had just opened, Vonnie startled as she saw Minnie, gray dress and dustcap, come through the door.

Catching Vonnie's eye, Minnie held her finger to her lips, and Vonnie looked down.

Taking a plate from the cupboard, Minnie filled it and sat down at a table and began to eat. Vonnie approached.

"Miss, can I get you anything?"

"Yes, please. A little salt…?"

Vonnie handed the salt shaker across the table. Taking it, Minnie whispered, "Change'a plans. Eight days. Back door."

Vonnie nodded. "Anything else, ma'am?"

"No, thank you," Minnie replied, politely.

When the plate was empty, Minnie left, flashing a small smile and a wink in Vonnie's direction.

The eighth day would be a Thursday. On Monday, in the warmth of the oil burner in attic room, Minnie and Denny made plans.

Denny, first. "All this beddin'. In the mornin' when we go, I'll carry some of it back to the wagon, so's it'll look more natural when we need to take it all."

"But, there's two more days…?

"Sleepin' on the bare floor won't be no problem. Warm, like it is."

"Maybe. I'm thinkin' we can do it. I been checkin' on where they sleep Laney, but I haven't actual seen her, yet. Vonnie's ready. Says she'll have Artie down to the back door, one way or the other. We can't say more'n two or three words at a time."

"Could be they'll let me see 'em tomorrow. Been five days, now."

But when Minnie came in to eat the next day, Tuesday, Vonnie, with frightened eyes, came close. "Got'a be tomorrow!" she whispered, as she walked away.

Minnie cut her eyes toward her sister, and mouthed, "Tomorrow?"

Vonnie vigorously nodded her head. Hobbling across the huge kitchen, she took two dishtowels from the rack and came toward Minnie.

"Ma'am, could you wash these? They fell to the floor and got dirty." Then, lowering her voice, "I'm bein' sent out on Thursday."

Fear clutched at Minnie's lungs. She hated last minute changes of plans. "Sure, I can throw 'em in with the rest." Then she added, "It'll be all right."

When Minnie had gone, Vonnie was chided. "Now, Amy, it ain't your call to gather up the washin.' You just tend to what you been told to do. You need to be ready to go out. This'll be your last day, today."

"Yes, Miss."

Taking a small knife in her hand, Vonnie bent as though to adjust the bandages on her foot. Clenching her teeth and closing her eyes, she gave a quick jab at the bandage. Then she tossed the knife onto the floor, where it clattered noisily.

"Ouch!" she yelled. "That old knife cut my foot!"

Miss Rush was just leaving the kitchen, and hurried back just as the red stain began to seep through the white cloth. "AMY! Whatever are you doing? You got'a keep a head on your shoulders when you got a knife in your hand."

"Yes, Miss."

"Well, get on up to the infirmary and get it tended to."

"Thank you, Miss." Adjusting the crutch under her arm, she hobbled slowly down the hall toward the kingdom of Nurse Brannon.

"Oh, darling, what bad luck! That knife must'a fell with the point straight down. Look at that puncture! Stretch out here on the bed and we'll see what we can do."

An hour later, Vonnie was still on the couch. "Miss Brannon?"

"Yes, dear?"

"Could I...? I mean, would it be all right if I peeked through the window to my brother? I ain't got to see 'im for days, and he'll be wonderin' if I still remember 'im."

"Why, honey, I don't see why not. He's sitting on his bed right now, and if you want, you can go in and sit with him for a minute. He'll probably go to the boy's dormitory tomorrow."

"He will? For sure?"

"Why, yes. He's doing fine."

"That'll be good."

Vonnie slipped through the door and clumped her way to Artie's bed. He grinned happily and started to come to meet her.

"No!" she whispered.

Sitting beside him, she spoke quickly. "I know you ain't got to see Denny, but he's gonna get us out. Tomorrow."

"Oh, goodie!"

"Shhhhh. Listen. You got'a get sick."

"Why?"

"They're fixin' to move you, and I won't know where you are. You got'a stay in here all day tomorrow. Set your shoes where you can get in 'im, and I'll sneak in and get you after dark."

Artie nodded, excitedly.

"Now, remember, you got'a be sick. Your stomach hurts. You got'a cry and say you're gonna throw up. You hear me?" Vonnie enforced her command with a small shake of his shoulder. "You be ready to be sick. You hear me?"

Artie stared with wide, concerned eyes. "I hear you. I feel sick right now."

"I can't stay no longer, so you remember, not tonight. Tomorrow night."

Artie nodded and crawled back under his covers, sniffing convincingly.

Vonnie returned to the nurse's room. Nurse Brannon looked up. "Was he happy to see you?"

Vonnie nodded. "Uh, ma'am, is it usual to be sick to the stomach when a body's gettin' over the measles? 'Cause my brother thinks he'll throw up."

"Really?"

"He just told me. I told 'im to lay back down and I'd tell you. Sometimes it goes away if a body lays back down, don't it?"

"Sometimes." Nurse Brannon had left what she was doing and looked through the window. Sure enough, Arthur Baldwin was huddled back under the quilt. He might need a little more watching. A day or two, anyway.

Seven

The bedding was all returned to the wagon and packed aboard on Wednesday morning. Denny went about his feeding and animal tending, and Minnie's fists rubbed up and down in the mountain of suds from the bars of yellow soap. Her mind was working on the fine points of her plan.

She was trying not to make good time, and several sheets were scrubbed and rubbed several times more than necessary. It was important that she not hurry.

227

At the evening meal, she had only the opportunity to give Vonnie a quick nod of assurance as she ate her meal of cornbread dressing made from chicken broth.

When it would have been time for her to leave the laundry room, she went, instead, to the bathroom and stayed as long as she could. The day-help filed out the door and went to their homes, and the live-in cook checked the stoves and put out the light.

Minnie came into the kitchen and huddled in a dark corner behind a cabinet. It was much too early to put her plan in effect. The minutes dragged by, and the ticking of the clock on the cabinet seemed to be drumming fear into her head. She felt her teeth begin to chatter, and she held her jaw in place with her hand. Wait... wait... wait...!

Finally, there was no sound. Stepping into the laundry room, she gathered a small armload of soiled bed sheets in her arms and waited. She should be able to hear anyone who crossed the kitchen floor.

Vonnie softly eased herself from her bed in the girls' dormitory and looked around. Everyone was asleep, even the night woman who slept on the cot by the door.

Holding the crutch under her arm, she crawled slowly between the beds and moved toward the door, not daring to breathe. Reaching up to turn the knob, the door swung back without a sound. Maneuvering the crutch through the door, she followed it and was finally in the dimly lit hall.

Standing, she fitted the crutch under her arm and moved carefully, positioning the wooden point of the crutch silently on the stone floor. No one was up, and the hall seemed a mile long, stretched out before her.

Working her way along, she reached the infirmary. It was dark, but she had been there so often it held no surprises. Carefully turning the knob, she slipped through the door. In the dim light, she could see Artie sitting on the edge of his bed.

When he saw her, he worked his feet into his shoes and tiptoed toward her. Silently they crept through the nurse's office, with Artie holding to her nightdress.

Back in the hall once more, she led him toward the kitchen.

A door banged somewhere down the hall, and they both stopped, clamping their hands over their mouths. Eyes wide with horror and fright, they stared at the figure approaching them. Miss Cantrell!

"Now what do you two think you're doin,' runnin' around in the dark'a the night? Speak up! Amy?"

"Yes, Miss. I mean, I'm sorry, Miss. It's just that my brother, here, he's been sick and ain't had all his meals. He's hungry, ma'am, and I thought it'd not be right to wake up someone to see if he could have a piece'a bread. Is it all right? 'Cause I can show 'im where it is and see he gets took care of."

"Well, I…"

"I always took care'a my brother and sister. I wouldn't be expectin' someone else to do what I could do. Is that all right?"

Vonnie's words sounded strange to her own ears over the frantic beating of her heart. Miss Cantrell was hesitating.

Vonnie managed more words. "Did I do somethin' wrong?"

Miss Cantrell was tired. She was especially tired of Amy Baldwin and was glad she would be put in service tomorrow. Mrs. Nester was agreeable to taking a girl on crutches, so she was going.

"I suppose," she finally agreed. "See he gets it ate and back in bed."

"Yes, Miss. I mean, thank you, Miss."

They stood aside for the supervisor to pass by them and then headed for the door. It was not so necessary now, to be silent. They had permission.

Into the kitchen they went, and Vonnie coughed loudly. At the back door, she slipped through, pulling Artie after her.

A change in the weather had brought one of the few snows that reached as far south as central Arkansas. It had sifted down from the clouds, sparkling flecks of silver falling around the mercury vapor street lamps, and settling wetly on the streets. A white sifting covered the streets like a dusting of confectioners sugar on the floor of a bakery.

Denny had brought one wagon up the alley behind the homes, and had tied the horses to a pole. Running back through the sifting snow, he quickly hitched up the other one and brought it up just behind the first one.

Gauging the distance, he brought the second wagon as close to the back door of the laundry room as he could. The other one he parked on the street, a half a block away.

With a pounding heart, he huddled, shivering, beside the wagon, training his eyes on the blackness of the door. Finally a sound, and two figures paused, then came running toward him.

Motioning them to follow, he hurried toward the far wagon. Then, seeing Vonnie with her crutch could not keep up, he grabbed her and slung her across his shoulder, flinging her shoe aside and sending her crutch clattering noisily on the stones of the alley.

Artie clomped along behind in his untied shoes.

The wet snow fell on Vonnie's nightdress, soaking against her back and arms, and Artie's head and shoulders were wet.

At the wagon, Denny crammed Vonnie under the storm flap, and Artie crawled in behind her.

"Wait now," he commanded. "I got'a go see if…!"

When Minnie heard the cough, she knew Vonnie and Artie were safely outside. It would be useless to get Laney until she was certain the others had made it. Holding the armload of soiled sheets, she walked quietly down the hall.

At the far end, a light around the door showed it to be ajar. Good. She didn't need any squeaking hinges. Pulling the door open a bit farther, she stopped, startled.

There, on a bed across the room, lay a woman seemingly asleep. It was a surprise. She had not thought of someone else being in the room. It was, however, too late to back out.

Several quiet steps brought her to the bed where Laney lay sleeping. Leaning down, she whispered, "Shhh. Shhh. Shhh. Minnie's gonna pick you up."

Laney opened her eyes just a peek, and saw the person in the gray dress. She heard the "Shhh Shhh Shhh" and she knew what that meant. That's what Minnie always said when her mama need to sleep, and Laney knew she was to play quietly.

The gray person had a nice whisper, just like Minnie's. It made her feel good, and she closed her eyes. She knew about dreams. Sometimes they were bad, and she woke up crying. Minnie would tell her everything was all right, and it was just a mean old dream.

So now she had a dream that was not mean. The gray person wrapped her and picked her up all gathered together in a wad, just the way she liked to be picked up. This was a good dream, and if she was very still, it might last.

"Shhh Shhh Shhh," whispered in her ears. Such a good dream! She cuddled down in the arms that knew how to hold her, and sighed with pleasure.

Minnie hurried, now. Time was very important. Then the door opened behind her.

"Stop, there!"

Minnie hesitated.

"Minnie Crowley, is it? What are you doing here? You should be through and gone home."

"Yes, ma'am. I know I should'a. The fact was, I was slow today, not gettin' done what I should'a. So I stayed late. I'm just puttin' these to soak, and I'll be out'a here."

"Well, now, you didn't need to do the gatherin'...."

Minnie thought fast. "Oh, ma'am, you know how it stinks when a measles youngen throws up. Hard to get the smell out when it's been let to get dry."

"Yes, well...."

"I'll take care'a this and be gone, ma'am."

"All right."

Laney heard the words, but that was all right. The person in the dream still sounded like Minnie and was still holding her like she wanted to be held. She squenched her eyes up tight, trying to prolong the dream.

Then the person was moving again. She was shifted to the person's shoulders, and the sheets were pulled away, but the arms still held her. Cold wetness fell on her, and she hugged herself against the person so the dream would not stop.

Minnie blinked in the sudden darkness then ran through the sparkling snow to the wagon. Denny stood inside the wagon bed and reached down for Laney.

Scrambling inside, Minnie drew on her coat, buried Laney in the quilts, telling her to Shhh, and grabbed the reins. In the distance, she could see the running figure of Denny, headed toward the other wagon. Laney, knowing the wonderful dream was still with her, cuddled into the cold quilts, and they were soon warm. And she slept.

Clicking the horses into action, Minnie directed them to follow along behind the first wagon. The clomp of the horses' hooves echoed in the silent night.

Miss Cottrell entered her own apartment and closed the door with determined finality, sighing a sigh of exhaustion.

Stepping up to the window, she looked out at the flecks of snow, tumbling and turning as they fell past the street lamp. They had the sparkle of fairy dust that she had read about in children's storybooks.

Finally, weariness claimed her, and she pulled the curtain panels together and fastened them, and in minutes, she was in her bed, asleep.

It was near morning, though still dark, when her eyes popped open with a sudden realization of what, without doubt, had happened.

First, how would Amy, in the girl's dormitory, know her little brother was hungry? And wasn't he the one with the stomachache?

Next question, how would the pretty, young washerwoman, hired only a few days ago, know that a sheet had been soiled? Especially one in the drawer room in the other building...? She'd have to check with the attendant there.

So, there was no more sleep for Miss Cottrell. It wouldn't do for the authorities to know she had let a child be kidnapped. There'd have to be a story. Perhaps an older couple came to claim them? Or... something!

When a dim light appeared behind her curtain panels, she looked out to see the snow. As usual, the snow had melted into the warmer ground, but the flecks of lightness had been followed by a peppering of sleet and freezing rain. She knew there would be no more sleep for her.

With yet another sigh, she drew on her corset and began to tighten the laces. It would take a lot of tightening of the whalebone stays to get through this day.

Down the hall and into the kitchen she went, and as she guessed, the kitchen door was unlocked. The "soiled" sheet had been tossed loosely into the laundry room, not put to soak. At this point, Miss Cantrell had no doubt as to what had happened.

She did, however, look out into the back alley. Faint tracks of wagon wheels marked the alley, and the ice casing had covered the garbage cans, the mop handles, and every weed along the fence. Also encased in ice was a girl's shoe and a crutch. Miss Cantrell walked carefully across the slippery coating and retrieved the shoe and crutch.

The only bright spot in her mind was that poor Ellen would now get her chance. But that would be after she had convinced Mrs. Nester that Ellen was the best choice. After all, Ellen was very careful, and Amy seemed to be "somewhat accident prone."

Somehow, she would get through the day. She always did.

She would tell the staff she had decided to release the children in their brother's custody (or perhaps an older family member showed up in the night?).

Nurse Brannon listened to the cover story, never doubting for an instant what had happened. She felt a pang of regret that she would not see the delightful Amy again.

Eight

The two-wagon caravan headed out of town on a route that took them due northwest, the exact direction of the blowing snow. Minnie blew against the frosted flakes that layered themselves on her lap and collar and caught on her eyelashes. The maid's dust cap now had great value. Its thickness snugged around her face and head, and she pulled it close under her wool-knit scarf.

They had hardly cleared the last house at the edge of town when the dusting of snow stopped and the sleet and freezing rain started. With weary discouragement, she watched the ice balls heap themselves on the rumps of the horses, falling faster than the heat of the animals could melt them. Her knowledge from childhood knew this was a very bad thing for horses.

Not only that, her hands could remember the feel of the thinness of Laney's nightgown as she had peeled away the sheets and dashed from the back door of the kitchen. Also, the bare feet. Something would have to be done immediately about that.

Without doubt Artie and Vonnie were no better clothed. Her mind inventoried the possibilities. Artie had another coat. Fortunately, it had been his older one that was left behind. Vonnie had her last year's coat but the sleeves stopped closely below her elbows. They had saved it, though, because it was still in good shape, and Laney would grow into it. Vonnie could manage with that until something better could be done.

Laney, however, had nothing. Being the recipient of hand-me-downs, there had been nothing else worth saving, other than the one left at the home. There were sweaters, however, and any sleeves were too long could be rolled, and she'd just have to stay under the quilts. Thank the Good Lord they had plenty of them, even though they had lost the one that had been wrapped around Artie on the way to the home.

With a sigh, she resigned herself. Sometimes there was nothing else that could have been done, and this was one of those times. The sleet burned and stung her face and she tucked the end of her scarf into the dust cap, totally covering her face. Her team would follow along without direction.

In her numbness, she wondered how Denny was getting along. Their last conversation in the attic room had been about which route to take. They agreed to take be best route along the southern bank of the Arkansas River. It extended into Oklahoma, and it would be a good way to avoid getting lost.

Suddenly, she felt the motion of the wagon cease, and the horses tossed in their harnesses and blew their breath… a sign that they knew they would be resting. Pulling her scarf from her face, she saw Denny hurrying toward her.

Denny's concerned voice called. "How're you doin'?"

Before Minnie could answer, he continued. "Sure would like to stop, but there ain't no place. Can't let these horses stop walkin.' Cold and wet as they are, they'd be sick, for sure. You doin' all right?"

What could she say? "I'm fine. We still goin' on to Dardanelle?"

"Might as well. It'd be three days to Conway, and the storm'll be over by then, either way. Dardanelle ain't no more'n five days. Only thing is, we got'a keep movin' all night. I'm hopin' you're up to it. Can't risk losin' a horse."

With cold-numbed hands, Minnie wiped the melted sleet from her cheeks and nose. "I can make it. How're the others? Come out without no coats, I 'speck."

"Yeah, just nightgowns. They're in the quilts and I ain't heard nothin' out'a either of 'em. Likely, they're the best off of the lot. I was just wonderin,' are those raisins where you could reach 'em? I'm thinkin' somethin' sweet might help us stay warmer."

Minnie turned and reached for the icy handle of the food box. An opened box of raisins was setting on top, and she handed it to Denny.

"Thanks. Now, Minnie…?"

"Huh?"

"You eat some, too." A command from Denny was an unusual thing.

"All right," she readily promised.

Denny turned and ran toward the rig in front of her team. Strange for him to be giving her orders about food. She didn't feel hungry, just terribly sleepy, but she had promised. Digging her non-feeling hand in the food box she located another box of raisins. How could she possibly get it open when her hands were so cold, and she was so sleepy?

SLEEPY! The very word startled her, and she sprang, bolt upright. Sleepiness preceded death by freezing. Standing up in front of the wagon beside the buckboard, she stomped her tingling feet and turned her body this way and that. She rubbed her cold hands against her face and eyes.

Reaching back in the food box, she located a paring knife. Jabbing it into the side of the box of raisins, she poked a handful of them into her mouth, holding them there to soften. The flavored sweetness of them filled her mouth, and her head cleared… somewhat.

The horror of it all was clear. After all they had been through, she could actually sit here and freeze to death in the sleet. At best, she could lose fingers or toes, and she was certain to need them. As soon as she could swallow the raisins, she poked her mouth full again.

As a mental exercise, she attempted to inventory the supply of raisins. Was it six boxes they had bought? Or eight? Anyway, they had eaten one in the attic room, one she handed Denny, and she was working on the third one. That left either three or five. When the children woke up, they would eat one whole box for breakfast.

What else could they eat? There were three peppermint sticks left. That would be good. No eggs. Next thing was water mixed with cornmeal or oatmeal, to eat raw. Add some sugar. It would taste terrible, but there would be no way to start a roadside fire in this sleet.

After an eternity, the sleet stopped. It was hardly a help, though, because the wind still blew fiercely, directly into their faces. Then a faint line of light made black silhouettes of the trees to the east. Almost morning.

Breakfast. That was the next hurdle.

She felt her head being turned. Small, icy fingers pulled at her chin, turning her head around. She looked back.

There stood Laney, standing on the wooden food box on her bare feet, her nightgown flapping in the wind.

"MINNIE! MINNIE!"

"Oh, darlin' girl! You can't be out of the quilts like that! Go back and crawl under the warm quilts."

"NO! NO!"

"Yes. Yes. You have to."

"NO! You'll go away from me."

"Oh, no, honey. I won't go. You go crawl under the quilt, and be warm."

Instead, Laney stepped over the back of the buckboard seat, holding to Minnie's shoulder to keep her balance. Stepping her bare foot on the icy seat, she was beside Minnie, and she plunked her bare bottom down on the solid sheet of ice.

Looking Minnie directly in the eye, she stated emphatically, "NO!"

Laying the reins aside, Minnie picked up the girl and took her back to the quilts, wrapping one of them snuggly around her, and, leaving a flap at the top to fall over her face, she carried her back to the buckboard.

The quilt wrapped bundle, leaning against Minnie, soon became quiet and still and a peek between the flaps revealed closed eyes. The quilt bundle pushed up against Minnie's side giving her a shred of warmth, and they rode along the gravelly road until daylight.

They had just pulled up a gradual hill, and at the top they could see a prosperous looking farmhouse. White painted fences surrounded the yard, and two barns were located behind the roomy looking house. Denny's wagon stopped in the middle of the road, and he came hurrying back to her.

"Minnie, I'm fixin' to go ask can we use their barn, today. The moisture ain't fallin' no more, and the horses can't stand the wind pullin' the warmth out'a their hides."

Minnie nodded wearily, relieved that a decision had been made that had not involved her. She watched as Denny hurried up the lane to the house. In a short time he was back, beckoning to her to follow.

A man stood at the corner of the barn and motioned them forward. Pulling into the generous shed room of the barn, they halted, side by side. The man called loudly over the whistling wind.

"You folks go on in the house. My missus is expectin' you."

Minnie stepped out of the wagon on aching, tingling feet and reached for the quilt wrapped bundle. Spilling out the end of the other wagon was Artie, his jacket tails flying, followed by a quilt wrapped

Vonnie, hopping across the icy barn yard on a bare foot, trying to hold her bandaged foot off the ground. An overbalanced misstep sent her scooting on the ice.

Denny had started to unhitch the horses and heard Vonnie's squeal. Leaving the horses, he ran to her, grabbed her and pitched her quilt and all, over his shoulder and hurried on to the open door of the farmhouse.

Maybelle Applewhite had just finished breakfast and was sitting at the table leisurely drinking her coffee when her husband had promised the young man he could stable his horses until the storm passed. Staring toward the front drive, she saw the two wagons turn from the road and approach.

"Good Lord a'Mercy! They got two wagons, and it looks like they got youngens. Henry, tell 'em to get on in here and get warm."

So she had stood at the back door of the porch as the woman (girl?) bundled in a coat, now marched woodenly toward her, carrying a wad of something (baby?) in her arms. Behind her was a boy in thin clothes, open jacket and shoes with their strings flopping.

Bringing up the rear was a man with what appeared to be someone slung across his shoulders like a sack of cowfeed. Bare feet and a white bandage preceded him into the closed-in porch. Speechless and unbelieving, she stared, then recovering her senses, she herded them into her warm kitchen. Denny set Vonnie on the floor, left, and went back to the barn.

Addressing the woman (girl?), she exclaimed, "Oh, honey, they…? You shouldn't… oh, those bare feet! Bring the baby… Oh, she's a big girl! Come, darlin,' put your feet up to the stove. I'll open the oven door. Aren't you 'bout froze?"

Sliding chairs toward the open door of the oven, that was sending delicious streams of warm dry air in the room, she looked at Minnie, her eyes begging for an explanation.

Instead, she got tears. Minnie looked around the large, warm kitchen smelling of warm biscuits and oatmeal, and tears of exhaustion began to stream down her face. Maybelle threw her ample, experienced arms around Minnie and led her to a chair.

"There, there, honey. You just sit here. Can you drink coffee? Sure you can! I had the thought you might be… then I see a little girl and not a baby." While talking, she had filled a mug with steaming black brew, spooned in sugar and poured a generous amount of cream. "Here, honey, you drink this, and I'll put on some oatmeal. These youngens look hungry."

Minnie lifted the coffee mug to her tear-wet face and breathed in the fragrant steam. Her eyes looked into the cup with the golden cream making swirls in the blackness of the coffee. A sip. Heaven must feel like this! The warmth of the drink flowed into her frozen throat and trembling stomach.

"Ma'am…?"

"Call me Maybelle."

"Miss Maybelle, I ain't got words to say… say what I want'a say. We'd just about gone as far… I mean, we…."

"Now, honey, don't you be tryin' to talk yet. You're stayin' here till the storm passes. I can see, by the look of the youngens, you come through a bad time. You just think about restin' and eatin,' and there'll be time for talkin' later."

The oatmeal plopped and bubbled in the kettle. With a large spoon, Maybelle scooped up a cup-sized lump of butter and tossed it in. Setting bowls down from the cupboard, she filled them at the kettle and set one before Minnie.

"Now, you youngens, you want'a slide up on that bench and eat?" She didn't have to call them twice.

"We're startin' with oatmeal, that bein' the quickest. Then, when you get warm, we'll make some eggs and other things.

The door opened, and Denny came in, followed by Mr. Applewhite.

"Son, you come and sit over here by your missus. I got your oatmeal ready. Nothin' like hot oatmeal to thaw out the insides."

Minnie, spoon in mid-air, glanced at Denny. Time enough later to straighten them out on the relationship. After what these people had already done, they were entitled to hear the entire sordid story. They were now a long way from Little Rock and its problems, and besides, these people didn't look like the kind who would turn them in.

A platter of scrambled eggs appeared, flanked by sizzling brown sausages. Steaming biscuits with berry preserves. Laney pulled her bare feet under her, making her tall enough to reach all the good stuff on the table.

Maybelle left and came back with a pair of high-topped, lace up shoes and four pairs of fuzzy socks. "Our grandson's leftover shoes," she explained. "His feet grow so fast, he was out of them in two months. Socks, too. Let's see if they fit."

She straightened Laney's legs and slipped on the cozy socks. It took two pairs, but the shoes laced up snug and comfortable. Maybelle looked sadly toward Vonnie. "I wish I had more."

Vonnie grinned, good naturedly. "I had one shoe on, but Denny pitched me over his shoulder, and I lost the crutch and fell out'a the shoe."

The explanation brought a smile to Maybelle's face. "Wait. I have an idea."

In a minute she was back with a pair of tall shiny black gum boots. "He out grew these, too. I was thinkin,' girl's feet are generally smaller than boys, and if she put them on with just socks…?"

Vonnie took the high-topped rubber boots and thrust in her foot. "Look! I can get my foot in even with the bandage!"

Maybelle smiled. "That should do you good until you can get shoes. Now, for sock…."

Minnie cut in, "Ma'am, I mean Miss Maybelle, socks we got I'll slip out to the wagon, and I can lay my hand right on 'em. I got'a bring in clothes, too, and get these youngens out'a their nightshirts."

When Minnie returned, Artie and Laney were playing with the grandson's toys, and Vonnie sat at the table clasping both hands around a cup of coffee. Minnie looked at the cup, then at Vonnie. Well, thirteen…? That was almost a grownup, and after what she'd been through….

Mr. Applewhite left and returned. To Denny, "You come by just in time, I'd say. Them horses has started to settle down their shiverin.' Another hour out in this, and I don't know…" He shook his head with concern. "Bein' in good shape, and not left out, they just didn't have the hide tough enough to be sleeted on. Bein' under blankets today and tonight, that'll put 'em right. 'Course, another day, that'd make 'em even better."

"I sure thank you. I don't know what we'd'a done." Denny was finishing the last of his biscuit with berry preserves.

Maybelle again. "I been thinkin'…" and she disappeared momentarily and returned with a coat with a furry collar. "This here coat'a mine. It's old but it's clean and warm. I was thinkin,' the sleeves'd come down over her hands, like, and be warmer. Leastwise, till you got to where you could get her a coat'a the right size. Stand up, honey."

239

Vonnie stood up in the gum boots and held out her arm. The coat enveloped her like a hug, and the furry collar stood up around her ears. The sleeves hung well below her hands. Maybelle studied her, critically, and finally nodded and smiled.

"I figure it'll be better'n a quilt, anyway. Now, that coat you had on, it'll work for the little'n."

It took most of the morning to relate the story, as they kept omitting horrible details, then remembering them. Maybelle listened as she peeled onions for the dinner stew. Her tears were not all from the onions.

Over the bowls of steaming stew, Mr. Applewhite reasoned. "This place where you're headed, you'll likely be farmin' some?"

"Wisht I knew. We're sort'a headed into a blind fog, tryin' to work it out as we go along."

Mr. Applewhite, again. "Leastwise, you'll be needin' to raise a kitchen garden. I'll tell you what. About seeds, I get this thing in my mind, wantin' to save the best seeds each year to plant the next year's crop. Seems I have so many that turn out good, I always save twice more'n I need. Now, if I was to let you look at 'em, there's sure to be some you could use."

Denny, coffee cup in mid-air, was definitely interested.

Mr. Applewhite nodded. "I was figurin,' the way you had to pull out all of a sudden, there'd likely not been time to think on plantin' seeds, much less gather 'em up. Good thing, too, 'cause I got more'n I can use, with just her'n me left."

"Well, sir, I'd be obliged...."

"Don't mention it! Now, I got garden stuff... carrots, peas, radishes and the like, and if I was you, I'd be thinkin' on plantin' oats for them fine horses'a yours. I got a good strain'a oats."

"I'd sure thank you. And I was thinkin', if you had a extra hundred pounds'a oats, or fifty pounds, whatever you weren't gonna need, I'd like to buy it off you."

"Sure, and I got plenty...."

"But I'll want'a buy it. You set the price."

"Well, I...."

"We got a little money. It was just that we didn't have no time, was why the youngens was in nightshirts."

"I understand. Well, if it'd make you feel better, I got likely two, maybe three, extra fifty pound sacks. Dollar each, that'd be three dollars. But now, son, you likely know this, but them horses need to be tied where there's dry grass from last year, if you ain't where they can get hay. Horses don't do too good on oats, alone. Messes up their insides. 'Course, I'm sure you already knew that."

They spent the day and the night with the Applewhite's, and were persuaded to stay over another day to let the wind lay.

Over breakfast, Mr. Applewhite observed. "Weather looks good. 'Course, that don't mean you have to go...."

Minnie intervened. "I reckon we ought to. This storm bein' past, could be we could get to Dardanelle before the next one comes on."

"You got a point, there. So we made up a few things...."

The few things consisted of almost four dozen eggs, (Oh, there'll be more in the nest this evenin'), a half a cured ham, (It'll be good to fill in when you can't make a fire with the wet wood,) and a dozen jars of home canned tomatoes, (Can't hardly make a good soup without 'em.). A huge bowl of fresh butter and a jar of spicy plum butter.

And there was last minute advice.

"I'm figurin' you know this, son, but when you see water over the road, you got'a test the ground to see if it's got a bottom in it. Some places got rock ledges, but some has holes that wash out, and you can't see 'em under standin' water. You'll want'a take care you don't get in there and break a wheel."

"Yes, sir. And I sure thank you."

"Don't mention it. I got three boys and a girl, all grownup and out on their own. There'll be somethin' happen to them sometimes, and I figure the Good Lord'll just have to have someone there ready to help 'em, like I was here for you. So you take care."

After being duly hugged and admonished, Denny turned his team toward the Applewhite's driveway, and Minnie followed after, waving as long as she could see the house. For a while, Vonnie, swathed in the big coat, sat on the buckboard seat, and then she crawled back on the quilts with Artie and Laney.

Minnie watched the backs of the horses and the end flap of the wagon moving along in front of her. Thoughts began to march along. Why were they going on this very long journey to a strange place, likely known only to the Good Lord? Where were their brains?

Dardanelle was three days ahead, and there were numerous small towns dotted along the road. It was certain there would be a place for sale, one that had a house of some sort. With the money they had left, not nearly as much as before the shooting, but enough… Surely, they could….

It was now the first of March, and spring was coming. Grass would be up in two, maybe three, weeks. Early gardens could be planted anytime.

Minnie allowed her body to adapt to the rolling jiggle of the wagon over the gravel road, dipping here and there into the fresh potholes. Barely sixteen, she was, and Denny was almost a year younger. What in the world were they doing, heading into something called Oklahoma territory with three younger children? Were they daft? Or just plain fools!

Nodding, she came to a conclusion. At night camp, wherever that was, she would talk with Denny. Happen they agreed, this journey could be over in a few days.

With that taken care of, she began to plan what would need to be purchased at Dardanelle. Something to make soup. Onions. If she put them in the quilts, she could likely keep them from freezing. Potatoes. No, they were so watery, they'd freeze for sure. The ones she had bought in Little Rock had to be tossed out. Maybe a few potatoes. No, rice would be better. They had all grown up on rice, living down by the river, and it could be cooked in so many ways. It was lighter to haul and didn't freeze. Maybe a hundred pounds of rice. But why buy so much if they were going to stop off soon and buy a place to stay? What was she thinking of?

Denny led the two-wagon caravan along, his mind full of thought. The first of March, it was, and he figured to be at least six weeks on the road. Here he was, not yet sixteen, headed… where? With a girl a few months older and three younger ones? Was he crazy? Or just plain stupid!

Come night camp, he'd just have to talk with Minnie. Likely there'd something else they could do, something safer and easier.

In late afternoon, they came to a small waterway, a tributary to the Arkansas River, flowing along beside them and then under a bridge. The bridge crossing the river was strong and wide, and it extended over a section of marshy land. There was a fair amount of space under the end of the bridge. Denny had been worried about the horses, even though the weather had faired up well.

Testing the space under the bridge, he decided it was a good place for a night camp. Pulling the wagons under, he loosed the horses to feed on the dried grass from last summer. In the protected places, small green shoots were appearing, and the animals worked their rubbery lips around to pull them.

There were dry sticks beneath the bridge, so a fire was soon crackling under the three-legged camp stove. A skillet sizzled as hotcake batter spread out on the hot surface. Sliced ham was rolled up in a steaming pancake to eat with their icy fingers. Then hot tea. They huddled around the fire, pulling their coats tight, and they held shivering fingers around steaming mugs of tea.

Darkness fell early, and the younger ones crawled under the quilts.

"Denny, I been thinkin.'"

"Me, too. Ridin' along lookin' at the backsides'a the horses gives a body a lot'a time to think. What you got on your mind?" Might as well discuss her thoughts before getting into the serious subject of whether they were doing the right thing.

"Denny, it ain't that I don't think we can do it, it's just that I wondered if we ought'a be doin' it. We're actin' like we were grown up, and the truth is, we ain't. And the little'ns…?" Her voice trailed away.

A pause. "Yeah. I been thinkin' the same thoughts. Now we got money, and I don't know what land costs around here, but we'd have enough for somethin.' That'd let us get in a garden, and I could find work at somethin.' We'll have to think on gettin' more money…"

"And school. Laney could maybe start this year."

"Dardanelle? Do you think? From the look of the map, it's a sizeable place."

"Good as any."

"Or maybe a smaller town."

"Could be even better."

"More tea? We can split this last cup?"

"Yeah, thanks."

"Small town, you think?"

"Maybe past Dardanelle. Need to put some space between us and…."

"Yeah… Couldn't hurt none."

"Well, I'll just hobble these horses. Wisht I had a blanket over 'em."

"Really need it?"

"It'd be good."

"Well, we got quilts aplenty. The way I see it, if we got no horses, we'll be in trouble."

"We can spare 'em?"

"Could be we have to, if the horses need 'em. We'll huddle together and make out. I'll sort out the oldest ones we got."

So the horses spent the night decked out in pieced quilts, keeping their body heat on their body. Whether or not it helped the horses, it helped Denny to sleep. Minnie was right. If they had no horses, stolen or otherwise, they were in big trouble.

It was a long night. Damp, cold and long. It was hardly light when Minnie crawled out of the quilts and set a blaze to the sticks. Denny joined her.

"I been thinkin' most'a the night."

"Me, too. What you got on your mind?"

"What to do. I keep thinkin' this way and that, and it'd make sense to stop here, but it's still Arkansas. They could still find us...."

"Do you reckon they're still lookin'?"

"Likely not. Still, there's the pull'a the territory. Seems if we started and don't get where we was started to, and then we fell short...."

"Like we failed? 'Course, it's just ourselves we'd be failin.' Nobody to consider but you and me, and them."

"True. I never learned much about growin' crops. Always figured I'd have somethin' to do with horses. But we got'a eat."

"The flyers say a body has to be 21 to get the land. Gettin' there in time for the run wouldn't be too important for us. Couldn't run anyway."

"No. But it wouldn't hurt, neither."

"If we decide to go on."

"Yeah, we might not go on. Seems it'd be easier not to."

"Likely. 'Course ain't nothin' ever been easy up to now. Reckon we could handle somethin' if it wasn't hard?" It was a weak attempt to speak lightly.

Denny grinned his wide handsome grin. He reached for the part of a mug of tea Minnie handed to him. "You got somethin' there, but right now I'd not mind tacklin' somethin' easy, just to see if I could get the hang of it."

Minnie fried thin suzette pancakes in the big skillet, stacking them tall in a warm plate as the others gathered around. A dozen and a half eggs were cracked into the grease and stirred into mounds of fluffy golden clouds. Rolled up in the thin pancakes, they were quickly gone.

The horses were warm under the blankets and seemed frisky and ready to be on their way.

The next night camp was behind an overhanging bluff, and the one after that in the mouth of a shallow cave. Then it was to be Dardanelle by nightfall.

Nine

Denny had studied the scraps of maps he had. The flyer had been many times folded and was becoming dog-eared. He really needed a new one. It appeared that Dardanelle was four days, maybe five, from the Fort. To be safe, he'd allow a week.

The schedule was still good. He did not consider that they had discussed looking at the small towns with the idea of settling. Somehow, he could not get the territory out of his mind. Even though he found himself sighing a lot.

Back by the river, he had known who he was and what he was doing. His 'day work' at the various farms had been well thought of, and paid for, and he had as many jobs as he had wanted, mostly to do with horses. There, he had been known and respected. Now he must fight with the elements, supplies, indecision, and the needs of four other people.

A storm had passed around them to the south, disturbing their night camp only with a wet wind that swirled over the river and themselves. The tributaries coming toward the Arkansas River from the south had swelled, carrying a load of muddy silt that stained the water brown.

Many low spots in the road had full bar ditches, and a lot of them had spilled over, running brown streams across the road. Most of these were shallow, and the horses hardly hesitated as they plunged on across.

"Git on up there!" he yelled, encouragingly. If he kept his team moving well, Minnie's followed on without a lot of encouragement from her.

Just ahead was another spillover. The horses pulled strongly into the stream of brown water, but reared their heads in surprise as they were pulled up, solidly. As the wagon stopped dead still, Denny yelled again, and the obedient horses leaned into the traces.

A sickening crunch and splintering tear sounded from the right front of the wagon, and the left rear corner began to slowly rise.

"WHOA! WHOA, UP THERE!"

The horses settled back, shaking their harnesses back into place. Looking down, Denny saw the splintered wheel as it settled into a freshly washed out pothole. With a groan, he sat down and settled his face into his open hands. Here he was miles from who-knew-where with a broken wheel and no spare, and even if he had a spare, he had no lift to help get it on. Sick to the pit of his stomach, he removed his shoes and rolled up his pants legs before he stepped into the icy brown water.

Minnie, moving along dreamily, heard the 'WHOA' and echoed her own, pulling back on the lines. The team obediently planted their feet solidly, and waited. Jumping down, she walked to the edge of the rushing water and watched as Denny removed his coat and pulled up his sleeve, running his hand along the axel that extended into the water.

Sloshing to the bank, he faced Minnie. "I done just what I was warned not to do. Mr. Applewhite said to me not to roll into the water without checkin' for holes. I didn't do it. Didn't seem like we had these edges'a ledge stone in the roads, back home. Should'a listened."

After a respectful pause, Minnie wondered. "Somethin' we can do…? That you know of?"

As the final nail that shut out any encouragement, his voice said, "No."

Vonnie, Artie and Laney had jumped down from the wagon and lined themselves up along the brown stream. Denny seemed to lose heart, and sat down on a nearby rock, burying his face in his hands. Minnie stood by, her mind racing. What to do, now?

Denny's muddy feet, red as a spring radish, were planted on the cold winter ground. The edge of his rolled-up overalls was wet, and the breeze whipped his shirtsleeves. He was silent, but Minnie had the impression he was a little boy who had run out of luck and was on the verge of tears.

Do something, Minnie. Hot tea. Might not help, but it couldn't hurt.

"This'd be a good time to make somethin' hot to drink. Artie, set out the stove. Girls, gather some little sticks. Don't get big 'ens, they'll be too waterlogged to burn. Here, Artie, set it up back here, out'a the wind. Vonnie, see if there's live coals in the bucket'a ashes. Good! Bring 'em on."

Scurrying around made her feel better, but Denny still sat with bare feet.

Calling Vonnie aside, she said, "Vonnie, honey, you got them boots, I want you to crawl up in the wagon and get Denny's shoes and coat."

Vonnie, now walking instead of hopping, splashed through the water and climbed into the disabled wagon. Grabbing up the shoes and coats, she sloshed back. Standing by the still-bowed Denny, she looked, questioningly, at Minnie.

Minnie stepped close. "Denny? Catchin' your death'a cold ain't gonna fix the wheel. Put on your coat, will you? And shoes? I've got tea a-fixin' to get your blood a'workin'... Denny?"

"I should'a listened. I did just what he said to not do."

"Yeah. And that bein' the first mistake you ever made, we're plannin' to hold it agin you the rest'a your natural life. The youngens and I, we had a talk, and we decided to go on without you. Who needs you anyway, after you made a mistake?"

The dark eyes raised above the cold, red fingers, and he grinned, somewhat sheepishly. "Wouldn't blame you if you did."

Minnie, sensing victory, called, "Vonnie, check and see if that tea's warm yet. Good! Pour a cup and bring it to your brother. We got plannin' to do."

Denny slipped into his coat and was tying his shoes as Vonnie appeared with the steaming drink. He closed his fingers around the warm cup. "Yeah, we got plannin' to do."

"You want I should go for help?"

"Could be. You could pull around. There wasn't no place in the back of us to get help, so it'd be best to go ahead. Now, I could go, and leave you here... or...?" The decision would be her's.

"Couldn't go on a single horse, could we? We'd be bringin' back a wheel."

"Yeah, and what's worse, we got'a have a lift to get the axel up. That, or unload everything."

"Likely have to go all the way to Dardanelle for that, huh? Couldn't hardly do that and get back here 'afore night."

"And this ain't a real good place for a night camp."

"I'm thinkin' it'd be best you go on."

"And leave you here all alone? We don't know what kind'a folks are around here."

"We could all go. Take all the horses and come back for the wagon."

"Yeah, we could, and they might not be here when we come back. We can't hardly afford to loose a wagon."

So they stood, staring at the tipped wagon, its crushed wheel completely under the brown water. Behind them they heard the sound of hooves, a lone horseman.

"Got troubles, friend?"

The tall man sat astride the horse and looked down at them.

Denny arose to meet him. "Yeah, got a busted wheel."

"Hmmmm. Slipped off the ledge, did ya? Wisht you'd'a' thought to check out for holes. Everybody around here knows about that busted ledge, and they go around it. Too bad you never thought."

"Yeah. Should'a done that."

The man leaped down and sloshed through the water in his high-topped gumboots. Pushing up his sleeve, he ran his hand down the axel. "Some good luck. You didn't bend your axel. All you're gonna need is a wheel."

"Yeah."

"Well, friend, you got another bit'a luck. Down the road a couple'a miles and there's a fellow that's got wheels. Got a lift, too. I could take you on down there, and he'd bring you back in the cart."

"Thanks! I'll take a horse out'a...."

"Naw, leave 'em be. Hop on back'a me. This old fellow ain't had nothin' to do for weeks and he'll be right on out. We'll just get on down there. Your women folks ought'a be safe, leavin' 'em here that long."

Minnie watched them go. There and back, she was looking at two hours at the least, and that was time to get a kettle of beans started. There was the bone and fat from the ham, and a lot of small sticks.

"Everyone bring wood. We got'a get somethin' started for supper."

Midafternoon the cart arrived with the wheel and the man from the livery.

"Buddy, you just stay over there in the dry. I do this all the time, and it wouldn't be no quicker with you a'helpin.'"

Gratefully, Denny sank down onto the flat stone and watched. His mind listed purchases to be made at Dardanelle. Extra wheel, lift, gumboots and . . . well....

Early evening they were on the road. "Could be you'll make it on in, but you'll be bad late. 'Course, it won't be no worse'n stayin here. Looks like rain."

Denny decided to go on.

And the farther they went, the more it looked like rain. Darkness fell but they kept rolling. From a small hill, they could see the lights in the windows in town, and that was when the rain started. For a while, they could hardly see the road, and both drivers were soaked to the skin and numb with the cold.

Then the rain let up long enough for them to see the painted sign at the edge of town. RIVERSIDE LIVERY STABLE. Thanks be to the Good Lord! Denny scooped the rain off his forehead with his icy fingers and squared his shoulders. There HAD to be room for them.

He turned the team off the road and up a driveway that was running full with a sheet of water. Straight under the shed he went, keeping as far to the right as he could to leave room for Minnie. Both wagons were in the dry when a man appeared.

"Two for the night?" the gray-whiskered man greeted.

"Yes, sir. And could we stay in the wagons? We're wet and...."

"Son, I don't really like to do that. It's been a habit'a mine not to let my shed be used as a roomin' house."

Denny's heart sank. "Then could you point us to a place that has rooms to let? I got the missus and little ones, and we're all wet and cold."

The old man stroked his chin. He was not without compassion. "Well.... come to think on it. I got a room right here. Ain't truly big enough for more'n one, but it's dry."

Denny excitedly sought to cinch the deal. "How much, sir?"

"Well, let's see. Don't rightly know, it bein' the room for my summer help, and it stays empty in the winter. I could... maybe... well, let's say two dollars for the night. No, make it a dollar fifty."

"I'll take it."

"Come to think on it, there's a oil stove in there. Ain't much to cook on, but it'll dry ya out."

"How much for the stove?"

"Ah, let's just bring up the price to two dollars and throw in the stove for nothin'."

"Yes, sir. And blankets for the horses?"

"Two bits each. Four of 'em, that'd be a dollar."

When Denny counted out the money, he doubled it. "I need two nights. This is the edge'a Dardanelle, ain't it?"

"Sure is. Ain't but a short walk, time it ain't rainin'."

The room proved to be twelve feet square. It might have seemed small to anyone, except to the travelers who had come in cramped wagons. To them, it seemed spacious, and warm, and the oil stove soon had the room steamy as their soaked clothing dried.

The half-cooked beans bubbled merrily on the tiny stove until they were soft, and, after eating, the travelers wrapped in their individual blankets and stretched out on the floor, thankfully breathing the warm, dry air.

The storm proved to be a usual early-March blow. By morning it was gone, and the sparkling rays of the spring sun glistened on the soaked world with startling brilliance. It was time to go shopping.

The second hand store was the first stop. It was always a good place for children's things, and occasionally other bargains could be had. Coats for the three little ones. Shoes for the girls, socks, that only had holes in the toes, and they could be easily darned.

Toys. A long trip was ahead of them, and small children had to do something with their hands. A tin doll buggy with a bent wheel. Easily straightened. Carved wooden animals... small, hard rubber horses. A rubber baby doll. A book of string games for Vonnie. It came with lengths of colored string, and the directions for making cat's cradle, crow's foot, Jacob's ladder and a dozen other things.

A whistle for Artie. (Come time we get there, I'll get me a puppy and train 'im to come when I blow it.) Sets of dominos with several lost. That didn't matter if they were to be used to build with. Dominos made fences to keep in the wooden animals, built towers and marked out roads.

Sweaters. It was surprising to find late bargains. Then, on to the farm supply store. Spare wheel, lift, boots (Minnie, I think you should have boots, too. Could be you'll need 'em when we get there.) Wherever it is that we get to.

Food supplies. Raisins had become a necessity, not a luxury. They were a cheap, filling dessert. Five boxes. Rice. Fifty pounds. Less than a pound of rice was cooked at a meal, so fifty pounds might be sixty day's worth. That would get them there, wherever it was they ended up. Gallon of molasses, a jug of bee tree honey, and two quarts of red jelly. Cinnamon, odds and ends. More matches.

The store had tall metal cans with a tight lid, one dollar each. Buy four… flour, meal, beans and rice, to keep out the weevils. Minnie circled the store over and over, her mind racing to project into the future to cover unknown needs.

Vonnie. "Minnie, back at the home, they had a medicine that came in a tube. Nurse said it killed germs…."

"Germs…?"

"Bad things that keep sores from healing. Called it zinc oxide ointment. I thought, could be it didn't cost much, and it healed good."

No, the grocer told them. Ointments were over to the drug store. It was fifty cents a tube, but they bought it, anyway. Also a tube of toothache medicine.

First light found them preparing to leave Dardanelle. At breakfast that morning, gathered around the toasty little stove, Denny had commented.

"Could be all kinds of little towns along the way. Couldn't count on livin' at the Fort, but the map shows a place close to it called Van Buren, and that ain't the only place."

Minnie nodded. "We'd want to see for sure they had a school. We got Artie and Laney…."

Denny agreed. "A good school. And the town'd need to be big enough to let me find work."

"Folks everywhere need horses. Could be, you could open a livery…?"

"That'd take time."

"We're young. Reckon we'll likely have all the time we need."

The extra pan of biscuits was turned out of the heavy skillet and wrapped in a tea towel for dinner. Dry clothes were folded away.

The horses were hitched, tossing their heads in their impatience to be on their way. Denny was glad he had paid extra to give them two

251

warm nights. The weather should be good for several days, at least to Fort Smith.

The little wagon caravan rolled through Elkins, Buckeye, Riverside, Morrilton, Carney, and Barling. It amounted to about a town a day, and a lot of miles. The nights were cold, but the wind was mild, and the weather stayed dry. All it took was enough quilts, and they slept warm in the wagons. The animals were protected with the older quilts fastened over them, and the wagons rolled on.

The Arkansas River took a wide turn, and when it was circled, there was the Fort, just ahead. It had post-stockade fences, parade grounds, practice ranges, and a small town beside it. Merchants and family members lived there, and several stores advertised that they could outfit travelers headed to the Oklahoma territory.

Denny, who had rolled through a different town each day for the last eight days, busied his mind thinking what he should get before leaving the Fort, and going into the unknown territory. He had the rifle and the handgun. Another, smaller, rifle would be good. Artie would soon need it, and what about Vonnie? Would there be a reason she should learn to shoot?

Maybe two more guns and a lot of shot. Ammunition weighed a lot, and the wagons were already heavily loaded. It was, however, necessary to have plenty of ammunition. There'd be hunting along the way.

He had more than two hundred miles to go and a month to do it in. The timing should be good, if he had no more bad trouble.

Axel grease. Extra wheel bolts. A hammer and a saw, because there would need to be a house sometime. Nails? Maybe a few. They were also heavy. A shovel and a pick, he already had. And a hoe… What else?

As the miles had passed under the wheels, his mind had sorted over items that had been packed at what seemed like years ago. Much of it had been packed by his pa, and he couldn't be for sure what was down there under the boxes and bedding quilts.

The Fort was noisy and crowded. They camped outside, and walked to the stores. Two guns, ammunition… a few other things. Minnie bought flour, meal, sugar, beans, and dried southern peas. In her mind, she tried to plan for food for three months. As a last thought, she picked up twenty boxes of raisins. You just couldn't have too many of them. And five quarts of peanut butter for energy. And with a sigh, another fifty pounds of rice.

It was the 22nd of March when they turned the horses toward the west. Tiny grass shoots gave a pale green haze to the low rolling hills stretching before them. The morning sun shone with golden spears of light, bouncing and sparkling off the rumps of the horses. The willow and cottonwood trees showed new leaves, and the small fruit bushes were in bud.

Bush cherries, sometimes called sand cherries, lined the road. The blackjack oaks would hold their leaves for another two or three weeks, but early flowers put in their touch of color.

Among the moist leaves in the groves of trees there sprouted mushrooms, their creamy globes sprinkled in drifts. The younger ones jumped from the wagon, gathering them in kettles, then running to catch up. Sautéed in butter, they made a tasty change in the diet.

Denny called to Artie. "Come morning, I want you on the bench along side'a me. Seems like it'd be time for you to learn to drive the team. It's a thing boys do. Girls, they got other things to do."

There was something else boys did. One afternoon, Denny and Artie took the guns into a woodland and brought back a small deer. It took a one-day layover to skin and fry up the meat, and chunks of it were packed in grease in the empty jars from Maybelle's tomatoes. Packed in grease, with the weather still cool, it would keep for weeks.

It seemed strange that there were no more tall mountains, only sloping hills, with small water streams at their base. By the second week in April, the hills had flattened into knolls, and there was a sameness to the landscape.

Patches of heavily wooded lands gave way to bare stretches, evidence of recent forest fires. The road was well marked, but there were only a few travelers. A lone horseman, a detachment of Cavalry Officers on patrol, a wagon camp set back in the trees. They called a greeting, but did not stop. Things were going too well, and there was a schedule to be met.

Night camp came early so the horses could graze on the fresh grass, and food could be cooked. The younger ones ran about, glad to be free of the wheels. Minnie and Denny stayed in the camp, acting like travelers twice their age. There was too much to think about to do otherwise.

On the second week of April, Denny's sixteenth birthday, they reached the mouth of the Deep Fork and were fortunate to find a ferry barge to get them across. Now, they had only to follow the Deep Fork, and it would bring them to the upper side of the Unassigned Lands.

The clear streams of Arkansas were no more. The water of the Deep Fork was murky, and when Minnie boiled it, silt settled out on the bottom of the kettle. She took to drawing their water late in the evening, and letting it settle until morning, before filling their water barrels.

On the nineteenth of April, the trail took them into a sizeable camp of wagons, buggies and lone horsemen. They had finally reached the territory, and these travelers were waiting for the day of the run. Camping at the edge of the group, they loosed the horses and Denny took them to the grass.

After darkness had settled, and the younger ones were asleep, Denny sat leaning against a tree, watching the fireflies draw golden lines on the dark sky. Night birds whistled in the trees, and small animals watched from the shrubby bushes, their eyes glowing as they reflected the lantern light.

"Minnie?"

"Yeah?"

"Seems we didn't never find the right little town to stop over in."

"Yeah. Times I wonder, did we do the right thing? We rolled into the towns, and we rolled out. Seemed like there was a rope, invisible like, pullin' on us to keep us movin.' I was knowin' we was thinkin' on stoppin' and still I bought a fifty pound sack'a rice, and then another one. Didn't make a lot'a sense, did it?"

"Hard to say. I been thinkin'. We been spendin' a lot' a money. I know we had to get things, and we lost some back in the home that was in the coats. I was wonderin,' do you know how much we got left?"

"Pretty close, but we can count it. There's light from the lantern, and we're a fair distance from the others."

Moving the lantern to a sheltered place, Minnie consulted her notes on hidden money they still had. Emptying her purse, she placed the bills and coins in a pile. Denny added his. Their reckoning came to one hundred twenty seven dollars and some change, and that was all. Where had it all gone?

Repairs? Overnight lodging? Clothes? Supplies? They hadn't bought a thing they weren't sure they'd need, except the little bit spent on toys in Dardanelle.

Minnie, seeing Denny's expression droop, suggested cheerily. "We don't know that it won't be enough. What else we got'a buy?"

"Land."

"What'll it cost?"

"Ain't no knowin.' Wisht I could make a run for it, but neither one of us could sign if I got it. Sure would like to be twenty one years old, right now."

"How far is it on to Guthrie? In a town, we could work, and maybe earn... something?"

"Yeah, and that'd be the best thing. It's been in my mind. We can't get free land, but we can buy, if we have the money. But I'm thinkin,' we can't get there before the run, on account'a that Cavalry officer won't let us in. We'll just settle back here and see what happens. These folks'll all get on out'a the way, and then we can make better plans."

With more confidence than she felt, Minnie agreed. "Sure we can."

"We're lucky to still have a lot'a food. Huntin' along the way helped to stretch it out. Stewed squirrel with rice and wild onions, that just hit the spot. And I see squirrels a'plenty all around here."

"We'll likely need 'em. Nuther thing, Denny. I been thinkin.' and I want a different name."

"Different name? What're you talkin' about?"

"Minnie... that's what I'm takin' about. That was my "little girl" name, and I'm not a little girl no more. My name's Isabelle."

"Hmmm. Isabelle." He tilted his head, surveying her critically. "Suits you. To my mind, you look more like Isabelle than Minnie. I'll match you. I'll be Dennis. Sounds more manly, don't it?"

With a grin, they shook hands on it.

Dennis went to tend the horses, taking Artie. Vonnie and Laney were with some of the other girls of the camp. Isabelle sat down on the wagon tongue and watched the bank of clouds pile up in the west. The evening sun was bright behind them, and each scallop of cloud was ringed with a band of shining light.

It made a beautiful picture, but Isabelle was not impressed. People could talk about silver linings all they wanted to, but if what they say was true, she was ready to turn a few of them clouds wrong side out. Things seemed a bit dull from where she sat, and she could use a little brightness.

On the evening of the 21st, a party was held around a roaring bonfire and everyone brought an offering to add to the celebration dinner. Isabelle took the peanut butter oatmeal cookies from her food box and added them to the other deserts. Everyone laughed and talked and ate and the children played, and then it was over. Much too soon, it was all over.

Ten

The morning of the 22nd of April, people seemed to gather in from everywhere. Horsemen, wagons and buggies were five to ten deep all along the line, and the two Cavalry officers paced constantly.

Near noon, the line formed in earnest. Those in the run sat on nervous horses and held their reins with sweaty hands, while those being left behind waited to cheer them on

The Officer stopped, and the crowd was instantly silent.

"Now you will listen for my gun. You will hear several gun reports, but you will not move until you hear MY gun." His voice was loud and firm with authority.

Then, in the distance, a faint shot was heard. Then a louder one, another, and finally a shot sounded that seemed only a few hundred feet away. It echoed into the trees, and all eyes were on the uplifted arm of the Corporal.

The sound of the near shot had hardly died away, when there was a wisp of smoke and a BANG! And the Corporal shouted, "GO!"

Yells and cheers rang out, echoing and rebounding along the Deep Fork River. Scrambling hooves dug into the stomped-on dirt, sending dust clouds into the waiting crowd. Pounding across the line in wave after wave, they fanned out and disappeared into the trees. What a thrilling sight!

Dennis watched with a mixture of excitement and sadness. If only he could have been a part of it…! But all he could do was settle down and wait.

By two o'clock they began coming back, excited and hurrying, trying to get their families onto their land, so they could head into Guthrie to file their claims. One by one, the wagons left.

By six o'clock, the disappointed ones began to return. One horse had broken a leg in a gopher hole and had to be put down. Its rider came limping back carrying the saddle, his dusty face streaked with what must have been bitter tears.

Another, and another, until there were seven families in the camp on the Deep Fork. In one of the wagons, a woman (girl?) was in the last stages of pregnancy. Several of the women had gathered around, wanting to help if they could, but the girl was so frightened, she could only scream when anyone approached.

Isabelle would have gone, but she felt she had nothing to offer, and if the older women were turned away, what would the girl do to her? Still, she watched, fascinated by the drama. What else was there to do?

In the late afternoon, the girl's man came back, disappointed. He spent a few minutes with his wife and disappeared again, practically leaving her screaming. How could he do such a thing? Isabelle was just trying to gather enough courage to approach the wagon when the man returned.

Hurriedly, he hitched a team to the wagon and looked around. As if on second thought, he shouted, "Could be I got good news. I heard tell of a town goin' up, four miles over. I checked it out, and it's true. They likely got building lots for sale."

Someone shouted, "How much?"

He shouted back, "Fifty dollars for five acres, and it's got a well."

"Fifty dollars? For only five acres?"

Dennis was hurrying toward the man. "They sure enough got tracts for sale?"

"They think so. They'll have a church and a school for my baby, and I'm on my way. Anybody that wants to, come on and follow me. Worse that can happen, is you have a place to camp for the night."

Dennis turned on his heels. "Artie, go bring up the horses, one at time. Minnie… I mean Isabelle, what'd'ya think?"

The response was immediate. "Let's hurry. Could be the best land we can afford. I'll sure like havin' a well."

Eleven

The sun was down, and the trails were shaded as they hurried with the hitching. One of the waiting wagons pulled in after the man, and Dennis was next in line. Isabelle was close behind. They pulled into a tree-studded lane, just as darkness fell. Lanterns greeted them, and a woman told them to make themselves at home, and then she climbed into the wagon with the screaming girl. Then another person came.

Isabelle walked part way toward the wagon before deciding they had help enough, likely better than she could give, so she stood in the shadows with the other women.

It seemed the baby was not quite ready to be born, so the woman told them all to find a place to camp, and she'd talk to them in the morning.

Suddenly, Isabelle felt festive. Hanging a lantern on a low limb, she rooted her hand around in the food box and came up with a small box of lemon drops.

"Gonna celebrate," she announced. "This is a party! There's five lemon drops apiece. Dennis, let's get that money ready, and be first to pay for our land."

Dennis grinned and nodded. "The man said it didn't have to be paid all at once."

Isabelle nodded. "I know. But ours will be. I don't want nothin' sayin' we don't get it, and if it's all paid, then nothin' can happen. That still leaves us $77.00, and that'll be enough. I'll really be glad for a well."

Before morning, sounds were very clear that the baby had arrived. Good! A few smiles and a bit of relief came at a good time!

Within days they were settled on their own tract. It was hardly an eighth of a mile from the place where a school and a church would be built. Five acres. At first, it seemed a bit small, but there was room for the horses, it had trees, there was space for a garden, and all they needed now was a house. Some kind of a house.

The town even had a name, Prosper.

Twelve

Then it was late on a Saturday afternoon a green wagon rolled by pulled by weary horses. Two young men slumped on the buckboard seat as it moved on past. The wagon was painted green, and on its side, white painted letters proclaimed KENDALL BROTHERS We Haul.

Hmmmmm. Dennis watched until it was out of sight. Dray Wagons? Way out here? And they said Guthrie was fourteen miles away.

There was a lot of excitement in the town when the most of the residents got there from where they came from up north. It seemed certain ones were sent on ahead to run for the land, and the rest of the town would follow. Thirty-five wagons appeared in the dusky dark and settled down for the night. The morning saw them spreading out and claiming their lots.

A sawmill was set up a mile to the west, and orders were taken for lumber, but the demand was so great, they could only get enough for an outhouse and a covered pavilion until everyone had some.

Dennis was going to make the trip to the sawmill to put their name on the list, but that night they were visited by two young men.

"Howdy, neighbors?" he greeted.

"Howdy. Thought we'd stop in. We live a quarter of a mile over." A hand was extended. "Kendall Brothers. I'm Chet and he's Manny."

"Dennis Baldwin. Glad to know you. You drive the green wagon."

"Sure do. You got a good lookin' wagon here. Good horses, too."

"Well, I...."

"What we come to say was...."

Before the evening was past, Dennis had agreed to go to Guthrie and haul freight under the name of KENDALL BROTHERS We Haul. It seemed the Santa Fe Railroad had merchandise coming in faster than it could be delivered. The Kendall Brothers had what might be called a contract to do the hauling, but they could really use another wagon. Their own three were not enough to deliver the goods ordered by the people of Guthrie.

They told him, "Could be the job'll only last the summer. 'Course, it could be longer. Depends on how things go. We thought'a you and on account'a your good wagon and team, and the way most of us come in lookin' for a way to make a bit'a money. The work's long and hard, and we get so tired we think we're gonna die, but the pay's good, and we needed that. You think about it, and let us know...."

"I done thought. I'll be ready. I'm needin' to work when I can."

"You ain't needin' to talk to your missus, first...?"

"My...? Oh, that's my cousin. Her name's Isabelle. Isabelle Crowley." The name sounded strange on his tongue, but he'd have to get used to it.

"Well, we'll see you later... Dennis."

"So long, and thanks."

He watched as the two fellows walked wearily away. "Hey, Minnie... I mean, Isabelle, I got a job!"

Isabelle's eyes lit up. "You did? Well... that'll be an answer!"

But after Dennis pulled out late Sunday afternoon, following after the green painted wagon, Isabelle remembered the sawmill and the necessity for getting one's name on the list. ,Dennis would not be back for five, maybe six, days. Couldn't wait that long.

Leaving the girls rubbing the washing in the big tub, she took Artie and headed west. Over a mile, they had said. Well, that was nothing, and it was such a lovely day. The May sun shone warmly, and small colorful flowers popped out all along the way.

After walking a half a mile, it was simple to determine which way to go. At intervals, a screech and a tearing grind rent the airwaves. Another tearing grind, then silence, and another grind. Artie pulled her forward eagerly.

At the edge of the clearing she stopped. Several young men worked around and over the logs, pulling them this way and that, hitching the horses to the large ones, pulling them up to the whirling saw and stacking the fresh, cream colored boards into piles. The whole woodland smelled of fresh sap.

Isabelle held to Artie's overall strap to keep him from running into the midst of the confusion. After the walk and the warmth of the day, she pushed her bonnet back, mopping her sleeve across her face.

She stood in a shaft of sunlight, her dress of pale green with white dots seeming cool in the shadows. Her light skin was rosy from the walk. She paused, watching the activity, deciding what to do next.

Andrew Green had just begun to work at the sawmill. It would be good to earn a bit of hard cash so he would be able to expand the horse training operation he managed with his pa. Breaking colts was a hard job, but not nearly so hard as rolling logs onto the platform, removing the slab sides and stacking them. Then, finally, measuring and dividing the dimension lumber.

He stood and flexed his aching shoulders, massaging his lower back. In stretching his neck, he looked around at the perimeter of trees, and at the stack of logs yet to saw. He swiped his sleeve over his perspiring forehead.

He saw a girl standing in the trees. Mirage, no doubt. He blinked his eyes and rubbed them, but the girl was still there. It was a certain sign that he had been working too hard. Clearly, his weary mind was only conjuring up images that he would like to see.

For his whole nineteen years of life, he had lived in the Oklahoma territory, hardly seeing a girl from one month's end to the next, except for his sisters. Then, suddenly, a town moved in only a few miles from him, and there were girls who lived there. If he walked down the section lines cut by surveyors, he could see them here and there, doing this and that. Real girls!

Some of them were married, but others were not, according to his friend who had come with the town as a driver and had decided to stay. The fellow, Dave, had told him there were a lot of single girls, mostly fourteen to sixteen as they usually married fairly soon after sixteen.

He had brought Dave home with him, and the fellow had fallen instantly in love with his sister, Mary Elizabeth, called Liz. Dave had told him about several of the girls, but they were very busy settling in, and so was he, with the sawmill on ten hour shifts. And now?

This very minute he had been thinking and planning how he could meet these girls. Clearly, his bleary, sawdust-grainy eyes were making up visions of girls, and his mind was believing they were real. Why would a girl be standing in the woods?

The fascinating mirage still held. This girl, now, was still dressed in cool green and half hidden in the shadows. She was very light skinned, and her red hair was piled on her head. A shaft of the May sunshine shot the red curls with a halo of glistening gold. One hand held to the overall strap of an active boy.

Well, if Andrew's mind was going to conjure up a vision, it did a good job, but why the boy? It was Andrew's vision. So why were his eyes seeing the boy? Could it be... hers?

Laying down his log tool, he walked toward her. It would be interesting to see at which point she would disappear into thin air. A step, another, then more steps.... Red hair. Dave had told him about Ellie Gunther and her red hair, and she was admittedly one of the prettiest girls in the town by common vote. Andrew had seen her at a distance. This girl did not look like Ellie, and besides, Ellie's mother had already put their family on the lumber list, so why would she be here?

Twenty feet away from her, he could still see her. What's more, she came toward him. If she was real, he should speak. Speak, Andrew, he commanded himself.

"Help you, Miss?"

"I hope so. I need to talk to someone about the list."

"List?"

"For lumber. I need some."

"Sure. I can help. You're… with the town?"

"Hmmmm, maybe. Anyway, I bought a tract."

All right, Andrew complemented himself. So far, so good. "Wonderful! How many in your family?"

"Uh, five."

"Parents?"

"No. Just me and Dennis Baldwin, and his younger brother and sisters."

"You and Dennis are… married?" Might as well be brave and find out, right off.

Her lovely green eyes clouded as she looked into his face. Thinking fast, she responded, "We got'a be married to get lumber?" If so, she could be very convincing as she still wore the ring, and she twisted it on her finger. The movement was not lost on Andrew.

Andrew sighed. "No, ma'am. You don't have to be married. Anyone can get on the list. Your name?"

"Isabelle Crowley, or Dennis Baldwin?"

All right, what did they have going on, here? "It's none of my business, ma'am, but this Dennis, he's…?"

"Workin.' Went to Guthrie with the Kendall Brothers to do haulin.'" She bit her lip apologetically. "Wasn't no one to come down here but me. I didn't think there'd be no trouble. We done had enough of that, getting' out'a Arkansas, and losin' pa."

"Pa? Your pa?" Andrew was determined to get to the bottom of this.

"Oh, no! Dennis, my cousin, it was his pa!"

"And mine!" put in the boy, straining at her grasp.

Ah, that was better. "You and this Dennis, you're… cousins?"

"Well, more like brother and sister. His folks raised me."

Andrew had been at least ten minutes talking to the girl, and she had not disappeared. That could be taken as a sign that she was actually real. His eyes saw but his mind had difficulty in comprehending.

"HEY, ANDREW! You got trouble?"

"NOPE!" he called back. "Just another customer." To the girl. "I'll put you down. Miss Isabelle Crowley? I can't say right off when you'll get the lumber, but…."

SAY SOMETHING ELSE, Andrew demanded of himself. You'll not get a better chance than this. His brain raked over every idea he ever had about girls, which was not very many.

"Uh, I could come by after work and let you know more about it. Which… Uh… tract do you have…?"

"Across from the school, eighth of a mile east. But you don't have to. I know I have to wait."

A call came from the sawmill. "Hey, Andrew! Come on with the logs!"

"I got a go. I'll be there. Maybe late, but I'll be there."

Trotting toward his work, he glanced back. The vision was still there. Ellie Gunther might be considered pretty, and certainly she was, but this one…! Such bright curls bobbing about on her head and eyes that seemed to pick up the cool green of the new spring leaves.

And he, the shy Andrew, had actually worked out a way to see her again!

Pulling Artie away from the fascination of the noisy machinery, Isabelle headed back to the town, her mission successfully completed. Andrew, he said his name was. Big, tall, and strong, with his weathered skin and dark, deep set eyes reminded her of Denny… no, make that Dennis. Eyes that were dark and thoughtful. And interested. In her?

That evening, he came. It was almost dark, and she was just straightening up the camp, ready to get the younger ones in bed. It seemed strange greeting someone without Dennis to take the lead.

"You know, Isabelle, I got a sister that looks to be about your age." He had reasoned that he couldn't stretch the lumber purchase into another visit to her, but if he brought Liz into it…? And Liz was just suffering to get acquainted with the girls in the town.

Isabelle volunteered, "I'm sixteen."

"So is she. Could I tell her about you, and maybe…? She comes to town sometimes, to talk with the school teacher."

"I'd like it. I don't have too much time, but I'd make some time to have a friend. A friend'd be nice. I don't think I hardly had one since my aunt died."

Andrew went home, whistling and light hearted, his weariness having mysteriously evaporated. Working this out should be like putting the last piece of the puzzle in place for himself and Liz, both. Before the land run, his sister had begun referring to herself as 'Liz, the lonely,' so this should work out well.

Dave Hill continued to come to Andrew's house, but he didn't need Andrew anymore. It was Liz he came to see, releasing Andrew to find things to do for Isabelle, who, with Dennis gone, was without a handy man around.

What a gift had fallen into his lap! There were the animals to take care of… the two bay mares, in perfect condition even after a trip of several hundred miles.

"Isabelle, could be you won't be needin' the horses for a while, and they could run in our pasture. It's fenced, and everything, and they'd be no trouble."

"Thanks for the offer. 'Course I'd have to wait and see what Dennis thinks. They're his, too."

And Artie had advised him, proudly. "My brother, he knows all there is to know about horses, and he's tellin' it to me. I'm gonna grow up to take care'a horses, just like he's gonna."

"Your brother, does he break horses?"

The boy's dark eyes were horrified. "Oh, no! He wouldn't never hurt a horse. He feeds 'em and takes care of 'em."

Idea! Say, it wouldn't hurt to make friends with this youngen…. obviously Isabelle was very fond of him. That would be another way to tie this vision of loveliness to himself. "I have a lot of horses. You'll have to come out to my house sometime and see my horses."

"I can come, now!"

"Well, maybe Sunday. You'll need to ask Isabelle, of course."

His "sister" smiled and nodded.

It was a busy summer for Isabelle, what with gardening and keeping everyone fed. Also for Dennis, gone for six days at a time and worrying about how Isabelle was managing. It was even hectic for Andrew, working ten hour shifts at the sawmill, thinking about how he could manage see more of Isabelle.

And Liz was as busy as anyone. A lot of her time was spent at Miss Sadie's house. The retired schoolteacher was preparing Liz to take the test for a teaching certificate, to be ready when the new school was built. With studying and all, being available when Dave (also working ten hour days) came to call, and spending time with Isabelle, it cut severely into her time.

Isabelle's lumber allotment came, and Andrew spent a Sunday, and, with Dennis helping, built a roofed pavilion, fourteen by sixteen, outfitting it with canvas walls until more lumber could be had. At least it was dry when it rained, and a lot more convenient than the covered wagons.

In the fall, Liz would start teaching the beginners at the school, and Laney would get to go. Later, other grades would be added. When the lumber allotments were available, Andrew left the sawmill and began to build buildings. Outhouses, sheds or whatever the owner wanted done.

By September, there was lumber for the school. Andrew and his pa worked every day on the schoolhouse with others coming when they had a minute. Girls came. The school was important to everyone, and there was a job for everyone. Bark must be stripped from the logs. Lots of work for anyone who could spare a minute and come.

Andrew's strong arm pulled the saw back and forth, cutting the boards to the correct length. He kept his eye on the cutting mark, difficult as it was to keep from looking around. A lot of volunteers were there, and among them were a lot of girls.

As Andrew worked, Caroline Kendall, almost fifteen, was interested in the scenery he created as his saw spit streams of sawdust with each thrust of his arm.

Gwendolyn Martin noticed the way his eyes, shoebutton black, crinkled in his face when he happened to smile in her direction. His dark skin was fascinating, and Gwendolyn was fifteen already. Clearly it was time to start looking around.

When she could spare the time, Isabelle was also at the schoolhouse. She watched Andrew's strong arms as he lifted the planks into place, holding them with one hand while the other pounded in the nails. Isabelle was almost seventeen, now, and a strong man was an attraction. If he happened to look the way Andrew looked, well... it was clearly time to do some serious thinking.

Thoughts such as she was having had their own problems. The young men in the town looked at her, and did not turn their eyes away, as men had done when she was younger... except for Harley. The thought of him sent shivers up her arms.

Isabelle watched Andrew working around her land, doing little things for her, and her feelings began to nag at her. She shouldn't be letting him do these things, because they entitled him to sit with her, and she could tell he was liking her more and more. A part of her was glad, but a part of her was very tense. What she didn't want more of was TROUBLE.

She thought about it at night, trying to sleep in the canvas-sided room with night birds and cicada crickets playing a symphony around her. And she dreamed.

She was a little girl, likely no older than Laney, and she was snugged in her bed in the back bedroom. She had been asleep, but the loud shouting aroused her.

Slipping down from the bed, she had padded in silent bare feet to the kitchen door and had stopped in horror. Harley was hitting Aunt Addie, and she was begging him to stop. She tried to get away, but he pulled her to him again. Finally, she quit crying, and slumped down to the floor.

For a minute, Harley stood looking at her, then took a dipper of water from the bucket and poured it on Aunt Addie's face. Little Minnie saw the drops, silver in the lamplight, as they splattered over the kitchen floor.

Harley had stared for a minute, then stomped off to bed. Little Minnie had wanted to run to her aunt, but her feet seemed nailed to the floor. She stood and stared, and finally Aunt Addie managed to sit up, and then she drew herself up to the table where she sat for a long time. Still, Minnie could not run to her, but stood in the darkness of the doorway.

A long time later, Aunt Addie stood up, and holding to the table and the walls, went into the room where Harley was.

Words welled up in Minnie's throat and she wanted to yell, "No! No! Don't go in there!" She didn't yell, though, because her throat was tight and dry.

An owl screeched in a nearby tree, and Isabelle woke herself up trying to say, "No! No!" Then she lay in the dark until morning, thinking. In her heart, she knew she had not only had a dream, she had actually re-lived what had really happened.

To little Minnie, the whole scene had been too horrible to allow herself to remember it. But now, the sixteen-year-old Isabelle remembered it in every clear and horrible detail.

There must have been a time when Harley loved Aunt Addie and was good to her. While they were courting, maybe… and at that time he likely did things to please her. She wouldn't have married him if he had been mean to her. So people change. And men change. How was it possible to know if a fellow was really what he seemed to be, or if he might change?

Andrew came, and he put up a clothesline with wire he brought from the farm, he put a curb around her well and a pulley overhead to make water easier to draw. He took the horses to his place, so they were no longer a concern to her, and he trimmed the low branches of some of the trees she wanted to keep, and he cut firewood from the limbs he removed.

He heard her say she liked chickens and didn't get enough eggs, so one day he came with two dozen baby chicks he had ordered, and Dennis had brought them out from the Santa Fe Depot. He had used an evening to make a pen so the foxes wouldn't get them. He had gone on home, so tired he could hardly walk. He certainly wasn't afraid of work.

He used his Sunday afternoons doing this and that and even took Artie to his place to let him pretend to help with the horses. Artie missed having Dennis around, and it was good for him to be with Andrew, wasn't it? But why would Andrew do it? Andrew didn't do that kind of thing for other nine-year-old boys. Likely the other boys would have had as much fun as Artie.

And what had brought on that strange dream?

As light broke in the east, Isabelle crawled from the bed and sighed from the weariness caused by thinking. She needed to find the strength to tell Andrew to quit coming, but, in spite of herself, she had begun to look forward to Sunday afternoons. Dennis always left early with the Kendall Brothers in order to be ready for work on Monday, and an evening with Andrew was pleasant… even fun, but it had to go. His coming could only lead to one thing, and that was too scary to think about.

Laney had started to school and talked constantly of "Miss Mary Elizabeth," as she was instructed to address Liz. The little girl sat under the trees or in the evening lantern light, marking on her slate with her chalk.

ABCDEFGHIJKLMNOPQRSTVWXYZ. It was a hard thing to get them all on her slate, but she managed. Occasionally upsidedown or sideways. Then, with a swipe of her cloth, they were gone, so she could write them again. Then she wrote small words, her wobbly letters forming what she had learned that day.

Sometimes Liz stopped by Isabelle's place for a few minutes, always heaping praise on Laney. "Never saw a youngen work so hard! Others get through with their work and go out to play, but that Laney, she wants more work! Miss Sadie said there were youngens like that, and that was one thing that made it such fun to teach school!"

And then Liz became serious. "Isabelle, it ain't none of my business, and you can tell me so, but I got'a ask. There was a time back in the summer I was thinkin' you liked my brother, and it seemed fun to think that maybe our children would be cousins. Course, I know things change, and you know what you want, but it don't seem like Andrew knows what he did to you that was wrong."

Isabelle swallowed hard. What could she say? She shook her head and silently buried her face in her hands.

Liz was apologetic. "Oh, I'm sorry! I didn't mean nothin.' It ain't none of my business. I think I said somethin' wrong, and I'm sorry, and I'll go away."

She waited a minute, and when Isabelle did not respond, Liz walked away, sorting over the words she had said. What had she said that was wrong?

When Isabelle realized Liz had gone, the tears began again. She wanted friends so badly, and now she had turned away Andrew, and even Liz. As she went about her chores, the matter weighed heavier and heavier on her mind. Liz really deserved an answer, but Isabelle did not know what to tell her.

It was in the early fall that Dennis told Isabelle, "I made arrangements for Andrew to help me to box in a cabin now that the lumber's come in. He's got trees on his farm that's got'a come down, and that'll make us three rooms, usin' partly boards and partly logs. I'll be takin' off a week to get it done."

"A week? And Andrew…?"

"Yeah, well, I don't know how to do it by myself, and he offered. I was glad enough to take 'im up on it. Then we'd be in the dry by winter. And warm."

The logs appeared, and the bark was skinned away with the drawknife. They were notched and fitted and pulled into place. The lumber was used for the floor and the roof, and Dennis brought home glass windowpanes. A real house!

Andrew certainly was handy about doing things. Seemed there wasn't hardly a thing he couldn't do. He came and worked with Dennis, she served them dinner, and he was polite… and thanked her, but that was all. He didn't say anything that didn't have to be said, and it gave Isabelle a sadness that seemed to pull her apart. Like a balloon set adrift. The balloon, when it left her fingers, was suddenly too high to retrieve, and it floated away on the nothingness of air. Fighting against the feeling of utter helplessness had made her continuously tired.

Then when she finally got to bed, she couldn't sleep, and lay on the quilts twisting this way and that. When at last she slept, the dreams came. On a Saturday night, she had fallen exhausted into her bed.

It seemed she had made up with Andrew, somehow, and they were riding together in his buggy. Darkness came, and they were hurrying home. It had been a wonderful day, laughing and light, and she sat contentedly as darkness fell around them. Then it was necessary to light the buggy lanterns, and Andrew had halted the horses while he lit their wicks and hung them on the hooks. He climbed into the buggy and turned to smile at her.

His face seemed different. His dark eyes turned to look at her. In the dimness of the buggy, they seemed strange, though familiar. Deep set and dark, heavily fringed lashes… so like Dennis' eyes… and something else. What was it? She turned to look him full in the face, and it was not Andrew beside her at all. It was Harley! The eyes had the deep, dark look that had been so frightening to her as a child! What had happened? How had she allowed herself to be alone with Harley?

As he reached toward her, she huddled into the corner of the buggy. He slid closer and with a quick twist, she squirmed away from his reach and leaped from the buggy into the darkness. Instead of touching the ground with her feet, she fell… and fell… and fell! Her own scream woke her.

In minutes, Dennis was in the room. "Isabelle! What is it?"

By the time he managed to light the lamp, she was sitting up in the bed, trembling and drenched with perspiration. Only a dream. The nightmare called Harley was gone, except in her own mind. There, he was very real.

"I'm sorry, Dennis. It was just a nightmare."

"Yeah, but what'd cause a nightmare? I'd'a thought you should'a had them while you had canvas walls. You got solid, hard, log walls, now, and doors you can close. No snakes or coons can get in."

"I know. I guess maybe…? Oh, I don't know!"

"You workin' too hard? I was thinkin' I'd be through by now, but the orderin' just keeps on. Looks like I could be workin' all winter, and it's such good money. But leavin' you with the youngens… here…?"

"I'm fine. Really, I am. It's just…." She hesitated. There was no way she could tell him the dream. It was his pa, and Dennis had already suffered enough for that. And Andrew. Dennis could never understand about him, either, and in addition to being a friend, Dennis needed Andrew. There were a lot of things Dennis had never done, and he needed help.

And Artie. Andrew seemed to like him, and Artie needed a man to be around, with Dennis gone so much.

And Liz. After that strange afternoon, Liz had not stopped by to talk. She smiled and waved from a distance and spoke when it was necessary, but it was certainly not the same. Isabelle's whole life seemed to be wrapped around this family, and the wrapping seemed to be falling apart.

Dennis still stood in the room, his shadow, made by the lamp, was tall on the wall. He waited, with a concerned frown on his forehead. His eyes were dark and deep-set, and he had developed the same jaw line as Harley. She had not noticed it, but the dim lamplight had brought it out, just as had the lantern in the dream.

Watching the concern in Dennis' face, she saw the difference. Only his features looked like his pa, and he couldn't help that. Dennis had always been her buddy… her brother, and that had not changed. She must somehow convince herself that Harley was gone.

"I'm sorry, Dennis. It just happened. I can go to sleep now, and…" Her words trailed away, but he waited for her to finish, "… and thanks for caring."

'Of course I care. I care a lot. Good night, then." He blew out the lamp and left, and Isabelle was alone with her thoughts. She had seen Harley buried in Little Rock. Now, she must find a way to bury him out of her mind. Why should the very thought of him cost her such a high price?

And she missed Liz. It was so interesting to have her drop by and talk about her day, and tell funny things that had happened. If she went to Liz and said… what? There'd still have to be an answer to the question Liz had asked. It was not fair that Liz should not know.

So the next day when it was time for school to be out, Isabelle put on a clean apron and a bonnet and tossed her shawl over her shoulder. She reached the school as the bell began to ring, and stood aside as the children spilled, shouting and laughing, through the door. Last to leave was Liz, with Laney holding possessively to her skirt.

Liz stopped short when she saw Isabelle.

"Liz…?"

Liz responded, "Good to see you, Isabelle."

"I was wonderin', could you…? Do you have time to stop by a while?"

"Well, I… sure I could."

They walked the short distance to Isabelle's house, with Laney walking between them, chattering about this and that. There was hot water for tea, and the cups were set out on the board that served as a table. She and Dennis had been reluctant to buy any furniture that was not absolutely necessary until they had made a winter and could see how the money lasted.

Liz, first. "How've you been?"

Isabelle sighed. She had decided she would be honest. "Up and down. Seems mostly down."

"Is there… could I help? Not wantin' to be nosey, nor nothin.'"

"Oh, you're not bein' nosey. Laney, honey, I want you to run outside and help Vonnie pull the late turnips."

Then Laney was gone, and Isabelle poured the water in the teacups. "A long time ago you asked me a question, and I couldn't answer it. Well, I…."

"Oh, Isabelle! You don't owe me no answer."

"Yes, I do. You're a friend, and you got the right to know. First, though, I got'a say some other things. I told you my aunt and uncle raised me. That's the truth, but there's Harley. That's the man that's pa to Dennis and the others, he was… well, there's not no good way to say it. He was a mean man. He never did act like a pa to his youngens, and he was mean to my Aunt Addie."

"Mean? Like…?'

Isabelle nodded. "Like hittin' and yellin.'"

"To his wife?" Liz asked, unbelieving of what she heard. "Why'd he do that?"

"Just mean, I guess. Well, I just found out more things he did."

"Just found out? I though he was dead!"

"He is, but he's still doin' things, in my mind. He was mean to my aunt, and I was so little, I didn't want to believe she was bein' hurt, so I forgot it. Now, in dreams and things, I start rememberin.' It's been forgot all these years, but I know it's true."

"Hmmm, well… What can you do?"

"I don't know. I say to myself I got'a find a way to bury him, 'cause I know he's dead. But there's more. I keep wonderin' what made him that way, and when did he start out bein' bad. It seems my aunt wouldn't'a married him if he was always that way, so that means he must'a changed. Does a fellow change from good to bad? That's what I wonder."

Liz sipped the tea and considered the problem. "I don't think so, Isabelle. I think he must'a been that way all the time, only hidin' it at first. Could be your aunt wanted to love him and didn't want to know how bad he was."

"I don't see how she could'a done that."

"Me, neither, but I can't see no other way. Now, my ma and pa, they picked each other because there weren't very many people that lived here when they were young. If there'd been others around, they might'a still picked each other. I don't know what makes people pick one person, and not another."

The door opened, and Vonnie called, "You want'a see these, Isabelle, or shall we put 'em in the root cellar right now?"

"You go ahead. Wash 'em first, though."

"Already did." And the door closed, leaving Liz and Isabelle alone.

Liz, again. "I looked around the town, at all the pretty girls that lived here, and Dave saw 'em, too. Still, he picked me to spend time with."

"But you picked him, too. You like him, don't you?"

Liz nodded, "Sure do. You know, Miss Sadie told me when she was young, a school teacher couldn't get married. She says it might be that way here, later on, but she said I was lucky no one in Prosper cares."

"You're getting' married?"

"Maybe. We're talkin' about it. Dave thinks… well, I don't want to do nothin,' till the school year is over. But we were talkin' about it."

"Liz, you like Dave, but what if he changes?"

"Why'd he change?"

"I don't know. Could be that some do."

"Nobody I know. Isabelle, are you thinkin' Andrew'll change?"

"Well, I…."

"That's it! You're rememberin' about when you were little Oh, Isabelle, my brother is the nicest, kindest person there is. He's never hurt nothin' in his whole life. You should'a seem him cry when the wolves got his little calf. Seemed like he was red eyes for days."

"Well, sure, a little boy'd be fond of his calf."

"Little boy? It was two years ago, and he was older than you are now. Pa thinks that's why he's so good with the horses, breakin' 'em to the saddle, and all. He's kind, and the horses know it, so they want to please him."

Isabelle smiled. "Artie says he wants to be just like Andrew."

"Yeah, and it'd be a good thing. Isabelle, are you changin' your mind about Andrew? You want me to tell 'im he can…?"

"No, not yet. Let me think about a way."

Liz helped her think. "I know what! You and the others could come to our house for Sunday dinner, and Dennis could come, too, and I could ask Dave. It'd be like a party! Say you will!"

"But, your ma…."

"My ma'd love it. She likes company."

Isabelle's mind searched for a reason and found none. "Well, we could…."

"Sure you could, and I'd need to tell Andrew we'll have company, so's he don't plan somethin' else."

"If you're sure…."

"I am. Now, there's somethin' else. I been wantin' to ask you, but I wasn't wantin' to butt in. I need help on somethin.'"

"Help? Sure, if it somethin' I can do."

"You can. I want to give a Christmas program, and Miss Sadie says I should ask somebody's mother to help out. She says it's a hard job to give a program, but they're a nice thing for the community and all."

"Program…?" Isabelle's mind brought up the little schoolhouse in southern Arkansas with its smell of peppermint paste and chalk and wet wool coats in the winter. "I love programs. The singing, and the poems and costumes and all the things. I like the Christmas songs… and everything."

Liz watched the transformation on Isabelle's face and knew she had found the help she needed. She went on.

"I can ask Liddy Palmer to play her accordion for the singin,' and you can help me teach the parts. It'll mean you have to come to the school some afternoons. You think you'll…."

"I'll make the time. I just love Christmas programs."

That evening, Liz confided in Andrew. "Isabelle and the youngen's are comin' out to Sunday dinner."

"She is?" Andrew's voice dryly indicated only small interest.

"Andrew, she's had some bad things happen to her, and she got scared. It's got nothin' to do with you, nor none of us."

"What happened?"

"I don't think it's somethin' I should say, and she didn't tell me much, but it all happened back where she came from."

"Dennis…?"

"No, his pa. But he's dead now."

"Oh. Good thing it wasn't Dennis. Not that I thought it was. Well, that'll be good."

"And she's gonna help me with the school program. Could be, you'd help us put up a curtain?"

"Sure."

"And about Dennis' pa…"

"Yeah?"

"Isabelle said for me not to say anything to you. The thing was, though, I just thought you ought'a know."

"Thanks."

The five of them had Sunday dinner at the Green's farm. Liz and Isabelle worked on ideas for the program, and Andrew and his younger brother took Dennis and Artie for a tour of the farm and the horse breaking and training business. Artie was too excited for words.

It was mid-December when the Christmas program began to come together. The manger scene, of course, would be the centerpiece, but the journey of the wisemen was a big part.

Sheets of cardboard from packing boxes were brought out from Guthrie by Dennis. Camels' heads were traced and features drawn and were made to be carried in front of the "wiseman" who rode them. Rope harnesses were fastened around the camels' heads, allowing the rider to turn the animal's head this way and that.

Gold crowns were a must and were created with more cardboard and a lot of yellow crayon.

There would be Mary and Joseph and the baby. There would be a palace (cardboard, again) where the king would send the wisemen away, telling them to let him know where the baby was, if they were able to find him.

On a Friday, the 20th of December, the whole town and a lot of the countryside gathered into the schoolhouse for the program. It began with each class showing something they had learned.

The beginners recited their numbers and their letters, and then, from a book brought to school by Alecia Carlile, they recited the alphabet poems.

"A" is for apple, that grows on a tree.
Some are for piggie, and some are for me.
"B" is for ball for the baby to play with.
"B" is for ball that the dog runs away with.
"C" is for chicken, with flappity wings
She scratches for worms and wiggley things.
On through the twenty-six verses they went, ending with;
"Z" is for zipper that runs on a track.
Just like a choo choo, forward and back.

Then they ran, single file, to the back of the room, making the choo choo noises of a train, and when they circled and ran back, the "engine" toot-tooted on a whistle. A whistle bought in Fort Smith for Artie Baldwin.

Loud and lengthy applause followed their performance.

The middle level took turns telling how Christmas was celebrated in other countries, and the older children sang certain Christmas songs, acting them out whenever possible. More applause.

During this time, a corner of the platform remained curtained off. At a certain point, several children disappeared behind the curtain, and a lot of activity occurred, evidenced by whispers and much waving of the curtain.

"Angels," older girls draped in white sheets, sang songs, ending with "We Three Kings of Orient Are." At the close of the song, the rippling of the curtain stopped, and it was drawn aside, showing Mary and Joseph and the baby, surrounded with sheep, easily identified by their "sheep ears" made of paper.

From the coatroom at the front door, the camels came, their heads waving this way and that as they sought the baby. Lightly, in the background, Liddy Palmer's skillful fingers produced thin strains of the song they had just sung.

Over the music, Betty Lou Kendall read the story from the Bible as the camels made their trip around the school classroom, back and forth, in their attempt to find Bethlehem. After an agonizing search, they finally reached the platform and placed their gifts at the feet of the baby.

Suddenly, a sheet-draped angel broke away from her place in the clouds and came to the wisemen. She announced, loudly, that they must not obey the king, because he meant no good to the baby. The wisemen thanked the angel and went back to the coatroom, where they left their camels, then returning as small boys, ready for the treats.

The tree had been decorated with chains and colored paper curls, painted sweet gum balls, and clusters of painted acorns. Under its branches were plates of molasses candy, popcorn balls, cookies made of nuts and raisins, and a giant box of store-bought peppermint sticks, compliments of the Kendall Brothers.

Isabelle had been assigned the task of getting the camels out of the coatroom at the right time and removing their costumes when it was over, and other than that, she had been able to watch the whole program.

She watched the young ones, Laney's class, her head bursting with pride as she heard Laney's voice in the lead. Not even a mother could have been more proud. Artie's voice was clear and loud as he told about Christmas in Norway and Sweden, just the way she had coached him in practice.

And the songs! She listened to the lovely background of accordion music and the voices of the older girls, and her thoughts drifted back to the little schoolhouse in Arkansas. It had been a lifetime ago, but she remembered the peace and happiness she had felt, only to have it dashed to shreds by her aunt's death that very night.

The two programs drifted together, and a tear formed in her eye. Than another one, and she was forced to apply her handkerchief to prevent a flow.

Andrew, who had stationed himself at the back of the school, stood beside her and wondered about the tears. There was a story back there somewhere, but it didn't matter. Easing his arm around her shoulders, he drew her closer. She did not pull away, and no one turned around to see them. Then, it was necessary for her to leave him and help serve the refreshments.

It was a bit of a letdown when Christmas was over, and the wet and dreary weather set in. Days of rain and wind were followed by days of weak sunshine, followed by a day of sleet and freezing moisture. It would have been a dull time, if there had not been Liz's wedding to discuss.

"I want a special white dress," Liz had insisted, and Dave had taken Liz and Isabelle to Guthrie to the catalog store to see the latest brochures. It had also been Liz's wedding plans that had finally pulled Isabelle through the loss of Miss Etta Garrett.

Isabelle had hardly settled onto her tract of land when she began to notice Miss Etta. Tiny, wrinkled and crowned with a fluff of snow-white hair, Miss Etta was daily helped into the big chair in the back yard of the tract next door. There she sat, spending most of the hours of the day under the tree when the weather permitted.

Isabelle raised her hand to wave, and Miss Etta raised her tiny hand and waved back. Then, one day as Isabelle finished hanging out the washing, the tiny, butterfly-like hand beckoned her. Isabelle crossed the yard.

"Honey, they say your name is Isabelle."

Isabelle admitted it was.

"Now, I know you're busier'n a pup with four youngens to follow, but I wanted you to know, that little girl's yours, she does pleasure me just to look at her. Honey, come closer. My old eyes ain't so clear no more. Yeah, folks were truthful. That little girl, they say she ain't your little girl."

Isabelle smiled and nodded. "She's my cousin. Her ma died, and I'm about all the ma she'll ever have. The others, they're my cousins, too. Their ma took me in."

"What a lovely thing to do! She took you in, and you took her little ones in. Now I know you ain't got the time to shoot the breeze with an old woman, but I wanted you to know the pleasure the little girl gives me. You, too, truth be told."

'Why, thank you! It's good to have a friend so close."

And it turned out that Miss Etta and Isabelle became very good friends. A sentence here and a moment there, and there was the time Isabelle picked in the pea patch nearby the big chair.

"Now, honey, time you get them peas picked, you bring 'em over, and I'll shell 'em for you. My old legs don't work too good, but my fingers work just fine."

"Well, I...."

"Humor a old woman, honey."

So Isabelle had taken the peas and two bowls and sat on a chair beside Miss Etta. The old woman had been right about her fingers. Isabelle could hardly keep up with her.

Miss Etta was a wonderful listener. The bright blue eyes tucked into the deep-set wrinkled eye sockets never left Isabelle's face as she told the old woman of the trip from the river and the circumstances surrounding it. The thin old lips puckered in sympathy, and her tongue sounded tsk tsk, as her head moved back and forth. "Such doings," she would exclaim.

And Miss Etta told her own story. She and her young husband had come west and settled in southern Nebraska in a place later named Providence Falls. There she had produced her family, buried her husband and had settled in to live out her days.

She had accidentally overheard her married son and daughter talking of the Oklahoma territory and their interest in going there but were concerned over Miss Etta. At her age, a trip would be hard, and their duty was with her.

She told how she had finally convinced them to make the trip, nagging at them and telling them that of course the trip would be hard. Life, itself, was hard when one reached her age. She finally convinced them that she would not be able to rest in her grave if she did not get to see the new land where her grandchildren and their future children would grow up.

Finally, they had consented, and here she was. The three weeks on the road had been spent mostly in her bed in a wagon driven by her grandson, but she had made it, and she now considered her life complete. She was clear in her mind that she was now waiting for God to decide to take her home.

"Can't think what it'd be that God is waitin' on. Got my youngens raised, as best I could, and see them raisin' up their children. Seems that'd be what a woman'd be put on the earth for."

"Oh, Miss Etta, you got time yet. Just see how you come out to your chair every day, and talk to me, and...."

"Sure, and you're right. Talkin' with you... that's..." There were no works to finish her thought.

And the dreams. "Miss Etta, how does a body get dreams to stop? My daytime brain knows there ain't no danger no more, but when I go to sleep, that's when things happen. Things, like when I was a little girl, and I keep wonderin' what bad thing it was that I done to lose my mama before I hardly got big enough to know her."

Miss Etta nodded in her understanding way. "That's the way of it, honey. Your little girl, she plays in the dirt, and she don't half remember where it was she got so dirty. She keeps playin,' not rememberin,' and when the day gets over, that dirt is still on her and her dress. You reckon that dirt ought'a stay on her the rest'a her life?"

Isabelle grinned at the joke. "Don't think I could hardly stand 'er if it did."

"That's right, honey, and what do you do then?"

"Why...? Well, I give her a bath, and her dress gets put in the wash."

Miss Etta nodded. "And you really don't care where the dirt come from. You just wash it off and pitch it out on the ground where it belongs."

"Yeah, well, that's the only thing to do..." Such strange talk!

Miss Etta smiled. "You got that right, and it's the same with your dreams. Them things you put up with have left their marks on you, and bein' so many of 'em, likely it'll take a while to get 'em all off. You'd not remember how they got on you, bein' you had nothin' to compare to. The fact was, though, that it happened and since you don't remember 'em with your daytime mind, they got'a be washed out while you sleep. Dreams washes 'em out."

"You sayin' all them things I dream, they likely happened?"

"Could be that, or could be your little girl mind thought they did. Or maybe it was something else just as bad. I wouldn't be worryin' about those old mean dreams. You just wake up and tell 'em you ain't got time to be messin' with 'em, so they need to just get on out."

Isabelle listened. The words, "old mean dreams" struck her with a stunning force. She had the vision of waking up the screaming Laney and holding her tight and telling her, "it was just a mean old bad dream." She would tell Laney to forget about the old dream and go back to sleep."

And Liz's wedding. "Your friend that teaches school, she'd got herself a weddin' comin' up. That'll be a good thing. That young man she's marryin,' he come down from Providence Falls as a driver and stayed. Fine young man. I been knowin' the Hill's, his ma and pa and the rest, ever since he was a tadpole. Fine family. She's doin' herself a good thing."

Isabelle had joined in. "Oh, her dress! You just got'a see her in her dress! Its white linen, cost a bundle, too, but her pa said she was to get what she wanted. She's such a beautiful girl."

Miss Etta nodded. "Yeah, and no purtrier'n you. Speakin'a you, ain't you a friend to her brother? Him comin' over here and doin' this and that for you?"

"Well, he just comes by, and he's… well, he takes my little brother to his house and…."

"You thinkin' he'd be takin' the little boy to have fun at his house if that little boy didn't mean a lot to you?"

"To me…?"

"Isabelle, honey, you got no ma, nor no grannie to talk to you, so you listen to me. You either pay attention to that young man that thinks he loves you, or you send him far away. The way I hear it, he's had good raisin,' and now he's grown up. He'll be needin' to look around at the girls in the town to find one to marry. Seems he started in on you, and looks like he's goin' about it the right way, doin' for you, and helpin' with your family."

"Yeah, well, Miss Etta… I need friends, but I…."

"You thinkin' he's not a fellow you can marry? If he ain't, you need to be sendin' 'em on 'is way, makin' sure he knows it. You're usin' up his lookin' time."

"His lookin' time? But, Miss Etta, he's never said a word about marryin.' About wantin' me to…? He ain't even thinkin' of that."

"Sure he is, and you know it. A girl don't have to hear the words to know they're comin.' It ain't good for a fellow to hear the word 'no.'

Better he be sent on before he hears it. That a'way you can stay friends. Happen he ain't the one for you, let 'em go, and you look around at the others."

"Oh, Miss Etta! I got so much to do! I don't know...."

"Sure and you got a lot to do. You had a load put on you that no girl should'a had, and that cousin'a yours, too. You two, both'a you, had'a grow up too quick, and that ain't a good thing. Fact is, though, that you can't go back and get what you lost. You can only get what you have now. So I'm a'tellin' you, it's time you was lookin' for help, and that fellow down the road, he could be the one."

"But I still got the youngens to take care of. Vonnie, she's a help, but she ain't hardly fourteen. The little'ns, they...."

"Hmmmm. You been keepin' them youngens hid when that young man's around? Could be, you ought'a tell him there's them that depends on you."

"Oh, Miss Etta, Andrew knows about them. He's been here...."

"Oh! So he knows, does he? Then I'd figure any plans he has for you, he'd put them into it. Sure, and you do have a lot to do, but it could be that he'd be help, 'stead of a problem."

"But...."

"I got nothin' to do but watch out the window and listen to the talk goin' on around me. No one wants to hear me, no more, and I says to the Good Lord, how come I'm still here? Could be he was leavin' me here to talk some sense into you, seein' you got no ma, or no one else."

Her eyes twinkled, and her wide smile rearranged the rows of wrinkles on either side of her mouth. "You'll forgive a old woman bein' blunt-like and talkin' the way I just did. Could be I ain't got time left in my life to be easy and gentle."

Her infectious smile was spread to Isabelle. "I'll think on it. What you say makes sense, hearin' it out'a the mouth of someone else. Reckon Andrew'd be smart enough to know I come with a family, at least for a while."

Miss Etta squenched up her eyes, as though to peer inside Isabelle's head. "The thing to think on now, is, do you love him?"

"Love? Well... I, uh..."

"Put it this way. Which'd be easier to say, 'Andrew, why not stop over, and we'll make popcorn balls', or "Andrew, you're takin' up time I should be doin' other things?'"

Isabelle nodded with understanding. Put that way, it was quite plain.

Miss Etta, again. "Or which would be easier to say, 'I got time to go for a drive on Sunday afternoon, happen you'd like to,' or, 'Andrew, you ever look at that Gwendolyn Martin, how pretty she's getting'? She keeps lookin' your way, and she'd likely spend time with you, if you want.'"

Isabelle swallowed hard. "I see what you mean. I got'a be friendlier, or let 'im find a girl who is."

Miss Etta reached out with her tiny, white-skinned hand and patted Isabelle's arm. "Don't reckon I could'a put it better if I'd'a tried."

Then it was time for Isabelle to put on the chicken she was cooking for their supper. It seemed as if they were hungry all the time, working hard like they did.

Isabelle didn't notice the light burning long in the Garrett house than night, but when morning came, she was the first to be told.

"Isabelle, honey, we got somethin' to tell you about Miss Etta. It was almost her last words 'afore she left."

"Left? Miss Etta?"

"Yes, honey. She passed on in the night. Said to tell you she was at peace, havin' said what she was left here to say. Now, them was her exact words, and they didn't make no sense to us. But we knowd we ought'a honor the dyin', and we promised. Wrote 'em down so's to remember exactly what she said. And she said for us to tell you good bye for her."

Miss Etta's daughter-in-law sniffed delicately and blinked her eyes. "She's one we're gonna miss, but it's a comfort to hear her say she was at peace. What else could a person want at the end of a long life?"

Miss Etta's passing necessitated a town meeting. Clancy Harper, the mayor, gathered everyone in the schoolyard. "Folks, it's come on us what we knew'd happen, sooner or later. It's just we were so concerned with the livin', we never gave thought... well....

"So, talkin' around to the ones that come down with the town, I feel like sayin' this. We still got two tracts that ain't been sold. You all know, it'd be the two that's got that Redbud Creek cuttin' across the middle of 'em. They're right back'a the one bought by the preacher's sister.

"Now, the ones I talked with, they all say one or both of them lots could be kept for a... we could use 'em for a cemetery. I wanted to have this meetin,' givin' everyone a chance to say their piece, even though they got no votin' rights. We can use ideas."

"Five acres? That'd last a long time."

"How close together was you plannin'…?"

"When it's full, then what?"

"Take all ten acres? That'd be a lot'a land to keep back…."

"Maybe not. Remember how the creek takes a strip out'a the middle'a them tracts? Ain't as much there as it looks like."

"Yeah, and that'd make a mighty purty place. Trees… creek… could be, we could set out some roses bushes or bridal wreath… or somethin.' Maybe later on."

"Who'd take care of it… like weeds and everything?"

"Everybody could take care'a their own graves… maybe?"

"Fence it, and turn in the goats."

"GOATS!"

"WHAT'RE YOU TALKIN' ABOUT!"

"Goats. There ain't nothin' like goats to clear out everything they can reach on their hind legs. Way I see it, we could put young goats on it early in the year and let 'em clean it up. Then, come fall, we could sell 'em in Guthrie, or to whoever wanted 'em. We'd save the money to buy more little goats, and then whatever else… we needed?"

"If there was money left, we could use it for headstones. That'd take the strain off the family, havin' to come up with the money for the stone."

"Yeah, and that way, every grave'd have a stone."

"But the goats…."

"Not hard to get. Miss Sadie brought a pair of 'em all the way from Springfield, Illinois. Could be she'd sell 'em to us for a start."

"Then all we'd need would be a fence."

The women of the town gathered next door, and Isabelle watched. Should she go? Or not? There seemed to be enough help that she was not needed. She really needed to check the chicken pen to see where they kept getting out.

Miss Etta. She couldn't really be gone. Just the day before yesterday, she had sat in the big chair, now, so forlornly empty. She had talked, and now she was so silent. She had been waiting for her time to go, and apparently it had come.

And, she, Isabelle, was Miss Etta's last concern. Leaving her a message that she now found peace. It was like a code, really. A message coded just for her, a special message, just for her alone. That made it very important, didn't it?

And the message? Chopping away all the extra words, it came out very clearly. Forget all the past. Let it take care of itself, and get on with her life. Begin to look for help, either Andrew, or, if she really didn't love him, someone else. Send Andrew away. Turn him toward Gwendolyn, or someone else.

The dewberries in the brambles at the back of her tract should be ripe. She could send Vonnie back there to get them. Or she could get them herself.

"Vonnie, sort out what jelly jars we have. I'll be comin' back with the first'a the berries."

"Sure."

Swinging the bucket beside her, her thoughts continued. Not now. I can't think about anything right now. After the funeral. After Liz's wedding. After… after… after…

She could hear the hammering. The nails were fastening together the box that would forever take the place of Miss Etta's chair. She walked on, the tears streaming down her face. They blurred her eyes and she could not see the path, or a snake, if there should be one. Lowering herself to a spot of green moss growing beneath a tree, she gave herself over to her tears. She covered her face with her hands and the tears flowed between her fingers and puddled in her palms. Miss Etta was gone. Another loss.

Isabelle felt so small and alone. Her mama had left so quickly there had been no goodbyes. Little Minnie Belle had been filled with a sadness she had not understood, but she had made the best of it. Aunt Addie had been a combination of friend and mother. Then she had gone.

Aunt Addie had tried to say last words to her, but young Minnie had refused to listen. That had not stopped Aunt Addie from going. She had tried to be brave, not to cry in front of the others, and if Denny had felt the same way, he, also, had pretended to be brave. A few private tears had happened, and there was the time on the road that she and Vonnie… but otherwise she had been careful to hide her grief. It had seemed best. There were things to be done, so she did not have time for crying.

Then Miss Etta. For someone she had known such a short time, Miss Etta seemed to be able to see inside her, turning her wrong side out with her kind words, allowing Isabelle to see herself. Such a comfort it had been! It was as though she had been carrying a heavy load, and someone came and lifted half the weight of it.

Now Miss Etta was gone, and the load was back on her own back. Leaning forward, she buried her face in her apron, folding her hands on the back of her head drawing her face even lower. Sobs shook her whole body, and the sounds were wrenched out of the depth of her heart, laden with grief, sadness and feelings of total aloneness.

On and on the tears flowed, and her throat ached from the tightness and the groaning sobs. She finally knew how to weep for her mama. Her mama had been taken away, not because little Minnie had been a bad girl, but because it was time for her to go, and the knowledge of that gave her the right to cry for the little girl she had been and the big girl she had become. She cried for the little girl who was sad and puzzled and saw so many sad things that she had to hide them inside herself, only to have them uncovered in her dreams. She cried for the girl whose childhood had been robbed by Artie and Laney, whom she dearly loved. It had not been their fault, but they had used up so much of her childhood.

Then the worse. She wept in grinding agony for the girl who must try to hide from Harley.

After that, Aunt Addie. A new, fresh flood of salty tears flowed as she relived the loss of her. Aunt Addie, the buffer between herself and HIM. After that, things had become ever so much worse.

There had been the problem in Little Rock, and the strange, unbreakable pull that she and Dennis had felt, the pull that took them through any number of places where they could have stopped, and doubtlessly lived well. There had been the many tears of weariness and frustration all along the way. Finally, in Prosper she had felt that she had reached home.

Then Miss Etta. NO! NO! She could not take another loss. No! No! No! The words forced them past her throat and into her mouth.

"NO! NO! NO!" She heard her voice pushing the words away from her mouth. Smothered against her apron, the words choked and gagged her. Swiping the tears from her eyes, she sat up and demanded of the trees around her, "NO!"

She felt a touch on her back, and a soft arm surrounded her. Startled, she turned face to face with Liz, sitting on the ground beside her. Tears were streaming down Liz's face.

285

"I don't know what's the matter, but I know its bad enough for my tears, too. I'm so sorry. Vonnie said you came back here."

"Liz…?"

"Is it Miss Etta? I know."

Isabelle nodded, moping her eyes. "Her, and others. Seems I keep lookin' for a mama and keep loosin' her. Sometimes I feel like I'm all…."

"Alone? Well if there's a thing I can sympathize with, it'd be that. I had a mama, and there'd be none better, but I know what it is to be lonely. Miss Etta must'a been really special."

"Liz, I can't go to the funeral. It'll hurt too much"

"Can't go? Oh, Isabelle, you can't say that! She'd want you to. You'd be so sorry, later. I'll help you. We'll go together."

"Well, I don't… know…."

School turned out for the funeral. The box made of new lumber was carried to the church, and Preacher Hap Palmer opened his Bible.

"Friends, this is the day of the first great sorrow for this new town. It is a sorrow for us but what a wonderful day for Miss Etta Garrett! Think, dear friends, of the glory all around her at this minute. No more pain…."

And the words went on, floating over Isabelle's head. Inside her head, she heard, "just old bad dreams. Leave 'em be. That's just the dirt bein' washed out'a your mind." Also, "you thinkin' that young man didn't see them youngens you got dependin' on you? Think he ain't considered that, when he set his eyes on you?" Then, "tell Isabelle I found peace."

Then a new thought, God must think I'm important. He let Miss Etta come all the way from wherever she lived, and He brought me all this way just so she could tell me last things that should'a come from my mama.

Thank you, God.

She sat between Liz and Andrew and rode with them down the road to the new cemetery. Red dirt was piled on the green of the new grass and the moss beneath the trees.

Liddy Palmer drew her arms gracefully in and out as she expanded the bellows of her accordion. The musical notes started whispery thin, growing and thickening into rich sounds that echoed into the surrounding trees. Redbud Creek ran full, flowing between its banks and over the roots of the trees of sycamore, cottonwood and willow. The clusters of ripe redbud seeds rattled in the breeze as though to tempt the birds.

Then the songs. "Shall we gather by the River, where bright angel's feet have trod…?" "In the Sweet Bye and Bye, we shall meet on that beautiful shore.."

Isabelle bowed her head forward, and the tears came. She felt an arm around her shoulders and realized it was Andrew's. A hand took hers, and she knew it was Liz's. Miss Etta was gone, but she was not alone.

It was over, and Andrew asked, "Isabelle, I got the buggy here. and if you can…?

Turning to Vonnie, Isabelle instructed. "Gather up somethin' for supper, will you, honey? I'll be gone for an hour… or two…."

It was a silent ride inside the buggy. The horses stepped lightly on the grassy ground, and the wheels made no sound at all. Overhead, the crows squabbled and squawked, the jays chattered, and the cardinals zipped and zoomed across the path of the buggy. Wasn't it said to be good luck when a redbird crossed one's path? Well, she could stand some right now. Turtles crossed and recrossed the trail that was fast becoming a road.

Isabelle sat in the buggy allowing the events of the day to flow over her in waves and then wash themselves away. Miss Etta had been right, and it was time for her to look after herself… Isabelle.Isabelle Minerva Crowley. If it was true that every cloud had a silver lining, it was time she turned a few of them clouds in-side-out.

"Andrew, I don't know what it'll be, but Vonnie'll have somethin' for the table. Whyn't you stop over?"

The aproned Vonnie slipped the spatula under the potatoes fried with fresh onions, stirred the sliced squash baked in butter and fresh spices. Stewed tomatoes and cornbread. She brightened as the two came through the door.

"Andrew! You stayin'?"

"If it's all right…."

"Oh, yes!"

Thirteen

Next was Liz's wedding. Half the time, that girl didn't seem to know what she was doing! Isabelle really felt needed.

There was this custom that came down from the north about having someone stand up with the bride and groom during the wedding. Isabelle could see the sense of it, as Liz, who always knew what to do, seemed at loss.

"Isabelle! I don't know! I'm afraid I'll do somethin' wrong!"

"No, you won't," Isabelle continually advised her. "I won't let you."

Then it was the day of the wedding. Liz's nervous hands had forgotten how to brush her hair, and Isabelle insisted she sit and calm herself. Having her hair brushed seemed to relax Liz somewhat, and finally the shining curls were pinned in place and a silky white ribbon was wound around them like a halo... the curled ends falling over Liz's shoulder beside the one ebony curl that was allowed to escape.

And the dress. White linen... white lace... glistening white pearl buttons. Expensive pearl buttons that marched from the neckline to the hem. Liz was so beautiful, Isabelle wiped her hand over her eyes to dry them.

Liz drank a cup of camomile tea while Isabelle slipped into her own dress, her best Sunday dress of pale blue with white dots. A blue ribbon tied up her shining curls, and she slipped her feet into her freshly polished, Sunday shoes.

With a last sigh, they stepped bravely out the door and headed across the street toward the church. As they came closer, they heard the music of the accordion being produced by the talented fingers of Liddy Palmer. The sound of it was like a chorus of bird songs on a spring morning. Then they were at the door of the church, and Liz hesitated.

Isabelle glanced at her. She was so beautiful. It was only right that she be told. "Liz, you're beautiful! I don't think I ever saw nothin' prettier'n you are."

Liz seemed to gain strength, and together they stepped through the door, onto the quiet sawdust. At the front of the church stood Dave and Andrew, side by side.

They walked to the front, and the music died away.

"Dearly beloved, we are...."

From the back of the church came a voice, deep and graveled, and insistent. "Wait a minute, preacher. I got somethin' to say."

An old man arose and headed toward them, and Isabelle's heart grabbed at her chest, taking her breath away. Then Liz's pa hurried after him, but the old man would not stop.

Liz whispered, "My granddad."

The old man stood beside Liz. "Mary Elizabeth, I got somethin' needin' to be done." Going on, he told about seeing Liz as a baby, and thinking she resembled his own mother, and then realizing he was wrong. His ma had been weak, but one had only to look into Liz's eyes to see she was strong.

He told of the string of pearls his mother gave him when he left home.

He told of his first wife... a girl from the Wichita tribe and how he had tried to give the pearls to her. When he finally knew she wanted beads of bright colors, he gave them to her, and she returned the pearls.

He took a beautiful strand of ivory pearls from the pocket of his overalls, holding them protectively in his gnarled old hands. A quiet fell over those gathered on the crowded benches, so great that the birds outside the window could be plainly heard.

The old man continued, "So, what I want to do is this. I still want'a give these beads to my Rose. I know she's gone, but there's a part'a her in them eyes'a yours, and I know now why she gave 'em back to me. They didn't match her. Shiny bright colors matched your Grandma Rose, and she knew it. These here, they wouldn't'a looked good on her, maybe like the feathers of a blue bird on a bird supposed to be all red.

"I kept these beads all this time, havin' thoughts about what to do, wonderin' this way and that, and then I saw them white beads all over your white dress, and I said to myself that I was doin' the right thing. So I got a present here for you, and it's from your Grandma Rose and from me."

A tear trickled down the dark, leathery cheek as he fumbled for the tiny catch which closed the strand of pearl. Liz's eyes were filling.

Then Isabelle knew why she was there. With strong, steady hands, she reached toward the old man, smiling, and she held out her hand for the necklace. Relieved, he dropped it in her palm.

Liz reached out and held the old man's trembling hands as Isabelle's steady fingers fastened the tiny clasp under the ends of the satin ribbon. The creamy white pearls lay softly on Liz's neck, completely matching the tones of her skin. They might have been invisible if it had not been for the translucent glow that came from the depth of each bead.

The old man extended a worn and calloused finger, touching the beads for one last time. Then he turned to face the waiting people. "That was all I wanted to say." Together, Liz's pa and grandpa walked back to their seats.

Liz pressed one hand against the pearls and touched the fingers of the other hand to her eyes. Swallowing hard, she sniffed softly.

Rev. Palmer began once more. Lifting the marriage book, he turned to the congregation. "Dearly Beloved, we are gathered here before God and these people to join this man and this woman…."

The service was short, but the party afterward was long and joyful, and after a respectful length of time, Andrew found her.

"Isabelle, I got the buggy here and I thought…."

At her smile and nod, they left together.

As he had the day of the funeral, Andrew headed the horses down the tree-canopied lane. Isabelle sat in the buggy, allowing the excitement of the day to drift over her and away. Liz had seemed so happy.

At the creek, Andrew stopped, allowing the horses to nose around in the grass. "Isabelle…?"

She turned toward him and smiled. He was such a thoughtful person. The buggy was there to take her away from the crowd, and he was beside her, strong and confident, to take away the bad dreams. He was terribly handsome with his tanned skin, his eyes of shoe button black, and his strong, square jaw. And his smile… Nothing at all like Harvey's… actually.

"Isabelle, I got somethin' to say. Could be, this ain't the best time to say it, but I got'a say it, anyway. I think you're the most beautiful girl I ever saw, and I've loved you from the minute I saw you standin' in the woods, down at the sawmill. The thing is, I want to marry you. Could be, you'll want'a wait a while to give a answer. It was just…well, I had to say…."

Isabelle's mind drew up a fleeting image of Miss Etta, smiling her pleased smile, her bright eyes sparkling. "Andrew, I'd love to marry you. I don't think I know of no good reason for waitin'."

Andrew's right arm felt warm and protective across her shoulder, and both her hands were gathered into his left hand. "Then we got'a make a trip to Guthrie to buy a dress and a ring. There wasn't no way I'd guess on the size. Now, when can we…?"

This was the last of May. It would take a little while to get used to the idea and to get ready.

"July? The first Saturday in July?"

Andrew was quick to nod. That was even sooner than he had allowed himself to hope for.

It was late in the afternoon, actually nearly evening when the buggy behind the patient horses was turned toward the farm belonging to the Green's, located just over two miles west of town.

And it was late in the afternoon that Emma Green, Liz's mother, feeling pensive and reflective from the loss of her daughter, walked out to her herb garden. Lowering herself to the stone bench Andrew had made for his grandmother, Emma settled herself.

The wedding. Her oldest daughter. It had been a beautiful thing, especially the part played by Liz's grandfather when he gave her the pearls.

She hadn't known David Hill very long, but he seemed to be a hardworking young man who knew what he wanted. And part of what he wanted had been her oldest daughter, Mary Elizabeth. She sighed, not of weariness or apprehension, but of restful satisfaction, as though she had walked a long way and was now resting before she traveled on.

The beginning heat of the summer had begun to render the oils from the aromatic herbs in the garden, sending out a pleasant blend of aromas. Bees, butterflies and Rufus hummingbirds were quick to take advantage of the early nectar. Emma had been satisfied with her life. When her father had given up and gone back to Missouri, she and her old Gran had stayed, and she had married Ben.

Raising five children had its problems, but so many things were easier now. She even had a school for her younger girls, ages eight and six, so she didn't have to teach them herself as she had her three oldest. Sally and Annie rode the gentle old mare to the schoolyard, and the animal was turned loose in the corral at the back of the school.

The little girls loved school. Emma had also loved it for their sakes and also because it made Liz so happy to be a teacher.

Then there was her second son, Clayton, now fifteen. Eager, strong, healthy and mostly good natured, he was happy to be handling horses, the family business. Bloodlines and speed were his interest, though he took his turn at breaking yearlings.

And Andrew. He was admittedly among the best at breaking and training, and there was a heavy demand for his animals. It was good that he had been able to work at the sawmill and at some of the house building, as it gave him cash money to expand the business. And it was good when a business was large enough for a father to expand and take in his sons.

Andrew said he was ready to start looking around for new animals, though it might take a while to find the right ones, and Clayton, with his own sawmill money, would be along for his valued opinion. Why, just the other day, Andrew had said....

A sound attracted her, and she looked toward the driveway curving off the surveyor's trail that had become a main road between the town of Prosper and the city of Guthrie. Watching, she saw the team and buggy pull into the yard and stop. Andrew was home.

Andrew circled the buggy and helped the girl down, being careful of her wide skirt. She still wore the pale blue dress with white dots that she had worn to Liz's wedding. Looking around, Andrew saw his mother in the herb garden, which was where he would have expected to find her.

Side by side, Andrew and Isabelle walked down the path, and Emma waited. As they approached, she studied their faces. Smiles. Her heart skipped a beat and then pounded double time. It could be good news.

When they reached the garden, Andrew said, softly, "I asked her, Ma."

Emma looked, questioningly, from her son to the girl. The head crowned with red-gold curls was ducked, slightly, with excitement flushing pink beneath her ivory skin. As she turned her head, the ends of the blue ribbon fell over her forehead. That was all the answer Emma needed.

Rising from the stone bench, she walked toward Isabelle. She wrapped her arms around her as though welcoming a lost child back to her home.

"Oh, darlin' girl, I hoped it would be you! I saw Andrew lookin' around, but there wasn't one that lit up his eyes like you did. For a while, I was afraid. But then you...? Such a beautiful, hardworking girl, and so brave, to make that trip from where you come from But here I am, squawlin,' and not lettin' you say a thing!"

Sniffing and wiping her eyes, she caught Isabelle's hand on one side and Andrew's on the other and walked them toward the house.

Turning to Andrew, "Son, did you…?"

"Not yet, ma. There'll be time."

"Sure. We got spice cookies, and I'll heat up some tea."

Isabelle was apprehensive. "Time for what?"

Emma turned to her son. "You could maybe…? While I get the tea ready?"

"But, ma… She just…."

Isabelle turned to Andrew and again demanded. "Time for what?"

"Oh, it's just ma. She's been anxious to know how you'd feel about the cabin, happen you said yes. I wasn't wantin' to say nothin' till we had a chance to talk, but there ain't no reason why."

Taking her hand, he led her toward the log cabin somewhat in back of the yard, not far from the herb garden. Walking through the door, Isabelle looked around at the large kitchen, and the even larger parlor with a roomy table along one side, fully surrounded with cane bottom chairs.

"Who lives here?"

"This was where we lived till ma wanted more room, and pa and me built the other house. Ma was wantin' us to live here, you and me. She was sayin' there was all this room, not bein' used. It's got these two rooms in the back that we used for bedrooms. And the porch, it could be boxed in. Likely Artie'd like it. And there's a room for Vonnie and Laney, and the other one could be for…."

He hesitated. Isabelle opened the door to one of the rooms. Large and roomy. A good solid bed with cast iron headboard and foot. She always liked ironwork. Windows… snowy white curtains. Braided rugs. The other room was just as nice. And a sleeping loft! Artie would like that better than any room.

She looked around at everything, trying to comprehend. It seemed that when she married Andrew, she could move into this wonderful house, and she would get to use all this nice furniture.

She walked into the kitchen and looked around. Nice cabinet, a pantry with shelves. A worktable, and a pump. A PUMP! She worked the handle and the water came out!

Somewhat dazed, she turned to Andrew. He held out his arms. "Isabelle, honey, forget all about it. I knew it wasn't a thing to talk on today. You don't have to live here just on account'a ma. She'll like you just as much if you live somewhere else. She shouldn't'a said nothin' till we had a chance to talk."

"Oh, I like it! I like everything about it! All this room…? And the water pump! I heard'a folks havin' water in the kitchen, but I never saw it except in Little Rock and the other towns."

Andrew sighed, greatly relieved. Ma was hoping so hard. "Now, we can change what you don't like. You don't have to…."

Isabelle nodded. "White curtains everywhere, like the ones in the bedroom. That's all the change I'd want."

Andrew nodded, "And if you change your mind…."

"That's all. Let's go tell your ma."

Isabelle was hugged again. "Oh, you sweet, darlin' girl…!"

Andrew watched and waited. "Isabelle, there's another thing ma's bustin' to ask. Might as well get it over with. She's sayin' with all the room we got here at the farm, couldn't we have the weddin' out here at the house. Liz didn't want to. She wanted the church, and if that's what you want…."

Isabelle looked out the door, mentally placing the people of the town in the wide yard, milling around the herb garden, and looking at the lovely cabin where she would live. "I want to be married here. I want to stand over by the herb garden, and I want everyone in the world to be here! I sure do thank you, Miz Green. You're bein' so good to me."

"Oh, sweet girl, you don't have to call me Miz Green, like I was a stranger. I could be Emma… or… well, you could call me 'ma,' not meanin' disrespect to your own ma, but us bein' so far out here…?" The question hung in the air.

"I don't remember havin' a ma. I always thought it'd be nice to have one."

And it was time to take Isabelle back home. Darkness had fallen among the trees, and the lighted lanterns swung with the movement of the buggy, lighting the way for the horses.

"Isabelle, you want I should come in with you when you tell the others?"

She thought a minute. "I think maybe, no. They'll be glad, but we been through a lot together, me and them youngens, and I'd like to tell them alone."

So he made his goodbye at the door and headed back west. Isabelle went into the little cabin.

There was an aroma of food, so they had eaten supper. A pan of fresh eggs sat on the boards being used as a table, so Artie had tended the chickens and locked them up for the night. She gathered their cousins around.

"I got things to say. Good things. Andrew has asked me to marry him, and we'll be moving out to the cabin by his house."

"Really?" Artie had difficulty believing such a wonderful thing. "We're for sure movin'? We gonna live there every day?"

Laney's eyes shone. "Annie and Sally's house! We can play, and I won't ever be lonesome!"

Isabelle's eyes turned to Vonnie, sitting quietly, a small smile on her lips.

Vonnie stood and walked to Isabelle and put her arms around her. "I'm glad. I truly am. I thought it might happen, and I'm happy for you."

"Thank you. You'll like it there. You and Laney'll have a big room all your own, and the kitchen has a water pump. It'll be really nice."

Vonnie nodded. "I'm glad you like it, but I won't be moving."

"Sure you will! Miz Green wants all of us...."

Vonnie's slowly shaking head stopped Isabelle's words. She regained her thought, "What're you sayin'? Sure you're goin.' You'll like it."

"I'm stayin' here. You and Denny brought me all the way over here, and I had nothin' to say one way or the other. That was all right, you done what you had to do, and it was good. All of it. But now I got my say. I like it here. I like this cabin, and Denny still lives here, and he'll have to have a place to come to on Saturdays."

"Oh, Vonnie! Alone? You only fourteen...?"

"Almost fifteen. You was takin' care'a ma and all of us when you was thirteen. Now, we been here a year, and I know what there is to do. Stuck in here between the Garrett's and the Hamilton's, there ain't a thing bad that can happen to me."

"But, food and such and...."

"Denny's got a good job, and it don't take much for me."

"Well, if you've thought on it…. 'Course, you can always change your mind, and the room'll still be there."

"I won't change my mind. I know what I want."

But Vonnie's decision took none of the joy from Artie and Laney. They joined hands and danced merrily around the room, squealing with happiness. Vonnie looked toward the dark window covered with faded curtains made from the scraps of an old skirt of Isabelle's.

Red. The ones hanging there were "all right" curtains, but she had never liked the faded flowers on the greenish background. They should be red, and she knew how she could get them that way. Ripe pokeberries. The beet-red juice of the berries would dye the curtains a bright and cheery red.

And that was just the start. A table. She'd tell Denny it was time to order a table. The cupboard shelves were all right, but she needed a workspace. Andrew was so handy, he'd build her some. All she had to do was ask. Before now, it would have been Isabelle's place to ask, but now she, Vonnie, had the right. Andrew would be family. Part of her family.

Now, in the parlor she would have to keep Denny's bed, but she wanted a willow settee and chair and some stools. The new preacher was very good at working with willow, and sometimes he had some things he would sell. She'd tell Denny….

Pillow cushions. The willow furniture would be covered with soft pillows that she would stitch up and fill with the fluffy leg feathers from the chickens they had killed. She had carefully saved them all. She'd piece a pretty quilt to cover Denny's bed.

Yessirree…! She knew exactly what she would do. She had heard, one time, that every cloud has a silver lining, and she knew they weren't talking about the clouds in the sky. The clouds they talked about were bad things, and she well knew about them. Her fingers massaged the scar, no longer painful, on her leg and foot. The burns and the knife had hurt horribly, but, because of them, she had still been where Minnie and Denny could rescue her and not in the kitchen of Mrs. Nester.

Well, if clouds had a silver lining, this was surely one of them. A quiet little house, all her own (except for Dennis, who was gone most of the time) and she could make any change she wanted to. She could cook what she wanted to eat, and she could go…? Well, she'd have to have a buggy of her own. That wasn't too much to ask, was it?

That evening she pulled on her gown and crawled under the sheet, her mind still on her wonderful life ahead. She was still thinking. Isabelle always had put things one place and left them. Vonnie knew she would change things around at least once a month. Isabelle cooked the food a certain way, and Vonnie liked to try this and that together, and sometimes she liked to add something new, just to see what it would taste like.

Finally, Artie and Laney settled down, and Isabelle went to bed. Vonnie's decision had taken away a bit of her happiness, just for a little while. It was hard to believe Vonnie was almost fifteen. It only made sense for her to want to stay where she could do things for herself. And Dennis? He would have someone to come home to… it could work out.

And weariness pulled her into sleep.

Andrew came for her in the buggy, and they were to go to Guthrie for the day. There was a ring to get and a dress for the wedding.

"The dress," he wondered. "What kind was it you thought you'd like to married in?"

She had thought, trying to picture herself in this one or that one. The picture was not clear. Maybe a white one, but not like Liz's. Maybe with a full skirt, and a lace collar, or maybe… So many maybe's.

Andrew came to her rescue. "Don't be worryin' on it. We'll get there and see the latest pictures in the catalog. That'll give you an idea. If Liz wasn't at the school, teachin,' likely she'd be a help."

Isabelle tried to think. A mile of silence, as the buggy swayed along the uneven roadbed. "What kind of a dress would you like?"

"Me? Well, I wouldn't want to say what dress you'd like to wear."

"But if you were to, what'd you think?"

Andrew reached for her hand. "Turn to me a minute. Yes, that would be right. If I was to pick a dress, it'd be the same shade'a green as your eyes. They look like they're the color'a the first leaves in the spring. Soft and fresh, just like when I first saw you."

"Green? You'd like green?"

"Unless you'd like some other color. We're out to get what you want. Ma says a girl ought'a get the weddin' dress she wants, if she can. Ma didn't get to have one, the way it was she got married. So quick, and all."

"Green. Light green, like new leaves?"

Andrew nodded. "Or apples."

"Apples?"

"Green apples, before they red up. Shiny and clear. The same color as the tree frogs in the creek. They set in the water and turn green, then climb the tree and turn gray. Green is the best."

"Green..." Isabelle pronounced, softly.

Andrew hurriedly added, "But it don't have to be green. I think a lot'a girls like to be married in white."

"I like green."

It had been over a year since the land rush, and there had been a lot of changes in the city of Guthrie. The city of tents, sticks and cardboard that had arisen in one day had quickly become a network of bricked streets, modest frame houses, mansions made of masonry with eastern money, stores that dealt with items needed to establish a life on the frontier, and hotels and places of amusement deemed necessary for a civilized life.

The Santa Fe Railway that dissected the town from north to south was the artery that brought the good life to the citizens of Guthrie. Sellers of this and that flooded the new town with their pamphlets, and brochures, and catalogs of general merchandise were displayed in "catalog" stores.

Two young brothers who had come down with the town had teamed up with a third brother into a cartage company with the unofficial contract to deliver freight for the railway. It was to these brothers that Dennis Baldwin joined, bringing his own well-built wagon and team of strong bays.

With the addition of the fourth wagon and the strength and endurance of the four young men, they were able to successfully crowd another hauling service from gaining a foothold in the Santa Fe freight business.

The young men were obliged to stay in the town for five and six day stretches, only seeing their families on the weekends, as the fourteen mile distance took too much time and energy to be traveled daily. For the first few months, they spent their weeks living in their wagon in a temporary livery stable, sleeping in them at night under a big tent. Then, late in the summer, the owner of the city lot and the tent housing the livery put it up for sale, opting to join forces with his brother in Oklahoma City.

Business had been good during the summer, and the four young men had scraped together enough money to secure the land, with a promise to pay in full by the end of the year. It became suddenly evident that something more would have to be done.

First, Dennis brought to the city the other wagon and team he had driven from Arkansas, and a young man was hired to operate it. Dennis, himself, stayed with the tent, caring for the animals and the many other horses whose owners had no place to keep them. Due to the shortage of places for horses to be kept and the absolute necessity of owning a horse for transportation, there was never a shortage of animals in the new "livery".

The first building was a twelve by fourteen shack with a small potbelly stove for heat and cooking, but it was adorned with a sign painted green with white letters, KENDALL BALDWIN LIVERY STABLE.

Expenses were cut to the bone, and long hours were spent in all weather, but by the first of the year, the last payment had been made. Next, the building began. As lumber had become more available, the entire perimeter of the lot was lined with stalls where animals could be kept more comfortably than under the canvas tent. Hay and grain were bought in quantity, and a small collection of light buggies were acquired for rental.

So great was the need for both hauling and animal care, and so strong was the desire of the young men to make a success, that by April of the next spring, they were again free of debt and able to let the hired help go, handling all the business themselves.

Dennis spent full time in the livery during the week. His love of horses and the experience he had gained in Arkansas stood him in good stead. But now that the livery had begun to board animals full time, someone must stay with them over the weekend. A schedule developed whereby Dennis and Manford (Manny) Kendall stayed in town one weekend, and Chester and Douglas Kendall stayed the other weekend. This gave each pair every other weekend at home.

The business was going well and Isabelle saw Dennis only every other weekend, but was fascinated by his success. It was what he had wanted, and he had never wanted anything else. What luck to join up with the Kendall Brothers! But she had never seen the new livery, a much bigger and better building than the twelve by fourteen shack, now used for hay and feed storage.

Andrew had promised that a visit to the livery would be the first stop in the city, and then they would visit the catalog store. There were, however, other businesses popping up like mushrooms along the streets of Guthrie. After a tour of the livery, they headed for the catalog store, but were sidetracked by a freshly painted storefront with a shiny new plate glass window and a sign proclaiming women's apparel for sale. In the window was a smartly dressed mannequin, hatted and gloved in the latest fashion.

Impressed, Andrew and Isabelle went in. There were, indeed, dresses. Every color and style, plain and trimmed, flouncy and chic.

"Can I help you?" A well-dressed young lady approached them.

"Well, we…" Isabelle began, but her words trailed away.

Andrew tried his luck. "That dress in the window, do you…?"

"Have it in her size?" the lady supplied. "I'm sure we do. Such a good choice. I think it might be the exact color of her eyes."

"Could we…?"

"Try it on? Certainly. If you'll sit here, sir, we'll take care of it."

Andrew sat. The tiny velvet-covered chair was fortunately stronger than it looked, and the spindly legs of it upheld him admirably. While Isabelle was gone, he had ample time to look around at the other offerings. There, hanging near him, was a white lace coat… or, maybe not a coat, but more of a… well, it was something that a lady would put over her shoulders when the weather was chilly, but not cold. He reached out to touch it, and it was so soft and light that he could hardly feel it with his fingers, and he thought even his breath would move it.

Then Isabelle was back. Andrew's first thought was of the time he saw her in the shade of the spring trees at the sawmill. Apple green. It fitted her smoothly from the neck to the hips and flared softly to the floor. The toes of her black shoes peeked from under the edge of the skirt.

The clerk stood back with a pleased expression as though she had created this masterpiece herself. "Lovely, isn't she?"

Andrew was forced to nod, yes.

"But if miss wants to buy it, there would be certain adjustments. A seam nipped here, and a bit shortened there," and she spoke, she pulled the fabric a bit, causing the drapes to fall more smoothly.

"How long…?"

"Oh, sir, this is the correct length. Nothing would need to be done… with the length…?"

"I mean, how long would it take to fix it?"

"An hour... maybe two. You could go to the tearoom for a while, or if you had other things to do? We could...."

Andrew nodded, and Isabelle was whisked away, leaving him to stare at the pink and white feathery things, the bolts of lace and ribbon, and sparkling buttons and pins. So many things! Where would a woman find places on her body to wear them all! But the shawl (cape?), that was a must.

Also, white shoes. They would, yet, need to go to the catalog store. And there was that other thing he wanted.

Shunning the tearoom, they went straight to the catalog store. White shoes and white stockings? Why not? More under things?

"But, Andrew, have you counted up what this'll cost?"

Andrew was no stranger to dollars and cents, and he already knew he would be obliged to forget about the new mares he hoped to get... or, perhaps he could get back the pair that had been used by the hired help at the livery. They would be good breeders. Perhaps he could swap out with KENDALL BALDWIN and make them the loan (trade?) of a pair of his stallions (well broke to the harness) as rental carriage horses.

While Isabelle looked at the colorful book, Andrew's mind shuffled horses. There was that pair of paints, cool temperament and with attractive markings. As a pair or singly, they stepped well, even strutted when necessary. It was all in the breaking and training. It could be, too, that he had others the livery could use... There were possibilities.

Anyway, there'd be a way for Isabelle to be dressed in that apple green dress on her wedding day. With the excitement akin to looking forward to a good meal when he was hungry, Andrew looked forward to the sight of Isabelle standing beside him before the preacher, looking as she had when he had first seen her.

There'd be a way. Come to think on it, there was that other pair of bay mares Dennis had brought over from Arkansas. They were being purely wasted hitched to carriages or used for short saddle trips to Edmond or Oklahoma City. He had sprightly young stallions who were better suited. If he could arrange a trade, there was the black stallion, descendent of the horse his granddad had stolen from the natives in Arkansas. Their bloodlines...? Well, he'd have to talk with Clayton.

Then, again, there was that heavy bay stallion his brother had insisted they buy. At fifteen, Clayton was good with form and bloodlines. Blending that with the four Arkansas mares… well, he'd just have to come over and do some talking, some evening after all four of them were through with work.

Isabelle was softly turning pages, writing this and that on the white order form. Andrew loved the serious look on her face as she weighted quality against price against appearance. With a sigh, she pushed the form toward him for his approval. He shook his head. Why would he need look at it? She would know what she needed.

"But there was that other thing you wanted to order. You said…."

"Oh, yes." Andrew took the thick catalog and turned to the farm equipment, centering in on the baby chickens. They could be ordered by the hundred, either pullets for egg laying, or mixed. He slid the book back to Isabelle.

"I know you like chickens. The ones in town, they'll need to be left for Vonnie and Dennis. You pick the kind you like, and we'll order a couple hundred, maybe three hundred."

"But… Doesn't your ma? I mean…?"

"I'm wantin you to have special chickens. Those wild things of ma's, they roam the woods, layin' where they take a notion, broodin' on the ground so the snakes and possums get the babies. There's a calf pen out back I'll be fixin' up for these."

"But, two hundred…?"

"Eggs. You know there'll be a market for the eggs we can't use. A trip to the city on a Friday? Or Saturday, if you was wantin' Liz to come along. Find a store that wants 'em, and they'll pay you, and you'll have money for buttons or fancies, or whatever you want."

"Hmmm… What'd we feed 'em on?"

"Whatever they can scratch up, and some waste grain. Maybe mash in the winter."

Isabelle was silent, looking at the pictures of the different breeds. She turned the pages slowly.

"Andrew…?"

"Yeah?"

"What you just said… would that work for Vonnie?"

"Well, yeah… sure. I don't know why not."

"Cause I was thinkin', she'll need a way to get a little money. Just for herself. Dennis, he'll help, but she'd like somethin' that was just her's."

Andrew considered it. Why not? He'd made the pen at the town house, and all he'd have to do was enlarge it a little. He could order the extra wire today.

"You pick out a hundred of what she'd like. Later in the summer we can get more. Wouldn't want her to think she had to...."

"She likes to work."

"Then get two hundred. They couldn't be much more trouble than a hundred."

Andrew paid for the order. There was still time, so they stopped at the tearoom. The smell of minty spices filled the room. Sugared fruit, flaky tea biscuits, tiny sandwiches of white bread spread thickly with fresh butter.

They sat on the fancy, wire-legged chairs around the tiny table. Isabelle looked up at the pastel walls, the heavy swaged curtains with flowered borders. So fancy.

"Last time I was in a café, Dennis and me, we sat in a wooden booth with wet feet from trompin' the streets. We thought a plate'a eggs was a gift from the Almighty, and a hot cup'a tea was all that'd save our fingers from breakin' off with the cold. I had a belly ache over bein' scared we'd not be able to get the youngens out'a the home, and the law'd have us in jail for tryin'."

Andrew had no words to respond. Isabelle leaned forward with her elbows planted on the table. She lowered her chin into her hands, and her eyelids drooped as she continued.

"And that Dennis, bein' only fifteen, was scared, but he was all we had to figure on how to take care'a the wagons and horses. He looked like a boy when we left, but by the time we got here, I kept forgettin' how young he was." A smile of pride flashed across her face. "It sure is good to see he got what he wanted. Seems he's so proud'a the business he's got, and he'd worked so hard, and all."

Isabelle swallowed hard, and her eyes turned serious. "And Vonnie, she'll carry a scarred foot and leg till her dyin' day, that bein' the only way she could think of to stay where we could get to 'er. And Laney, she still talks about the drawer where babies came from. I got no idea what she means, but I know she saw somethin' that scared her."

The waitress in the pink dress with a ruffled white apron came to them. Smiling, she handed them a small folder that was the menu. "I'll give you a minute to think..." and she was gone.

Isabelle glanced toward a glass-covered case filled with delicacies. "I'd like those, the ones with white icing, and that mint tea."

While the food was being brought, Isabelle returned to her reminiscences. "I got nightmares out'a the trip and the things before it, and it seems Artie was the only one that didn't get hurt. Seemed good how he was always laughing and jolly and helped get Laney and Vonnie in a good humor. He's gonna love the farm and the horses. He thinks you and Clayton hung the sun and moon." Then she grinned and asked, "Did you?"

The tea biscuits arrived. Isabelle, remembering her growling stomach as the plate of eggs and gravy arrived in the Arkansas café, took a biscuit and nibbled it. The light sugary flakes of richness crumbled in her mouth, melting into nothingness. Imagine, spending money for something that melted in her mouth! Sighing with pleasure, she looked around. Such a wonderful place!

The green dress was ready, and Isabelle must try it on again, just for the fit. While she was gone, Andrew picked out a bolt of shiny white lace ribbon, a string of clear, glass beads that reflected the color of whatever they were near, and busied himself before a tray of rings, glowing and sparkling in their velvet nests.

She was back. The dress that had seemed to barely fit before, now fitted perfectly, better than a second skin.

Andrew pointed to the shawl (cape?). "Put that on, will you?"

With a smile and skillful fingers, the clerk draped the filmy web over the dress. Andrew nodded, handing the clerk the ribbon and the beads. He beckoned Isabelle to the tray of rings.

Isabelle looked over the display, and then picked up a solid gold band, smooth and glowing.

"Are you sure?"

"Sure. I got work to do, and I want to wear it all the time. I don't want no sets to get dirty or messed up. Or fall out."

While the clerk figured the bill, Andrew mentally inventoried the stock of animals in the pasture. If KENDALL BALDWIN agreed and the mares bore the way they should, that, and the two year olds he had coming up...? Say, maybe Dennis could arrange a sale or two. He was certain to be in position to hear of folks who wanted to buy well broke ponies. Anyway, whatever it took, Isabelle was going to look the way he wanted her to.

The buggy headed for home. The early June sun shone warmly on the back of the buggy and on the rumps of the horses. The buggy swayed gently, sleepily, into the branch-covered trail cut by the surveyors a year and a half ago. Wheel traffic had worn ruts in the soil, smoothing and hardening it. Such changes in a year!

Isabelle pulled her feet up under her skirt and settled into the corner of the buggy. Her eyelids drooped, closing away the green eyes. Red-gold lashes lay on her cheeks... on the rosyness of her skin. Curls had escaped their ribbon and flattened against her forehead or corkscrewed in a delicate fringe of rosy-gold.

Her hands lay in her lap, pale against her skirt. Andrew pictured the gold band on her finger, and ripples of excitement played along his arms.

His. One more month. A busy month of work at the sawmill, and then he would quit that job and tend to the horses. He and Clayton, they were determined to make a success, and if young Artie... well, there was a lot of time for that.

From the height of excitement came the drop of contented relief. Isabelle slept all the way to Prosper, past the church and the school, and into the driveway of the three-room cabin he had helped to build.

"Isabel? Honey?"

Fourteen

Liz had a new dress for Isabell's wedding. It was light pink with darker pink roses, and ivory lace trimmed the neck and sleeves. Above the lace, she wore the glowing pearls and a radiant smile.

And Isabelle. The shimmering folds of the green dress were lifted over the red curls and settled onto Isabelle's shoulders. The fitted sleeves hugged her arms, and the ruffled edge on the sleeves fell over her wrists. The low waist of the dress settled onto her hips, and then flared in soft folds above the shiny white patented leather of the new shoes.

Liz worked the brush through the red curls, drawing them to the top and securing them with the lace ribbon. After cutting her own hair as a child, Isabelle's hair had never again been long. Brushing small wisps of hair around her fingers, Liz piled the resulting curls into a rosy cap. The shorter fringe of hair was separated into flock of ringlets grouped across her forehead and around her ears.

The strand of clear glass beads picked up the pale rosiness of her skin, as well as the shimmer of green from the dress. Liz's fingers adjusted the beads and stepped back. Would it be correct to comment on the excellent taste of her own brother in his choice of the clothes, as well as the girl? Perhaps not.

"You look beautiful, Isabelle! That dress....!"

Isabel cut in, "Andrew liked it. I'd'a been happy with anything."

The girls could hear the people gathering outside the log cabin. Emma had been baking for days, and tables laden with sweets decorated the yard, hiding under tea towels against the summer flies. Jugs of tea had been lowered into the crystal water of the spring to make them as cool as possible. The heavy aroma of coffee wafted over the whole scene.

Dave and Andrew waited on the stone bench of the herb garden with Preacher Palmer for company. Nearby, Liddy Palmer's accordion sent out haunting notes that echoed into the canyon behind the garden. There were sounds of an occasional whinny of a horse or baa of a calf, newly separated from its mother. Chickens pecked and clucked, scratching among the herb plants.

The people visited in pairs and groups, always watching the door of the cabin. Vonnie, alone, waited inside while Isabelle was being dressed. She had inspected the cabin, and it was nice, but the town house was best for her. Starting tomorrow, she would turn it into her own. Dennis wouldn't care what she did, and Manny Kendall would surely be impressed with her skill.

Andrew's gift of the baby chickens had sent her dreams spiraling. That's what the town lot had room for, and any eggs Hewett's store could not use, she would send to Guthrie. With the money, she would have nice clothes, like the other girls in the town, and she could buy some things for the house.

She watched Isabelle being transformed into a beautiful picture. She was happy for her cousin. Isabelle deserved any good she got, and if it hadn't been for her, no telling where they would be by now. Vonnie studied Isabelle's smile... sweet, dreamy and faraway. Is that what happened when a girl fell in love...? Whatever that was? Liz had looked the same way.

Well, she had other things to do. Much better things.

Finally it was decided that Isabelle was ready. Vonnie left the cabin and walked to the preacher. Conversation stopped, and eyes were turned on her.

The preacher took his place, and Dave and Andrew left the safety of the stone bench. Vonnie took her place with the crowd where other girls stood. A sound came from the front gate… likely a late comer. Heads turned and watched as Dennis and Manny Kendall left their horses at the gate and walked toward Vonnie. Vonnie watched, and smiled softly.

Handsome Dennis, his easy stride bringing him toward her. Closely behind was Manny Kendall. Very tall for seventeen. Chiseled nose… square jaw softened by the hint of a dimple. Smile lines on either side of his mouth.

Vonnie watched, and when Manny's eyes found hers, he was quick to smile and turn toward her. She returned his smile, then her eyes lowered, dark-lashed and dreamy. He stopped and stood beside her, with Dennis on his other side.

The cabin door opened, and the pink flowered dress came through. Liz's dark hair was pulled to the nape of her neck and secured with a clasp of pink stones, catching sparkling light from the noonday sun. She paused, and Isabelle followed.

The shiny white shoes were planted on the green grass with slow steps, and the flared green dress flowed around her like the swirling water of Redbud Creek when the spring rains filled the banks. The white whisper of the cape floated over the slim shoulders, and the fitted sleeves of the dress were as filmy as summer clouds above the new green of willow trees in the early spring.

The cut glass beads caught the light, glistening like diamonds… better than diamonds. A breeze caught the curled ends of the lace ribbon, tossing them against the white web of the cape.

Andrew, standing beside Dave, stared with adoration. If it took the sale of every horse he owned, it would be worth it just for this moment. The soft notes of the music stopped, and Isabelle was by his side.

The preacher opened his marriage book. "Dearly beloved, we are gathered here before God, and these people to join this woman and this man in holy matrimony. Andrew, do you take…?"

So quickly it was over, and the accordion bounced into a lively waltz. Laughter and congratulations sounded through the crowd.

Vonnie helped Emma take the tea towels from the tables of food. Dennis and Manny pulled jugs of spiced tea from the water of the spring, and others poured coffee into mugs. Most of the guests brought their own mug, to be sure of having one.

Dennis came to Isabelle.

When they had left the Arkansas town, from his height he had looked slightly down at his cousin, but now, a year and a half later, she barely came to his shoulders. Was this tiny, rosy-faced girl the wildcat who had braved life in Arkansas and had kept them together on the trip? It had to be, but to his eyes, now sharpened by separation, it seemed almost impossible. Without her, where would he be now? Where would any of them have been?

Swallowing a lump in his throat, he gathered her into his arms, startling both himself and her with his emotion. His own sister, Vonnie, whom he loved dearly, would never be as close to him as Isabelle. For months, they had worked as one mind for the survival of themselves and the others. He was sublimely happy for her.

Releasing her at last, he wiped his eyes with the back of his hand, and she had sniffed and been handed a handkerchief by Liz. Dabbing her eyes, she smiled up at Dennis, her eyes soft and dreamy.

Embarrassed by his own emotion, he turned toward the tables of food. There was Manny, talking with Vonnie. His sister smiled, her eyes crinkling with pleasure. Vonnie, almost fifteen years old! Already!

Caroline Kendall stood beside Vonnie, and when he glanced her way, she smiled and extended the plate of sandwiches toward him. Hmmmm, that Caroline had turned into a right pretty girl. Saucy chin, twinkly eyes and a strong nose and forehead. How could she manage to look so much like Manny and still be so pretty?

Isabelle was hugged and congratulated by the women. Emma hovered protectively, basking in the glow of the festivities. Isabelle was now hers and a woman with daughters like Liz and Isabelle… ? Well, she must have done something right!

Clayton nudged Andrew. "I'll get the chores," he muttered under his breath. Andrew nodded his thanks, as Clayton left to join a group of the younger fellows… and girls.

The party lasted the rest of the day. Isabelle finally had to change out of the green dress into something more practical for a lawn party. She returned, still radiant, in the pale blue with white dots.

The sun lowered, and Dennis and Manny had to leave. The others left in pairs and groups. There were evening chores to be done. Vonnie and Caroline left in Caroline's buggy, chattering happily. Dave and Liz had to leave, and finally the preacher, alone, was left. He and his wife and their son and five daughters stood around his wagon.

He shook hands with Andrew. "Son, you got a good girl, and I'm happy for you." Then he was gone. He had said all there was to say.

Isabelle moved around among the tables, gathering the dishes and putting away the remaining cookies and candy. Emma joined her.

"Isabelle, honey, you go on. You got'a be tired. I'll take care'a this. It'll be no trouble."

"No, I'll help. Then it'll be only half as much trouble."

Emma's arm tightened around the girl's shoulders. "You dear, sweet girl…!"

Andrew walked aimlessly across the yard and into the barn. Clayton had finished with the milking and had gone to check the spring-born colts in the far pasture. Seven of them had entered the world safely, and there were another six to go. With the four mares from Arkansas, there would be…?

Oh, well, tomorrow was another day, plenty of time to discuss it with his brother. Certainly not today. Turning, he returned to the yard just as Isabelle left his mother's house. Taking her arm, he led her to the door of the cabin and scooped her into his arms.

Feather light. Lighter than a newborn calf, trying to stand. Lighter than a new leather saddle tossed over the back of a horse. Lighter than….

Kicking the door closed behind him, he looked around, and remembered that Laney was spending the night with his little sisters, and Artie was going to be allowed to sleep in Andrew's old room at the big house.

Andrew stood in the kitchen with Isabelle still in his arms, marveling at how well she fit. He smiled as a silly thought passed through his mind.

Would it be possible to stand there forever, just holding her?

Probably not! Oh, well….

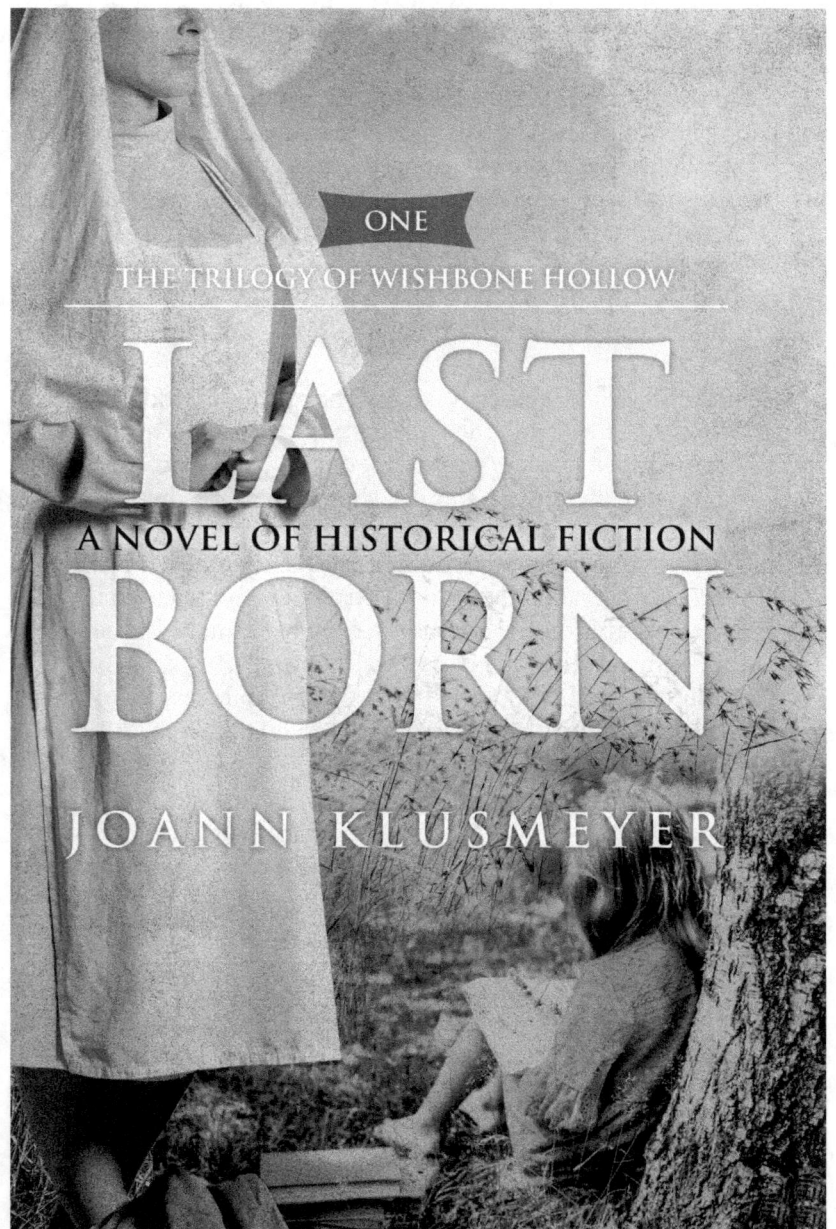

ONE

THE TRILOGY OF WISHBONE HOLLOW

LAST

A NOVEL OF HISTORICAL FICTION

BORN

JOANN KLUSMEYER

Last Born

Rowenna's future destination was pretty much set when she received the Christmas book as a gift for her tenth Christmas birthday. Bernard and Loretta Moffat made it a point to give a Christmas book to each child every year as long as each of the youngens was at home. After that, he (or she) was on his own.

An even dozen youngens seemed to be a handy number for a family, so it was thought that Rowenna's sister, Jadeen, was intended to be the last of the family, but when you get a good thing a'goin' it could be a chore to get it stopped. Besides that, as precarious as it was living on the steep mountains, one should plan on an extra kid to 'make up for the one lost over the hill'.

Growing kids in Arkansas was rather like growin' morning glory flowers. They look good on the fence, but when they're climbin' the cornstalks, chokin' off the tomatoes, and trippin' the horse a'tryin' to plow 'em out, then it might be good to take another look at 'em.

So Jadeen had her nose out of joint for a while, they say. But then she saw the value of someone littler to blame with breakage and other disobediences. Another thing… it was number thirteen girl who thought up the idea of callin' her 'Jade', and that boosted her rating up a notch.

And then their pa, who may not have been the busiest bee in the hive, must have listened to Ma and her bit of wise reasonin'. "Just look at it this way, Bernard; if you were thinkin' on someone bein' around for our old age, forget that. Just look around and see how the youngens are gettin' away faster'n we can produce 'em.Sophia's headed off to Fayetteville, and Laverne is packin' up to go somewhere. Only thing that's kept her here this long is the stage plays."

And Pa seemed to have said, "Loretta, my little sweet pea, it could be you got somethin' there."

Kid number eleven, Laverne, was arguably one of the best heroines the Wishbone Hollow Magic Curtain Theater ever had. She could die and leave the audience weeping and sopping up their tears. Also lining up at the door to see her do it again.

Laverne outgrew Wishbone and ended up about three hollows and two ridges to the east at a place called Eureka Springs. They made her an offer she couldn't refuse. Sometimes she got to die at two or three theaters at a time if they could just get their schedules of performance right.

But then, right after Jadeen, number twelve, was born, here came Rowenna, pink as a baby piglet and dimpled as a brand new golf ball. It soon became evident that she possessed the Moffat hard-headedness.

The people of Wishbone shook their collective heads. No good would come of that, for everyone knew that thirteen was an unlucky number... especially for a Moffat, who was related to the Hopkins. All except Granddad Hopkins, actually the retired Reverend Irvin Hopkins, Rowenna's maternal grandfather.

Preacher Hopkins was actually retired from the local church, but his words around town still carried a lot of weight. Two other relatives sided with him in defense of number thirteen, and they were his two widowed sisters, Sophrenia and Cecilia, who ran the Thimbles and Spools sewing shop along with their cousin, Georgiana.

As the parents were still rather busy with kids number seven to twelve, the older generation had a chance to cast their influence over that last child... number thirteen. The old ladies had room for her to crawl about in their workplace, and Granddad was handy for an afternoon to sit with Rowenna and her cousin Wally, a year and a half older.

Back to the Christmas gift book and its permanent influence on Rowenna. The little girl got her first Christmas book at age two and ate pages seven through ten before she recognized the dog, cat and piggy pictures on the pages. By that time, Laverne, the actress, had learned to read a few words and pointed to them as she read the one-sentence stories to her sister.

Rowenna was hooked. Robert, who was next older than Laverne, could read quite well, loved a challenge and took on the word recognition effort. By age four, Rowenna was receiving 'real' books and reading them without much assistance.

Also at about age four, she discovered the value of her cousin, Wally, five and a half, and they stuck together like a pair of magnets. Maybe it was their size at first, but later, it was identical interests. Wally was a belated chick hatched after four teenage sisters had practically flown the nest. Their mothers being sisters-in-laws, naturally these two youngest were flung together at family gatherings and at church and such.

THIMBLES AND SPOOLS

One particular location in the town of Wishbone was both home and the place of business of two widowed sisters and their cousin.

The house originally belonged to Georgiana, but it would be unseemingly for one old lady to be alone, so Sophrenia and Cecilia moved in with her. There was plenty of room, of course, as that was where Georgiana had reared her family. Six rooms close to the foot of the hill. It was not intended that they be in the center of town, but Main Street sort of crowded in between her house and Possum Creek. So there they were, right in the thick of it all.

Handy, though. They just added a display room to the parlor and stocked it with every known item required by anyone who sewed… along with trimmings and thread… and they were in business. A few patterns rounded out the offering, except for the hand-pieced quilts mostly bought by the 'summer people'.

Good advertisement, it was, to have the quilting frame hanging from the ceiling to be admired by the 'summer trade' who wandered into the shop. It was even more enticing when the three gray-haired ladies, with the proper number of wrinkles, were wielding a needle at the time. The quilt in the frame, however, was not, and likely would never be, for sale. It was purely for show. The ladies were nothing if not showmen… beg pardon, show ladies.

The shelves were laden with beautifully pieced and quilted coverlets made by skillful hands living all the way up the hills in every direction and a few from the nearby hollows. The ladies of Thimbles and Spools made their money on commission sales, and they were master salespersons.

So, back to Rowenna and Wally. The pair were grand-niece and nephew to the three old ladies and were welcome guests. They created the need to keep the cookie jar full. The two well-known children from well-known families created conversation material for the three as well as other locals. And conversation was the 'mother's milk' of mountain relationships.

A pair of wooden rocking horses had their stable under the accounts desk and made trips around and under the quilting platform manned by the trio. The horses themselves were advertisement for the carpenter shop over on Larkspur Lane.

Any comment from 'summer people' on the attractive wooden creatures (authentic from teeth to mane to tail to painted hoofs) produced a business card for 10% off on the purchase of one. Of course, any customer could get at least 10% off on any purchase, but 'summer people' were not supposed to notice that.

When the team of Rowenna and Wally were six and seven and a half, they were fully trusted to make the short trip to the WM (Wilkinson's Market) for some little item the ladies were out of. Like everyone else in Wishbone, the ladies 'ran a tab' at the market. It simplified matters, because small children could then perform the shopping trips without the use of, and possible loss of, actual coins.

The fact that the small town was transverse twice by small mountain rivers brought home the fact that coins dropped in the water could be more or less considered to arrive somewhere over in Oklahoma. This fact also necessitated that each child learn to swim almost as soon as he could walk.

When the team was eight and nine and a half, they were trusted to make a trip over to the Big Three for a ready-made lunch for the Thimbles ladies. Age and excessive poundage, gradually acquired over the years, made unnecessary trips rare as long as a pair of young legs were available. And all it cost was a pair of ice cream cones while they were there.

The Big Three consisted of three small diners, each offering specialty items only and located in almost the dead center of town

To start the food conversation, Sophrenia quietly mentioned, "What's for lunch?" which was short for "It's too hot to cook, and the youngens want ice cream."

Georgiana, after a polite pause, countered with, "Well… if we've got nothing started, I could go for a piece of fried chicken."

That was not a surprise to the other two, and she usually ordered the wishbone even though it was priced higher. Cecelia, who rather liked a surprise sometimes, alternated her orders.

"I believe I'll have the soup. When I send the pint jar, I get more than when I get it in that there paper bowl."

"It's not paper, I keep saying. It's a formed cellulose container."

Cecelia nodded. "Yeah, like I said… that paper bowl. It's the same stuff that the paper wasps use for their hives, only it isn't made with wasp spit."

"Right, but we don't know what the bowl maker uses. Maybe it's his own.…"

"Hush," shouted Sophrenia with her fingers in her ears. "I don't want to hear that. It's nasty, and we're about to eat."

"Not if you don't decide what you want."

Sophrenia, with an injured sniff, "I already know. I want cold ham and slaw. It's too hot for hot food."

Cecelia, with a toss of her gray ringlet hair, "I hadn't noticed anything ever bein' very hot by the time those two get back here, crossin' Possum Creek and all."

Then Georgiana, with a whisper, suggested, "Better than goin' there ourselves, remember? And none of us seemed to want to fire up the stove."

Rowenna and Wally continued to sit on the porch, swinging their bare feet over the edge and waiting for the words to settle and preparing their tastes for ice cream. This banter of words was a game perfected over the years. The game was well-known by the children and all three ladies knew the rules and there was never a winner.

Georgiana decided she'd also have slaw, and Cecelia would have a biscuit, please, and she'd flavor it with her own jelly.

The matter now settled, Rowenna ducked inside the store for the soup jar and the cloth bags for the food, and they were off, bare feet padding the worn paths and the very warm boards of the bridge over Possum Creek. They skipped along in the shade of the store awnings to the path over to the Big Three huts.

The home-churned ice cream turned out to be chocolate today… a favorite. There was never a choice of flavors. You ate what was made for that day, or you didn't. Almost everyone ate. The ice cream hut was very skilled in its specialty and used actual cream, sweetening it with half bee-tree honey and half sugar, and their chocolate was the brown powder that came from a fifty-gallon keg, ordered in by the WM especially for this customer.

The children did not loiter over the ice cream. It was to be eaten quickly or it became liquid… though it was still very tasty when the last drops were drunk from the bowl. Collecting the ordered items from various of the three huts, they were off again.

The pair, racing along on a 'high' from the sugar and fat, felt they had been well paid for their services.

Cecelia peered with interest at her soup. Always thick with vegetables and flavored with meat broth, it was also always a surprise.

Like the flavor of the ice cream, the variety of the soup was entirely the choice of the maker... and if you didn't want that flavor, there was always home-prepared chili with beans that was always made exactly the same way. It was made from a 'secret recipe,' and no chili-lover had ever complained. Or at listened to if they did.

The lady with her gray-streaked hair in a knot on her head smiled with satisfaction. Broccoli, squash, and corn in a tomato broth flavored with the leftover sausages ground into a pulp. A favorite.

Summer people usually viewed it with a puzzled frown the first time they ate it, but only the first time. Any decent soup connoisseur would give it a 5-star rating without a second thought.

Food delivered, the messengers scurried off for further summer amusement, and their great aunts bowed their heads over their food. It was their habit to be thankful.... mostly for the bountiful blessings from their Lord, but partly because they didn't have to heat up the kitchen. Firing up the wood-burning stove wasn't so bad in the winter... in fact, it was quite cozy, but come summer... well, that was another story!

GRANDDAD HOPKINS

Though he had been retired for more than five years, the old man still felt a kinship with the church that he had helped to erect. Somehow it seemed to be as much a part of his family as the dirt between the two streams of water that came together to make the wishbone shape of the town. Necessary real estate surgery required that much of the mound of dirt must to be scraped away to make a level foundation.

Several donated mule-drawn dirt-slips spent days... yea, weeks... on the project. Help from ANY source was begged for the many and varied jobs, the greatest of them being the laying aside of all useable stones that were uncovered.

The mountains of northern Arkansas could yield a massive amount of what was once volcanic rock. The hard mineral chunks came in all-broken-up shapes and also in massive boulders the sizes of the mules themselves. Centuries of being impregnated with minerals had painted the stones with various colors and patterns.

A fact was, one had to do something with the stones, and the building must be constructed of something, so an argument could be made that God had provided the durable chunks of this material specifically for his house.

Usable stones laid aside, the unusable remains were piled for use in walling off the streams and filling in holes. Like so many of the first buildings in that mountainous area, soil was scraped down from the uphill side to fill in on the lower side to make what was hoped to be a fairly level building plot.

So the Wishbone Congregational Community Church was born on a scrap of useless, donated land and carefully reared into a solid building that would seat at least 75 standard-sized people and provide standing room for almost that many more when necessary.

Local labor created the benches and pulpit and closed off a couple of rooms for children's classes. A stockroom was hooked onto the rear for whatever seemed not to fit anywhere else, and that room acquired the name "Office" and was loosely used for that purpose by the current pastor.

With great thanks to his Creator, the recently licensed Irvin Hopkins had moved in, so to speak. Actually, he lived with his wife and family across Tarantula River, sometimes called Spider River. Tarantula sounds too dangerous. A small, wooden footbridge joined his front yard to that of his beloved church.

All of that was then… and now it was later.

So now Granddad, the preacher, was retired, and when the pair, Rowenna and Wally, reached ten and eleven and a half, it was time for Granddad to take over some of the responsibility for their training that was being ignored by the tolerant great aunts.

The first duty they were taught to assume was care of the church yard. Somehow among the stones there came an everlasting crop of something called a sand burr.

Now, Granddad Irvin was ever the preacher, and he saw spiritual lessons in just about everything, but the clearest and easiest to understand was the sand burr.

"Come over here, youngens, and we're gonna look at this plant. God had a reason for it or it wouldn't be here, so I reckon it is here for a lesson."

Wally immediately found something to object to. "Ah, Granddad, we done saw those things, a'pickin' 'em outta our feet."

"I know that, but now you're gonna see 'em a different way. See here how those blades look just like the grass all around 'em? Well, that's the way sin is. It sneaks in without callin' attention to itself, and it don't make burrs right off. It's gonna wait till it has good roots and can make a lotta burrs so fast that no one can pick 'em all off."

The girl and boy hunkered down beside Granddad, looking at the innocent-looking plant in a different light. Rather clever of it… it seemed.

Granddad continued. "And see here how those blades get thick and spread out, bein' shorter than the other grass, so it don't get itself mowed down? It's hidin', just like sin. And see here where the joints are on the stem? It's tryin' to put down new roots, so it can use up more of the nutrition in the ground. Just like sin takes up a lot of a fellow's time… if he lets it."

The two pairs of young eyes now viewed the clever plant with even greater respect.

"And another thing. See here how I can gather all those blades together and pull, and they break off in my hand, leavin' the root right there in the ground. Can you guess what that reminds me of?"

They turned their eyes to Granddad, shaking their head. There was no way they, with their limited experience, could guess what Granddad could be thinking of.

The old man nodded with satisfaction. There were very few occasions so satisfying as having two pairs of your young flesh-and-blood family hanging onto your every word.

"That reminds me of how some folks think they can just be good all by theirselves and that God will not notice they still have their old sinful nature that they were born with. That plant is tryin' to fool us into thinkin' it's been killed, but I'm going to put a marker right here, and we'll look at it next week."

They were now even more impressed. Imagine…! That was a really smart weed.

Granddad nodded with emphasis. "That there's like some folks thinkin' God won't notice their old sin nature. But they're wrong there. God knows, and until folks' sins are forgiven, they can't even ask God for help to get rid of them. Now come on over here and see this."

Granddad moved over a couple of yards and knelt down by another sand burr plant. Taking his sharpened Winchester knife from his pocket, he straightened the longest blade. The sharp shininess of it sparkled in the morning sun.

The old man's fingers gathered the blades of the plant and thrust his knife into the ground beside the roots. Slicing sideways, he severed the roots below the ground and lifted the plant and clod together. Two pairs of eyes examined the hole and watched Granddad knock back the dirt into the hollow space.

"Lookie here, now. See that bunch'a roots? Almost like a brush for being so many. That plant really wanted to grow there, but my knife wouldn't let it. That there's the way God is with his words. They're like that knife and he is like my hand. He's done told us what to do and how to do it, so now we have the book he had some men write down. That book is the knife to cut away the roots of sin after we ask God for forgiveness."

He looked squarely into each of the pairs of eyes. Yes, it looked like this lesson took… but he'd have another chance at them next week when they examined the marked plant. Bright youngens… these two. He was planning to be proud of them as they grew up. That might take some effort on his part, but he was ready for whatever it took.

"Now, we could go over to the Big Three and have ice cream. It's time they got it made, but there is a problem…."

"Problem…?" Surely he would not disappoint them after that long, absorbing lesson.

The old man sighed with resignation. "Bein' that both'a you don't like fresh peach ice cream, there'll be no use goin' over there."

"Aw, Granddad…!" and they pounded their fists lovingly on the old man's shoulders and each reached for a hand to help him to his feet. Getting him up was a bit dicey… sometimes… but once he got going, he was fine.

Granddad paid for the ice cream and walked on to the 'spit and whittle bench' where a few others his age were gathered. The older fellows often gathered there to watch the 'summer people' go by… and to wonder, with many words, what the world was coming to.

- END OF EXCERPT -

Additional Book Series
by Joann Klusmeyer

The Great I Am Bible Story Series for Kids
6 books

The Young Pioneers Adventure Series for Kids
5 books

The Wentworth Triplets Mystery Series for Young Teens
3 books

The Footsteps in the Canyon Adventure Series for Young Teens
4 books

The Burnt Tree Junction Historical Fiction Series
6 books

The Ozark Mountains Historical Fiction Series
7 books

The Taming the Wilderness Historical Fiction Series
4 books

The Sheltering Stones Historical Fiction Series
5 books

The Trilogy of Wishbone Hollow Historicial Fiction Series
3 books

www.ingramcontent.com/pod-product-compliance
Lightning Source LLC
Chambersburg PA
CBHW071845020726
47502CB00003B/604